THE HARTLEPOOL MONKEY

www.rbooks.co.uk

THE HARTLEPOOL
MONKEY

SEAN LONGLEY

Doubleday

LONDON · TORONTO · SYDNEY · AUCKLAND · JOHANNESBURG

TRANSWORLD PUBLISHERS
61–63 Uxbridge Road, London W5 5SA
A Random House Group Company
www.rbooks.co.uk

First published in Great Britain
in 2008 by Doubleday
an imprint of Transworld Publishers

A CIP catalogue record for this book is available from the British Library.

ISBN 9780385612531

Addresses for Random House Group Ltd companies outside the UK
can be found at: www.randomhouse.co.uk
The Random House Group Ltd Reg. No. 954009

The Random House Group Limited supports The Forest Stewardship Council (FSC),
the leading international forest certification organisation. All our titles that are
printed on Greenpeace approved FSC certified paper carry the FSC logo.
Our paper procurement policy can be found at www.rbooks.co.uk/environment

Typeset in 11½/17pt Minion by
Kestrel Data, Exeter, Devon.
Printed and bound in Great Britain by
Clays Ltd, St Ives plc.

2 4 6 8 10 9 7 5 3 1

Mixed Sources
Product group from well-managed
forests and other controlled sources
www.fsc.org Cert no. TT-COC-2139
© 1996 Forest Stewardship Council
FSC

To Esme Longley

Part I

Dr Simon Legris

1

Africa

I AM SITTING ON A LOG WEARING MY HAT. THE JUNGLE HAS many noises, and every time I hear them I fail to recognize them. Every day I am reborn into this terrible place. I have been struck by melancholia, but I have transcended any lethargy. Although Jacques tended me through the first bout, I doubt his commitment too much to try a second, no matter how much I would welcome the cool damp embrace of this humour. The jungle is cruel and all I can do is trudge its cluttered emptiness. I follow Jacques. I have nothing else to do. I have lost everything. I have lost my master, my clothing, my enquiring instincts and I strongly suspect I have lost my sanity as well, although that still provokes a certain amount of debate.

So far as my Young Master and my clothing are concerned, they both fell victim to the foul humidity of this place. They have fallen into the loam that makes up the forest floor, a loam so deep and rich it masks every footfall. How I long for the rumble of carts in the filthy streets outside my windows or the crisp rap of heels upon a polished floor. I once had a pair of particularly elegant shoes. I have never been a dandy but these shoes were my pride. I bought them when I came into my position as the personal physician of the Duc Ladurie de Bretagne. They were an emblem of my triumph and now they have returned to the soil. So have my coat, my britches and my shirt. Everything is gone apart from my hat. It is all that prevents me standing naked in this hellish Eden. I have my hat, my musket, six balls, some powder and Jacques. They are the only things between my destruction and me.

The jungle is constantly changing, rotting and rising in twisted forms. I find myself changing with it, until I can scarcely recall what I was. Take the bees. When we first arrived here (by 'we', I mean the Young Master, Van der Veer the hunter, Lieutenant La Roche and me, twenty native bearers and a boarhound), I was immediately struck by the bees. They were so very wondrous, having no sting and subsisting on drinking our sweat, that I became convinced that they craved salt. I spent many hours observing and dissecting them in order to ascertain whether there were any peculiarities in their intestines that differentiated them from their European cousins. I took many notes. I drew diagrams. I preserved specimens. All gone, now. Lost, presumed decayed. And now the pitiless insects merely annoy me. I would wave them away but I really cannot summon the strength. Stingless and weak, they inspire only contempt. Like me, I suspect. Like the European bee, I am diminished by my sting. Like the European bee, I have no place in this wilderness. The irony is not lost on me and it is only because of this that I have some small hope I may not be insane after all. All evidence points against this, but while there is hope surely there must be sanity?

I do not think that Jacques will leave me to my fate. He is an honourable little fellow. We talk for hours about the nature of things and he recognizes that obligations are terms of the great contract that binds all men together in society. He owes me and he knows it. I saved him from a terrible fate, when I was strong, before it all rotted away and I was left with nothing but a three-cornered hat. I recall it well.

2

Simon

MY NAME IS SIMON LEGRIS. I WAS BORN IN THE CITY of Rennes and in my infancy I found myself with neither mother nor father to protect me. The cholera that precipitated my destitution propelled me into the care of my aunt, a woman whose popularity among the gentlemen allowed her little time to indulge her maternal instinct. I became a solitary child, immersed in furtive reading as I hid myself about the house while my aunt entertained her callers. Deaf to all but the thunder in print, I lived inside myself, until I began to occupy so much physical space that my presence became an inconvenience to her. She was not cruel, my aunt, and the debt of gratitude she owed my parents' memory meant that she cared for me well until I became a hindrance. She compromised between my presence and abandonment by sending me to acquire an education.

The monks who were to provide me with this commodity were austere men who allowed no frivolity to survive their walls. The first casualty was my given name. Like the memory of my parents' faces, it faded until it was reduced to irrelevance. My years among the brothers were ones of joyless growth. Despite my aunt's unspoken wish that I should become one of them when I came of age, I was but an average theologian. I had no father on earth, and found in this absence the concept of the father intangible hard to assimilate. The fervour that made Jesuits escaped me, while I found the relentless burden of obligation hard to bear. I knew God's peace only as I knew of India. I was told it existed yet I had never been there.

The benefit I derived was a rigour of analysis. While other more diligent students expended this upon the nature of the Trinity, I discovered the world around me. I had spent so long inside that the duty to maintain the college's vegetable supplies was like an awakening. I soaked in the world of nature as the Breton drizzle soaked into my clothing. Poised above the cabbages, I noticed the insects and worms and found them marvellous. I became fascinated by the mechanisms of life, an interest that was derided as wool-gathering before being channelled into the study of medicine. I left the brothers for the university without God in my heart. There was no room for him among all my creditors.

I was a good student. Goaded by constant reminders of my need to exhibit gratitude, I applied myself diligently. I became proficient in the setting of the broken, the application of the leech and the amputation of the putrid. I sawed, salved and drained away five years under the lowering reminder of the workhouse I had so fortunately avoided. I drank only in moderation and my occasional forays into carnality were solitary affairs. I was to better myself, so to lower myself would be to turn my back on my undeserved fortune.

The search for self-improvement led me to join what was then called a philosophical society. At first my involvement was limited to listening at the edges of conversations between confident, solid young men. I became a receptor of received opinion, listening and processing the vocabulary of my new countrymen in what I discovered to be called the Republic of Ideas. I found vindication. There was no God. I had always suspected as much. There was Reason, a goddess whose heretical love of an explanation for all the mysteries of my monastic youth would have left my former carers dreaming wistfully of burning posts and thumbscrews. Best of all, there was virtue in what I had always been led to believe was a simplicity that could be dismissed with the catch-all phrase of 'the marvel of creation'. My love of worms, plants and other denizens of the kitchen garden had a name. It was a science. Its study put men in touch with the simple nobility of man unblemished by corruption. I was not a daydreamer. I was a botanist.

I read of social contracts, of natural men and of the need for justice and liberty. As I assimilated the concept that betterment was the birthright of those capable of improvement, I sloughed off my deference. With this renaissance came the realization that if I did not owe the Church my gratitude, it had no right to my parole. My good behaviour was mine to withhold.

I did not become a fully fledged libertine. I still drank moderately but with slightly increased frequency. I invited company to what had previously been a lonely and mechanical ritual. Only the richer students could afford a relationship with providers of this intimate service. My mistress's time was rationed and strictly timed. I felt no guilt at my mortal sin. I rather enjoyed this final parting from the manual rigours of monastic contemplation.

Finally I was judged to have been educated to a level at which

I could practise my profession without putting my patients into such mortal danger that my reputation could harm the practices of my fellows. I acquired the soubriquet 'Doctor', and in so doing gained something to stand next to Legris. I was glad it had found a companion.

After I became M'sieur le Docteur I decided that the treatment of the sick was simply a way to fund my study of nature. I understood the mechanics of healing but my heart remained in the kitchen garden. This realization set me upon the quest that sooner or later every follower of Hippocrates pursues: the search for a wealthy invalid whose essentially spiritual ills could be cured by the application of complex and expensive remedies.

My attempts to find this golden patient were initially unsuccessful. While I knew the quarry I pursued, I had no idea where one was to be found. My attempts to expand my practice beyond the merely comfortably afflicted were thwarted at every turn by my lamentable ignorance of where the really well-heeled sick sought relief. Disconsolate, I sought refuge in increasing the frequency of my moderate indulgence in the pleasures of the flesh. My practice enabled me to attend bordellos of a quality that in my student days had seemed as elusive and attractive as the Garden of Earthly Delights. At last I could afford a mistress.

Claudette was a willing girl. She had some small local celebrity, her father having been hanged for the murder of a tax collector. While his act was secretly applauded, this approval did not extend to a willingness to support his progeny. His estate was confiscated and the hitherto pampered Claudette was cast out on her own resources. I was able to afford her only because she was unaware of precisely what those resources could command. She was in her teens, with broad hips, a full chest and blonde hair. I was delighted to find that this was a consistent feature. She was blessed with a simplicity of soul that combined exquisitely with her diligent professionalism. She was literally capable of anything. Only my monk-caged imagination set the horizons of our union. I chose and paid the fee. She was mine for as long as I could afford to keep her.

I overlooked the contractual foundation of our love. She was soon bought from under me. I was convinced that I could win her away from her aristocrat by the force of my ardour alone and followed her to Paris. She would allow me an occasional memento of happier times while her new lover was at Versailles, but I remained discontented. I sought her womanhood as a man but found it as a physician. Paris was a city where freedom could go to a provincial girl's head. What liberty could be more intoxicating than freedom of choice, when its every exercise could lead to romance and enrichment? Sadly, this very choice was to prove her temporary undoing. One of her plethora of clients was ungentlemanly enough to leave her with the English Disease. She came to me weeping and, once treatment was successfully completed, begged me most attractively to accept her gratitude as payment. I had a young man's faith in my skill as a healer. I accepted.

This act of mutual charity paid dividends. Claudette enjoyed the society of like-minded young women. They talked shop, passing her discovery from one to another. Soon, as the pox traversed one end of her circle, my name followed at the other. I had no energy to accommodate such frequent thanks. Ultimately I was forced to accept payment in cash.

They proved a generous clientele. I was soon able to afford consulting rooms and a servant. While these were not in the smartest location, their unremarkable façade gave them the discretion that my patients required. I gained a reputation as a specialist and my client group widened. I began to treat the patron as well as the patronized. The small sign on the outer wall of my building, 's. LEGRIS–MÉDECIN', was reassuringly anonymous.

My increased wealth allowed me to begin a modest collection of natural curiosities. I kept these in my consulting rooms, as I felt they gave the place an air of scientific enquiry that would distract my patients from the nature of their treatment. I imagined that their eyes played over the glass cases containing what I considered to be rare and exotic preserved flora and fauna, distracting them from the discomforts of the cure. I hoped that they realized what a man of learning and philosophical insight it was who was now engaged in the task of infusing their genitalia with a tincture of white mercury.

Proudest among my exhibits was a 'wild man of the woods' – an ape of medium stature, covered with coarse dark hair. He had been taken from Africa, just south of the Slave Coast. I would often contemplate him between examinations and note the similarity of his generative organs to those I had recently scrutinized. His face was flat, with a prominent jaw. It had an intelligent air and bore a slight similarity to Brother Jerome, the monk who had supervised my punitive excavations in the vegetable beds. I attempted to conceive the creature in its habitat. Its diet and society were a mystery to me. There were a few in Paris, kept as pets or show animals. I sought them out and realized that captivity had robbed them of their nature. Their behaviour was not their own, but that which they had learned from the society of men. I saw in that a parallel to the fashionable hypothesis of the Noble Savage and contrived a desire to travel to the forests of their origin. I fantasized about the tumultuous acclaim that my writings on this subject would bring but recognized my ambitions for what they were. An expedition to *terra incognita* was beyond my purse. Only a venereal-disease epidemic of biblical proportions could provide me with the funding for such an enterprise.

I wore my life in Paris with a comfort that neither monastic nor student apparel had ever afforded me. My practice was successful if never truly lucrative. I attended lectures and debated their content in the wine shops. My collection grew through acquisition and as a result of my own limited expeditions within France. I became the proud owner of a wild boar of domestic origin and a crocodile from Egypt that cost the dizzying sum of fifteen livres. They, and my wild man, stood in my surgery, monuments to my scientific curiosity. My dreams of the Slave Coast and the golden patient settled into the silt. I was resigned to being a bourgeois pox-doctor.

Urchins would follow me, singing:

> Doctor Simon I'm unwell
> It's love that's brought me down
> Open your bag and make my cock
> The cleanest in the town.

I ceased to notice them. The pompous fury that at first drove me to chase them down the street with my stick soon departed. I discovered a fondness for drink that consoled me and, with its warming embrace, put any frustration to one side.

3

Reynard

I WOKE TO THE SOUND OF KNOCKING. MY HEAD POUNDED with brandy. The din continued and I lay, expecting my servant to answer the door. To my increasing rage, no footsteps creaked along the corridor. The thunder rolled on. I got to my feet, pulled my coat about me and staggered to the door, my brain slewing from side to side in my skull like mercury in a glass jar. My mouth tasted as foul as if I had slept with a beggar's toe in it. I threw open the door and was instantly blinded by the pallid early-morning sun. An urchin stood before me with a stick in his hand. He regarded me with undisguised insolence.

'What do you mean by hammering on my door at this hour?' I snapped.

The boy recoiled. I had a brief moment to savour the belief that my gravitas had forced him to rue his impropriety before a slight breeze from the street blew the stench of my breath back in my face. I stifled an impulse to retch.

'It's not a hammer, it's a stick.'

I glared at him. 'What do you want?'

'I have a message from Miss Claudette. She wishes you to attend upon her.'

She had recently forbidden me to call on her uninvited. She had a new client whose terms of engagement included paying her a stipend to ensure exclusive access to her affections. While my love had no instinctive respect for the law of contract, the penalty for a breach being discovered would cost her sorely. She calculated that a physician's pleasure was less of a loss to her than a duke's coin and so I was exiled. I was not distraught, as this was not an unfamiliar situation to me. It was, however, inconvenient and frustrating, not to say expensive as, although for nostalgia's sake Claudette would indulge me without payment, her guild sisters were less generous and I frequently found myself on the horns of a horrid dilemma. Would I spend my scant resources upon a woman or an exotic specimen? I had recently purchased the jawbones of a gigantic shark – which now smiled from the walls of my consulting rooms with a most satisfactory air of ironic menace – so I had been forced to revert to monastic practices for many weeks.

I turned to run to my toilet when the wretched youth distracted me with an irritating dry cough. I paused and saw him standing with hand outstretched. I seized it in my strongest grip and pumped it in the English fashion, thanking him warmly for his service before retreating behind my door. I cleaned myself and changed my nether garments to the sound of his shrill cursing.

When his voice or inclination failed him and the street became silent, I left.

I have always detested walking, never more so than in Paris. I picked my way through the piles of dung in the streets, waving my stick menacingly at the numerous villainous looking dogs that seemed to congregate in the city during the summer months. I joined the flow of people, until I found myself at Claudette's lodgings by the theatre. I was admitted and was relieved to see that her paymaster was not at home. Mademoiselle Claudette greeted me with a languid wave.

'Ah, Simon, how good of you to call. Some wine?'

She was quite the grand lady. All traces of the Breton were erased from her voice and her dress showed an expanse of white flesh that would have had her in the pillory in a less enlightened time. I accepted a glass. She motioned for me to sit beside her. I rose and as I walked towards her I became aware of a low growling.

I stopped. The noise continued and rose in pitch. I froze. Beneath the couch lay what I recognized at first glance to be a fine specimen of the European wolf. It had a most alarming array of teeth which it displayed with what I took to be most unsettling aggression.

'Claudette. It's a wolf. There's a wolf under your couch. Do not try to move – it will enrage it. We must stand in silence until it falls to sleep.'

She laughed and scratched the creature behind its ear.

'Oh, he's just Reynard. Alain gave him to me. He wants me to pose for a portrait as Diana the virgin huntress. Reynard is to sit at my feet. I will be quite naked, you know. Isn't that the very thing? He is devoted to me. Quite the jealous lover, aren't you my dear?'

She patted his hackles affectionately. The creature turned and licked her hand.

'Claudette, Reynard is a name for a fox, not a wolf.'

She pouted. 'He's my wolf and I will call him what I please, Simon. Anyway, he is why I called you here.'

My heart sank. Did she expect me to treat a wolf? I had no intention of examining it. I was about to protest when Claudette rang a small silver bell. Her maid entered. I noticed that her arm was bandaged.

'Take Reynard to the kitchen, Sandrine, if you please.'

The maid took a chop from her apron and wafted it towards the wolf, which got to its feet and padded nonchalantly out of the room, shooting me a look of undisguised contempt as it passed. I sat next to Claudette and she rested her hand upon my arm.

'I need you to look after Reynard for me for a few days.'

I blanched. 'Claudette. I cannot do this. It is impossible for me to care for a wolf in my small apartment . . .'

She cut me off. 'It's just he gets so jealous, Simon. Last evening Alain came to visit me. He was going to take me to the theatre. I was so looking forward to it. Well, we were just about to be intimate. Alain had nothing on when Reynard flew into the room and attacked him. He was forced to leap from the window, the poor man. He stood in the street hiding his privy parts with his hat until Sandrine readmitted him. He was beside himself. He has sworn never to return until Reynard is gone. It's really most inconvenient.'

I warmed to Reynard at once.

'He wears his hat?'

'The poor man is losing his hair. He's ever so sensitive about it. I believe that is what hurt him the most. Choosing which of his indignities to cover.'

She giggled and for a moment we were co-conspirators.

'Anyway, Simon, you like animals. You could study him. It

would only be until the portrait's finished. He'd be at the studio with me all day. I'd be ever so grateful.'

She leaned forwards, fumbled with my belt and looked up at me. Her eyes were mischievous and her upper lip curled lasciviously. I felt my resistance crumble but said nothing.

'Ever so grateful.'

I abandoned myself to watching her head rise and fall in my lap. I would do anything for her. She stopped abruptly and caught my eye.

'So you'll take him?'

'Yes, Claudette, yes. Oh yes.'

She resumed and within moments I had become the wolf's guardian.

I spent the next week as part of the pack. It was a fascinating experience. I was not the leader. Each night, as I lay on my bed-chamber floor writing my journal, I could hear my leader's heavy breathing from my bed. He slept.

My journey home was an eventful one. I had Reynard re-strained at the end of a rope as I left Mademoiselle Claudette's, of that I am sure. At first the wolf did not take to his confinement and we had a fine tussle, with him first dragging me forward at breakneck speed and then sitting as immoveable as a gravestone in the road. The former I countered by sitting myself, and ruined a good pair of britches that had cost me over a livre. The latter I countered by putting the rope over my shoulder and heaving him along like a bargee. This was to be our first trial of strength. A wolf is no featherweight and by the time he had relented I was quite pink in the face. Reynard took to lagging behind me, casting baleful glances at my back that made the hair on the nape of my neck prickle. The rope was frequently slack and I believed him defeated. I ceased to pay him any mind.

I was diverted by thoughts of Claudette's gratitude. We were passing through a butchers' market before I realized that while I still held to my end, Reynard had parted with his. My thoughts were interrupted by a shout. I glanced sharply to my right and saw him. He was standing on a cart with the carcass of a lamb under his paws. I noticed that it was fully prepared and table-dressed and found myself remarking inconsequentially that it was a fine choice that the beast had made, although a little extravagant. The butcher was waving a cleaver at him. The wolf raised his hackles. His lips pulled back in a grim smile and he growled. The butcher fell back.

Enough is enough, I thought. I had already proved myself his master in our struggle with the rope and I prided myself in understanding the mentality of the pack animal. I drew myself to my full height and bellowed. 'Reynard. Put that down and come to my heel, sir. You are a bad wolf.'

Mimicking his mannerisms, I bared my teeth. I had read the most recent works in the *Journal of the Scientific Academy* and I was convinced that, as I had earned his surrender in the past, he was mine to command at will. I had not realized that what I had taken to be surrender had been merely a tactical retreat. The beast picked up the lamb in his jaws and looked me squarely in the eye. As he turned, just before our eye-contact broke, he raised his left leg and urinated copiously, then dawdled insolently away. The crowd parted before him.

Unfortunately the crowd did not remain parted for long. Cries of 'Seize him!' and 'He was with the wolf!' began to sound. Rough hands grabbed at my coat and I realized that I was confined. I tried to explain, to offer apologies, but I was not to be heard. Finally, I was confronted by the butcher, an odious man. I immediately noticed the small particles of raw meat roosting in the bristles on his chin.

'You owe me money. Your fucking wolf has stolen an entire lamb. That's three livres you owe me, you bloody lunatic. Bringing a wolf to a butchers' market. You ought to be locked up.'

Words failed him. I tried reason. 'Sir, I apologize. I had no idea the wolf would steal your wares. In fact, I was so lost in thought that I did not realize I was in a butchers' market at all.'

This seemed to provoke the crowd. Hands went through my pockets, searching for my purse. I remembered with relief that I had enough money to pay the stallholder's really quite outrageous price. I resigned myself to the loss of my money and had almost found consolation in the thought that a piece of meat of that size should keep even a wolf of Reynard's obvious vigour satisfied for a few days, when I remembered that I had left the purse in my consulting rooms before setting off to meet Claudette that morning. It was only a matter of moments before my embarrassment was discovered and . . . Arrest? Worse?

The baying of the crowd changed in pitch and I was suddenly released. I staggered, falling to my knees. It was Reynard. The wolf was bounding through the market crowd. People threw themselves from his path, overturning stalls and sending their neighbours crashing to the ground. He halted before me, snarling at my captors. I got to my feet and followed him through the crowd. Despite my superior reason I had become the subordinate. No one followed us and after the crowd was some distance behind us he fell into step with me. I was able to guide him back towards my home.

*　　*　　*

My servant had always been a remarkably lazy man. The simplest task would usually take hours if not days to complete. I had kept him in employment only because his remarkable set of symptoms defied my skills and I felt obligated to retain him until I could dismiss a healthy man without notice. He professed a crippling back pain that he bore with a painful fortitude that it was beyond my powers not to notice. To my surprise, the arrival of a wolf in our household effected a miraculous cure. Within a matter of minutes of Reynard's introducing himself by urinating against his legs, my man had packed his belongings and departed. I pondered his headlong flight along the road with personal and professional satisfaction. I decided to write of his case but was undecided whether to hypothesize shock as a cure for rheumatism or malingering.

The next day I awaited the arrival of a grateful Mademoiselle Claudette, but she did not come. On the third day I gave up hope. By then Reynard and I had established the parameters of our relationship and, although I say so myself, our leader ran a tight ship but he could not have done so without my wise counsel.

Leadership had its privileges. He occupied the bed and the best chair. He recognized my ability to light the fire and prepare food, which naturally I would let him eat first. We would groom each other. He paid particular attention to my wig, spending many hours nibbling it with his incisors. He was active at night, which was fortunate as, after the meat-market experience, I was concerned about the danger of his taking exercise during daylight. I found it convenient to conform to his activity and left the house rarely during the day. We would wander the streets at night. On one of our excursions I met a watchman. It gave me a shock, but fortunately I was able to convince him that an exceptionally large dog accompanied me. My suspicions that the authorities would frown upon wolf-keeping were correct and I was too afraid to return home directly. We wandered for hours until cockcrow drove us back inside like the restless dead. The next night I was too shaken to take to the streets. We paced the apartment and fell into a fitful sleep at dawn.

Disaster struck! A woeful, sorry, unfortunate day that left me the most undeserving hero. If I could relive any part of my life, I would relive that day and shun brandy. I was writing in my journal, lying on the floor of my bedchamber, while Reynard slumbered peacefully in my bed. After re-enacting my past week on the page I felt such an overwhelming sense of melancholy that I concluded that my humours must be quite out of balance. I was bilious and required a warming draught to restore equilibrium. What better than brandy? Oh God, I don't believe in you but if you exist, allow me never to be a drunkard again for all the harm a little indulgence can cost.

It was the brandy that allowed me to sleep through that evil hour. I had observed during my night rambles that wolves, or at least this particular wolf, are greater scavengers than goats. Reynard would eat literally anything, no matter how vile. He would swallow it with great gluttony. But his iron stomach failed him that night. I could only imagine his attempts to escape before he defecated all over me. Because I slept I could not help him. Because I was drunk. I was caked in wolf dung by the time I woke. I opened my eyes to a sight so horrible it turns my stomach to recall it even now. The stench caught my throat. The air was filled with noxious vapours that made my eyes stream. I stripped and scraped as much as I could from my naked person before gathering my poor clothing on the foul blanket. I wiped my feet upon an undefiled corner and tiptoed to the washroom. There I scrubbed myself with a fury until my skin was raw and my hair stood from my scalp.

I shivered and cringed back into the bedchamber. The wolf slept. The stench that overpowered me and was causing me to tremble at the knee bothered him not at all. I gingerly bundled clothing, blanket and those portions of the carpet that were contaminated into a parcel. I knew I had to take it away. It could not remain in the apartment. My neighbours would be sure to notice and become inquisitive. All evidence had to be disposed of if I were to avoid being denounced as a wolf-keeper. I had to take it far away and dispose of it somewhere where it could never be traced to my door. Then Reynard had to go. I had cared for him in a manner that would make any reasonable owner very grateful indeed. And she had better be grateful, I thought to myself as I dragged the evil-smelling parcel over my shoulder, barely suppressing the urge to vomit and soil myself simultaneously. I was owed a lot of gratitude. So lost was I in self-pity that as I left the building I forgot, in my haste, to secure the doors.

I disposed of my burden by dropping it into the Seine. My filthy task accomplished, I retraced my steps. As I neared my destination, I became aware of a commotion ahead. A grand, gilded carriage of the sort that only the very wealthy could own seemed to be in some distress. I could hear the frantic neighing of the horses and the thunder of wheels as it careered downhill at a terrifying pace. I saw a streak of grey running alongside the lead horse. I heard savage baying that seemed somehow to remind me of my native Breton forests, and I knew.

I was doomed. My wolf had assaulted someone of enormous wealth and influence.

Oh God, Reason, or who or whatever you are, I cannot bear to recall it. Yet I must. It is carved on my memory like some vast, shameful monolith. I knew that I could never speak of it again. I had made myself my own sole confidant because to know this secret was to possess the key to my ruin. The lead horse fell and the carriage tipped as Reynard fell upon his prey like a . . . well, like a wolf. The coach hit the ground with a rending crash and slid in a shower of glass splinters and sparks. It came to a halt with another crash against a wall and shattered. There was a pause, a moment of complete tranquillity, then pandemonium descended. Half the crowd set off in pursuit of Reynard, while the rest thronged to the coach to offer assistance or watch. For my part, reason came to me as if a cataract had been cut from my eyes. I sprinted to my surgery and feverishly packed the tools of my profession into my physician's bag. I then joined the crowd around the coach and forced my way to the front with cries of, 'Let me through, I'm a doctor.'

I assessed the passengers. One was a youth who looked to be in his late teens – obviously noble. He had been thrown from the coach when it overturned. He was unconscious, his arm was broken, but he was breathing. The remaining passenger was of more concern. He was a man in his mid-forties. The side of the coach was lifted off him. He lay motionless. His eyes looked glassy and there was blood in his mouth. Yet he was still alive. I turned him over and saw a shard of glass protruding from the small of his back.

'Make stretchers and carry them to my rooms. Follow me.'

I strode off and a group of people fell in to step, carrying the two casualties on pieces of their coach. I prayed that Reynard had not emptied his bowels before his bid for freedom. Fortunately there was no trace of him. The operation on the older man was a qualified success. I cleaned and stitched the wound, but while my patient was lucky in that no vital organ had been damaged, his backbone was broken. He would live, but he would never walk again.

I patched up his son, which required little skill. I learned that he was a count and that he and his father, a duke, were travelling to Versailles from Brittany but had become lost in Paris. I revealed my origins and we made smalltalk before I told him of his father's condition. The youth became quite tearful. He looked at me in a way that showed his breeding rather than his tender years. His voice shook but he controlled himself.

'Look here, Doctor. You're a Breton, and I know that were it not for your skill my father would be dead. He's going to need looking after. What do you say? Are you the man for the job?'

I looked around my rooms. Finally, from the horror of my week as a wolf-keeper, I had found him – the golden patient.

'You'll have to leave your practice and come to live on the estate. We'll compensate you well for that. How does a thousand livres sound? With five hundred a year salary. Accommodation as well, naturally. You'll be part of the household.'

I could not look at him. I glowed with shame. He embraced me. I ceased to be Dr Simon, companion of whores, and became M'sieur le Docteur Legris, personal physician to the aristocracy. My only regret was that, with this change, I was forced to abandon my Claudette. I could not see her again for fear she would connect me to the wolf.

4

The Golden Patient

IN THE WEEKS THAT FOLLOWED, I APPLIED MYSELF TO THE treatment of my new master's wounds. I was able to stave off infection by using a tincture of brandy, both externally and, when mixed with extracts of poppy sap, internally. The best aid to recovery is sleep. My treatment ensured that he slept well and often. In his waking moments I tested his reflexes and was sad to find that he was dead from the waist downwards. At first he bore this with amazing fortitude, commenting to me as I pricked his feet without response that if a man were given the choice between losing his legs and his head, only a fool would select oblivion over incapacity.

To my relief he seemed to have no recollection of the events that had brought him under my care. I knew that the day would come when it was no longer possible to shield him from the truth of the accident, but staved this off as best I could by telling everyone who came to visit him that the shocking truth (which was the talk of Paris by now) could only serve to upset him and thereby delay his recovery. As he grew in strength this became increasingly untenable. I toyed with the idea of keeping him permanently drugged but dismissed this as incompatible with the Hippocratic oath. Besides, I had to show some success in my treatment to be assured that the offer of permanent employment remained.

I took comfort in human nature, which abhors a vacuum of information with such fervour that it will seek to fill it with the most wild and ridiculous theories. The most popular explanation was that Reynard had been driven into the centre of the city by the increase in wandering brigands and beggars taking up residence in the Bois de Boulogne. This caused an outbreak of random violence against the itinerant poor that did little to improve the chances of solving the mystery, but I had no doubt provided the perpetrators with an excuse to behave in a manner to which they were already inclined. One journal speculated that the wolf had escaped from the Russian Embassy. This was based upon little more than the fact that wolves are apparently prevalent in that country. A mob formed at the gates. The ambassador was pelted with stones and worse, before the irate populace were dispersed by Swiss Guards, who had to be dispatched from their barracks in the Louvre. No one seemed to hold the opinion that the creature had been released upon the city accidentally or that it had been kept locally. In fact, wholly untrue sightings were reported daily. Only three held the true secret: Claudette, Reynard and me. I would keep it to my grave. I prayed that Claudette had the intelligence to realize that my exposure meant her own ruin. Reynard had not been found. I wished him luck and the absence of a homing instinct.

The Duke made good progress. The fever that so often accompanies a wound of such gravity broke and I felt constrained from sedating him further. Finally, the day arrived when I could keep it from him no longer. I had just helped him to the commode and had turned my back when he asked me.

'Legris.'

'Yes, Your Grace?'

'I recall the carriage turning over, as you know.'

I knew what was coming and kept my back turned. Now I was sparing him my blushes of shame rather than preserving his dignity.

'Yes, Your Grace.'

'How came it to overturn, Legris? You see, my memory fails me. I can recall the coachmen driving at speed. I distinctly recall telling them to slow down after my son had encouraged them to drive at a reckless pace. I can remember no other vehicle. I can hear the horses screaming, feel the crash, then my memory is as dead as my legs.'

I gulped, hiding it with a cough.

'Your carriage was attacked by a wolf, Your Grace.'

There was a silence.

'You never struck me as a man with a sense of humour, Legris. Do you think that is funny? Is this some kind of treatment? Are you hoping to shock the feeling back to my feet by enraging me with your idiotic attempts at merriment?'

He was becoming quite apoplectic and I feared for his condition, but the lesser of the two evils seemed to be to continue. He would dismiss me if I tried to shield him from the truth by claiming that I had spoken lightly.

'It is nothing of the kind, Your Grace. And you are right. I have never had a reputation for wit. I speak the truth. A wolf attacked your carriage. Only a step away from the Pont Neuf.'

I steeled myself. I was never a great liar. My face would flush and betray me. I was relieved His Grace remained on his commode, so I could hide my deceit behind my back.

'No one knows where it came from. Of course there are many tales. People love to speculate, you know. They say wandering thieves drove it into the city, although why they would want to do that I cannot say. Or that it escaped from the Russian Embassy.'

I tailed off. There was silence behind me. I turned and saw my Master seated on the commode with his head in his hands. His legs had already grown spindly and stretched before him, useless, pale and withered.

'Are you all right, Your Grace? Do you require any assistance?'

He sighed and looked up at me. I could see his eyes were moist and this affected me far more than the sight of him as a stoic invalid.

'Take me to bed, Legris.'

So I did. He turned his face to the wall and lay there, acknowledging no caller and taking no refreshment. There he remained for the next three days.

Many people came to visit the Duke. I managed a very profitable sideline treating their ailments. He was too unwell to leave my consulting room, where I had made a bed for him, and his habit had been to receive visitors lying in his bed. The revelation of the wolf brought this to a close. He would not dismiss them: they attended and he ignored them until they left of their own accord. All save his son, whom he dispatched about his business with the greatest of violence.

I, of course, remained. I sent for food. It remained uneaten. My attempts to engage him in conversation went unanswered. Our intercourse was confined to his requests to be placed upon the

commode, in which I took heart. I had heard of cases of melancholia
(and I was convinced that this was what assailed my patient) that
were so severe that the sufferer would lose the will even to do this.
I resolved to balance out the bilious humour that dominated him
by creating a hot, dry atmosphere and by prescribing a warming
draught. He would accept my ministrations and bore the heat
with fortitude although it was barely tolerable. Only my respect
for his station and my position kept me in my frock coat while I
attended upon him. I was gratified at my diagnosis, as after three
days of treatment he spoke to me. It was a surprising question. I
was expecting him to demand that I extinguish the fires or open
the window, as I myself was weak with the heat.

'Do you believe in God, Legris?'

I hesitated. This was the sort of interrogation that could
produce an unfavourable answer. I thought of professing faith,
as I had noticed the crucifix he wore on a silver chain round his
neck. But I discounted this. I owed him honesty in all matters save
one.

'No, Your Grace. Cholera took my parents when I was a child.
I always found it hard to believe in a benevolent creator who
had robbed and abandoned me so. That is not to say I have no
experience of religion. I have lived among monks.'

He cut me short. 'I do. Or at least I did. Life has always favoured
me. I was born a noble of the sword. I have marched to gunfire
and, as I thought, there are no atheists where the shell flies. I have
always found it easy to have a faith that teaches that all is ordained
and part of some great plan that we cannot hope to comprehend.
Very similar to soldiering, don't you see? Obey orders and it will
be all for the best. I have faced death, and the prospect of being
crippled in battle, and my faith gave me the strength to resist my

fear. Illness, an accident at the hunt, a duel – all these I could withstand. But a wolf – a fucking wolf in the middle of Paris – makes me, the Duc Ladurie de Bretagne, of the sword, of the cavalry, of the Court of His Highness King Louis the Fifteenth of that fucking name, dependent on a motherly duck of a man like you to evacuate my bowels. Well, it must be some kind of a joke. I believed in God's plan. I cannot believe in a plan that would cripple me so lightly. I have no faith. When the rank and file lose faith, they desert. I have nothing but contempt for deserters.'

I knew the balance of my life teetered on the fulcrum of my answer. I remembered past disastrous attempts to say the right thing. I was paralysed with indecision and, to my horror, blurted out the first thought that came to me.

'I have told you my beliefs, Your Grace, so I shall not repeat them. I believe them, and in my world there is no God. If you believe, then for you he exists. I have heard it said that God exists as a creator but, as the Supreme Being, no more concerns himself in the fates of individual men than His Majesty enquires whether I am happy in my lodgings. He is like a clockmaker who constructs the perfect mechanism of his world then allows it to run on. The clock runs, chimes and will do so for eternity, with every event contributing to the greater whole.'

I had no idea where it had come from. Something I had read, perhaps? Overheard somewhere? Oh, seven million barrels of shit – I had just told my prospective employer, who was understandably out of sorts after being crippled in an accident that I caused because I wanted to fuck Claudette, that he was a cripple because it was part of some divine plan. I could have wept. I dared a glance at him. To my surprise he did not seem to be enraged. He contemplated the view of the courtyard from my window in silence. I could hardly bear to breathe in case this broke his reverie. Finally he turned to me. There was a new life in his eyes, although he did not go so far as actually to smile.

'A clock, you say. Very good.'

I stood. I wanted to say something but did not trust myself not to unravel this peculiar advantage. The Duke returned to his contemplation. More silence. I became conscious of a desire to empty my bladder. I could do nothing. I started to hop from foot to foot in what I hoped was an inconspicuous manner. The poor quality of the floorboards made each footfall sound as if I was dancing on a drum.

My Lord Ladurie de Bretagne drew me sharply into focus. He nodded curtly to me. 'Carry on, Legris.'

I was dismissed. I fled to the privy in a state of corporeal and intellectual flux.

I am pleased to say that my patient recovered rapidly from his melancholia. Although he would never regain the use of his legs, the wound itself was healing nicely. I was able to advise my charge that he would soon be well enough to travel. I had hoped to be swept to Versailles, but this was not to be. My new employer – for he was kind enough to engage me on another generous stipend – decided to return to Brittany. My terms were simple: I was to attend to the family's medical needs. This would undoubtedly give me ample time to pursue my botanical studies. Versailles would have been an ideal, but I was aware that its rarefied environment made it highly unlikely that I would come across a specimen that truly engaged me. Indeed, I felt that I had learned more in three days in my rooms in Reynard's company than would be possible in three years at Court. I had always aspired to aristocratic patients, but on reflection, the prospect of seeing nothing but aristocrats and servants, to be a servant myself, filled me with dread. The Duke and his son made me feel quite uncomfortable enough. Herds of their like were unthinkable. At least the women would be more affordable in Brittany, particularly to a man of means like me. I would return to the west in triumph. I was not coming home. I was arriving.

5

Matters of Honour

THE JOURNEY WAS NOT TOO ARDUOUS. I WAS GRATIFIED to find that if one travelled as part of an extremely well-connected entourage, one escaped the lice, stomach complaints and weariness that characterized the experience for less notable wayfarers. I felt positively invigorated as the carriage turned from the highway. I was scarcely able to restrain myself from craning my neck from the carriage window as we passed between elms that stood sentry on either side of a long driveway that rivalled the road in width. The coach turned to the left and I caught first sight of my new home. It was a hot day and, unusually for Brittany, the sun smiled down from a cloudless sky. The great gate was already open and as we drove into a courtyard that seemed as large as the Louvre, the sun's rays were reflected from the pointed, conical turret roofs, turning them silver. It was as if the chateau was my Master's wealth made solid, proclaiming to the world that here resided the Duc Ladurie de Bretagne, a man of power and influence.

I was escorted to my chambers, which were located at the west and rear of the building. I was to occupy rooms at the top of a former watchtower, which had the curious feature of being square at its base, but becoming circular at the third floor. Here my apartment was located. I found a circular room, which, I was told, could serve as a library and laboratory, a bedroom one storey above and facilities to bathe and conduct my other ablutions. I found the curved walls a pleasing novelty, like being an imprisoned damsel in one of the chivalrous romances that Claudette so relished. My quarters commanded a magnificent view over what I at first took to be my Master's lands. Lush, verdant fields that stretched towards the coast. I did not appreciate that the full extent of the Duke's estate stretched from the Atlantic coast in the west to La Manche in the north. I had always wanted to be a rich man. Luck had brought me to a place that showed me the poverty of my ambition. I had not known the meaning of wealth before. The riches that had been the object of my modest aspirations barely qualified as crumbs from the Duke's table.

The chateau was not merely a monument to the wealth of its owner. The Duke was Master of the Royal Horse, and his estate was devoted to the training, rearing and upkeep of these animals. They were provided with a chateau of their own to the west of the main courtyard, complete with an imposing Grecian aspect and chiming clock. I have never been a keen horseman. I am too short to cut an imposing equestrian figure and I am not comfortable rising above the natural height of a man. I am happy to be transported by the horse, but I need the comforting distance of a coach and coachman before I can be entirely at peace with the arrangement. Soon after my arrival, my natural antipathy for the creatures was confirmed by the discovery that my duties were to include treating those injured while attending to the horses' welfare. I could not have imagined how frequently this would occur. I confess I have not come across an animal that causes more hurt to those around it. My Master would have caused fewer fractures, bruises and abrasions to his servants if he had taken it upon himself to breed lions.

I slipped into the routine of life at the chateau without much difficulty. I tended to the horse-damaged as and when the need arose, reviewing the various patients in the mid-morning. I attended His Grace and the other members of the family when they had need of my services. I inspected the Duke's injuries daily and found that they were healing well, as far as they could. The wound on his back had formed a scar and showed no sign of opening or infection. I had hoped that there would be some return of sensation in his legs, but this was not to be. I manipulated them, pricked them with pins and salved the line of his backbone to no avail.

During these sessions I had the opportunity to converse with my Master and develop a small understanding of the man whose life I had so drastically altered. We shared many aspects of character, although the differences in our station in life ensured that these had developed in diverse ways. Both of us had a curiosity about the natural sciences. My own delving into the realm of nature was constrained by my lack of funds. His knew no such boundaries. His collection of curiosities was unrivalled. It had an entire gallery to house it, and still had outgrown its home. The exhibits ranged from European fauna that the Duke had gathered as a hunter – including a wolf of such villainous aspect as to make him twin to the infamous Reynard – to exotic specimens such as a white tiger and an Indian cobra that he had purchased through agents.

The responsibilities of public life and military service had prevented the Duke from travelling as broadly as he desired, but his deep pockets had allowed his enquiring mind to roam the globe vicariously. A constant procession of agents and dealers came to the chateau. All were competing for his favour and his wallet, all selling some variety of curiosity. I was privileged to be able to observe these exchanges and was even consulted on occasion. The world of the specimen-collector was peopled with as many charlatans as upright men, and I prided myself on my ability to spot a dissembler. I knew from my own experience that His Grace, although master of the horse market and the battlefield, had a forthright disposition that hampered his ability to discern if a secret was being kept from him. I flatter myself in thinking that I was able to save him from some very unwise purchases.

We spent hours discussing the merits of various hypotheses. His experiences breeding horses led him to believe that the nature and capabilities of all creatures, including mankind, depended upon breeding alone. I did not share this view, preferring to draw a distinction between the physical and the moral. I could accept that one inherited one's physical self. But I believed one to be master of one's own moral development. We compromised upon the idea that the capacity to develop may be inherited, but there would need to be some empirical study before a decision could be made one way or the other.

The Duke had read the English philosopher John Locke. This had affected him greatly, giving him a desire for experimentation. He had in mind taking the children of a hanged thief and raising them in virtuous surroundings to establish whether it would be for the greater good to nurture or hang the families of all convicted criminals. He was in the process of drawing up detailed plans for this exercise and eagerly consulting the local magistrates to find a suitable candidate.

As we debated the morality of the human species, I found myself faced with a dilemma of my own. I was forced to concede that a cure was beyond my skills. I did not think that any other physician could do better. There are some cases that even the greatest and most gifted scientist cannot affect. Sadly, with this discovery came the unwelcome recognition that my work was complete. In the absence of a cure, what need is there of a physician? I had grown acclimatized to the luxury of my new position and would sorely miss it if I declared myself redundant. Luckily for me, fate intervened and made me indispensable once again.

The Comte La Latte, my Master's son, was the child of his first marriage. His mother had paid the ultimate sacrifice in bringing him into this world and for many years my Master grieved for her and did not remarry. Despite his physical resemblance to his mother, the Young Master was resolved to follow in his father's profession. This met with the obstacle of an unprecedented period of peace and stability that denied him the battlefield. At the time of my employment he was twenty-three years old, and was finding the leisurely existence of the peacetime soldier somewhat of an anticlimax. The youthful humours that make a soldier stand firm in the line of battle boiled within him and, as is common in these cases, sought relief. There were two arenas in which such relief could be found: the boudoir and the field of honour. In my Master's son's case the two became linked.

My role in the history of the Young Master as a lover and duellist started at almost the same point that I realized I was unable to cure his father. I sat in my tower, contemplating the anatomy of yet another fractured femur and wondering how I could remain in situ without actively misleading my employer, when a servant entered to tell me that my presence was required. I made my way to the salon, where I saw my Master. He had borne his own ill-luck bravely, but seemed reduced by worry. I hastened to him and, on checking his pulse and temperature, found him to be slightly fevered.

'What ails you, Your Grace?'

'Legris, my wife was a brave and honourable woman.'

'I am sure that is so, Your Grace.'

'Characteristics she passed to our son.'

He lit a pipe and drew reflectively, allowing the calming vapours to soothe him as I had so often prescribed.

'She was also a profoundly stupid woman. Not a problem while she lived. I married her for her looks and her lands, not her mind. Sadly, this is a characteristic that she passed to our son as well. I have just heard that the idiot has been apprehended in a liaison with the Comte d'Armentières' mistress. While that young woman's virtues are famously freely given, my idiot son decided to avail himself of her good nature in the family chapel at Versailles while his rival was at prayer. I understand that the confessional capsized and deposited them both in the bosom of his family in a state of undress. Both had been drinking – a fact that my son confirmed by gallantly vomiting on the Count's shoes. The lack of discretion alone required satisfaction. Unfortunately, I know d'Armentières. He's a bloody good shot and the better swordsman. My son is brave and will no doubt make a good show of things, but I fear that that will not be enough and I need you to travel to Paris to see if you can repair any damage he may sustain. I hope that there is enough left of him for you to treat. You will take horse and ride for Paris tonight.'

This was a great honour. I knew I had become the family physician and my presence and stipend were secure. I did not protest that I could not ride nor that I was terrified of horses. It did not seem to be the right time to do so. Within moments I was clinging to a horse and hurtling through the night at alarming speed.

I do not recall much of the journey. This may be because of the many blows to the head I sustained falling from my mount. I recommend two days' ride, much of it in darkness, as a means of learning the art of horsemanship. The horse was of a relatively placid disposition. It would run, I would fall, whereupon it would stand and wait for me to pull myself to my feet and remount. It would run and the process would be repeated. By the time I arrived at the tax wall, I was so addled I did not notice that the usually heavy traffic had ceased and night was falling. I swung myself from the saddle, savouring the rare moment of doing so voluntarily, and entered the building.

The interior consisted of a long room, lit by two rather poorly made lanterns. There was a counter, at the head of which sat a woman. She was of middle years and was of the type from whom life seems to have leached the good nature and vitality. Her hair was dyed red, framing an ill-natured countenance. She wore a stained dress beneath a blue uniform coat that had been made for someone twice her stature. She glowered out beneath the brim of a three-cornered hat from eyes so sunken that they seemed to be positioned at the back of her head. Her scrawny arms lay upon a ledger that she was scratching at venomously with a balding quill. It was as if the bones of one of the former residents of the Innocents' Cemetery that had been transferred to the new ossuary had taken both life and public office. I stood in front of her, and thinking I would minimize the inconvenience to us both, held a livre in my hand to indicate that I wanted to pay quickly and be on my way.

I waited; the only sound the scratching of the quill upon the ledger. Finally, the woman said, 'Wait, wait, wait. Everyone waits for the tax collector. Such a long wait with the night falling.'

I was relieved. I decided to try a pleasantry. 'Madame, we must all wait in life. Patience is a virtue to be cultivated. Now, if you would be so good . . .'

Her head snapped round and she snarled at me, baring brown, uneven teeth. 'How dare you address me!'

I protested that she had spoken to me first, but in vain.

'You, Monsieur, with your high-and-mighty wig and your brocade coat. You come to my office and address me out of turn in your stupid Breton accent. Who do you think you are? I am engaged in important work here. All the receipts for the day must tally in this ledger. If they do not – anarchy! You distract the good governing of the kingdom with your prattling. When I am finished and have time to deal with you, then I will ask you what you want. Do you understand?'

I stood in silence, shaking with rage. I did not dare to give this impertinent crone the dressing down she richly deserved. She had the power to thwart my mission, to refuse me entry to the city, to call the police and have me carried off, even. I had to remain calm. I waited, every scratch of the quill a lash across my face and a victorious drum roll of her petty tyranny. Finally, she looked up.

'Madame, I wish to enter. I am Dr Simon Legris, personal physician to the Duc Ladurie de Bretagne. I am on urgent business for my Master. I have only the tools of my profession and my horse.'

'That will be eight sous.'

We both surveyed the gold coin in my hand.

'I cannot change that. You must return with something smaller.'

The blood pounded in my ears. For a moment I was literally paralysed. There was nothing I could do but stalk off into the night and find something to buy to produce the change. I went to an inn. The innkeeper seemed unsurprised by my indignant recital, and charged me at least three times a fair price for a very ordinary bottle of red wine. I returned to the customs post to find it closed.

The morning was a grey line on the horizon as my horse and I finally entered the city, poorer in cash but richer in the variety of parasites we had acquired at our insalubrious lodgings. I made my way to the Hôtel de Châtelet, where I was to meet the Young Master. I had never met someone facing death before and I was intrigued to see if there were any physical changes that could be observed. He was taking breakfast as I arrived, seated in a well-appointed guest room on the first floor. I noted that he was not pale, and did not seem to have suffered any reduction in his appetite.

'Ah, Legris, do come in. I trust my father is well. Why has he sent you to Paris?'

'Your father is as recovered as his condition permits, sir. He is put in jeopardy not by his own health but by his concern for yours. You are to fight tomorrow?'

'Oh, that.' He gestured dismissively. 'You don't mean the Old Man has dragged you all the way from the family seat because of that, do you? It's not serious. A little gunplay then either I walk away with honour or I don't walk away at all. I don't expect some-one of your station to understand, but I am surprised that my father has sent you to try to talk me out of it.'

'He has not sent me to talk you out of it. I have come to attend to your needs if you are fortunate enough to survive. You are right. I do not understand the desire to die a painful, violent and utterly unnecessary death. No other animal does this. Even great predators such as bears or lions will not fight to the death over a mate.'

The Young Master looked smug. I realized that he thought that he had found an answer to this point.

'Isn't that proof that we stand above the other animals in the natural order of creation?'

I was nonplussed. What could he be talking about?

'The fact that we alone will die for love or for honour. For an ideal. For an abstract. The rest of creation may die for food or territory. Only man, and indeed only man at his highest and most noble, will die for these.'

I paused. While there may have been a certain vestige of an argument in what he was saying in general, I was sure that the lofty idealism to which he referred did not apply to his situation. I was powerless to resist an impulse to deflate him.

'That is, of course, correct, sir. However, I would venture to suggest that if a lion, tiger or even a baboon had defiled another's lair and concluded its invasion by voiding the contents of its stomach over its rival's paws, it is likely that the result would have been violent, regardless of their lack of ideals and nobility.'

The Young Master's face betrayed no indication that he had the slightest idea what I could be implying. I have noticed that many people share the inclination to cast the particulars of that which has brought them to the brink of some crisis out of their minds. He simply could or would not relate his inability to drink without casting all restraint to the winds to his predicament, preferring to look upon his impending annihilation as a great, chivalrous adventure. The example I had given him had as little meaning to him now as an anecdote about the mating behaviour of stoats. I have found that this trait of character is at its most pronounced among those whose early years have been devoted to the martial virtues. A religious upbringing has a similar but distinct outcome. It will tend to produce a sanctimonious and long-suffering victim.

He smiled at me and said, 'I dare say it would, Doctor.'

The duel was to be fought at dawn in the Bois de Boulogne. I rose before the sun and prepared my medical bag. The Young Master was in a good humour and passed the journey joking with his Second, a witless young man who repeatedly expressed regret that it was not his turn to face death. By the time we arrived at the field of honour his regret at this could not match my own.

It had rained. Birch trees surrounded the clearing, their white bark glittering through the morning mist. The staccato sound of droplets falling upon leaves ground at my nerves. The Comte d'Armentières' party had already arrived and set up camp in the centre of the clearing. A small but not inconsiderable throng of spectators surrounded them. We walked towards the Count and his party, with the Young Master and his Second leading. They comprised the Count, another nobleman who had obviously come to assist him prepare his weapons, a third, older man who was to act as invigilator, and a woman. This last intrigued me and I paid her great attention as we walked towards them. Could she be the lady whose virtue was at the heart of this affair? All I was able to distinguish at a distance was her blonde hair, set off very fetchingly by a black gown and veil. She stood to the side and did not engage in conversation with either man. As we approached and the two Seconds greeted each other, she was finally close enough for me to make out her face. I caught my breath. Claudette. This could spell my ruin. I must not betray that I knew her. Surely she could not be stupid enough to acknowledge me? My heart hammered. I could not discount the possibility that she would greet me and the whole tale of Reynard would be exposed. Fortunately, she seemed not to recognize me. I could not help but feel a sting of humiliation at how quickly I had passed from her memory. It mingled strangely with my relief.

I had never witnessed a duel before. It is a grim business, as extinguishing life always is, whether for honour or punishment. The two protagonists were summoned together. The third man asked each whether their differences could not be reconciled. Both men replied that they could not, d'Armentières grimly and the Young Master with such good humour that I could barely restrain myself from slapping his face.

The Seconds handed each man a loaded pistol and retired. The two stood back to back and, at the invigilator's command, walked ten paces, turned and fired. Both fell, both clutching their heads. I ran to the Young Master. Blood poured from his nose, and I noticed with some surprise that there was a bullet hole in his clothing at the level of his heart. I cut away the cloth to find an ugly weal but no wound. His heart still beat and I could detect breath at his lips. I resolved that his best hope of recovery was to be taken to a place where I could examine the source of his head wound and treat him as he rested. I called for a stretcher and as we loaded the unconscious body I looked around the clearing. It was plain that d'Armentières was dead. His party stood in silence, looking down at his prostrate form but making no effort to staunch the puddle of blood growing around him. I looked back to the Young Master and was relieved to note that his stretcher was being loaded into our carriage. I hurried after them.

As I turned to leave, I caught Claudette's eye. She winked at me, grinned and blew me a kiss. I was unsure whether this was because she had recognized me at last or because her wanton nature compelled her to treat all men who crossed her path as potential clients. It was with some regret that I was forced to reject the possibility of renewing our acquaintance as too dangerous.

It did not take me long to restore the Young Master to health. This was not because in his case a head wound was unlikely to prove fatal, as his father unkindly remarked when I made my report on my return to Brittany. Rather, it was one of those few instances that made me feel that my lack of faith in the Almighty might be misplaced. If there is a God, he certainly watches over the Comte La Latte. The bullet had been fired with unwavering accuracy. It had struck him in the heart. Fortunately, the flask of Calvados in his breast pocket had interceded. The force of the impact caused the flask to collapse. This, in turn, propelled the cork from its neck at some velocity. It flew upwards, imbedding itself in the Young Master's nasal cavity, causing him to cry out, fall to the ground and swoon. The procedure required to extract it was gratifyingly simple. It caused the young man sufficient discomfort to make him regret fighting the duel at all, which was my intention.

The philosophical and theological implications were wide ranging. If God could protect individuals, why protect the Young Master and not my parents? Did God, if he exists, have some special affection for idiots? Why idiots? Were they most directly in his image? If so, was God an idiot or was the Young Master under the protection of a specific god of fools? Clearly, d'Armentières was no fool. The Young Master's shot had passed cleanly through his right eye and removed the back of his skull. Why was he unworthy? All in all I was happy to conclude that if I was incorrect in my atheism, then this was evidence of such stupidity that I could demand divine protection as my right.

My return to the chateau was to prove both shortlived and eventful. The Duke had developed an interest in Africa, particularly the idea that creatures that had never been seen by civilized men existed in the interior of that massive continent. I believe that his injury had caused him to spend an unhealthy amount of time ruminating upon his own mortality, as his latest obsession seemed to be to procure the discovery and presentation of such a creature that would, in return, bear his name. This ambition led to a procession of would-be explorers, all presenting their plans for some or other expedition. Many of these were lunatics – for example, the man who, by counting all the numerical values of the words in the Book of Genesis and converting these to a set of coordinates, claimed to have established that the Garden of Eden was located in the howling northern ice deserts. Others were dreamers whose desire for discovery was matched only by their lack of ability to organize a trip to market.

My Master was convinced that only one candidate belonged with neither the lunatics nor the fools: a Dutchman from the

Cape Colony named Van der Veer. He was a tall, well-built man who matched to the letter the popular view of how an explorer and hunter should look. He had a large scar running from his right elbow to his wrist, which he explained was the result of an encounter with a lion. His proposal was simple. He wished to travel to the mouth of the great river that reached the sea beneath the Slave Coast and from there to the interior by boat and foot. His purpose was to hunt down and capture great reptiles, which he had heard the native peoples of that region talk of with some fear.

Van der Veer had never seen these animals himself but had with him a collection of teeth and other small bones that he explained had been bartered with the native tribesmen who occupy the settlements at the river's bank. They had traded them with more reclusive peoples from the centre of the forests that cover the continent's heart. My Master passed these to me for my opinion. I found them to be strange artefacts. They were certainly teeth, curving, wickedly sharp, smooth and about the same length as a man's hand. They seemed reptilian in origin, or at least came from a carnivorous creature and resembled those of a crocodile more closely than any other animal of my experience. Yet they were not constructed from a substance that could be described as bone or horn. They seemed to be composed of stone, as if some gorgon had petrified the creature from which they came – and what a creature that must have been. If the teeth that I held were of a similar proportion to their owner as a crocodile's were to its size, the beast from which these had been extracted must have been at least fifteen strides in length. I checked them carefully for any indication that they had been cast or carved, but could find none. As far as I could tell these were genuine.

I passed my opinion on to my Master, who seemed overjoyed. He summoned Van der Veer and told him that he should put together a detailed proposal for his expedition for his perusal. If the plan were sound, he could count upon the Duke's patronage and support. The Dutchman was typically phlegmatic, grunting his assent and promising to return with all the details set down in writing within a month.

I was beside myself with excitement. It had always been an ambition of mine to travel to Africa to pursue my interest in the natural sciences. It seemed that this dream stood some small chance of being realized. I waited for an opportune moment to ask to be included among the explorers.

Once again, fate was to conspire against me. I adopted the direct approach and asked my Master if I could go. He refused me. My services were paid for and my presence at the chateau was required. I was left in no doubt that my absence would result not only in my dismissal from my comfortable office but in my being unable to practise my profession in France again. I hesitate to say I was trapped. If I was a prisoner, it was in a gilded dungeon to which I had always aspired. Although it irked me that the realization of a dream should be dangled before me only to prove impossible, all in all it was not hard to reconcile myself to my fate with the consolation that I, Simon Legris, would have the first chance to examine the specimens when the explorers returned.

No one could have taken the stupidity of my Master's son into consideration with the weight that, without doubt, it deserved. The fact that he had been saved from certain death by what was little short of a miracle served to restrain his behaviour for less than six months. Once again I found myself in receipt of a late summons to my Master's presence.

'Legris, he's done it again.'

'Done what, Your Grace?'

'My son is to fight another duel. This time with the Chevalier Renault.'

I drew in my breath sharply. The Chevalier was a famous duellist. As a young man he had spent some time at his family's plantations in Louisiana and had acquired some of that country's barbarous customs. He was in the habit of recording the lives he had taken by scoring a notch upon the weapon that had been the engine of his unfortunate victim's demise. Now a man in his third decade, the butts of his duelling pistols were rumoured to be so disfigured that only his hands were calloused in a way that allowed him to hold them without discomfort.

'Why does the Young Master have to fight the Chevalier?'

'I am almost too embarrassed to tell even you, my friend and servant. You will be aware that I am contemplating arranging a wife for my son in the hope that she will provide me with an heir able enough to take on the management of my estates?'

'You had not taken me into your confidence in this respect before now, Your Grace.'

'Well, I am. Do you know why? No? Because my son, although a worthy and courageous young man, has not the intellect to realize that there is a difference between losing something because of one's own irredeemable stupidity and being cheated of it. The fool has convinced himself that he is an expert card player, a view that he holds tenaciously and in the teeth of the evidence. So far as he is concerned, if a man is to defeat him consistently, it must be by way of foul means, as by fair the idiot believes he is invincible.'

I ventured a question. 'Your Grace, are you sure that he is as bad as you say? We should at least acknowledge the possibility that he has been cheated rather than been stupid.'

My Master dismissed this suggestion with a sharp bark of laughter. 'Legris, my admirable progeny only mastered counting beyond nine at the age of seventeen. His memory is so poor it remains a miracle that he is able to find his way to the privy in a house he has occupied since his birth. I have never been much of a card player, preferring to gamble on horses and exploit a medium about which I know more than my opponents. I understand numeracy and memory are essential prerequisites for success at cards. Clearly my son takes a different view of gambling to me, preferring to play a game at which his foe has all the natural advantages. Anyway, not content with losing enough money to require me to bail him out again, he has accused Renault of cheating. Naturally, the Chevalier demanded satisfaction.'

'How does he say that he was cheated?'

'Oh, this transcends stupidity. Apparently my son was cheated because his opponent realized that there was no such card as a thirteen of diamonds, while he did not. If his dear, witless and departed mother had been kind enough to leave me with any other children, I would be content to abandon him to his fate. As she did not, I feel an obligation to dispatch you to Paris again to try to salvage his broken, but one hopes still living, body. That is, if you cannot prevail upon him to abandon this lunacy and apologize. He cannot remain. With his rutting and his idiocy I swear to God he is more goat than man. In the unlikely event of his survival, I want you to bring him back to the west.'

My journey was uneventful, lacking the alarms and falls of its predecessor. I was used to the horse now. It differed from the wolf in that it was not a pack animal. It was not necessary to dominate it to have it do one's bidding. It had become used to me during our last journey together, and set off at its usual amble, secure in the knowledge that if it reached the various inns we had stayed at, there would be food and shelter. Finally, I found myself at the excise house awaiting entry to Paris once again.

I was not surprised to see my nemesis ensconced behind her table. She looked even more corpse-like than at our previous encounter and sported a large, unattractive canker on her upper lip. She and I regarded each other, her undisguised loathing augmented by an uncomfortable spark of recognition. I recalled our previous encounter and judged it unwise to attempt to initiate proceedings. We regarded each other in silence. All the shutters were barred. The day's heat had not dissuaded her from lighting a fire, raising the temperature to the borders of that which the human frame is able to accommodate. I felt pools of perspiration well up into the small of my back and under my arms, causing me to fear for the propriety of my appearance. A rivulet burst the banks of my wig and meandered slowly to the end of my nose, where it hung, poised like some unpleasant stalactite. The heat caused my head to spin. I feared that I would faint and placed my hand upon the table to support myself.

'Take your hand from this table. Have you no respect for the property of your King?'

She lunged forwards and struck me upon the wrist with her ledger. I was incensed. The blood flew to my cheeks, compounding the effects of the hideous environment. The pulse in my temple hammered out a tattoo with the violence of a military band. I drew myself up to protest at this intolerable insolence. I was able only to emit a short, rodentine squeak before woman, fire, table and ledger spun around me, drawing me into their vortex. I fell to the floor.

When I came to my senses I found myself propped against the wall with my horse standing over me wearing the expression of mild anxiety that is typical of its species. It was utterly dark. The customs-house door was securely barred and the city closed to me. I pulled myself to my feet. My head throbbed and I recognized that I would need to drink copious amounts of water to rebalance my humours. I took the horse by the bridle and, with the infinite care I was forced to exercise to prevent myself from voiding my stomach, led him slowly to our vermin-contaminated lodgings.

I attended upon the Young Master the next morning. He was in his habitual good humour and, on noticing my feverish appearance, enquired about my wellbeing with the utmost solicitousness. I was far too embarrassed to recount the full history of my encounter with the foul woman the previous day and asserted that I had suffered dehydration but was now in fine health.

'So, Legris, have you come to render me your invaluable medical assistance at my father's behest?'

'I have indeed, sir. Your father is most displeased about this latest matter. He bids you consider your position. You have accused the Chevalier in error. Neither you nor he should face death as a result of your mistake. A wise man would apologize. Your noble father urges you to take a sagacious course.'

The Young Master smiled at me, his eyes as utterly guileless as those of a child. 'Well, Legris, I can't deny that I was wrong about the method. But consider this: if I was not right in the generality of my accusation, then why did Renault fly off the handle so? An innocent man would not have been so enraged. Further, he had won eighteen of eighteen hands and I cannot accept that that could be done without recourse to deceit. In any event, it's all in the past. He insulted me, called me a buffoon before company. There were even ladies present. What man of honour could suffer that?'

I was unsure whether it was the extent of his folly or the lingering effects of my ordeal of the previous day that caused my mind to reel. It occurred to me that his late mother must have been stupider than his father's description of her conveyed for their union to have produced such an offspring. The Young Master continued to survey me. His face wore an expression of heartfelt pleasure at his own rhetoric. He glowed with good humour and vacuity in equal measure. I tried the balm of reason, but to no avail. He could not acknowledge that his own behaviour in accusing the Chevalier of theft had in any way contributed to the situation. Fight he must and fight he would.

There are those who believe that ritual is the means by which the mysteries of life are revealed. The truth is to be found among the repetition of patterns of behaviour that have been set down as milestones on a path. I cannot agree. My experience is that these patterns are set down to hide the emptiness of that which they surround. Take the duel – this was the second I had attended. It was identical in form right up to the moment that the protagonists turned and fired.

I was sure that this was as much a ritual as any performed by priests or freemasons. It shared the elements of repetition and disguised the fundamental truth, that a man would kill another over a game and an unkind word. I say that it was identical to the point that both men turned, because then it was that the protector of fools who seemed to watch over the Young Master intervened again. The Chevalier Renault marched the ten paces at the invigilator's count with his pistol held level with his face. I could not detect a tremor. The Young Master retained his affable air, but his shaking hand betrayed him. Both men reached the limits of their perambulation and turned, with the Chevalier spinning sharply upon his heel and bringing his gun down. He was wearing boots with a somewhat high heel, and this minor vanity proved his undoing. His heel caught. He fell as he turned, the gun discharging low.

The Young Master doubled over, falling as well. He discharged his pistol harmlessly, the ball crashing through the foliage above. I ran to his side and saw that he had been struck in the groin. I cut away his britches to reveal that his escape had not been complete. The wound was not mortal but the shot had severed the right testicle. I applied a compress and arranged his conveyance to a place at which I could repair the damage as best I could. No infection set in and he was fit to travel in three weeks. It was a slightly diminished and greatly chastened young man who set out for home with me.

I have found that the worst for someone else has sometimes worked out the best for me. My Master summoned me on our return and called upon me to report upon my doings in Paris. His concern was simple: 'Tell me, Legris, did my son continue with his duel out of a sense that he could not withdraw without compromising the family honour, regardless of where the blame for the challenge lay in truth?'

He looked at me expectantly. I knew that my reply could not fail to wound and distress him. I considered lying to save his feelings, but rejected this. There was no doubt that he would speak to the Young Master, if only to admonish him. The son was too much of a fool to realize that his own interest lay in perpetuating this lie.

'Sadly, Your Grace, this is not the case. I followed your instructions to the letter. I pointed out to the Young Master not only that he was wrong in fact, but also that his own action had led to the challenge. He maintained the view that his only error was to have misidentified the method by which he had been cheated. He would not withdraw. Once again, it was only an uncanny stroke of fate that saved him.'

I set out the facts of the duel and my Master became very grave. 'Legris, what can be done to save him from himself? If he is allowed his own leisure he will be dead within the year without a doubt. No man can hope to rely upon that level of good fortune to insulate him from death. I fear that nowhere in the civilized world could be said to be out of harm's way for my idiot son.'

The first germination of an idea stirred in my mind.

'Your Grace, you say the civilized world?'

'Indeed I do. The boy will find a reason to have someone kill him anywhere with a primitive sense of honour. Even the English . . .'

I pretended to be deep in thought.

'Out with it, Legris.'

'With what, Your Grace?'

'Don't take me for as big a fool as my son. You have some idea in mind?'

'Well, Your Grace, if one were to take your son away from the civilized world, one could remove the likelihood of his throwing away his life on some cretinous point of honour. If, for instance, he were to go to, say, the Slave Coast, he would be far away from the duelling field but also in an environment that would test his metal and ensure that the soldierly virtues were maintained.'

'I suppose you are about to say that you would reluctantly agree to accompany him and keep him out of needless trouble, eh?'

I pretended to demur but he had seen through my device.

'Very well, Legris. If the Dutchman can convince me with his plan, you may go. Take the boy with you and do make sure that he stays out of trouble.'

I left my Master's chamber with a small caper and danced my way to the rear of the house and my tower. Keep him out of trouble? What could be easier? After all, we were going to a place where no cards were played, no ladies plied their charms and no noblemen flaunted their honour. It all hinged upon Van der Veer's producing some kind of coherent plan. I went to my bed with a song, and dreamed of Claudette.

I was not disappointed by Van der Veer's plan. Whatever the likelihood of our coming across his giant lizards might have been, his ability to put together a plan to find them spoke of a clerical organization of mind that his rugged man-of-nature appearance belied. He had even gone to the trouble of locating a ship and obtaining the price of her charter. He attended the chateau in the company of its first officer, a somewhat moon-faced young man by the name of La Roche. The ship, the *Force de Nature*, was a schooner and would be available at Roscoff should we wish to embark.

There were pages of finely detailed costings, lists of provisions and a voluminous portfolio of quotations which my Master spent a great deal of time considering. La Roche and Van der Veer enjoyed the hospitality of the chateau while he did so, spending their time hunting deer and wild boar with the Young Master. While no one acquired any injuries, I had the opportunity to get to know Lieutenant La Roche rather well, and I confess lasting confusion about his choice of naval officer as a profession. It was not that he lacked courage – in what he perceived to be good health I had no doubt that he was as brave as a lion. His flaw was a love of luxury and comfort that sat at odds with what little I knew of what my Master referred to as the 'martial virtues'. I observed this when he returned from one of the numerous hunting trips. I was at rest in my rooms, and had just settled to a particularly rewarding piece by the blessed Jean-Jacques and a glass of Calvados when he entered without announcing himself.

'M'sieur Doctor, I am afraid I am injured.' He appeared to be in distress and I was concerned.

'Pray come in. Sit upon my couch. Tell me, where are you hurt?'

He gave a sigh that spoke of torment borne with quiet courage. Then he cleared his throat, a mannerism that I have always found irritating.

'I am injured at the hunt. It is my shoulder.'

'Pray remove your coat and shirt. Allow me to inspect it.'

He pulled off his topcoat with the air of a man removing a layer of skin. Breathing heavily, he pulled down his shirt to reveal ... nothing. I examined the area closely and could find no visible bruising, no wound and no swelling.

I was perplexed and expressed this. 'Pray show me how you move it to cause the most discomfort?'

He rotated it slowly anticlockwise; puffing and blowing like a porpoise. I observed no muscular or skeletal defect.

'How have you sustained this, er, injury?'

'It was the gun. I swear, Doctor, it had a kick like a horse. I feel as though my shoulder has been pounded with a tenderizer.'

I probed his joint. I could detect no dislocation. Surely he could not be complaining of that soreness that is the inevitable consequence of vigorous exercise? I could find nothing that required treatment but thought it politic to send him on his way with something to distract him. I instructed him to stand with his face to the wall and rotate the arm towards it while I prepared a poultice from the remainder of the loaf I had enjoyed with my supper and the fortunately solely liquid contents of my commode. When I encountered him the following day he professed it to have been most efficacious.

La Roche consulted me for a number of complaints while he stayed at the chateau. He complained of the flux – I diagnosed wind; and when he feared a tumour – I found a hangover. In my experience most men – and I include those fortunate enough to be able to say that they are neither aristocrats nor soldiers – traverse their daily lives in a constant state of trivial discomfort. They do not complain. They are prevented from doing so. Fear of ridicule, a sense of manhood – it is hard to define the source of this reticence. The ancients called it stoicism. La Roche was so bereft of this characteristic that he could have had it removed by the great Galen himself.

The irritation La Roche caused me was trivialized by my anticipation as my Master cast his eye over Van der Veer's plans. I was not alone in my disquiet. The whole company awaited his decision. He called us all together in the great salon. He reclined upon a couch adjacent to the fire while we all – the Young Master, Van der Veer, La Roche and I – sat upon high-backed chairs, our status determined by how far away from the great fireplace we were obliged to place ourselves. He was to pronounce judgement. We waited beneath the painted ceiling for his verdict. It was in our favour. We were to leave for the Slave Coast as soon as the wind and tide were propitious and all necessary arrangements could be put in place.

I had travelled from whores' doctor to personal physician of a great family. Now I was to make a voyage of discovery. I felt momentary disquiet. After all, I was to achieve my ambitions as a direct consequence of my own misdeeds. I had been taught to believe no good could come of it. The rational man in me arose and put these fancies to flight. This was superstition unworthy of a man of science who was to journey to the heart of Africa. We men of science acknowledge the random nature of events.

6

Africa

IT HAD BEEN AT LEAST THREE MONTHS SINCE OUR arrival and we had wandered like Israelites. I say 'at least' because the place seemed to rob one of all sense of time. We meandered aimlessly through the jungle. Our guide, if that is the correct word, claimed to have a purpose, but if that was so, it was as inscrutable as God's. I did not believe in the Almighty, and I was beginning to lose my faith in Van der Veer.

While the Young Master, La Roche and Van der Veer went off searching for the great reptiles that the Dutchman swore lived in the vicinity, I would stay to observe the ape colony. These were wild men of the forest apes – *Panus sylvanus*, to give them their scientific name. A large tribe lived near our second camp. They were shy at first, their nocturnal hooting and chattering the only sign of their presence. They would show themselves from time to time only to flee into the trees when we approached. I begged the others not to shoot them as I wished to study their behaviour and feared they would decamp altogether if some of their number were harmed.

Our camp was deep in the heart of the forest. There was little to do. At that time all enjoyed good health save for one of the bearers who had suffered a broken leg. I had no desire to go hunting, so I was able to put my strategy to the test. I knew that at least one animal would tolerate the presence of man. I reasoned that the force that prevented a man from becoming a wolf's breakfast was not affection. Nature is too harsh for affection to play a part. It was habituation. The man is spared simply because the animal is used to him. He blends so closely into the scenery of the creature's life he ceases to be anything other than scenery himself. I resolved to make myself a part of the forest. If my smell alarmed the apes, they must become so used to it that it bored them.

This necessitated a campaign of utter idleness. I must confess that I rather enjoyed it. While wood was gathered, water was drawn and the hunt for the giant reptiles continued, I sat in my chair beneath the tree favoured by the tribe and read. It was extremely agreeable to sit in the shade and enjoy Monsieur Voltaire's splendid *Candide*. I rose to take my repast with the others to avoid confusing the apes with too great an abundance of scents. I was so excited that I could not restrain myself from sharing my theory with my companions, who gazed at me gravely when I spoke to them directly but seemed to avoid my society. This was ideal. I could not see the tribe through the foliage. But I knew they were there. The serenity of my vigil allowed me to monitor their subtle approach. I could hear them talk, and I am convinced that they did talk, in their fashion. They tested the distance and approached, finding me neither threat nor mystery. Finally they were so unafraid of me they felt safe to risk the floor around my feet. I had finished my book and played no active role in the upkeep of the camp for some weeks in the name of my research. I was ready to have my attention claimed.

The tribe numbered twenty, of which fewer than half were adult males. There were seven females, ranging from a fearsome and rather stout matriarch to a lithesome nymph of the jungle. Then there were the children, four of them. I could not forbear from naming them. Marie was the youngest, much doted upon. Gaston was her older brother. Suzanne was the coy, older girl on the threshold of womanhood. And there was Jacques. He was a young man at our first meeting. He stood taller than the others and held himself more erect. The others in the group were covered in a thick pelt, save for their faces and behinds. Jacques was a far less hirsute creature. Were it not for the cast of his brow and his easy place among their society I would hardly have credited him part of the same species and classified him as some separate genus of naked ape. They were a hierarchical society and the children were able to live in freedom because they had no place to defend. Jacques was at a time in his development at which the hour of his having to earn his rank was at hand.

The life of the females and children was an idyll. They wandered, grazing upon what they found among the leaves. They enjoyed the protection of the males of the tribe and allowed them to compete for their affections. It was among the gentlemen that competition was at its cruellest. There was a leader, Louis (what else?). There were his lieutenants. Then there were the rest. They would strive against each other to rise above their status. All of them were locked in eternal conflict, settled mainly through furious display before one or the other capitulated. Each had his place and was destroyed by ambition. They viewed those above them with a furious envy and those beneath with fear.

The apes became so used to my presence that they would gather round my chair, hooting and grooming each other. I sat motionless, afraid that movement of any kind would scare them back into the canopy. I was friendliest with the tribe's children, who used me as a source of amusement. They would sit upon me, Marie in Jacques' or Suzanne's arms, Gaston fooling and tumbling, ever the clown. And then it changed. As sudden as a fashion. Jacques slipped over the imperceptible barrier into manhood and his existence was transmuted from the ideal of the Noble Savage into something else. What I was to observe made me certain that there is no nobility. There is only power and with it the hatred that makes creatures feel that they must make each other aware of their power. So did Jacques reach manhood and fall out of favour. As soon as the other males sensed Jacques to be a child no more, they started to notice his many differences. Their attention turned to scorn, and their scorn soon became condemnation. I could not understand how these seemingly simple creatures could demand such homogeny, but demand it they did. Once Jacques was old enough to be a rival, he was judged and found wanting. Retribution was swift, heresy seeming to be their severest crime. The great males, those who were not part of the constant struggle for status, instigated it. As in the world of men, the leader played no active part in matters. He sniffed at Jacques, then turned his back. He made his wishes known and delegated their execution to his lieutenants. I had called the second largest ape Richelieu, and it was he who acted as his sovereign's right hand. He seized poor Jacques. He did not hurt him but cast him among the pack. They let out a great yell and fell upon him. I raised my musket. I drew the sights over the nearest and paused. How could I intrude upon them? If I killed one to save the other, I would compromise their society. My intervention could produce a distortion that could destroy precisely what I sought to save. Then the pack seized Jacques by the arms and wrenched them apart. He let out a scream, a shout of rage and defiance, and before I was able to restrain myself my finger tightened on the trigger. A report. An ape fell.

The remainder fled. I ran forward to pick Jacques up in my arms. I would carry him to the camp. I had saved his life. He was my charge, my responsibility. He lay stunned both by the assault of his former comrades and by the musket's explosive interruption. He got to his feet unsteadily. We looked at each other. His eyes were liquid and deep. I was convinced we both knew that my intervention had bound us together. I extended my hand. He took it, not as an equal shaking hands in the English fashion, but as a child may take the hand of a nurse. At that time, you see, I had the strength. I had saved him and it seemed only right and proper that I should be the senior.

My new parenthood coincided with an acknowledgement that the giant reptiles no longer frequented this part of the jungle. We were to move camp, deeper into the heart of the forest. I was excited. I had Jacques, already establishing himself as part of the family of our expedition. La Roche and the Young Master had taken him to their hearts. They were constantly bribing him with food. He proved an apt pupil. To my surprise he seemed to have an ability to remember the names of things. I was not sure whether this was merely phonetic or showed some deeper understanding. They would ask and he would fetch. Money, a bottle, food. He seemed to enjoy the game. My interest became most acute when I overheard La Roche send him to his tent to fetch something particular. Jacques returned with 'the green jacket lying next to my bed upon the pile of my hunting clothes.' I was astounded. I confess that I felt obliged to check the interior of La Roche's tent to find out whether the coat he had returned with represented the only choice. My findings were unexpected. He owned many sets of clothes. So it was not random. Jacques could learn the meaning of simple human speech. But then so could a dog or a horse. It was an indication of intelligence but no more than an indication.

I was not sorry to move from our encampment. I feared that Jacques remained in danger while we stayed in the tribe's territory. We wandered deep into the forest, always searching for signs of the giant reptiles' presence among the great trunks, peering for their tracks in the green half-light. None did we find, yet still we wandered, until Van der Veer led us to a bitter and unhealthy place.

The humidity made walking as difficult as wading. It became impossible to distinguish the rivulets of sweat running from our foreheads and beneath our arms from the water that fell from the very air upon our clothing like rain. Our guide followed his plan, and we wandered towards an evil place. It was La Roche who first discovered it – a great brackish lake, its dark waters shrouded in a permanent haze of mist and insects. The latter were most troubling, as they were mosquitoes or some similar bloodsucking genus. The air was filled with the low whine of their passing and a great deal of time was occupied slapping them away, as they settled to their repast. A moderate disrobing was almost essential to cope with the oppressive heat, yet to remove even a stitch left a banquet of exposed flesh. It was a hellish compromise.

Most significantly, there were tracks. Vast, three-toed tracks leading through the mud to the water's edge. The hunters were delighted. I was able to confirm that their origin was reptilian, although I added the caveat that I believed them to have been made by crocodiles, albeit of a prodigious size. It was decided that here we would stay. I argued in vain that we should move to dryer ground. I must confess, I was exhausted and found the enthusiasm of the others so overbearing that I could not muster the spirit to counter it. I surrendered to them, against my better judgement and against my solemn oath. I did not do enough, and this weighs on my conscience as heavily as the wolf. I have never been a deliberate villain, yet my omissions have had consequences far beyond my anticipation. We pitched our camp. As the bearers erected the tents and the hunting party cleaned their weapons, I sat with Jacques. He looked around him with wide, fearful eyes and clasped my hand. I felt him shiver. I squeezed his hand reassuringly. He seemed comforted and soon fell into a fitful sleep.

Once again, our lives settled into a routine. Our new placement at the water's edge gave me many rewards as a natural scientist. The hunters went on great expeditions. They did not return empty-handed, although their prey remained fauna that were already known to science. The giant lizards of Van der Veer's tales and the calcified jawbone remained elusive. They captured crocodiles of a size that would have made me green with envy had I seen their bodies displayed in Paris in any consulting rooms but mine. They seemed less than impressive in the forest.

I spent my time with Jacques. I was increasingly convinced he had a remarkable capacity for learning. At school, I had acquired the habit of speaking to myself, when I was isolated from my fellows for long periods as a punishment for daydreaming. It was not as if Jacques actually responded. That would have been miraculous indeed. He would look at me as I spoke, staring at me with an intensity that made me speculate occasionally that, if he did not understand my words (and how could he, indeed?), he was struggling to do so. He was quietly pushing at a great wall standing between him and comprehension. Impossible? Incredible, perhaps? It seemed somehow plausible in the green half-light.

Jacques was a phenomenal mimic, this was true. La Roche had a particularly irritating mannerism of leaning forward, nodding and making a noise that fell somewhere between a cough and a grunt. 'Hoom hoom,' he would go. I half expected him to search for truffles. To my great amusement Jacques took this on. His 'hoom hoom' was so true to the original that I felt confused about whether I should praise his ingenuity or chide him for his impudence. Predictably, the Young Master and Van der Veer thought this a great sport and would engage him in conversation just to hear him 'do' La Roche. He would regard them with the same solemn concentration as he did me when I spoke to him of elephants and other fauna. He seemed to understand their purpose and play up to it.

I am not a bad physician. I am diligent and I keep abreast of others' discoveries. I had anticipated disease on the expedition, but that which I had predicted was confined to maladies that affect slaves and Europeans in the Indies. I had imagined that, as the climate was similar, so would be the consequences of inhabiting it. Foolishly I had thought there was nothing in nature that man had not encountered. In the fetid depths of that forest I was to be proved disastrously wrong. I did not realize it at first, but as I have reflected upon the events of the outbreak, I am increasingly convinced that, had I heeded the only warning that Jacques was able to give us then, the whole episode could have been avoided.

Jacques and I had taken to making an early-morning walk along the shores of the lake. This was the time at which many of the forest's inhabitants took the waters and I was able to observe some fascinating creatures: apes, monkeys, wild dogs, pigs and even a solitary porcupine of a species and appearance I had not seen recorded. They were all shy and would flee once they detected our approach. Jacques was as light-footed as his wild fellows and could come close to them. He could never teach me to walk as cleverly as he. The only creature I was ever able to approach was the little monkey. We came upon him at the water's edge. He was seated and solitary – itself unusual, as his kind were gregarious and busy. I attempted to stalk him, following Jacques' lead, expecting him to flee to the canopy at any moment. I reached an arm's length of him and realized I had not the faintest idea of how to capture him. I could make out his markings in detail, and could see that he was quivering. I interpreted this as tension and believed him about to bolt when suddenly he vomited, copiously and in an alarming shade of blood-flecked black bile. He collapsed in convulsions and I scooped him up, wrapping him in my coat. I decided that I would keep him. I thought he would probably die but I was intrigued and wished to compare his symptoms with those of the unfortunate men whom the bloody flux brought to mortality. I anticipated dissecting him.

As I carried the little body towards the camp, Jacques set up a terrible howling. He plucked at my sleeve and waved his finger from side to side in a gesture of disapproval I vaguely recognized as my own. I shrugged him off. I noted that dreading the presence of the sick, a facet of the society of the lower orders of humanity, appeared to be mirrored in the animal kingdom. I resolved to study this in Jacques. I had in mind some kind of treatise. It could be argued to fly in the face of the idea of the Noble Savage that was very *courant* when we set off, but in one sense it seemed to support it. After all, a natural man is only one of nature's many creatures.

I put the little monkey in a crate at the edge of the encampment. I wanted to observe him as the disease ran its course. I had hoped to house him in the vicinity of my tent, but this proved unacceptable to my companions. His symptoms included the violent and regular evacuation of his bowels, producing more of the blood and bile I noted in his vomit. I fed him water and a little bread soaked in wine, but to no avail. I had given him a bed of coats, hoping that he would rest comfortably and regain his strength. The coats were mainly mine. I confess that I borrowed one of La Roche's. I had hoped to return it laundered without his noticing, but this was not to be. He came upon me removing it from the crate and grabbed it from me, stalking off to his tent cursing. The monkey seemed to vomit and defecate all the fluid from himself, reducing himself to a shadow of tendon, skin and bone. Finally, he expired.

I began my dissection the following day. I noted that the creature's stomach had ruptured – a similarity with the flux. I had hoped that Jacques would assist me, but since I had brought the little monkey back to the camp he had taken to avoiding my company. He stayed at the far side of the perimeter, spending his time with the hunters. It was only after the dissection had ended and I had buried the remains that he deigned to seek me out.

His behaviour was really quite extraordinary. He approached me cautiously, sniffing the air around me, then circled me three times. It was as if the fear he had displayed had caused him to regress. I had not seen him so feral since I rescued him from the wrath of his tribe. I allowed him his inspection. He seemed to find what he was looking for and accepted me. He returned to my tent and we resumed our morning walks.

La Roche consulted me two days later. I was not surprised to see him. I watched him as he approached and noted a slight awkwardness in his gait. I predicted he would complain of rheumatic pain, probably in the shoulders and upper chest. The sort of low-level discomfort that an officer in His Majesty's Navy really ought to have borne without complaint. Jacques was seated at my side. He gave a soft 'hoom hoom' at La Roche's presence, as if identifying our visitor.

I confess I was not kind. La Roche told me of the pains I had predicted and in an attempt to cure his hysteria I prescribed him a violent emetic, believing that a good purge would do him no ill and distract him from his fantasies. He took to his bed and I, thinking my treatment to be responsible, paid him no mind. Three days later the others began to remark upon his absence. At first I minimized their concerns, but when the good lieutenant failed to emerge some two days later, I became concerned enough to check my supplies. I was reassured to find that I had not miscalculated the dosage I had given him. It was capable of causing mild vomiting only, so I concluded that his sensitive disposition had compounded the effects to produce a disproportionate impact upon his wellbeing. I resolved to eject him from his undeserving sickbed with a great surplus of hearty good cheer and a firm recommendation to exercise.

I realized my error as soon as I entered his tent. The air was heavy with a sweet smell, decay mingled with excrement, bile and sweat. La Roche lay on his bunk. I approached him and placed a hand upon his forehead. He was aflame with fever. He opened an eye and seemed to take in my presence. I noticed that his eyeball was dull and arid.

'Doctor . . .'

There followed a great retching. I located the chamber pot and caught his vomit. I put the pot to one side and wrapped him in a blanket. He started to tremble uncontrollably. I looked towards the pot and saw that he had vomited red-flecked black, bilious and foul with the consistency of Sauce Hollandaise. I recalled seeing its like only once before. It could not be! No disease prevalent among beasts could pass to man. It was surely some form of flux or dysentery. I had read the literature and I knew that the only course was to purge the ill humours and to cool his person with cloths soaked in water.

It was no good. Poor La Roche did not last the night. I purged him, but my treatment seemed to accelerate the course of the disease, turning him into little more than a husk, wizened and lined like an ancient leather bag. The bones of his face made prominent ridges and hollows. I stayed until the end. It was my duty to share his suffering. It was beyond my skill as a physician to cure him but I eased his passing by moistening his lips and throat. I emerged into the grey dawn mist after the final convulsion had released him from its grip. Van der Veer and the Young Master were sleeping, huddled around the embers. Jacques was nowhere to be found. He was probably scavenging for food, although he was sensitive to atmosphere and the air was filled with melancholy. La Roche died with his mother's name on his lips. And mine. If I had faith's consolation, I would feel his last breath like a lash across my shoulders. I felt only empty. Weak. Insignificant.

My comrades awoke. I told them and we went to the tent together. I washed what remained of Lieutenant Etienne La Roche, first officer of the ship *Force de Nature*, twenty-two years old, explorer, hunter, unpublished poet and milksop. While the others looked on, I dressed him in his uniform. For all their martial pretensions they were less comfortable in the presence of death than I. For my part, I was grateful that the poor man was beyond the reach of the imaginary pains that so plagued him in life.

I inherited command in the face of this tragedy. I placed the Young Master in charge of the gravedigging party. He was relieved to have a role in proceedings. I heard his shouts through the canvas walls of our comrade's mausoleum, as he rounded up the bearers and set about his commission. Van der Veer trailed out, muttering about life going on and hunting for breakfast. I was alone. I was overcome with tiredness and could not help shaking. I tried to keep the word 'epidemic' from my mind, but it surfaced like the corpse of a drowned man.

The gravediggers returned. The natives remained outside the tent, but I was aware of their disquiet. They muttered to each other in their barbarous tongue and waited. Van der Veer and the Young Master assisted me in carrying La Roche to his resting place. We bore him on his bunk. We were lucky that Van der Veer was a large, strong man, as we were three and lacked a bearer for each corner.

The natives formed an aisle from the tent door. As we emerged from the gloom, the light struck my eyes and I was temporarily blinded. I failed to notice the consternation La Roche's corpse caused among our servants, mistaking the crescendo of babble for an outpouring of grief. When I realized that the hubbub was not what I had at first supposed, I was afraid and my hands dropped to my pistol. Then I recognized it. It was fear. They were afraid. The shouts coagulated into motion as they fled. Within moments they had melted into the forest. We were alone, we four. One down and three to carry him. The word burst to the front of my consciousness. Epidemic. They feared it, because they knew it.

We buried La Roche. None of us could think of anything to say, so he went to his rest without a kind word. I, at least, was too preoccupied with my horror at our plight. I passed my panic off as the muteness of grief. I was relatively sure that the Young Master lacked the depth of perception to comprehend how utterly we were fucked. We were stranded, without guides or bearers and in the centre of the most terrible, hostile wasteland. We might be dying.

We sat around a fire. None spoke. I became aware of a small frame leaning against me. A hand scrabbled for mine and took it. Jacques had returned. Whatever our fate was to be, he had decided to share it.

Van der Veer was the next to fall ill. It took a few days for the rest of us to notice. I believe he refused to acknowledge the symptoms himself. I became aware only at the point at which he was no longer able to conceal his vomiting by retreating to the trees. I confined him to his tent. I had no faith in my ability to affect the course of the disease and concentrated on maintaining his comfort in the hope that his own resilience would save him. It did not. Within days he had taken on the leathery, desiccated look that had characterized La Roche towards the end. I felt obliged to sit with him, a witness to the failure of my own knowledge. His mind wandered and he spoke in many languages. I was able to understand his French, but my Dutch and English were not equal to the task. There were moments when he was entirely lucid. He would curse me and weep. Finally, he called me to him. It was clear to me that these moments were his last.

His voice was weak and hoarse. 'Doctor, I wish to give you something. It has not helped me but if God is willing and you survive it may bring you great wealth.'

I was intrigued and leaned towards him. He smelled foul. The stench caught the back of my throat. I could not help but flinch. He noticed this and gave a strange croaking cough which I realized was a laugh. His hand clawed at his clothing and removed a piece of paper. He handed this to me.

'I had this from a hunter in the Cape. He told me it came from a traveller who traded with the nomads of East Africa. These men wander the continent with their herds. It is a map. It shows the location of King Solomon's mine, the source of his legendary wealth. Take it. May it bring you more luck than me. I regret nothing more than the day that I left my life as a clerk in the service of the East India Company to follow its journey.'

Phlegm rattled in his throat. He thrust the paper into my hand. I put my head to his. He tried to spit in my face but had not the strength. He abandoned himself to the dark and was still. I digested this revelation. Van der Veer was a clerk. Not a hunter, explorer or man of action but a clerk. He had deceived us all. Used us as tools to follow the map to wealth. He had told us nothing of this before his death. I was convinced that, had we found the mine, he would have killed us all. There could be no other explanation for his reticence. I should have been enraged, but the horror robbed me of emotion.

I opened the map listlessly. As soon as I saw the contents I was overcome. Great shudders shook me. I could not draw breath, such was the extent of my laughter. I recognized it. I had seen it before – well, if not it, then its stablemates. No doubt whoever had drawn it had also prepared similar ones showing the location of Arthur's tomb and the resting place of the Holy Grail. This whole horrific adventure was based upon one man's gullible greed. I wanted to see the creatures of this place; my master had wanted to get his son out of harm's way; the Young Master had wanted to hunt the great reptiles whose very existence Van der Veer had invented. He had read our desires and used them to follow his own. No doubt he had kept the map a closely guarded secret. No doubt this prevented him from learning that it was a forgery.

I decided not to tell the Young Master. I was afraid that the realization would puncture his indefatigable optimism. There seemed to be little point in stripping away his illusions, when we were both utterly doomed. He, Jacques and I spent our days foraging, and every time he mentioned the prospect of finding the giant reptiles, I felt as though I would weep. I did not have the strength to cope with my surviving human companion if he slipped into despair. God knows, his remorseless good humour was difficult enough to bear. If he realized that we were both going to die in a wilderness that we had been lured into as part of an idiot's scheme, I feared that I would be forced to cheat the disease and danger of this terrible place by killing him myself.

The illness struck the Young Master two weeks later. I nursed him till the end. Once again I could not save my patient. Once again I was covered in the most vile bodily fluids but remained in the rudest of rude health. I found myself kneeling by a sickbed as my last comrade rattled and slipped out of life. I turned from physician to spectator, powerless to prevent the march of the disease and unable to discern its workings from observation of its victims. From time to time I would prepare food or hot beverages, thinking that these might provide comfort and sustenance to enable the body to fight off the ailment with its own strength. These would always be accepted by my patient but rejected by his traitorous body. I was in despair. I could be drenched with fluids, reek of death and yet be unharmed. I began to long for the companionship that illness would bring me and to regard myself as cursed. My good health lay upon me like the mark of Cain.

My Master's son left his life as grey light began to penetrate the canvas wall. I had not slept for many days and had slipped into a reverie in which the small points of light that danced in my fatigued eyes became the points of a brilliant chandelier. A flash of movement caught my attention. I turned to see the Young Master standing by the bed, ankle deep in the pools of vomit and excreta that I had not the strength of purpose to remove. He looked down as if noticing this for the first time. His eyes met mine, yet he stared past me towards something that distressed him. He coughed. I leaned forward, putting my arms around him to support his weight. His last words convinced me that my sanity had deserted me. 'The wolf!' he cried. 'The wolf!'

I left the tent. I took all I could carry. It seems a petty conceit now. I packed my books, my specimens and my journal. I packed my clothing. I shouldered a musket and filled my pockets with powder and shot. I could not bring myself to bury the Young Master. His remains probably rest in their canvas mausoleum still, if the jungle has not absorbed them. God knows, it has absorbed everything else. I could not face him. How he knew of the chain of events that had placed our feet upon the road to his death I do not know, but I could not suffer the condemnation of his dead eyes.

Jacques took my hand and led me away from this terrible place. We talked about many things, Jacques and I. He was sympathetic, although sometimes he did not seem to understand my distress. Indeed, I noticed that when I was in despair and could not speak, a state that would often last for days, his obvious impatience with me seemed to mirror my unsympathetic treatment of poor La Roche. I asked myself whether this was mimicry or something more. It was certainly irritating. I even told him to leave me. He would not. I am glad he was so forgiving, as I had earned little forgiveness. If he were to have heeded me, I would have been lost. I had nothing save my hat and my ape. My companion.

7

Hope

I WAS AFRAID THAT I WOULD FORGET HOW TO SPEAK. WHEN I was a child I would often speak Breton to my parents. Now I am a man, I can hardly recall the basic structures of that tongue. I can understand it, or at least I am pretty certain that I would understand it if I moved in the kind of circles where it is used. I never use it, so it has ceased to have any use to me. There is a small part of the human stomach that is similarly unemployed. One school of thought is that it was used to digest the grass and leaves that Adam and Eve ate in the Garden of Eden. Whatever purposes it once had, it serves none now. It has fallen into disuse, atrophied like a bedridden patient's limbs. The point is that if something is left to its own devices it fails. Nature seems to abhor idleness and deals with things that have outlived their purpose with the utmost ruthlessness. She is a utilitarian goddess. That which cannot work loses its right to exist. If I were a religious man I would hold this joylessness to be evidence that God is a Protestant.

It concerned me that I was forgetting how to communicate with other men. It had been at least three months since I began my wanderings. I confess that I had ceased to count the sunsets as time had decreasing relevance to my existence. So it could have been as many as six months, even a year. Ten years would not have been out of the question. I stopped counting after three months. One day was very much like another, as Jacques and I wandered the silent forest, eking out our living among its inhabitants. I noticed that I ceased to dream, but I resolved not to lose hope. It was all I had. My clothes were gone. I was naked save for my hat and my dream of rescue. If that were to have rotted into the undergrowth to join my britches, shirt, shoes, books, education, manners, literacy and pride, I would have been naked indeed. No man could stand to be so exposed. I clung to my hat and my hope.

Jacques had gone foraging and I was fiddling with my tinderbox, trying to coax a small flame from tinder I vaguely recognized as the third page of the second chapter of *Candide*. It was damp, so I was both surprised and delighted to succeed. I had become used to failure. That day I did not fail him and could hold up my head in the green gloom as being less burdensome. He was my saviour, Jacques. My little hairy redeemer, guiding me past snakes, away from crocodiles and showing me the wonders I had always sought.

So, I spoke to Jacques all the time. My voice would sound odd, muffled by the leaves and the loam. I started by wishing him a good morning every day and progressed to sharing my observations with him. I could not write in my journal any more. It served a far more utilitarian purpose as kindling. I spoke to

Jacques in its stead. I recorded my experiences for posterity by confiding in him.

He started to reply. I know that apes cannot speak. I know this in the same way that I know that I cannot have a conversation with an ape. I hold this truth to be self-evident. I always admired the symmetrical elegance of the great postulation 'I think therefore I am.' But as I discussed breakfast with Jacques, it did not make me feel secure. I knew that apes do not talk; yet, I was discoursing with one.

He was frowning at me and expressed concern that I was not taking enough water when the air was so hot and humid. I replied that I had my bottle and would drink as we walked if I needed sustenance, as I preferred to be burdened with the inconvenience of carrying a bottle to that of marching through the ground-scrub with a full bladder. I was pleased to notice he, at least, seemed to burst with vitality. He had grown since I first made his acquaintance and now stood level with the bridge of my nose. I am not a tall man nor, indeed, a vain one, yet I did hope he had reached his apex. I could not bear him to tower over me, although I was forced to acknowledge that this would have reflected our respective status at that point.

Jacques was a more than adequate conversationalist. Was I imagining him talking? Had the unending solitude and the death of my companions driven me mad? Jacques left to find a stream for us to follow. I sat on a tree-stump to recuperate before he returned. Descartes' theory is all very well when one has the comfort of others sharing one's perception. Even if they owed their existence entirely to me, their approval was affirming. If only someone else could have heard Jacques speak.

*   *   *

We followed a rivulet for days. Jacques caught fish and found edible roots, which I roasted in the embers of our campfire. The trickle became a stream, which became a sizable flood. Jacques explained that we must always keep close to water. The green light and humidity gave an impression of plenty that was utterly false. It was possible to die of thirst among the lush vegetation. I was happy to see such a huge amount of water. All the while, I could hear a noise that spoke to me across what seemed to be aeons. It roared and crashed and reminded me of childhood. I could not place it. I had ceased to trust my senses and asked Jacques if he could hear it too. He agreed, shrugging. He sniffed the air and could sense no danger, so to him the noise was of no importance. Yet it bothered me. It made my little hope tingle, but I could not explain why.

There was something strange about the sunrise. The world I lived in was green. But the days became a lighter green and, one day, the morning brought the lightest green I had ever seen. I looked up and was amazed. There were snatches of blue among the canopy. I felt a voyeuristic thrill at catching a glimpse of this new colour, as if I had seen between a woman's thighs as she crossed her legs in public. It was a portent.

The ground had a subtle slope to it. It was in our favour, and Jacques and I rejoiced in its assistance. We hurled ourselves along the riverbank, hooting and shouting as the blue infiltrated the green above us. There was a thunder that was not the same as the thunder that precedes downpour after downpour. I shrieked like a savage and ran towards its source. The land dropped away. I could see blue above me. Mist was rising from the water. I recognized what I saw and realized the drumming came from that which I could no longer name as being a waterfall. I threw myself into the river and felt it sucking me into space. The blood coursed through me and I felt every tiny particle of my skin register each minor current and rivulet as I was propelled into space and crashed to the pool below with a very satisfying fountain.

There was an unfamiliar azure tinge to the water as I opened my eyes and began to fight my way to the surface. When I broke out of its embrace, I was temporarily blinded. The light was intense. I shut my eyes to see a bright red backdrop. Scattered images of a wide blue sky, a treeline and the ocean were projected on to it. I could hear Jacques' ragged breathing next to me. He had surfaced. I forced my eyes open and saw the sea. The sky. For the first time in God knows how long the air around me was bright and every sound rang in my ears as crisply as an envelope being cut open with a sharp knife.

I was speechless. I looked round and realized that we were not alone. Two men stood at the water's edge. They regarded Jacques and me with some concern. I saw every detail of them. They were both in blue uniform. Both wore wigs. The taller had blond hair emerging at the sides of his peruke. He was in his late twenties. His teeth were poor and I could see a greasy mark upon his embroidered waistcoat. He had been eating fried food and had wiped his hand upon his clothing. The other was older and stouter. He had a three-cornered hat. I cast around and saw my hat floating upon the water and snatched it up. I swam towards them and emerged from the river, hat in hand. I followed their gaze and for the first time I was ashamed of my nakedness. I had no idea what to do and so took refuge in formality. I held my hat over my privy parts and bowed.

'Doctor Simon Legris at your service, gentlemen.'

The smaller man stared at me. I felt my emotions rush upon

me like some unstoppable juggernaut. I fell to the ground in tears and did not resist as they raised me to my feet and led me across the beach by the hand. I was pleased to feel Jacques' little hand in my other, his touch a note of familiarity in the disconcerting reality of an answered prayer. I heard my rescuers remark on the loyalty of my pet and abandoned myself to unconsciousness as I was manhandled into a rowing boat. My last vision of the Slave Coast was of its receding with each pull of the oars. Jacques was still holding my hand. We were going home.

I had spent so long yearning for someone to talk to that when the opportunity arose I found myself curiously tongue-tied. I took my meals in the great cabin, along with Captain Broullard and his officers. The captain was a Norman and typically taciturn. Conversation was at best sparse, confined to that which was necessary for the efficient running of the ship. Our intercourse was limited to his demanding my name and nationality, which I surrendered freely, and an assertion that I had been tremendously fortunate. Had he not been swindled by a shipping agent and forced to put to shore on that wild coast to replenish his inadequate supplies, I would have remained undiscovered. The officers and crew followed their leader's example, with the result that the atmosphere aboard was dour, affording me the leisure to reflect in silence that my fortune seemed to be procured at others' expense. This left me with little opportunity to reacclimatize myself to the company of men other than in the absolute rudiments of politeness.

I have always enjoyed lively discourse and took to spending more time in my cabin with Jacques, who was becoming a proficient conversationalist. He had a ready grasp of the abstract, and while he had no independent knowledge of such things as liberty, I was happy to use the medium of our discourse to provide him with instruction. As the wind blew us back towards an uncertain future, I took refuge in playing Socrates to my small, simian Plato. I noticed that Jacques was unwilling to leave the cabin, preferring to remain in solitude when I left to take my meals at the captain's table. He seemed to be unsure of how he should behave among men and hung in my shadow on the rare occasions he ventured out. This saddened me. I recalled the natural charm of his behaviour in the camp, among the Young Master, La Roche and the others. I became concerned that by teaching this child of nature some of the ways of civilized men, I had made him conscious of himself, where he had previously been conscious only of his surroundings. Our roles were reversed. He needed me here as much as I had needed him there. Unfortunately, his new-found self-consciousness rendered him completely unable to speak in front of anyone but me. This, in turn, brought me no closer to resolving the dilemma of my putative insanity.

It was not my only dilemma, and possibly not even the most pressing of them. Every day was bringing us closer to France and when we arrived . . . well, where were we to go? I suspected that my Master would not be best pleased with my discharge of his sacred trust. I had gone to Africa with a mission. I was to keep the Young Master out of harm's way and bring him safely home. Not only had I taken him to a desolate, disease-ridden tropical hell, I had mislaid him and had had the singular misfortune to have survived myself. The possibility of passing Jacques off as the Young Master flitted across my mind, only for me to reject it as further evidence on the side of my lunacy. I pictured the scene. The carriage approached and was ushered through the gatehouse. Retainers caught the bridle of the leading team. A footman in the full livery of Ladurie de Bretagne brought a set of steps to the carriage door. I alighted and caught the Master's eye.

'Your Grace, Africa has been an ordeal that has changed your son.'

It didn't bear thinking about – and I couldn't even flee. My conscience wouldn't permit it. Since my path crossed that of the Master's family, one had become a cripple and the other was dead. I had produced a higher rate of attrition upon the Ducs Ladurie de Bretagne than the English had managed throughout the Hundred Years War. I confided in Jacques, but he was of little help. Seeking his counsel was a measure of my desperation. Our discourses were always the same:

ME: Oh God, Jacques, what am I to do? Shall we return to Paris and my practice?

JACQUES: I will follow you and do as you say.

ME: Or shall we go to Brittany and report to my Master? It would be the right thing to do, after all. I had a sacred trust and even in my failure I owe my Master the courtesy of reporting his son's death. It would be a painful meeting for us all, but I must confess that I think that it would be a catharsis. The Master must be beside himself. I have heard from Captain Broullard that we have been away from France for seven years. Can you imagine his torment? His only heir gone for so long without even a word. I cannot believe that the worst has not crossed his mind already. Perhaps it will be a relief to have those fears confirmed?

JACQUES: Why did your Master send you to Africa with his hair?

ME: Heir, Jacques. H E I R. It means the person who takes your name and property after you die.

JACQUES (after a long pause): Am I your heir?

ME: I do not know. I suppose so, although I can see some legal impediments. Anyway, Jacques, what am I to do?

JACQUES: I will follow you and do as you say.

There are those who say that enunciating a problem is the first step to its resolution. I believe them to be wrong, or at least blessed with lives in which their problems are not as intractable as mine. Jacques and I would take our constitutional upon the deck. I would walk and he would play in the plethora of bewilderingly named ropes, swinging and climbing. He became somewhat of a favourite with the crew because of these exploits. They cheered him on to new heights of recklessness, calling him over and trying to tempt him with food and tobacco. He did not go to them. He was either lost in this jungle of rope and wood or by my side. I had been concerned that he was unhappy. His little brow was perpetually furrowed during our exchanges. These excursions allowed him to delight in the purely physical and seemed to restore his equilibrium. Not so for me. As we walked on (or in his case capered above) the deck I began to notice changes. The sea turned from blue to grey. There was a freshness to the breeze. I asked Captain Broullard our location and was told that we were rounding the Spanish coast and would be entering the Bay of Biscay the following day. We would dock in St Malo three days hence, if the winds were favourable. Jacques and I continued our circular conversations in my cabin. I was no nearer a solution.

We rounded Cape Finisterre. I could see the shadow of the coast and it was a glorious green. Not the intense verdancy of the forest but a subtle, pleasing shade that spoke to me of oysters and cider. I was filled with a longing to sit outside a tavern and feel the texture of crêpes with stewed apples and Calvados in my mouth. I could not face the dirt and crowds of Paris. I had spent too long in alien environments and I wanted to stand with my feet upon the soil of my birth. I wanted to go home. I would face the Duke and would repay my debt by doing so. I wiped a tear from my cheek and turned to Jacques to tell him this. His reply was predictable. He would follow me and do as I said.

8

Homecoming

CAPTAIN BROULLARD WAS A KINDLY MAN, DESPITE HIS forbidding manner. He gave me a small purse to get about my business with the injunction that I was to repay him once I had found my feet, and waved away my thanks with a terse, 'Mind that you do, now.'

I would have preferred to travel by coach, but this proved to be beyond my limited means. I was forced to renew my acquaintance with the horse. It transpired that I had not lost my ability to remain in the saddle. Jacques rode behind me, clutching on to my waist with all his might and almost crushing the wind from me when our steed lost its footing and stumbled. The chateau was two days' ride away, which left me with ample time to distress myself about what awaited me when I arrived. I had come to the conclusion that I was about to be made the subject of *lettres de cachet* and locked up in the Bastille, a fate that filled me with a gloomy lassitude from which the searing pain in my buttocks and thighs brought on by riding provided only a moderate diversion.

I dawdled. I sampled salt-reared lamb as we passed Mont St-Michel. I ate mussels cooked in cider within sight of the Young Master's house at Fort La Latte.

It was early summer and I took some comfort in the familiarity of the countryside. Jacques was full of questions. I explained farming to him, pointing out meadows, livestock and fields of crops. He was particularly confused by the practice of keeping animals, asking me whether the cows were the farmers' friends. No, I told him, the farmer keeps the cows to take their milk and sometimes to eat them. 'Milk?' he asked. 'What is milk?' We stopped at a farm and I introduced him to milk, as well as a pungent cheese I had purchased. He drank the milk speedily, covering his face with it until he looked prematurely aged. He was less than enamoured of the cheese, taking an enormous bite then spitting it the width of the road. I noticed that his tastes ran to simplicity. He preferred fruit, vegetables and bread. He was particularly enchanted by apples and would ask to stop at every opportunity so that he might acquire them.

On one occasion we were accosted by an aggressive farm dog. It ran up to us, barking and snarling furiously. Jacques sprang into a tree to escape and refused to come down until apples had been purchased and the dog was safely tied. Later, as we rode on to the west, he asked me whether the dog was wild. No, I replied, the dog belonged to the farmer. He enquired whether the farmer would eat the dog. I laughed and told him that the farmer kept the dog to guard his property and that other sorts of dog were kept for hunting. We rode on in silence. Finally he asked me if people kept animals just as friends. I told him that people kept animals for many reasons. Some were friends, others were to show and educate. All fulfilled some purpose, whether this was emotional or practical. He should not worry about this, I reassured him. Animals could not understand what was happening to them. More silence. I could tell he was mulling this over.

I sat in my old room in the tower contemplating how it is part of the condition of man to expect the worst. I can recall my home-coming, for that is how my Master styled it, in curious detail. I can smell the horse's sweat, hear the whine of dragonflies over the moat and feel the tingling in my fingertips as I anticipated a general command to place me under arrest. It did not come. A man whose broken arm I treated when he was but a youth took my bridle and greeted me effusively. A curious group emerged from the main gate to see what the commotion was. I recognized one. My Master had aged well. Were it not for the wheeled chair in which he propelled himself with the utmost dexterity, one would be hard pressed to see him as the vision of grief I had ex-pected. Next to him stood a woman. She was at most half his age and wore an expression of teasing curiosity. She carried an infant in her arms. To her left was a line of five young children. I am no paediatrician, but I estimated the oldest to be some six years. I dismounted and approached the Master, Jacques at my side.

'Your Grace, I am the bearer of bad news. Your son is dead. You are without an heir. I tried my utmost to save him but the pestilence that had struck him down was too terrible. I, alone, came from the forest. I wish I had died with him, but my fate was to nurse my companions to their ends and never to fall ill. I cannot pretend to understand why . . .'

My Master raised his hand to silence me. I stood awaiting some terrible pronouncement.

'Legris, I am delighted to see you. I have mourned my son these past seven years. I did not expect to see him again once I received the news that the ship had returned from your rendezvous empty. I feared that I had lost both a son and a physician. I am overjoyed to find that I was wrong. I am not the only one who has been under a misapprehension, it seems. You say that I have no heir. Well, may I first present my wife, the Lady Caroline.'

He indicated the woman holding the infant. I knelt and kissed her hand.

'I met her when I was involved in a lawsuit over the payment of compensation to the family of that unfortunate young man, La Roche. Her father was the judge who ruled in my favour. Although her family only passes for nobility, being of the robe rather than the sword, they have that singly ennobling characteristic of a fortune.'

He turned and smiled at her. She stuck out her tongue at him and they laughed together. I appraised her. She was a striking girl with very dark hair and pale skin. Her nose was perhaps a little too long for her to be classified as a real beauty, but her full lips and green eyes made more than amends.

'Now, Legris, if I may present my offspring. Louis, he's five years old.' The oldest child bowed. 'Charles and Jean, they're twins – both four. Etienne is three. Cyril is two and the youngest . . .' He indicated the infant, '. . . my little Henri, well, I forget how old he is but he is quite a recent addition as you can see. So, far from being without an heir, I have six.'

'Your Grace has been busy.'

I cannot abhor enough my tendency to say the first thing that comes into my mind. As soon as the words left my lips, I knew that I had been over-familiar. I closed my eyes and awaited the storm. There was a most non-aristocratic giggle. I opened my eyes again to see that the Lady Caroline had placed her arm around the Master's shoulders.

'I'll say he has been busy, Monsieur. He would keep me forever confined, this Master of yours. Sometimes I have to flee up a flight of stairs where I know he cannot follow to enjoy a few moments when I am not with child.'

They laughed together. I did not know whether to join in and decided that I would maintain a servant's dignity. I stood and watched them together and realized that, while I had travelled to the ends of the world, my Master had found all he needed. He was happy with his new wife.

He addressed me. 'Legris, what is that?' He pointed at Jacques.

'That is Jacques, Your Grace. He is an ape of the Slave Coast. He has been my true companion these last seven years.'

I turned to Jacques who was observing proceedings with wide eyes. 'Jacques, I present my Master, the Duc Ladurie de Bretagne, his wife, the Lady Caroline, and their sons . . . You'll forgive me, Your Grace, but I cannot recall all the names.'

Jacques was always a prodigious mimic, and put this faculty to good use. He bowed like a courtier. There was great consternation among them.

'He understands?' my Master asked.

'Oh yes, Your Grace, and has speech as well. He is a remarkable creature.'

A bell sounded within and the Young Masters all assumed pleading expressions. The Lady Caroline – I suppose I should begin to refer to her as my Mistress, in the non-Claudette sense, of course – rounded on them with a severity that I suspected was somewhat of an act. 'You can all find out about Doctor Legris and Africa later. It is time for your lessons. Go. Quickly.'

She followed the children as they slouched reluctantly into the building, leaving me, the Master and Jacques alone. The trepidation that had kept me from my sleep for many days left me and I yawned.

'I am so sorry, Your Grace. Forgive me. It has been a long journey.'

'You may leave us, Legris. I will have your old rooms made ready. Attend me in the salon after you have rested and dined. Oh, and bring your . . . companion with you. There is much I wish to ask you.'

So I came home. Back to my circular room in the tower. Back to my books. Back to my effects. I lost no time in putting aside the seaman's clothing that I had been forced to borrow and dressing myself in a pair of culottes, a brocade shirt and a rather handsome coat. I felt this befitted me as the personal physician of a powerful man. I found that my clothing was a trifle too big. It hung about my frame and rustled like sails as I walked. Had I been diminished by my experiences? I decided not. I had lost my belly and become a spare man, but I was back where I belonged. I had kept my oath. Jacques ranged around my rooms, picking up books, running his fingers over the teeth of my shark jaws and investigating the borders of our territory with his species' thoroughness. There was a discreet knock and a servant entered carrying our repast. We dined together as the sun set over the stables. I lit my pipe and felt at peace.

Jacques and I made our way to the salon. I had dressed him in a shirt and britches. The sleeves hung only to the mid-point on his forearm while the knee britches reached his ankles. He

certainly cut a curious figure, but I calculated it to be the lesser
affront for him to present himself to the Master thus attired than
with his genitalia uncovered. My Master sat by the fire. He motioned for me to join him. I was provided with a very fine glass of
Armangac.

'What happened?'

'It was a disaster, Your Grace. It transpired that Van der Veer
was the basest of charlatans. He was not even the Dutchman
he claimed. He was an Englishman possessed of a forged map.
He hoped to bring us all to King Solomon's mines, but instead
brought us to an evil place. We fell sick. Or rather, they fell sick, as
I seemed immune to the malady. I nursed them all as they died. La
Roche, Van der Veer, the Young Master. Our bearers fled and we
could not carry enough provisions to take us to safety, even were
we to have been fortunate enough to find a road out of there. I
was left alone. Well, not alone, as Jacques was with me.'

'Where did he come from?'

'He was cast out by a tribe of his kind. I saved him from their
wrath, then he saved me. He found me food and water as we
wandered the forest. I would have perished were it not for him.
Eventually we found the coast and the good Captain Broullard,
whom I must repay.'

'What is he? You say he can talk.'

'Indeed. He is a fluent conversationalist.'

I gestured to Jacques, bidding him to approach. 'Jacques. Tell
the Master your name.'

'My name is Jacques.'

My Master's jaw hung open in a manner that was most unbefitting. He shook his head. 'Am I hallucinating?'

'No, Your Grace. He really speaks. I spent many hours talking to him as we went about our wanderings, as I feared that I would lose the power of speech unless I exercised it. When he replied for the first time I thought I had lost my mind. It was only when we came aboard the ship that I knew I had not.'

'But what manner of a creature is he? Can he reason? Is he merely a mimic?'

I turned to Jacques, who was observing the Master with some alarm. 'Jacques, tell the Master what you are.'

He hesitated. He looked confused and raised his arms in an eloquent shrug.

The Duke smiled at him. 'Very good, Jacques. You certainly understand more than many men I have met. Would you go back to your rooms? I need to speak to Doctor Simon alone.'

Jacques nodded and padded off on his bare feet. The Duke turned to me. 'Well, Legris, you have returned with a prodigy. He presents an interesting question for an enlightened man, does he not?'

'What question would that be?'

'What he is. And by extension, what are we? Consider. He has the power of speech. Good, many will say, but so do parrots. He can reason. Well, would come the reply, it is merely a question of degree and not characteristic. Many dogs will ponder a problem – usually how to get a piece of food. They will go through the process of trial and error to achieve their goal. Reason is not the exclusive characteristic of humanity. Most animals possess this faculty in some form or other. He is advanced for his species, but no more than that.'

'Do you say he could be a man, Your Grace?'

'I have absolutely no idea. He could be. The real question is what makes a man, is it not?' My Master turned his face to the fire.

He sat in silence. It had been some time since I had enjoyed the status of retainer, so it took his discreet cough for me to realize I had been dismissed.

It was as if I had never left. I slipped back into my life as the resident physician, treating the maladies and injuries of the chateau's inhabitants. There was nothing to challenge my skill. The business of the horse farm meant for the most part that I expended my medical skills setting broken bones, a task that I had considered beneath me and properly the preserve of a barber-surgeon. Yet it did not irritate me as it used to, and I found that I was in a state of curious repose. I had achieved that which I wanted. I had journeyed to the Slave Coast. I had found myself the golden patient, albeit one who showed a refreshing lack of hypochondria. I was happy to live out my life among splints and bridles, concentrating my curiosity upon the question of Jacques.

He was very shy, preferring to live in my shadow rather than venture among men alone. And I had not realized before how strong he was. A cart overturned, trapping one of the grooms beneath its wheel. We went to assist, Jacques carrying my bag of instruments as this was heavy and the sun was high and hot. The man's workmates had gone to fetch blocks and tackle to elevate the burden that was crushing his leg into the soil. His foot and shin stuck out perpendicular to his knee. I could tell at a glance that unless he was freed the pain would send him into that dreamlike state that is death's aperitif. I gave him a glass of poppy juice to ease his pain.

'Jacques,' I called, 'pass me my severing knife and saw.'

He put his head on one side and looked at me quizzically.

Sometimes his unquenchable curiosity could be a little trying. Time was of the essence and I responded sharply. 'If this man's leg remains under the cart he will die. Observe his eyes. They are open but see nothing. The will to live is draining from him. I must sever his leg to stand any chance of saving his life. Hurry now.'

He came to my side without a word. He grasped the edge of the wheel in both hands.

'Jacques. Don't be a fool. If this man's companions could not free him how can . . .'

He clenched his teeth and set his strength to his task. He kept his back straight and lifted with his legs and arms. To my astonishment, the cart lurched upwards. His face shook with the effort and he gestured to me to make haste.

I dragged the man away and knelt to assess his injuries. A crash behind me signified that my assistant had let his burden fall. There was an ugly gash across the man's shin. It hung open like a dog's mouth and I could see slivers of white among the scarlet. I folded my hat and put it in his mouth so that he would not sever his tongue when the pain of my treatment struck, then, grasping his foot between my knees I wrenched the shin around until it lay true to his knee. My patient gave a muffled howl and surrendered himself to unconsciousness. A blessing, I thought, as I had little faith in my ability to save his life, let alone his limb.

Jacques brought my bag, and I removed those slivers of bone I could find with my forceps while he ran to the house to find cobwebs, a treatment that I have found curiously efficacious in stemming the flow of blood, despite my having learned this from the monk who presided over the infirmary at my place of education rather than through the study of pure science. I cleaned the wound with brandy, and by the time the Duke's men arrived with a stretcher his leg was bound and splinted. As we walked back to my tower together I recalled Jacques hurling great branches from our path as we navigated the forest. It had seemed no more remarkable then than his ability to scale any surface. He was a creature of his habitat, after all, and had the abilities that nature had bestowed upon him to survive it. Here, among neat haystacks and orchards, it represented something extraordinary. He was stronger than any man. Did this make him less than human? I do not believe in God and I cannot believe that his spark would illuminate an ape, were I to accept even the theoretical possibility of his existence. I resolved to bring this to my Master's attention when we met to discuss the matter next.

The patient clung to life for two weeks before abandoning his struggle. I was filled with a new lassitude that had begun to strike me each time my skills were inadequate to the task. I took to my rooms, diverting my mind by reading. Jacques was at my side, leaving only to fetch my repast from the kitchens. It was a grey and stifling summer, with the spectre of a deluge ever hidden behind iron clouds but never revealing itself. The occasional breezes were ripples in the moist air. They provided no refreshment. I sat, book in hand and glass by my side, ignoring the unpleasant sensation of my perspiration sticking my shirt to the back of my chair. The books failed to divert me. Food and wine no longer delighted me. They were sustenance and no more.

I had feared imprisonment, and now found myself incarcerated in a Bastille of my own melancholy. I tried to free myself but could not muster the vigour to do even the little tasks that are the mark of freedom. I did not bathe, and my beard grew as thick as it ever had in Africa. Jacques seemed to notice my aroma. It would have been impossible for him not to as I was able to remark upon it myself although it seemed distant and detached from me, like a memory. I saw him wrinkle his nose as he approached with my meal tray. His expression seemed to be one of delight rather than disgust. This intrigued me enough to break my silence.

'Why do you smile, Jacques? Am I not unpleasant to behold, unwashed and unshaven?'

He paused. His expression was indecipherable as he searched for the words to express his emotions. 'I do not like to see you sad. I am sad because I am your friend.'

I was thunderstruck. I had no idea that he was capable of such tender emotion. He could feel sympathy. Empathy, even. It was as if I was precipitated into a sudden frenzy of activity.

'Jacques, draw my bath and prepare my shaving things. I must speak to the Master as soon as it is possible. It is a matter of great importance.'

He ran to his tasks. As I stripped I folded my shirt with great precision and handed it to him. I was sure I could detect a tear in his eye, but he turned from me and busied himself with the razor and strop.

I entered the salon as the sun was setting. My Master sat in his chair gazing out of the window across the courtyard, his favourite hound at his feet. I followed his eye and saw the Lady Caroline and her attendants entering the chapel.

'Come in Legris. Sit, pray. I was thinking about God. You see my wife attending vespers? She is a devout girl. I believe she misses her father's house despite all I have given her. She has rededicated the chapel to St Yves. He's the patron saint of lawyers, you know. I believe I have told you that her father followed that profession.'

'You did, Your Grace.'

He sighed. 'It troubles me, Legris. I am afraid that she is un-happy and wants to return to her family.' He petted the dog's ears. I could see that this introduction gave me the perfect opportunity to raise the issue for which I had sought this audience.

'Your Grace, I do not think you have much to fear. Lady Caroline seems blissfully happy to me. The fact that she misses the place of her birth speaks not of her dissatisfaction but of her tenderness and humanity. Why, as Captain Broullard's vessel came in sight of the Emerald Coast I was moved to tears. Is not the love of one's home the most sincere emotion?'

My Master considered this. 'You have the most extraordinary ability to provide words of comfort, Legris. I have not forgotten the universal clock that you told me of when I was recovering from my wounds. I am convinced that had you been of noble birth you would have been a courtier. I am relieved that you were not, as this would have robbed me of a fine physician.' He laughed.

'You are correct, of course. When I went to fight Frederick and his Prussians as a young man I kept a stone from the wall of this very house in my locket to remind me why I was in this peril and to guide me home. It was a great comfort to me. I should not doubt my wife. She has given me no cause to think any ill of her. Like all old men with spirited young spouses, I fear that a vigorous young man will put horns upon my head one day. It is a blemish on my character, I know. I sit in my chair and dread her infidelity. It is as if I want it to happen, so I can act out the revenge that I have contemplated for so long. Ridiculous! I am like the character in that play by the Englishman. You know, the Moor general who kills his blameless spouse because his jealousy blinds him to her virtue.'

'Your Grace's profusion of offspring leads me to believe her satisfied.'

'Spoken like a true courtier, Legris. We will see you in Versailles yet! You have a matter to raise with me, I hear.'

'It concerns Jacques, Your Grace. I have given the subject of his nature some great consideration. I had a conversation with him today that I feel will answer this question once and for all. I have been in a dark and melancholy place since I was unable to save the man I treated. Today Jacques told me he felt sorrow. I am sure it was not the sorrow he feels because he misses his native land, but sorrow for me. What mere beast could be capable of such empathy? Your Grace, I am certain that there is a spark of humanity in him that is capable of consuming his bestial beginnings. It is fanned by his exposure to men. He is being educated into human society.'

I finished my speech and fell into a triumphant silence. I thought that I had made an unassailable argument. I noticed that my Master's expression did not speak of his anticipated whole-hearted agreement.

'Legris, I can accept your account but not the hypothesis you seek to draw. Regard my hound. He is my favourite. When you and my son set out on your journey he was just a pup. I came across him when he escaped from the kennels and managed to penetrate the kitchen's defences. He should have been whipped but I was taken by his audacity. I took him into the house and kept him as a companion. The days turned into months. I was alone. I do not fear solitude, but I was deprived of the company of my son and of the only servant I employed in whom I felt I could confide.' He inclined his head towards me.

'I became morose. The dog was forever at my side. I noticed

that when I was at my grimmest, he took on a doleful expression. When La Roche's family took me to court and I met Caroline, my mood lightened. So did that of the dog. When I was at my happiest following the birth of my children, the dog recognized this and took them into his heart also. Even now he accompanies my older sons on their expeditions hunting squirrels and rats. He does this because it brings me pleasure. He has the empathy that you say marks out your Jacques as unique. He remains a dog – a noble, loyal and intelligent specimen, but a dog all the same. I do not doubt Jacques' qualities. He is a singular ape. It will take more than an ability to articulate qualities that all the higher animals possess to convince me that he is more.'

Our interview was over. I left my Master observing his wife converse with the curate on the chapel steps. He had a vulpine expression. I resolved to speak to him again. I was concerned that his jealousy might indicate an excess of bilious humours, as he had no cause for it that I could discern. If this was the case it was a medical problem worthy of the physician's art. As it transpired, I was to find another soon enough.

A pregnant summer gave birth to a stormy autumn. Rain fell in sheets, creating havoc with the harvest. It was a hungry time elsewhere, by all accounts. We heard of bread riots in Paris and the larger provincial cities, but there was no privation on my Master's lands. He was a rich and prudent man who had laid grain aside to provide for such an eventuality. The Lady Caroline was true to her faith and instrumental in ensuring that, while the people may have been hungry, there were no scenes of starvation or riot.

The weather kept Jacques and me confined largely to our tower, where we prepared treatments for the fevers that I was sure would ride upon the back of the cold and damp. Our excursions were rare and usually limited to visiting patients and apothecaries, the nearest of which that carried any of the stock I required was in Rennes. We would ride to collect our orders. This gave me an opportunity to continue my observations. I was struck by Jacques' discomfort when his singular appearance drew the stares and pointed fingers of those whom we passed on our way. I took this to be a sign of his growing self-awareness. While I found this heartening and resolved to bring it to the Master's attention when we spoke, it also created something of a practical difficulty. I could not stand to see Jacques upset, yet I could not leave him, for although he was getting bolder in his exploration of his immediate surroundings his shyness made him utterly dependent upon my presence for reassurance.

I considered shaving his face, but rejected the idea as failing to obscure his features. It was a problem that occupied my mind as I loitered in the hallway awaiting another audience. My eyes fell upon a canvas that depicted the aftermath of battle, and I noticed a man whose face was encased in bandages among the wounded. I knew he was a French dragoon by his uniform, but of his face one could see nothing. I had found a solution. Jacques was reluctant to adopt it at first but, reassured of this device's humanity, he allowed himself to be swathed before we set out on our next journey.

We returned in the early evening to a scene of much terror. My Master's favourite hound had become enraged and had attacked one of the children. The Lady Caroline greeted me. She was in a state of hysteria. I ran to the child's bedchamber to find him covered in blood and lying quite still. I waved my hand before his face and was concerned to see his eyes did not follow it. His forehead was cold. I caused blankets to be placed upon him and the fire stoked to provide a fierce, tropical atmosphere to balance this excess and cleaned his wounds. I was relieved to find that they were superficial. The dog had removed a piece of flesh from the child's cheek, but as he was a well-nourished young man I concluded that the muscles had not been subjected to great damage.

The shock of the astringent seemed to revitalize him and the child cried most piteously, bringing forth a great lamentation from his mother and her ladies. I hastened to reassure them that this was a good sign, as it allowed air to enter the lungs and showed a resilience of spirit that boded well for his recovery. He would have a scar, certainly. I introduced a note of levity by telling the Lady Caroline that I was not unaware that ladies found the marks of honourable combat attractive in a young man. She did not seem to find this as consoling as I had hoped – a fact which led me to speculate that my Master's praise for my apposite turn of phrase may have been misplaced. Her look of disapproval was so withering that I packed my instruments and left with a precipitation quite unbefitting a physician whose patient had survived.

I slumped into my chair exhausted. Jacques approached me, decanter in hand. His expression was concerned. I gestured to him to pour me a glass of brandy. He allowed time for it to soothe me before asking what had happened.

'Nothing of great importance, Jacques. The Master's dog has bitten the face of his oldest son. I have treated him to the best of my skill. The child will live, but will be scarred upon the face.'

His relief was palpable. I sat in silence. I could see he wanted to ask me something and I left him space to do so.

'Doctor Simon, what will become of the dog?'

'It will be shot, I expect.'

'But supposing the child was horrid to it and it bit only to defend itself?'

'That does not matter, Jacques. If an animal kills or hurts a human, it is always put to death.'

He seemed as if he was trying to articulate something, before abandoning the effort and going to retrieve my repast from the kitchens. I paid it no more mind, reasoning that when he felt able to ask his question, I would satisfy his curiosity.

I had noticed that Jacques had an aversion to going to the stables. I tried to accommodate this, as I was all too well aware of its source. The stable hands were a rough crew, men whom my Master had chosen for their ability to tend his horses not for their refined manners. Oh, they treated me well enough. I had saved too many of their limbs and livelihoods for them to make an enemy of me. But they could be unkind to Jacques, shouting names after him, which I was sure his sensitivity made it hard for him to bear. I had little fear that it would go beyond name-calling. They liked to pit dogs, badgers and all other animals of a moderately ferocious nature against each other, it was true. They did not regard my friend as anything other than an animal. I had overheard speculation about whether he could overcome various creatures in combat. I ignored it. Jacques' strength alone should keep him from serious harm.

So I did not send him on errands there unless they were vital. One such was when I dispatched Jacques to the stables to enquire of Monsieur Duval, the head stockman, if it was necessary for me to attend one of his men who had fallen from a hayloft. The man was unconscious for half a day, but seemed to be recovering with rest. I should have gone myself, but I had another duty. I was obliged to change the dressing on my Master's son's face, a task that I had to do first, despite the servant's greater need. Also, it was raining. I did not rejoice in the thought of the walk to the grooms' quarters as I had just managed to dispel the chill of my earlier outing. I sent Jacques. There is no point in having an assistant (I hesitate to call him my servant) if he cannot be called upon to assist.

It was getting dark and Jacques was still absent. I had begun to be concerned enough to consider venturing into the rain. I sighed with much fortitude as I pulled my cloak around me and set off to find him. It was rare for us to exchange cross words, but this would be one such occasion if I found him to have become distracted by something. Although he was developing quickly, he had no sense of time passing. I believed his conception extended to daylight and darkness at best.

I heard the shouts even as I approached the stables. There was a note of drunkenness about them, which did not bode well. I quickened my pace. The door was open. I did not announce my presence. A group of stablemen was gathered around a stall. It had been blocked off at one end by planks, turning it into an arena. I would be most displeased if Jacques had allowed this barbarity to deflect him from his purpose. I moulded my features into a suitably stern expression and advanced upon them. As I did so, I heard a familiar cry of alarm over the snarling of a dog. It was a cry that I had not heard in France and it took me some time to place it. It was he, my Jacques. It was his cry of distress. I had not heard it since I saw him set upon by his tribe. I was filled with an uncharacteristic rage.

I have never been a violent man, but as much as any man I

am a descendant of the wild Gaels who fought Caesar. I seized a pitchfork and advanced as quickly as I was able. The men were perched upon the stall's sides to give them a better view of the spectacle. I jabbed the implement into the nearest one's buttocks. He fell to the floor. The others turned on me. I should have been afraid. I am a small man and had only primitive armaments. I was alone and they were many. Yet I had no fear. I had transcended my limitations; such was the force of my anger.

I pulled another to the floor and screamed at them, 'You bastards. I know every one of you. I will have your jobs. Your families will starve. You will regret this moment, I swear it.' I rounded on one of them. 'You, release him immediately or I will kill you where you stand.'

The man hastened to obey. In fact, my command required little other than permitting Jacques to scale the sides. I realized with disgust that they had kept him confined by forcing him back each time he had tried to escape. I noticed that Jacques had a cut to his hand. A classic wound of defence. I was so angry I could hardly see.

'You had better go home and pack your things, you vermin. I will speak to His Grace the Duke presently. That should give you time to explain to your kin why they are destitute. And as for you all, you cunts, I look forward to spitting in your begging bowls when I pass you by.'

I turned on my heel and strode back to the chateau with Jacques following in my wake. Even brandy took time to compose me. I finished dressing Jacques' wound before I could bring myself to speak. 'What happened?'

'They gave me an apple and made the dog fight me.'

'But why did you not fight them? You are strong, Jacques. Easily a match for them. None of them could have lifted the cart.'

He was silent. I could see his struggle and waited. There was no response. He yawned and I noticed that he looked exhausted. His eyes were liquid. I was filled with pity for him and disgust with my fellow man. I dispatched him to his bed resolved to take this matter up again when he had recovered from his ordeal.

I sought an audience with my Master. After I had explained all, he pronounced his judgement.

'Very well, Legris. I cannot abide cruelty. I have no wish to loose such a valuable servant as you, also. You will leave unless I punish these men, you say?'

I nodded my assent.

'So be it. I can find a stockman behind every hedge between here and Caen. A physician is a rarer breed. I will dismiss them. I will not cast their families out if they have able relatives in my employ and live as my tenants. I will remind them that they will join their relations were they to harbour them. Does that satisfy you?'

I confirmed it did. My Master continued. 'This incident raises wider concerns about our little debate, does it not? What sort of a man would permit himself to suffer these indignities when he had the resources to escape? I am reminded of the ox and the slaughterman. The ox is the stronger. If he chose, he could gore, trample and destroy his executioner. Yet he does not. He has not the will to resist. The capacity to protect one's dignity is unique to humanity, I think. Contemplate this and we will meet again. I am anxious to hear your response once it is formulated.'

I left my Master's company and returned to my room to speculate about the nature of man. I was not as blind to the contradictions of this exchange as it seems my Master was. It was unjust. Seeking vengeance and punishment was an act so foreign to my nature that I believe this was the first time I had ever done so. It did not leave me feeling powerful or satisfied, just curiously cold and sick. Jacques' tormentors deserved their punishment. Of that I was certain. They would be dismissed and dispossessed. No doubt some had played a lesser role than others. In my anger I had demanded a collective punishment and that is what they would receive. It would not occur to them to resist. Spectator and perpetrator would languish beneath the lash of my Master's displeasure without murmur. What could they do? They could not protect their dignity yet they were indubitably men. My Master relied upon the absence of the very characteristic by which he defined himself to govern his lands. I picked up a volume and sought consolation in the blessed Jean-Jacques Rousseau.

'Mankind was born free but everywhere lies in chains.'

Then it came to me. The spectators among the men might lack the power to resist, but they would certainly see themselves as being unjustly treated. That was it. What defined a man? Why, it was obvious. A man was born free. He may be in chains, but every passive slave's quietude hid a Spartacus. If Jacques could see he was the victim of unfairness then I would have won my argument. I needed my Master to accept the terms before I embarked upon my experiment, but I was convinced that he would, and that Jacques had the capacity to rise to the challenge.

I approached the Duke the next evening. I was armed with a plethora of philosophical works, and expected to have to be at my most persuasive. My Master was surprisingly amenable to my argument, accepting the conceptual difference between being unable to rectify an injustice and being able to perceive one. He even went so far as to provide the illuminating analogy of an army living off the land of a conquered population. We devised our plan. Jacques was notable for his primitive honesty. He had no possessions. I cared for his material needs, which were simple. I had instilled in him a respect for other's property. He knew it was a serious thing to be a thief. I was to allow him to see me place some coins among his belongings. These would be 'discovered' and he would be accused of theft. I would fail to protect him, despite his knowledge that I could confirm his innocence. He would come to know the dual agonies of injustice and betrayal. His reaction would determine our debate. If he proved capable of expressing anger at it, he would be a man. I would have won.

I set about my duties with alacrity. Jacques rose before me and prepared my breakfast. As soon as he left for the kitchens I took up my station by his cot. On his return, I asked him if he minded my storing a purse under his mattress. His only concern was whether it would cause him discomfort. I reassured him that all would be gone before it was time for him to retire that evening. He shrugged and poured my coffee. I had just lit my pipe when there was a thunderous knocking at my door. It was the Duke, accompanied by his bailiff. I feigned astonishment and asked why my chambers were so invaded.

'I have been forced to intrude upon you, Doctor. A very serious allegation has been made against your servant. I have spoken to a witness who has accused him of taking his money.'

'Not Jacques. He is incapable of such dishonesty.'

'Then you will raise no objection to my man searching his belongings?'

'None whatsoever,' I retorted curtly. 'Proceed. It will take no great time as he has hardly a thing to call his own.'

The bailiff made a great show of overturning Jacques' sole chair and hurling his few clothes across the room. Finally, his attention was directed to the bed. The bedclothes were dispatched unceremoniously. And now the moment of truth. With a great flourish the mattress was cast to one side. The seeker gave a cry of triumph and brandished the coins in the air.

My Master turned to Jacques. 'So, thief, you stand condemned. What have you to say to this?'

Jacques looked perplexed. He turned to me, his eyes wide. 'Tell them, Doctor Simon. Tell them I am no thief.'

I turned my face away. My expression would have betrayed me. 'I will not lie for you, Jacques. If you have betrayed our Master's trust it is you who must face the consequences.'

Suddenly I was hurled to the floor. Jacques, my little, mild-mannered friend who would not resist his tormentors, had attacked me. I was so happy that I could barely muster the strength to protest. It was only after the bailiff had struck him upon the head that he was able to control his fury enough to hear my words of praise and delight. He seemed mollified, and accepted that what I had done was necessary, although he described it as cruel. I was forced to placate his misgivings with a gift of his beloved apples, but even then it took him many weeks to recover his trust. My Master and I took this as further proof of his humanity. For my part I was rewarded with a gift of a thousand livres and a horse. Jacques, now a man, was given a modest salary and permitted to serve me my wine as the Master and I met to discuss other matters of interest. He was provided with a family name, LeSinge, and a suit of clothes in the livery of the family Ladurie de Bretagne, as befitted a man in service. He wore it with a pride that almost equalled mine at seeing him.

9

Arrivals and Departures

J ACQUES' HUMANITY MARKED THE PINNACLE OF MY HAPPINESS.
It was as if I had been reborn. I started to experience the
renaissance of a chapter of my life I had believed to be closed.
I had long periods during which my services were not required,
and I found myself recalling Claudette with a fondness that was
not entirely nostalgic. I attempted to sublimate these desires by
taking an interest in the business of the chateau. I even attended
some of the procedures that were necessary in the maintenance of
horses. In a purely advisory capacity, you must understand. I am
no mere veterinarian. Jacques accompanied me to a few births,
which I found quite affecting.

It was no good. I could not rid myself of the desire to find a
mistress. Jacques' constant presence at my side precluded even the
momentary relief of monastic practices. I felt compelled to make
my way to Rennes in search of female company. Why should I
not? I reasoned that these urges were natural. Their return surely
signified my return to good health. I was a successful physician

and a mistress was not only what was expected of a man in my position. It was a right as inalienable as freedom of assembly.

I found her. Marie was her name and she was, as I found out to my horror, young enough to be my daughter. She was as dark as Claudette was fair and was her equal as a libertine. She made my trips to the apothecary's a positive pleasure. Naturally, Jacques no longer accompanied me. He had found a new independence and did not seem to resent being left behind. He was always overjoyed at my return of course, and took great pleasure in telling me of his exploits in my absence. It was as if his elevation to the ranks of humanity represented a coming of age. He had ceased to be a child, or at least ceased to be childlike. He was becoming a young man. We still enjoyed each other's company. If I were given to extravagant phraseology, I would say that he was like a son to me.

I returned one day from visiting Marie to find the unexpected. Although my Master was undoubtedly a man of great learning and had been a patron of the natural sciences in his youth, since my return from Africa he had been somewhat of a recluse. He could be said to prefer the company of his family to that of his peers. The loss of his eldest son seemed to have reduced the impulse that had led to the chateau becoming a place of pilgrimage for those in search of a wealthy backer for some project or other. Those visitors who did come were connected to the business of the horse farm. He had cultivated his status as an invalid carefully to absolve him of the duty of spending his time at Court. There was no great traffic between my Master's house and Paris, so it was a great surprise to return that day to find a rather magnificent coach and four in the courtyard. It was decked out in the royal livery, which caused me some concern. The sovereign was traditionally wary of aristocrats residing away from Court, so I had been given to understand. I feared that my Master's visitors brought a summons that could only signify the end of my idyll.

My trepidation was tinged with curiosity. It was this that led me to depart from precedent and enter the chateau by the main door. I lingered in the hallway to see if I could discern any of the conversation within the salon. I rationalized that this was not exactly eavesdropping, as I did not place my ear to the door or deploy any of the traditional subterfuges of espionage. I merely stood for a while, admiring the portraiture. If I happened to overhear anything, well, it was hardly my fault. An intense conversation was taking place. I could hear the Master's voice raised in exclamation from time to time. I could discern that he did not seem to be caught up in fury or filled with resignation, but the details were lost. I returned to my rooms feeling uneasy.

My Master summoned me to the salon in the late evening. He was alone and seemed to be in a state of some excitement.

'Legris. We are to go to Paris.'

It was the news I had feared. I masked my unhappiness.

'I am concerned that Your Grace's health precludes such an arduous journey. Although there is great merit in your offspring being educated in the manner suitable to young noblemen, I fear that the demands that the journey would place upon you could prove intolerable. I am a physician of some skill, as Your Grace knows. I would be happy to give my opinion to those who have brought the summons.'

My Master laughed. 'You have my interests at heart as ever, Legris. Had I simply been summoned to Versailles I would not hesitate to call upon your, ah, professional judgement. But it is not a summons that has been brought. It is a convocation. I have been instructed to attend the Estates General. The King has called the three strands of the nation together to save France from the mire. I answered my King's call as a young soldier. Who would have guessed that I would be asked to put on my armour to defend the nation again as an old man? I will take my place as a noble of the sword. I am prepared to do my duty. Sadly, this means that I will have to leave this place for a while. You will come with me, of course. I cannot do without my physician. Paris is a very unhealthy place. There are many preparations to make. You must make sure that your bag of tricks is replenished before we depart.'

I was not sure what to make of it all. I was not unhappy to be going to Paris once more. I was even slightly excited by the prospect of being present at such an occasion. It is not every man who has the opportunity to witness history being made. My main concern was for Jacques. He had settled well into the life of the chateau after the incident with the dog, and I was worried that the sheer magnitude of the greatest city since Rome would disquiet him. I resolved to make my own preparations and to let Jacques decide for himself when the time came for us to leave. I hoped his loyalty to me would overcome the natural fear of the unknown. I did not want to be parted from him.

The preparations subsumed the entire household. There was a state of eager confusion similar to that which had surrounded my departure to Africa. Amid all of this, we received our second visitor. His arrival was not as glorious as the first. He came on foot, having been deposited by coach at the gates. He cut a rather muddy and travel-worn figure. His coat was stained. I noted that it seemed to provide a history of his recent and not so recent dining habits. He was corpulent, and the exertion of his arrival had more than moistened his wig and neckerchief. He was an autumnal man. I use the word because at first glance his face seemed to be composed of mounds of the berries that load the hedgerows in that season. His cheeks were as purple as the blackcurrant, latticed with broken raspberry veins. His skin was bulbous and uneven. The effect was crowned by his eyes. A vivid strawberry red surrounded an iris of the same faded blue as a September sky. If his appearance was unprepossessing, his manner had the confidence and grandeur of Caesar himself. He knocked upon the main door with his cane, demanding an audience with the Master. I expected him to be dismissed rather curtly but even though my Master was not renowned for his hospitality, he was ushered in. I busied myself with my rounds among the sick and injured, but I found them a poor distraction. My perfunctory ministrations betrayed my preoccupation with the stranger's identity.

I returned to my rooms and paced. I was no nearer working out who the individual was when I was called to attend upon my Master. Jacques and I made our way to the salon to find them deep in conversation.

'Legris. This is Doctor McCreadie, an Englishman. It seems that our fame as a patron of the natural sciences has spread as far as Albion.'

I regarded the man. Perhaps his appearance spoke of some voyage of discovery rather than the degradation I had supposed. The name seemed familiar. I dredged my memory but found nothing other than a vague sense that I had heard or read something of it.

'If your fame as a patron has reached England, Your Grace, it has done so in a manner that is entirely consistent with any other aspect of civilization.' I turned to face the visitor. 'Monsieur, I fear you are too late. The Duke's fascination with expeditions has cooled since his oldest son met his end on the Slave Coast. You must continue your search for a backer elsewhere.'

My Master looked displeased. 'There is no need for discourtesy, Legris. Doctor McCreadie is a member of the Royal Society in London. He has been telling me of his expedition to the High Andes and the singular phenomenon of the winged serpent.'

Then all was clear. The Royal Society, winged serpents – I could recall exactly where I had heard the name McCreadie. It was all I could do to repress my laughter.

'Ah yes, Doctor McCreadie, I recall reading of your exploits. Your serpent was not as winged as you led many to believe. A large snake, the wings of a vast native bird called the condor, a needle and some thread proved to be its genesis, I believe.'

It was hard to discern whether he flushed with anger or shame, for his face was a network of puce that allowed the physical manifestation of such emotions a ready hiding place. His voice was steady, with a note of conciliation.

'You are a well-read man, Doctor, but you seem to be appraised of only part of the story. Let me supply the remainder. I set out to discover the fabled golden city of the mountains. My journey took me to many of the ruined cities of the Romans of that continent, whose barbarity was eclipsed by that of the Spaniards. I noticed that many of their statues depicted the winged serpent. Curiosity about this beast led me to ask my guides where it could be located. They took me to lonely and desolate places. I maintain that I have seen these creatures from a great distance but their nesting sites proved elusive. I was determined to capture one so that it could be displayed for the edification of my fellows. I essayed this for months without success. My funds were short. When it seemed that I would have to forgo this discovery because of the tiresome bonds placed upon me by less enlightened men who had expected a golden return from my expedition, I chanced upon a group of native hunters. They were able to sell me what I took to be a genuine specimen in good faith. My horror that it was a forgery far surpassed that of the Society. I have come to request that your Master permits me the chance of salvaging my reputation.'

He had made his pitch. I turned to my Master in some anxiety. My experience of the English and their expeditions had been soured somewhat by the man I could not help but refer to by his assumed name of Van der Veer. I hoped that the Duke would adopt a deserved scepticism. I had no need for my alarm.

'My dear Doctor McCreadie, I fear that my physician is correct when he says that I have lost any desire to fund or equip such undertakings. You may enjoy our hospitality for a while, though. Time will be short, as I am to travel to take my seat in the Estates General before long. You may find while you are here that there are wonders to be discovered without the need to travel to the ends of the world.'

McCreadie's face assumed a miser's interest. 'I am grateful, Your Grace, but to what could you be referring?'

'Why, my physician has a servant of a most singular nature. Legris took part in the expedition to the Slave Coast that claimed my son's life. He was the only survivor. He returned with an ape that attends him as a manservant – a unique creature. Although he has the appearance of his species, he is able to speak and reason. Indeed, after some debate we have decided that he is a man.'

'I would be honoured to meet such a creature.'

'You may. Step forward, Jacques.'

Jacques emerged from his station at my shoulder. He walked to the centre of the room awaiting his command.

'Doctor McCreadie is fatigued and hungry, Jacques. Pray fetch him some brandy and fruit.'

Jacques turned smartly on his heel and went about this errand, leaving McCreadie open mouthed. He returned with a decanter, three glasses and a basket of apples, which he placed upon a table. McCreadie watched him in silence throughout. His face was expressionless.

'May I examine him, Your Grace?'

'Indeed you may.'

Jacques allowed himself to be prodded and poked, opening his mouth on request.

'The roof of his mouth is hard, as in a man. Apes have no such organ. This leads me to conclude that you do not have an ape that has become a man but rather a man that has the outward appearance of an ape, if you follow?'

I said nothing. The same thought had occurred to me before. My Master nodded enthusiastically. 'What does this signify? How could this have occurred?'

'Well, Your Grace, there is a school of thought that states that the period spent within the womb is that which allows us to establish our physical appearance. I do not speak of heredity. That simply provides nature with the bricks and mortar from which the edifice of life is constructed. I speak of the way that the mother's experiences throughout gestation can influence the character and appearance of the child. For example, if a child is of an even disposition it would be safe to conclude that the period of confinement was tranquil, would it not?'

We muttered our assent.

'Yet if the child is fractious this could be caused by the influence of a discordant existence upon the mother. But these are just what could be described as the ordinary influences that fall upon every child before its birth. There are some cases in which the shock faced by the mother has been so great that its aftermath affects not only the shape of the offspring's character, but its physical form as well. I have seen reports of such cases. One of the most notable took place in my own native Scotland. Have you heard of the Fish Boy of Arbroath, the Scottish merman? No? Well, putting it briefly, the child came from a family of fishermen. Such was their disadvantage that the poor mother's assistance in pulling in the nets could not be dispensed with in the early stages of pregnancy. She continued to go out on the boats with her husband and kin to catch herring. One such voyage ended in near tragedy. The boat was upset by a grampus, which attacked it most aggressively. Luckily other boats were at hand. The beast was driven off and the shipwrecked were rescued. No more thought was paid to the incident save as an example of a fortunate escape until the child was born. He had no legs. Instead of the two limbs his parents confidently expected to find, there was a fishlike tail. Most significantly, where his feet should have been there were flukes that stuck out to each side like those of a grampus, not above and below like a codfish. The inference is clear. The trauma of the mother's near death at the hands of the whale was so great that her son took on its physical aspect.'

I could not restrain myself. 'What became of the merman?'

'Why, he was cast out by his family. He was taken to the University in Edinburgh where he died. I have read records of his dissection. I can assure you that they support my theory. I believe that this must be your Jacques' history. Consider the plight of the family of natives to whom he was born. The mother escapes death at the hands of an ape by the narrowest of margins. The child is born. His birth and survival are miraculous and yet his appearance serves only as a terrible reminder of mortality. Savagery and superstition cause the parents to fear their child. A terrible fate hangs over those who murder their young in almost every culture. You will recall that the ancients imagined that creatures called the Furies haunted infanticides until they were driven mad and destroyed.'

We nodded sagely.

'The parents take the only course open to them. They abandon their child in the forest, hoping that they will be spared divine vengeance if the agency of his destruction transpires to be wild beasts. He is saved, as Romulus and Remus were saved, through adoption by the beasts who were intended to be his nemesis. This man who acts as your servant is a prodigy. He is living proof of this theorem. How else could he have learned the ways of men?'

My Master and I cogitated this oration in silence. I was forced to admire McCreadie's reasoning. It made sense. My debate with the Duke suddenly took on a most unwelcome aspect. Had we spent our time debating the nature of humanity as a philosophical concept when the question was confined to the physical? It was an appalling prospect. I began to develop upon my instinctive dislike of our guest – a task that was greatly assisted by his next remark.

'If Your Grace would permit me to dissect the subject, I would be in a position to confirm my initial diagnosis in full.'

Dissect Jacques! The idea was monstrous. If he was a man then the course this Englishman proposed was murder, pure and simple. I began to protest. My Master raised his hand to silence me and addressed our guest coldly. 'I do not know what passes for governance where you come from, Doctor, but let me assure you that here in France we still regard murder as one of the more serious crimes. I have no intention of permitting you to murder my servant, even if you would be doing so in a spirit of scientific enquiry.'

'Your Grace, of course I intended no slight upon your country or person. I would be honoured if you would allow Jacques to accompany me to London. I would present him and my theory to the Royal Society.'

I was concerned that my Master would acquiesce. I had under-estimated his distaste for the presumption of his inferiors.

'We may be less enlightened than you English claim to be, Monsieur, but you will find that we have abolished our feudal ways some time ago. Jacques is not a serf. He is a free citizen of France who happens to be in my employ. I give you the privilege of asking him to accompany you to London. If he chooses to do so, I will release him from my service for the duration of his stay there. If he does not, then he will remain here. Jacques!'

'Yes, Your Grace?'

'Do you want to go to London with Doctor McCreadie?'

Jacques paused and seemed to weigh his options before shaking his head violently. He walked to his station behind my chair with his nose in the air, studiously avoiding the Englishman's eye.

My Master roared with laughter. 'Well, there you have it, McCreadie. Jacques will not come with you and that is an end to the matter. You may stay here until we leave for Paris. Now I intend to join my wife. I will bid you both good evening.'

It does not do gratuitously to offend one's fellow men of science, even those as loathesome as I suspected McCreadie to be.

I suppressed an entirely natural impulse to jeer at him. Instead I bade him a courteous good night and made my way to my tower. I believe I successfully disguised my desire to caper as I went.

I noticed that McCreadie took every opportunity to ingratiate himself with Jacques. My duties as physician and the need to prepare for our departure took me away from the chateau. I was most extraordinarily busy. And I was neglecting Jacques. He was not alone in this – I had not seen Marie for some weeks. Every time I returned, I found Jacques had been presented with some other bauble. He acquired a wooden chest to contain them. He had nothing of real value – a toy soldier, a glass apple, a watch (broken) and a model horse. But he discovered a peculiar pride in these. He described them as gifts and told me that he must treasure them because they were 'tokens of Doctor Mac's esteem.'

I did not trust McCreadie, yet I could find nothing other than my visceral dislike for the man to justify my aversion. I feared I was becoming jealous. The thought that I had become envious of a man because he showed kindness to my servant appalled me. I consoled myself that his time here was short, as we would be leaving for Paris soon. Yet I could not prevent myself from feeling an angry unease when I saw them together. I decided to absent myself from their company, as revealing my baser emotions would reflect upon me badly. I had time for one final trip to Rennes before we departed. It would be pleasurable to see Marie. I had appetites that Jacques could not quench. His distance from me increased daily, and I was often left with the feeling that I was the subject of discussion between McCreadie and him during which I was described in less than flattering terms. At least Marie would be happy to spend time in my company.

On my return, my chest was as full as the apothecary's purse. I was unnerved by Jacques' absence as I rode into the courtyard. He was in the habit of greeting me effusively. I wondered with dark humour if he was with McCreadie, receiving some 'token of esteem'. My alarm was increased by my Master's manservant who delivered me an order to join him in the salon even as I dismounted. There was no time for me to change. I hurried to join the Duke even though I was travel-stained and weary. McCreadie was there. My Master's expression was angry. I had never seen him like this. It was not the anger of a man who had lost his temper but a white, cold thing that could be wielded like a sword. There was no sign of Jacques. My surreptitious attempts to locate him did not pass unnoticed.

'If you are looking for your servant, Legris, you will not find him here. He has betrayed my trust most monstrously. If it were not for the intervention of the good Doctor McCreadie, then I would not have arrived in time to prevent him committing an act of outrage upon my wife.'

I tried to speak. I was filled with an incomprehension that struck me dumb. I opened my mouth like a drowning man but my Master cut me short. 'Oh yes, Legris, your Jacques has shown himself to be a viper at my bosom. I had become so distracted by his humanity that I neglected to recall that not all men are benign. McCreadie's theory that he was born a savage has proved true. He has acted the savage tonight and paid the price. I found him in my wife's private chambers. He was bathing in her bath, quite naked and unashamed. I am sure he meant to ravage her as she retired. McCreadie has told me that he talked of her frequently and with great impropriety. I am angered that you did not see fit to bring this to my attention yourself, or was it an attraction that you shared?'

I protested. 'Your Grace, I have never heard Jacques mention the Lady Caroline in any other than the most respectful manner. He has never seemed to possess any carnal impulse whatsoever. If there is a viper, then it is a beef-fed viper of England. Do you not see that you have been bent to his will? He seeks to have you turn Jacques over to him so that he can return to London triumphant.'

'Then he will be a very disappointed man indeed. I have had my men whip him and drag him from my lands behind a horse. I do not care what has become of him. I do not know where he is.'

I could see that McCreadie had been ignorant of this. His expression changed from one of reptilian self-satisfaction to one of alarm. I raised my arm and pointed to him.

'See, Your Grace. I accuse him. He has the face of a liar. Were his kind not always the most infamous and subtle of deceivers? My poor Jacques. Where can he be? I must go to him.'

I turned and ran from the room. I rode all night, circling the countryside, ever alert for any sign of him. I found none. I returned to find that my Master had not taken McCreadie's deceit lightly. Like all great men he prized his reputation. It is unwise to make a fool of someone with such power. McCreadie had been whipped and driven from my Master's lands upon a donkey. He had been tied upon its back with his face pointing towards the animal's tail. The means of his departure may have excelled that of his arrival in its indignity, but I found that this was scant compensation. My Jacques had gone. I waited for word of him, reasoning that one so distinctive could not get far without attracting attention. None came. I packed my belongings to go to Paris like an automaton. I had expected to be filled with anticipation at the great events to which I was to be privileged to bear witness, but I was as damp and empty as an abandoned house. Even that last hope that we would meet again faded as we left Brittany behind. My only wish was that he would come to no more harm without me to care for him. Please keep my Jacques safe.

Part II

Claudette

10

Reflections

I CAN STILL REMEMBER THE FIRST TIME I REALIZED THAT MEN looked at me. It was the day before midsummer and the fair had come to our village. They had pitched by the stream where the women went to do their washing. The travelling men had stripped to the waist to hammer in pegs. When my friends and I brought the laundry to the water, we were forbidden to speak to them, even as they whistled and called to us. Naturally, being good girls, we did what our mothers and fathers had told us. Joséphine and Marie-France would not even look at them directly. They lowered their eyes as we passed them but still managed to take in their hair, their muscles, their skin – their very maleness.

They would shout out after all the girls, those gypsies. You would have had to have been a whiskery grandmother with breasts like a nanny goat's udders to have escaped their attentions. Even so, I knew I was being singled out. '*Jolie blonde,*' they shouted, 'come and kiss me. *Je t'aime. Je t'adore.*' Who else could they mean? Their accents were strange and, to my thirteen-year-old ears, exotic. I would never have dreamed of replying. My father would have been furious. Yet, I would not do as my friends did and scamper away. I was too proud. I was La Belle Claudette, the prettiest girl in Moncontour.

When they shouted after me I pointed my nose to the clouds and sauntered past as if they were beneath my attention. As soon as we were out of earshot, my friends and I fell into each others' arms and giggled like the village girls we were. I did not really understand what we were laughing about then, but I knew that I possessed something that made me special and I could not wait to see what I could do with it. That night I was so distracted by my thoughts that I dropped the butter churn and was sent to bed. And I never did get to go to the fair.

I understand men. There is only so much to know, after all, and I have spent a lot of time with them over the years. I am sure I would know as much about needlework if I had ended up a seamstress. It's just a question of professional pride. There are three main types: the romantics, the knights errant and the gourmets. Romantics are the most irritating. They have a tendency to confuse the carnal with the spiritual, which can have a girl ducking proposals of marriage. Knights errant are dull, and a bit of a challenge. They see poor little Claudette as a damsel to be rescued. They often don't want to spoil the purity of their intentions by the act of love itself, which is fine by me. Money for nothing, you might say, although I find the effort of looking heartbreakingly beautiful and remaining awake while they preach at me to be an ordeal. Although it can be quite fun putting temptation in their path. You know, a glimpse of thigh as a hem rides up during the sermon, a view of my chest as I lean forward to have something explained to me. I do need things explained. I am a woman after all.

For all their nobility men do find it hard to ignore that I am beautiful and available – a fatal combination, even for the chivalrous. And as for gourmets, they want a mistress. No romance; just a girl who looks good and indulges them. Someone better than they have at home. They prefer to take their pleasures *à la carte*, which can be quite tiresome. Their redeeming feature is a willingness to pay virtually anything if the menu pleases them. Which it does. Always.

I can't say that I like men, exactly. I certainly don't dislike them. They're just so terribly disappointing. I'm like every other girl, I suppose. I'm just waiting to be swept away by my great love. He will fold me in his arms and our passion will be so strong I won't mind if we live in a ditch or a chateau, so long as we are together. I can't imagine it, somehow, because I like nice things far more than I have liked any of the men who have brought them to me. I still hope that my love will come one day. It's a nice daydream and I always find it sustains me when a client is little short of unbearable. Hope: you may live in it, but you can't live on it.

I had two men when I left Rennes. Well, two-and-a-half if you counted Hypolite d'Armentières. I had other clients, obviously, but these two were my regulars. I say half because I saw Hypolite only rarely. When I discussed business with the other girls I would call him the assassin. He would arrive without warning, sheath his blade quickly and leave without a word. Only the purse on my dresser and the imprint of his rosary upon my breast bore witness to his passing. He was a deeply religious man, I'm sure, and regarded visiting me as a fall from divine grace. More of an occasional than a regular, really. The first real client was my doctor,

Simon. He was a small permanence in my changing world. He was my first client and I suspect I was his first altogether, which would explain his appearance in Paris. He swore he didn't follow me and he was quite sweet in his way, always making marriage proposals. There were hazards in my line of work that meant knowing a good doctor was very useful indeed. He cured my pox and got rid of any unfortunate accidents for me. He was so well acquainted with my nether regions in his professional capacity that his devotion to them in mine was really quite touching, and he was very considerate. Marriage was out of the question. He simply couldn't afford me and his sheep's eyes did get irritating after a while. I preferred him as an occasional indulgence. Adoration is like chocolate. It can make you feel unwell unless you show some restraint.

My second was a gourmet. Alain de Ladurie, Comte La Latte, no less. The son of a duke. He was a Breton too, so we had that in common. His family was very grand and he was full of his noble destiny. Never tired of telling me about this ancestor or that who died in some battle or another. It was all very dull, and I had to restrain myself from pointing out that they all seemed absolute liabilities and should not have been let near a couple of drunks fighting in the street, let alone the glorious field of battle, or whatever he called it.

He had one redeeming feature, though. He was enormously rich. Rich enough to demand exclusivity. His family had been oppressing the peasants and taxing the fishermen since the Capets were on the throne, so he could give me a great deal. This meant Simon had to be sent about his business for a while. Not a problem. I knew he would wait. All I ever had to do was snap my fingers. He was undemanding, which is more than could be said for Alain, who saw himself as a renaissance man, a soldier and a patron of the arts. He decided to have me painted. As Diana the Virgin Huntress, no less. Not only did I have to be naked while this was going on, which I had expected, but I had to have a wolf at my feet to complete the tableau, which I had not.

The wolf was a problem. It was devoted to me, of course, but had bitten everyone else, including the artist, my maid and my neighbour. Alain thought this was hilarious at first. He would laugh about it as he disrobed. Unfortunately the wolf also demanded my undivided affections, which eventually led to the great warrior leaping from my window wearing nothing but his hat. He had to go, of course. The wolf, that is. Given the choice I'd have got rid of Alain. The creature was not much of a conversationalist – which can be a blessing in a gentleman. I was mildly amused by the irony of the comparison with poor Simon. It's always the ones you prefer who can't afford you. The solution was to bring them together. I didn't anticipate much resistance. Simon was always very easy to persuade.

I had two men, did I say? In the blink of an eye, I found myself with none. Alain called on me. He wasn't making much sense, as usual. He swore me to secrecy about the wolf, gave me a purse then ordered me to wait for him. His father had had some sort of accident and they had to return to the country. By the time he got to the details I had stopped listening, so I never did get the full story. It was a very large purse, so I resolved to be the devoted mistress. At least until it was gone.

And Simon. Well. The most predictable man in the world had actually done something surprising. He'd disappeared. I was feeling a bit melancholy and I thought I would get him to call on me. I thought a bit of adoration would cheer me up. I sent a boy to his rooms and he'd gone. No forwarding address. Nothing. It was unlike him, and I was almost concerned. I didn't like the thought of his coming to any harm.

But I digress. Enough about men. I may not have gone to the fair all those years ago, but I remember Marie-France bringing back a mirror some gypsy had sold her. She was convinced it was magic. It was a cheap thing, no bigger than the palm of your hand. The frame was copper, although it had been polished to a high shine and the gypsy swore it was gold. I still have it somewhere. I can be so sentimental. The man told Marie-France that she should go to the churchyard, spin three times widdershins and look into the mirror with the moon behind her on midsummer night and she would see her true love. I had to try it for myself, of course.

I climbed down the trellis and went with Marie-France and Joséphine. We were all out without permission. God knows, our parents would have beaten us black and blue if we'd been caught. Still, into the churchyard we went, shaking with laughter at our own daring. Marie-France went first, then Joséphine, then me. They both saw village boys and I have no doubt that they saw the future as they were both as destined to be farmers' wives as I thought I was in those days. When it came to my turn I looked as intently as I could. I said I saw the blacksmith's son. I can't even remember his name now, although he was considered to be the most handsome boy and mine by right. In truth, I saw nothing but my reflection.

11

A Good Time Had By All

I WAS AT A LOOSE END AFTER ALAIN'S SUDDEN CONVERSION to being the devoted son and Simon's dropping off the face of the earth. The purse tided me over, but it wasn't just the money. Frankly, I was bored. I could have sat in waiting for my lord and master's return like a dutiful little wife, but I always thought my attraction was that I was not. Dutiful or a wife, that is. I needed a bit of excitement. Nothing too intense. Just something to help the days pass and keep up a healthy cash flow.

If a girl wants a good time she has to go where they're being had. So, off to the theatre I went. It was always a good night out. Of course, I would never really pay attention to the play. It's the excuse not the reason. I like to dress up. Looking good is important to me and when I make the effort there's no one who looks better, though I say so myself. The fashion then was for great big diamond necklaces. They were designed to flow down your body like a river. You know, like the one the Queen was supposed to have got herself into a spot of bother over with that Jeanne de la Motte character. Alain had bought me one as soon as I'd asked. It wasn't cheap, but he knew that a contented girl is a friendly one. I wore it over a black gown. I looked in the mirror before I stepped out to the carriage and thought to myself, 'Claudette, if you spend the evening alone, then they've put something in the wine.' I don't like to boast, but experience has taught me what the gentlemen like. They like me.

So, I sat through the play. Some Austrian nonsense about a great lover and his conquests. A lot of caterwauling and very little action, but very *à la mode*. As usual, it was failing to capture my attention, but I had a nice little box seat that gave me a good view all around the place. Very useful for scouting the talent, and it put me on display. I had a glass of Chablis and some oysters, which I was trying to eat in a ladylike manner while sitting on my own – a woman of mystery. All in black which offset my blonde hair and my diamonds a treat. I could feel a good few eyes on me and I smiled the sort of half-smile that I knew would be taken to promise pleasures unheard of in the marital bed. In the box to my right there was a pair gawping. I'd looked them over out of the corner of my eye and they seemed to be the sort of upper-class fools that were my meat and drink. There was an old one and a young one, scarcely more than a boy. The latter's coat and gold buttons suggested that he was worth considering. I prefer them young. The older they get, the more demanding they become, but a youngster can be relied upon to be suitably grateful. Plus, you can never underestimate the advantages of getting the deed over with as quickly as possible.

The interval came. My little admirer rose to his feet and I turned to catch his eye, at the same time sensually slurping an oyster from its shell. I licked my lips and smiled at him. He turned as red as his velvet chair. It was all I could do not to laugh out loud, but I mastered myself. They don't like the idea of being found funny. It never pays to upset the clientele before they are well and truly on the books and can't help themselves but to come back for more. I studied the programme as Papa looked over to me. I didn't catch his eye, as I don't do parties. Not that I have any objection to it, I just don't have to. I'm a one-man woman. One at a time, that is.

Sure enough, there was a little knock on the door of my box. 'Come in,' I said, all husky and with the slight Breton accent that the customers find most becoming. He was very nervous, and stumbled as he took the two steps to cross the floor. It had obviously taken him all his courage to come to the door in the first place. Well, little boy, I'm worth it. I asked him his name and he told me it was Henri, younger son of some count or other from Alsace. He was part of the Comte d'Artoise's retinue and it was his first time in society. I took his hand and pulled it to my chest. It looked like a grand romantic gesture but in reality all I was doing was letting him feel that I was every bit as good as I appeared to be – and by the sight of the strain he was putting on his brocade culottes the message was received loud and clear.

He asked if he could call on me, and at first I was suitably reticent. After all, a lady has to care for her reputation. I let him talk me round. It's always best to let the gentlemen feel like they've made a conquest. People look after things they've had to work for far more carefully. He scampered off to rejoin Papa when the orchestra started up with yet another interminable overture. There was a spring in his step which the fact that he had to bend forward to disguise his erection couldn't hide entirely.

The play ended and I was making my way to my carriage when

I overheard two men talking about me. They were remarking on my necklace, that magnificent piece that hung to my groin. One described it as a river of light. His friend, acting the wit, told him that it was remarkable to see the way that the river flowed from its source. I could almost have smiled until I turned to look at them and realized that they were somewhat down at heel. Both in uniform but obviously living on their army pay. Quite beneath my notice, really, and the contempt in the remark irritated me. I smiled my half-smile and they both looked hopeful.

'Sir,' I said, 'it is one thing to know that a river flows from its source but quite another to discover that source for oneself. Such an expedition requires a courage and wealth few men possess.'

I turned on my heel and left, swaying my hips seductively and pulling my skirts up high enough to give them both a look at my ankles – all in all, a good evening. It's not unlike being royalty when you think about it, my line of work. I needed an heir as well. Just in case Alain decided to play the dutiful son for too long. I couldn't leave myself short, now, could I?

It's amazing the way things can go full circle. I started off with two regulars: rich Alain who knew I was his mistress, and the hopeless Simon who wanted me as his wife. Simon may have disappeared without trace, but Alain had come back and I found myself juggling again. Little Henri was devoted to me. He procured me a set of rooms near the rue Cordeliers. It was not my part of town and it was full of some truly awful people – journalists and so forth. The whole place abounded with these ghastly characters writing and printing their tracts about the despicable drinking, whoring and spending their betters got up to at the expense of the common man.

The thing that annoyed me was that they presumed to judge the likes of me. I used to come to the apartment in all my finery, but I could feel their little glances and hear the horrid remarks that peppered their conversations – all said in the sort of voices that you just know are for your benefit. It was a simple jealousy thing. They didn't so much hate me as hate themselves for wanting me, like drunks blaming the tavernkeeper because they've pissed themselves in the street.

There was a particularly nasty, monkey-faced character called Marat, who never missed the chance to stare at my chest or denounce my corruption. He used to be a doctor, I'm told. He couldn't be up to much if he wasn't capable of earning a sous in that profession. After all, even Simon managed that. It could have made me quite angry, if I had the inclination, but I never lose my temper.

I have seen what having no control can do and I don't like it. It was only for a moment and it caused a lot of pain to everybody. My father was a hot-headed man, red-headed too, as it happens, and true to the type. He was a farmer. Not a tenant, a real farmer. His one weakness apart from the temper was that he was very close with his purse. Parting with money hurt him. Taxes were a burden at the best of times and, like all farmers, Father tended to play his prosperity down. Then he got caught. Some pissant little tax collector found out he was holding out on the Sovereign and it looked like the galleys were going to be where he ended up. But no. Not content with disgrace, Father had to go for ruin. Beat the taxman to death with a grain flail. Not a worry in his head about who saw. There were twenty-seven witnesses at the trial. Broken on the wheel, hanged and his property forfeit to the Crown. Temper temper.

The rue Cordeliers crowd were harmless enough, though. The police came and closed them down from time to time, which was all very entertaining as they cursed and swore a lot. They lacked the balls to do anything else, which I quite admired. If all my dear Papa had done was have a bit of a tantrum I wouldn't have been in my line of work in the first place, would I? I only went there to meet Henri and I stayed for the shortest time possible. I took to dressing down to get there and, as you know, I like to live well. It was all a means to an end and Henri paid very generously for his pleasures. He was young, so it didn't take long. He overtook Simon as the client who proposed to me the most, bless him.

I tried to explain that if we were to marry, then his dear father would cut him off without a sou and then what would we do? He seemed to take this on board for a few weeks before giving me the doe eyes and bended-knee routine again. Honestly, aristocrats! It was a mystery to me how they ended up in charge, because the ones I met were never exactly bright. Perhaps it gets bred out of them.

Talking of stupid, Alain went from strength to strength in that department. The idiot discovered what he called the field of honour. He decided that he wanted to fight to the death practically everyone he met who didn't show him the proper respect. Alain thought he sat at the right hand of God himself and, frankly, I've had meals that were more intelligent. It was a fatal combination.

I tried reasoning with him but even his bloody wolf would have been more sensible. I came to the conclusion that he was a short-term investment. It was only a matter of time before someone lost their patience and killed him, which made keeping little Henri interested all the more important. They could never meet, of course. I thought that there was only one man in France stupid and vain enough to fight a duel over a whore's fidelity, and that was our Alain. Sadly, there was only one other capable of accepting his challenge in the hope of winning the said whore's hand in marriage. In one sense at least, they were evenly matched. I told them both I was visiting my mother at the convent to explain my absences. It was a pain to keep all of this up, as I had to remember exactly what I said to each of them and not mix the two up. I became rather good at it. I put this down to being a farmer's daughter. You have to keep your livestock from hurting each other and ruining your investment. It's just good husbandry. Common sense, really.

I wanted no part in Alain's foolishness. He asked me to accompany him, but I declined every request. I did not want to encourage this suicidal pursuit. It seemed very bad for business. I saw him fight once, and no spectator was more surprised that he was victorious. I only went because I felt slightly responsible.

Alain had paid me what he, no doubt, regarded as the enormous compliment of inviting me to Versailles. I hated the place, personally. Too countrified, and I detest travelling. It was a dull afternoon. Alain and his cronies drivelled on at each other interminably and I became bored. There was nothing to divert me but wine, so I drank almost as much as he did. Usually I hate to lose control but we were both as drunk as dragoons when his friends departed, and Alain always let the drink bring out his romantic side. We found seclusion in a confessional. I swear to this day I had no idea whose chapel we were in. Why would I lie? No one was more shocked than I to see Hypolite d'Armentières glaring down at me when the damn thing overturned. I was so bewildered that for a moment I thought I had mistaken my clients and dreamed the whole afternoon. It was only the sound of Alain's vomiting that brought me back to my senses.

There are some questions to which violence is the answer, and whether Hypolite was more enraged by the assault upon his romantic or religious sensibilities fell into this category. A duel would be fought. Both parties insisted that I attend, and I graciously accepted their invitations. I told Alain I would make my own way to the field of honour and Hypolite that I would travel with him. In all honesty I did not expect Alain to survive, but I didn't want to cause him any offence. His opponent was a famously violent man and, if he were to be believed, had the Almighty on his side. Alain was hardly the favourite, but it looked like a good idea to spread my bets. Miracles can happen, so I'm told.

This particular field of honour was in a clearing in the Bois de Boulogne. I was there, all in black with a veil like a grieving widow, when who should come bustling into the arena behind my lord and master, clutching his medical bag in both hands and peering around through his spectacles for all the world like an anxious, motherly mole, but Simon. He took one look at me and only just managed to hold back a squeak. I couldn't resist licking my lips and blowing him a kiss. I don't know why I do these things, I swear.

He was obviously very taken with the solemnity of the occasion, because he looked scandalized. He always did have a tendency to get all maudlin about man's noble destiny. It was all I could do not to wet myself laughing. I knew I could rely on him not to say anything. It looked as if he had finally landed himself what he used to call a 'golden patient'. He was not about to confess to his new boss that he'd had his mistress now, was he? Simon liked his home comforts too much to risk them for me. It was the last time I saw him and I sometimes wonder what became of him. I do hope he managed to stay out of trouble. Sometimes I think that he's the only man I've slept with that I don't consider a complete fool.

It was almost a relief when Alain told me he was going to Africa. He was starting to become extremely tiresome. I showed him just the right amount of regret, and promised to wait for him. Naturally, he left me looked after and I intended to keep myself available for as long as that lasted. I didn't expect to see him again. Alain was the sort of person who couldn't help putting himself in harm's way. You hear so many stories about how dangerous it is out there and his plan seemed positively lunatic even by his standards. He was going to hunt giant lizards, he told me, but he didn't even know exactly where they were or what they looked like. I expected they would kill and eat him, if they were fast enough to get there before he accidentally did the job himself. I promised to wave him off at the dock, but in the end I did not go. I do hate to travel. That's why I hardly ever visit Mother. Really, I mean.

I got by on the money Alain left me for the next couple of years. I never heard from him again, so I suppose my prediction came true. Little Henri came to his senses and realized that I wasn't the material wives are made of. They all grow out of that one in the end, apart from Simon. And of course I had a new admirer. He was very rich and the fact that he was over seventy years old didn't put me off too much. I lay under him as he did his business, and I could feel his heart hammering against my chest. It sounded like soldiers running up a narrow street. His name was André and he was up from Provence to take part in all the new politics. Very high-minded, which had the unfortunate side-effect of making him want to educate me about liberty and virtue.

I listened and pretended to be too empty-headed to understand what he was going on about until he stopped. I hated this sort of nonsense. It was all very well for people like him with all his money to talk about equality and liberty. As far as I can see everyone's equal to the height they reach while they're standing on their fortune. If you haven't got any money you're free to starve, so the pox take your liberty. As for virtue, well, don't get me started. How he could go on about the noble beauty of simple pleasures taken by the pure of heart while reclining on my bed, drinking champagne and watching me sitting naked at my dressing table combing my hair, I do not know. I asked him if he meant that I was his equal, giving it all the wide blue eyes, and he ruffled my hair. Poor little Claudette can't understand all the big, important words, he cooed. He carried me to bed. I writhed and groaned as if it was the best I had ever had. It wouldn't do to disappoint my betters, now, would it?

I didn't like him much, but he was like every other man I'd ever known. I could tolerate him, but it was a constant struggle between what he could give me and how much he annoyed me. It was hard sometimes but I never lost my temper, however much I might have wanted to. Fortunately going out to Versailles for the parliament business stopped him getting too underfoot. I didn't see him for days on end. In fact, I didn't even realize he had died until his lawyer came calling. I had a legacy, he explained. I took in the lawyer's coat and shoes and noticed they seemed reassuringly expensive. I opened my eyes to let a tear roll down my face, tracking its way through my powder in a very attractive picture of grief. The lawyer moved his chair next to mine and tried to look down my dress. I could smell tobacco and coffee on his breath. It wasn't what you could call attractive, but by no means the worst. I wriggled my hip and leaned forward slightly to make sure he could see before asking him how much. Well. I had never really fainted before, although I pretended to a few times. There's a first time for everything, I suppose. I live in hope. When I came round he was solicitously patting my hand while staring at my thighs. My dress had ridden up when I fell. I got to my feet and adjusted my clothing. No point in advertising. It wasn't for sale any more. I was a lady of independent means.

I should feel more grateful to André than I actually do. He left me enough money to set myself up in business. I had a very high-class establishment on the rue Saint-Honoré itself. Twelve girls, a chef who used to work for the Duc d'Orléans – until I paid him more – and even a string quartet to accompany the gentlemen as they dined and took their choice. My father always taught me to go into the business that you know. A rare piece of good advice from the man who ended the family fortunes so conclusively. The new thinking could easily have fooled me. My old friend Théroigne got completely carried away with it. Started calling herself 'citizeness', of all things. Rode off to storm Versailles with her tits out and a load of washerwomen in tow. I knew her when she was a working girl and she'd have done better to keep her head down. She was always good at that. It was obvious she would meet a bad end. No, André taught me that underneath all the fine flowery language they were the same old snobs and all the worse for hiding it away. Give me a brocaded dandy over a duke in a tanner's coat any day. I could never abide a hypocrite. At least the Alains of this world were honest parasites.

I'd noticed that a lot more of the clientele were making a run for it. The King had a go himself. He got caught, of course. The others seemed better at it. As the sole criteria for membership of the aristocracy seemed to be stupidity, I can't be surprised by the fact that the greatest of them all turned out to be so idiotic as to take one's breath away. Imagine trying to pay for a meal under a false identity with your name and picture on the coins you're paying with! It was not good for trade, though. All the best customers went and there were some people about at the time who disturbed me.

Remember that monkey-faced little reptile Marat? He of the sweaty palms and high moral values? Well, he was a great power in the land for a bit. Always looking out for the enemy within. It didn't surprise me that some young girl managed to stab him to death in the bath. Oh, I know the official story is that the little snake met his martyrdom trying to uncover plots against the people, but I'm sure the only thing he was trying to uncover was the girl's chest. Why else would such a great big important man see her on his own, eh? No great loss, however it happened. Thing is, what followed Marat was infinitely worse. I had a shrewd suspicion that all his virtue and patriotism were so much hot air. I'd seen the way he used to look at me when I was meeting little Henri and I'm sure he'd have been happy to dirty himself with a plaything of the aristocracy, provided he didn't have to soil his revolutionary purity by paying for it.

The people who came to power next were bloody dangerous. A whole mob of them broke into Salpêtrière Prison that September and killed all the whores. Just a bunch of street girls, you understand, but I could see the writing on the wall. What with all my business running off to Vienna and London as well, it was time to make myself scarce.

There's no point in leaving home if you can't take a few home comforts with you. I'd worked very hard for what I had and I had no intention of starting from scratch. I was not about to repeat anyone else's mistakes, let alone my own. So, the first step was to get my cash out of the country before I went myself. The powers that be took a dim view of anyone fleeing the revolutionary paradise they seemed to think they had created. And there was nothing that looked more as if your commitment to this particular version of brotherhood, freedom and equality may have been less than wholehearted than being caught with a carriage full of plate and coin.

Fortunately I had a very wide circle of acquaintances, some of whom were in the diplomatic profession. We seemed to have avoided war with the Americans at that point. Even the collection of maniacs in charge then could see that taking on the entire world at once was a bad idea. There was a rather pleasant little man called Ben Franklin whom I knew briefly when he was in Paris. (He preferred being naked to wearing fine clothes.) He introduced me to quite a few of his countrymen, and I kept in touch. The Ambassador's Under-Secretary was a regular at my little soirées right until the end. It was a simple matter to call on his assistance to get the money out.

I even found a buyer for the house. Another client, of course, the builder Palloy. I'm sure he paid me considerably less than market value. Cash for a quick sale. No more than you'd expect from a man who made his third fortune selling off bits of the Bastille. He'd been locked up himself. So, I'm sure he could see the writing was on the wall for me and took advantage. If I were a vindictive woman, I would've marked his name in the punishment book, but I've never had time for that sort of thing.

Life's too short anyway and would have been a great deal

shorter if I'd allowed myself to get distracted. Time to move on. I quite fancied the idea of the New World. It wouldn't be a new beginning, exactly – stick to what you know, and all that – but I was quite looking forward to it. I just had to get myself to Roscoff, and then it was New York for me. I had arranged travel to Brittany on the pretext of visiting Mother, who was in a rare old state after the government closed the convent. It was amazing how much I'd come to rely upon her, really, considering how little help she was when I was a young girl. One should never underestimate the importance of family. She was an unreliable excuse for a mother, but her reliability as a mother for an excuse couldn't be over-stated. Once I got west, it was only a short trip to Roscoff, where I was to be a passenger on a ship called the *Orion* bound for New York. I'd never been to sea, although I had known a lot of sailors. I hoped that the motion of the water didn't make me sick. It's so unattractive.

I have had an eventful life. I don't regret a minute of it. The problem with having done so much with so many people is that you can never predict when you are going to come across someone again. I do my best to avoid causing any upset, so chance meetings are usually no problem. My carriage was on its way out of the city when we came across one of the numerous patrols of Revolutionary Guards. In my experience these people are more of an irritation than anything else, all moustaches and shouting with very little between the ears. My paperwork was in order and I didn't anticipate being detained for long. After all, what possible interest would they have in 'Claudette Benoit, actress and farmer's daughter, travelling to visit her elderly ex-nun of a mother?' I handed over my documents and waited. It didn't even alarm me when I was asked to step out of the carriage. I assumed the guardians of the Revolution wanted a look at the actress before sending her on her way.

As soon as my feet landed on cobbles and I got a good look at the man in charge I knew things weren't going to be simple. Do you remember that bloody wolf? Well, before I managed to palm him off on Simon he got me into trouble with the police. Bit one of the neighbours. Alain sorted it out for me. I assumed that money changed hands because no more was ever said about it. The guardsman was a slab of beef with a face like a laundry bag and a smell about him that said 'Police'. The very same individual who took Alain's money to piss off and forget his duty to the equally well-bribed wolf-bitten drab who had denounced me. And as I met his eye I realized that he had recognized the Comte La Latte's mistress from all those years ago. I was in custody as a suspected assister of émigrés within seconds and off to bloody Salpêtrière, which was a shock I can tell you. Very uncomfortable lodgings for a working girl, given recent events.

I was sitting in my cell wondering how I was going to get out of this mess when my captor returned with another obvious policeman. I kept my eyes lowered to show him my new-found modesty, but I took him in. I knew the type. I could practically hear the jingle of bribes in his pocket as he sat down opposite me. He was not in uniform, which gave me some hope. Not a Revolutionary Guard, then. A man who could be tempted? He asked me my name. I told him I was called Claudette. This was usually enough. Not many girls in my profession need more than one name. He asked me if I had a family name. It was on the tip of my tongue to tell him 'Benoit', when it occurred to me that I may be able to play the same game as my old friend Théroigne. Time to flex my roots and act the ravaged daughter of the virtuous peasant.

'I have no name since the aristocrats killed my father and forced me into a life of shame.'

The policeman looked at me, then laughed. 'You'll do, girlie. Come and see the boss. He's got a proposition for you.'

I was relieved to see the back of Salpêtrière. I'd never been to prison before, and I had no intention of going back. Whatever the 'proposition' might be, it had to be better than waiting to be murdered by a pack of hypocrites who thought that killing me was going to stop them fantasizing about screwing me. I made no plans to get out of this one. I was going to play it by ear. Plans have an awful habit of going wrong for the most stupid reasons. You have to take these things in your stride.

12

A Very Secret Service

THERE'S AN ART TO BEING A WHORE, AND BEING A GOOD fuck doesn't amount to over a quarter of it. The real skill is not being shocked by the client's requests, however insane or ridiculous they may be. It's helpful if you can pretend that the sort of perversion he's suggesting is exactly what your heart desires as well. I've always been rather good at this. It's a talent that I find very useful when I'm not working. Never more so, I can tell you, than after my release into the custody of what turned out to be the Committee for General Security.

The policeman took me to a set of offices near the Hôtel de Ville. I was ushered into a room where I waited, alone. It was 'revolutionary Spartan'. No books, no pictures and damned uncomfortable chairs. I assumed that this was where the mysterious 'boss' did his business. I looked round for some clue about how to play the man when he decided to put in an appearance, but there was nothing to go on. He was either the greatest revolutionary hypocrite in the world – with an apartment filled with stolen furniture and twelve whores to do his bidding elsewhere – or he was a real fanatic. If I had stumbled upon one of those aristocrats who had given up their titles and become revolutionaries I knew exactly how to behave and what the 'proposition' was going to be. If not, well, who knew? Someone like that wasn't going to spring little Claudette from prison just for a fuck. Whatever happened, I was pretty sure I was safe for the time being. I was needed for something, and as every girl knows, you're at your richest when the gentlemen say they need you.

Usually, men stare at me. Polite ones try to hide it, but they're all the same really. They know that it will cost them and they're trying to work out if it's worth their investment. It is. This one didn't spare me a glance below the neck, just caught my eye and stared into my face until I looked down. It wouldn't have done to seem too bold, I thought. His eyes were watery blue, and blood-shot. You could almost have mistaken him for a drunk, were it not for the most singular intensity in his gaze. The man did have the look of the fanatic, but there was also something different about him. The skin on his face was stretched tightly over his skull, giving the impression that whatever animated him was also eating him from the inside. He was no bellowing, moustachio'd guardsman. In fact, the closest I had seen to his type was the priest who tried to persuade me out of my ways of vice and temptation back in Rennes when I was just seventeen. He genuinely wanted to save my soul and turned down the temptation I put in his path. They had a lot in common, Father Michel and Commandant Bouchier. They both wanted to infect me with the thing that consumed them. Neither managed it, although I would have to say that of the two Guillaume came closer. They had the same manner, as well. I know that Guillaume killed many men, but when he spoke to me his voice was gentle.

'Tell me your story, Claudette. I know a lot about you,' he gestured at a sheaf of papers on the desk, 'but I find that the facts often fail to contain the essential information. Don't try to deceive me. I know a great deal about what brought you here. What I need to know is what you are and whether you can be of service to the people of France. Lying will be counterproductive. I have the ability to send you on a short and painful journey, but I dislike unnecessary violence. Pray don't place me in that position.'

So I told him. Not everything, of course, but enough. I told him about my father, about Moncontour, Rennes, Paris and how I became what I am. About the men. Even about Mother. The only thing I held back on was the money. I had no doubt that he was serious about what he would do if he caught me out. I thought that if he didn't know then I wasn't going to tell him and silence tells no lies. If he had no idea I had any money he'd be less inclined to watch me too closely. A poor sparrow can't fly far, after all. He said nothing until I stopped, then looked at me in a silence that made me feel so uncomfortable that it took every bit of my self-control to stop myself filling it with prattle.

'This I know, Claudette. I know about your father and your, er, career. I know that you maintain your mother in a modest style since her ejection from the life of a parasite that the Church permitted her. What I would like you to tell me is how you feel about your life.'

Well now, there's a question! I knew it all hung upon my answer. He knew that idleness is the mother of philosophy and only aristocrats are idle. If I told him I had no feelings, then he would see I was no idle aristocrat and I would live. Tell the client what he wants and pretend it was your idea all along.

'Feelings are for those with the luxury of being able to afford them. You know my history. Tell me when I have had time to sit and think about how I felt? If I had let myself feel, I would not be able to work as I have worked. If my father had been a calmer man, then I could have told you how I felt about being the prettiest bride. I cannot allow myself to feel as I know I should.'

He smiled. Right answer. 'Well done, Claudette,' I thought. 'Another satisfied customer.'

'I have in mind that you will play the aristocrat. I see from your history that you were briefly an actress before you became, well, what you became. Did you change your profession because you were a poor actress?'

Now I genuinely did want to be an actress when I left Mother in the arms of Jesus. I tried it for a bit and I was talented. I've always found it easy to pretend to be someone else. But too little money, and the men – well, if I was going to be leered at and pawed by oafs, it was going to cost them a lot more then two sous on the gate, I can tell you. If he had been as clued-up about me as he thought, he'd have known that. His confidence seemed rather foolish, and all the more reassuring for it. It's hard not to laugh when you hear someone say something stupid, but then I've spent most of my life managing not to laugh at men and their ridiculous little vanities.

'Monsieur, you speak of me changing my profession as if there is any difference between actress and prostitute. For years I have let men touch me, let them use me. The very sort of men who put me where I would have to endure their caresses to survive. As you know my life, you will know that I was a very good whore. I believe this speaks of my skill as an actress more than anything I could say to you in this room, don't you? As for aristocrats, well, you know where I have been.'

I put on my best 'Versailles' accent and looked at him down my nose: 'Even a man of your obvious lack of breeding should know that one can only learn how to conduct oneself by associating with the right sort of people. Now fetch me some wine. I am fatigued after my journey and I did not find my last lodgings at all congenial.'

He stared at me as if I'd slapped him. I started to worry that I had overplayed my hand until he smiled again. 'Got you!' I thought. 'Whatever scheme you have in mind, I'm obviously irreplaceable. You can't find better, so give up trying.'

So I became Claudette, Comtesse d'Auray. It wasn't that hard. Far easier than empty-headed little Claudette who didn't understand all the important things her lovers talked about. Guillaume's men attended me, and I was forced to live my role by ordering them about and berating them. A hardship, as you can imagine. They were an odd assortment. There was Jean-Claude, my deliverer from Salpêtrière, whom I had identified correctly as a policeman. He was what used to be called a thief-taker. A man I could understand easily. He had been a policeman before the Revolution and was a practical, violent and greedy man. I could recognize the survivor in him and knew that I had self-interest to appeal to if the need arose.

Then there was Jacques. He was a little, slight man, standing no taller than my chin. He was cursed with such a beard that he needed to shave at least twice a day, which made him seem older than his years. I call him a man but he came across as if he was little more than a boy. Jean-Claude told me that he had been a thief, whom Guillaume had recruited when his skills became necessary for the cause. I expected to find the disrespectful charm that most thieves seem to possess, but it wasn't in him. If I had to use a word to describe him I suppose it would be sweet. Jean-Claude told me he was dangerous and violent, but God knows I never saw that side to him then. The boy was either one of Guillaume's success stories or he was the best actor I have ever met. He spoke like a book of the great man's political sayings, when he spoke at all. He did most of his talking with his hands or his face, nodding, shrugging and grimacing in a way that left you in no doubt about his feelings. The few times he did speak, it was in a whisper. I put this down to his being shy. He liked me, but I think not for the usual reasons. That part of him seemed not to exist and I was told that he had been in love with another thief. She was in custody and refused to take on his new beliefs with appropriate sincerity, so little Jacques had given her up. He told me he had been the devoted manservant to a great family's physician. He had done something to upset them, and been chucked out on his ear for his pains. He knew about my past, or at least the edited version of bereavement, disgrace and rescue by revolutionary service that struck a chord with my new employers, and seemed to think this made us kindred spirits. He was an ugly little soul, but you never know when someone who can climb any wall might come in handy, so I flirted with him. This made him devoted to me, although how much I could rely on him I did not know. As for Guillaume himself, I didn't see him again until much later. He was out and about – putting his great plan together, I was told.

His plan was to use me as bait. Degrading, I thought, but I couldn't disagree that it was clever. There was a character who specialized in freeing condemned aristocrats and spiriting them away to England. The Revolution wanted him caught and cut, and as quickly as possible. The problem was that there were so many aristocrats waiting to get the chop that it was hard to predict where he would strike next. That's where I came in. The villain was supposed to be English, and everyone knows that the English like a beautiful, brave French girl and think she must fuck like a bitch in season. I had only ever met one Englishman then, but he certainly lived up to type and very profitable it was, too.

Guillaume's plan was that I would go on trial as a conspirator against the French people. The evidence against me would be partly true – the men and the sex – and partly false – my devotion to the King and activities spying for the émigrés and the Austrians. I would be convicted and condemned. They would catch the Englishman when he came sniffing around to rescue me. Simple. By this time I was repeating so often the 'good-girl-wronged-by-a-bad-world' rubbish that played so well with Guillaume that they all assumed I was another convert. So I wasn't too concerned about what would happen if he didn't show up. If he did, well, then it rather depended on how things went. I'd never been to England but I was sure that I could make my living there, no trouble. It would be easy to have my money sent back from America. If Guillaume and his lads won the day, then this daughter of Marianne would have to bide her time a little longer, wouldn't she?

They did love their pornography, those stern, moral men of family values, I can tell you. It was standing room only. The prosecutor was a funny little man called Fouquier-Tinville. He was the mainstay of the Tribunal, and I was disappointed when I saw him. He looked like the sort of man who devotes his life to his geraniums and is occasionally cruel to his wife. Not the avenging angel I had been led to expect. I caught him looking at me before it all started and asked him if he liked what he saw. He flushed, and I laughed at him, telling my guards loudly that when my father's clerk had once looked at me in the same way, I had had him flogged for his impudence. It made a fine spectacle, and got the crowd in the galleries well and truly interested. I smiled at them, and blew a kiss at my would-be tormentor, who took refuge in his papers.

It was straight in with the sex. The first question was whether I knew the Marshall Lafayette. As it happened I did, although sadly not professionally, as I had been told he was a generous man. 'Yes,' I replied.

'And did you have relations with him when he was trusted with the defence of France?'

This was too good to miss. 'Not immediately.'

This seemed to put my prosecutor off his stroke. 'What do you mean, "Not immediately"?' he asked.

'Well, I don't like just to get down to it as if I'm your wife going through the tedious burden of my marital duty. I like to be wooed. First he kissed me, then he suckled at my breast, and then he put his head between my thighs and kissed my sex. I could feel my legs tremble with desire for him. My pleasure was made all the sweeter by the thought that the Austrians were advancing a step to every lick of his tongue. I expect you could have heard my screams of pleasure in Vienna.'

There was a rumble in the gallery. Row upon row of scandalized faces pressed nearer to avoid missing a single word.

'And when he had finished, ah, giving you your pleasure, Mademoiselle d'Auray, did you ask him about the plans for the defence of our Mother Country?'

'Again, not immediately.'

'I hesitate to ask why not?'

'If that's your idea of hesitation I pity your wife, Monsieur. It's hard to ask a general about military manoeuvres with his baton of office in one's mouth. Most unladylike as well.'

'You are from the west yourself, Mademoiselle. Do you know Charlotte Corday?'

I put my hand to my breast and looked down, sighing. 'Ah yes, little Charlotte. A lovely girl.'

He looked as if I had slapped him on the arse. 'Lovely, you say. You are aware she assassinated that most brave tribune of the people, Marat.'

'And brave as well. I never loved her more than when she sliced that monstrous hypocrite. I knew him too, but I've never been in the habit of screwing my way around the farmyard, so our acquaintance was never as rewarding as that I enjoyed with General Lafayette.'

'Did you pay Mademoiselle Corday to assassinate Marat?'

'Not in cash.'

'But in some other way?'

'When I first met Charlotte she was a little girl up from the country. I took her in. She had no idea about matters of romance so I showed her the ropes, in a manner of speaking. She'd never been with a man when you cowardly scum killed her, but I can do more with my mouth to give a young girl what she needs than any poor excuse for a man in this hall. Charlotte did what she did for love of me. That was to be her reward and I hope she sniffed my scent on her fingers for one last time before she took her final journey. I know I did.'

There was outrage in court. The trial continued for three days in much the same vein. By the end of proceedings I had defiantly confessed to sleeping with the King and Queen (together, separately and with the Dauphin looking on), Mirabeau (who took me up the arse as I bent over a copy of the Constitution), Talleyrand (true! – but who hasn't? I had to hold back on the details because it could have got Théroigne into terrible trouble), Generals Pichgru and Dumouriez (at the same time), and practically the whole émigré Court. In fact, had these idiots not been so preoccupied with imagining my lewdness, they might have realized that all this enthusiastic sex actually left me with very little time for treachery and espionage. They didn't. My confessions to passing military secrets I had gained in my various conquests to the Austrians, English and Prussians were accepted in full.

There was a queue that stretched around the corner by the time the Tribunal decided it had heard enough about me to deliver a verdict. I took my sentence of death with a fiery courage my father would have approved of. If this had been for real it would have been the sort of suicidal gesture that he was prone to making. When the Tribunal asked me if I had anything to say I took the chance to describe them as eunuchs before being dragged off in chains to the Temple Prison, damning them to Hell and shouting '*Vive le Roi!*'

As I was being loaded on to a tumbril Jean-Claude caught my eye and winked. This fierce and stern revolutionary guard leaned towards me, squeezed my backside and whispered, 'Well done, Mademoiselle. A grateful people salute you.'

I rather enjoyed the trial. The best thing about it was that my role let me say things to those horrible, small-minded moralists that I had wanted to say since my rue Cordeliers days. I never lose my temper really, but oh God, it can be such fun pretending.

13

Rescue

S O I WENT BACK TO PRISON. NOT THE HELLISH STEW OF Salpêtrière this time, but a rather well-appointed room in the Temple, as was only fitting for a lady of my station awaiting her fate. It might have been quite an enjoyable experience staying there if I had had the time to linger and get to know my fellow prisoners, but this was not to be. My protectors arrived as soon as I was locked away. I heard the orders through the wicket. Jean-Claude and Jacques were left out in the cold, guarding my door. I heard a key turn in the lock and Commandant Guillaume Bouchier, he of the icy smile and pure, revolutionary heart, stepped into my chamber. I noticed he was clutching a bottle of wine and two pewter cups. 'Hello,' I thought. 'Has the great man had his fires stoked by the reports of my trial? Surely not.' Still, there's no accounting for taste. It occurred to me that a stolen moment in a cell with some damaged goods he'd saved from the predatory enemies of the people could be exactly what would appeal to him. I doubted he'd have payment in mind, so I consoled myself with the thought that he was a man whose right side was worth cultivating and arranged myself most alluringly on the cot. Good husbandry, again, you see. They're more like dogs than cattle, these revolutionaries. It made sense to have the pack leader eating out of my hand to stop the lesser ones getting above themselves and becoming over familiar.

It turned out I was wrong. Unusually. You can always predict the gentlemen by expecting the worst and in most cases you'll be right, but with the bold commandant all he wanted to do was talk. And talk. Now I have had more politics talked at me by more men than most. A hazard of my profession and the times that we lived in, you might say. I have heard more about sacred duties, liberty and equality from the customers than I care to remember. Assuming I could.

Guillaume was different. He didn't try to fuck me, or even lay a hand upon me. It wasn't that he was a eunuch, or even that his tastes ran to boys. I could tell that he was interested. It was all over his face. I worked out much later that he was waiting for me to make the first move. He was trying to prove that he was different from all my lovers by giving me the freedom to choose him, rather than him picking me as if I were the most succulent cake in the baker's window. It's a pity that he wasn't more forthcoming as I would have taken him up, for the novelty value more than anything else. That's the problem with living in changing times. No one's sure what the rules of the game are. By the time it's all been settled, chances that might have been are long gone and there's no point in wondering how it could have all worked out if you'd known about them. It did put me on the back foot at the time. I'd never met a man who could restrain himself from trying his luck and I wasn't sure what to make of it.

It was a long conversation, made remarkable by the fact that I played an unusually active part. I wasn't convinced that he was right about how things ought to be. It struck me that all his nonsense about free trade meant was that merchants would become rich and the rest of us would have the freedom to starve, sell ourselves and generally get by as best we could. No change there, then. He told me that America would be the first attempt, and that if the Revolution here stayed true to its purpose, we would see a new world in which the wealth of the nation belonged to the people. Nice idea, I thought. You only had to look at the creatures that carried out my trial to see where things were really headed, though. And then he said it. The one piece of politics that I have ever thought had some point to it. He looked into my eyes as if he was trying to make me understand by the force of his will and told me: 'Claudette, there are two wars. One we fight against the English and their allies, and one we fight against ourselves. Whoever wins the first will be able to draw up the map of Europe in their image for the next hundred years. Whoever wins the second will be able to educate a generation to believe whatever version of France suits their purposes. It's too late to go back. The King is dead, and even if we lose our war against the world, they will never be able to bring him back. Our Revolution isn't a goal, but a womb. The winners of these wars will say how this child is raised. The only certainty is that those who pick the losing side will be swept away by the waters when they break.'

Food for thought indeed. I was turning this idea around in my head when there was a sharp rap at the door. I looked out of the window and saw dawn had coloured the dirty rooftops like a red rim around a tired eye. Guillaume answered. It was Jean-Claude, who snapped out a military salute while passing an insubordinately knowing look across his commanding officer's creased clothing.

'The execution party has arrived, sir.'

I managed to steal a look past Guillaume's back. I could see two people – a guard, complete with moustachios and pike, and an old woman. She was there to hold my little hand and steal my dress after I got the chop, I supposed. Guillaume and Jean-Claude exchanged glances, and my political educator rubbed the back of his neck with his kerchief. Not a gesture that put my mind at rest, I can assure you. He examined the warrant before dashing out a signature. He leaned down to pull me to my feet. Our eyes locked for a second, and he winked at me then dragged me upright. I felt my misgivings ebb. All to plan and all right on schedule. I played my part. I shook his hand from my arm, every inch the unbowed aristocrat. I looked around me, taking in the lads and the new arrivals before spitting on the floor.

'You, sirs, I will see in Hell,' I announced. 'May your method of arrival there be more painful than mine. I understand the English hang their criminals. I do not doubt that they will invite you to your last dance before long.'

The guard took me by the elbow and steered me down the corridor. I shook him off and walked ahead. He was a tall man, and I found myself having to trot to keep in front of him. I looked at him, but he was eyes front, forward and correct as if he were on the Champs de Mars. We left the building and crossed a courtyard to the main gate. The guard presented papers to the gate turnkey. The gates swung open and I was being loaded unceremoniously into the tumbril when all hell broke loose. I caught a glimpse of Jean-Claude kicking a man in the face as the gate slammed behind us. I could hear shouts and a solitary

shot as the driver whipped up the horse and our cart lurched
forward.

For the next few minutes all I could do was brace myself
against the side of the cart and hope that I wouldn't be thrown
into the street. I came to the conclusion that the driver had gone
mad, as we thundered along, almost overturning at each corner.
I could barely take in where we were going, but noticed that we
seemed to be heading towards Les Invalides and not la Place de la
Révolution. At last he reined the horse to a shuddering halt and
pulled into a courtyard where another cart was standing. I stared
around. This was not what I had expected. I noticed that the
old woman seemed to be taking off her clothes, while the guard
pulled off his whiskers. The driver jumped down and took up his
station on the second wagon. When I turned round, the guard
and the old woman had transformed into two men, both dressed
in working clothes and both obviously no older than their mid-
twenties. Then the driver spoke to me in the most English French
I had ever heard.

'Mademoiselle d'Auray. You must hurry up, if you please.
You are perfectly safe and among friends but we must make
our escape before we introduce ourselves properly. You must
change your clothing. My manservant will assist you by holding
up a screen. Let me reassure you that we are gentlemen and your
privacy will be absolute. Sadly, my manservant must also cut off
your magnificent hair, as you must become our apprentice for
the day. A painful duty. No civilized man likes to spoil a thing of
beauty. Still, better to lose your hair than your head I say, what?'

He laughed at his own wit. He was obviously in charge because
the others guffawed with far more vigour than the joke demanded.
I found myself behind a filthy blanket putting on the sort of rags

that I would not have permitted my scullery boy to wear. His companion, who had been dressed as an old woman, told me to sit. He spoke to me rapidly as he cropped my hair. It was obvious that he was no Englishman. His accent was unfamiliar, but he spoke French as though it was his mother tongue.

'Mademoiselle, please to keep your head to one side so I don't remove your ear. Thank you. You are a driver's apprentice. We'll call you Claude to avoid any confusion. When we leave, please sit between me and my friend who had pretend whiskers. Say nothing if we are challenged. I will talk for us all. Now the other side. Good. If you will be so good as to smear some of this mud on to your hands. Can't have them on display so white, fine and ladylike, can we? People will talk. A bit to your face, if you please. You know that the Germans think that this improves the skin? What could improve on perfection in your case, though? Who knows? Are we done? Good. Let's away.'

I couldn't help but run my hands over my scalp as we rolled through the streets at a more sedate pace. It felt unfamiliar, like a shorthaired dog's coat. I found that feeling my hair rise and prick against the palm of my hand calmed me. My rescuers were a silent lot. No words were exchanged as we reached the edge of the city and a picket of guards. The driver whistled to himself as a sergeant stepped into the road and signalled to us to halt. I knew that here was when I was in most danger. I was not too concerned about capture. I had done my part and Guillaume would vouch that I was a patriot. I thought of unmasking myself, but my new companions did not seem the surrendering kind. The last thing I wanted to do was start some kind of free-for-all. I could be hurt, or worse. I had absolutely no inclination to join the loathsome Marat in the list of glorious revolutionary martyrs.

I had nothing to worry about as it turned out. The rescue party were very professional. Papers were demanded and handed over. The sergeant was no fool, and picked up upon the 'foreman's' accent.

'And you, Citizen, you are not a local man?'

'Indeed not, Sergeant, although I have had the honour of living in the greatest city in the world since the American War. I am Québecois. When war broke out with our old enemies the English I rushed to enlist. Sadly, my war was not as victorious as history would have us believe. My Quebec remains in English hands and I have come home to the Mother Country to be among Frenchmen. One day I shall return.'

'Your cargo?'

'Bones, Sergeant. Bones of the good, the bad and the rest. Coming from Les Invalides and going to their final destination. Not a happy load, but surely not the first.'

The sergeant narrowed his eyes suspiciously. 'These loads come with a whole load of people seeing them off, usually.'

'Yes, but we thought we'd get this dropped off in time to get back to the square and watch the People's Razor make its shaves for today. That girl's due for the chop. You know, the countess who'd screwed half of Versailles. Everyone's talking about her, the wicked aristo whore. Supposed to be a real sort. Me and the lads wouldn't want to miss that, now, would we?'

The sergeant laughed. 'You've left your beds early for nothing.'

'How so?'

'She's only escaped, hasn't she? Helped by that bloody Englishman. We'll get her though. Every guard in Paris is on the alert for them. A man with moustaches, an old woman and a girl. They won't get far. You be sure and keep a look out. When we get them I can promise you a show at the guillotine well worth getting out of bed for.'

The foreman shrugged. 'Probably have to bloody work when it's on, though. Ah well, my brave boys, you heard the man. Another wasted day. Let's get this lot dropped off and we can be in the tavern by noon.'

We were on our way. The wagon wound through rural roads until we came to a small track leading up to a house. It was derelict. I could see the ribs of its roof through broken slates. We stopped. The Québecois dismounted and began to uncouple the horses. I looked around me. Better stay in character, I thought. I addressed the Englishman in my best and most frosty tones.

'Monsieur. There is no doubt that I owe you and your companions my life. But, you cannot expect me to stay here.' I gestured at the broken-down building. 'Why, for one such as me this would be dishonour. I would rather die than lose my honour by hiding among beggars.'

They exchanged glances and laughed. The Englishman took my hand and kissed it with quite unnecessary chivalry.

'Mademoiselle, in a week's time I hope to have the honour of presenting you to the highest in society. For the moment, all I can offer you is the humblest hospitality. I have found that the credit to which an English gentleman should be entitled is passing thin among your countrymen. We have to spend a bit of time living on our wits before I can have the honour of squiring you around Hyde Park. The hounds are in full cry, as you no doubt heard the good sergeant tell my manservant. We must be as cunning as the fox until I can arrange matters, and any self-respecting fox goes to earth when he hears the pack. Follow me, I implore you. I am not about to squander a life I have risked a great deal to save.'

He took me to the back of the house and down a steep hill. A tunnel had been hollowed out of one side and, stopping to light a lantern that was concealed in the shadows, he led me beneath the ground. We walked until the tunnel widened into a chamber. More lanterns were lit and I took in my surroundings. It was a curious place. The walls were rough, but the furnishings reminded me of my own establishment. There was a chaise longue, a mirror, and a number of beds, all made up with silk sheets. He gestured to the chaise longue and poured me a glass of wine. I arranged myself and put on my most neutral expression. Better see how the land lies with this lot before deciding what to do, I thought. He kept silent until the other two came in, now joined by another man. They stood in a line, like soldiers waiting for an inspection. The Englishman knelt at my side and took my hand.

'Mademoiselle d'Auray, I am Sir Hubert Lovell, of the Hampshire Lovells and late of His Majesty's Grenadier Guards and the Ontario Loyal Volunteers Militia. May I present my servant, Bertrand,' he indicated the Québecois, 'formerly corporal of the militia.'

The Québecois bowed and I inclined my head slightly.

'Tom Jenkinson, my gamekeeper.' The driver. 'He doesn't speak a word of French, I'm afraid. Good man with a rifle and dashed useful to have on board in a scrape, I can assure you. And good old Perry, or the Right Honourable Sir Peregrine Hawkwood to give him his full title. Served together in the Americas, Perry and I, don't you know.'

The 'guard' kissed my hand and murmured that he was overjoyed to make my acquaintance. They talked together in English before the two retainers set about preparing a meal. I kept quiet, acting the poor little woman shocked by her deliverance from certain death, and I really did need some time to decide what to do. There was no point in thinking about escape. I had no idea how to get back to the surface, for one thing, and my rescuers looked like they knew their work, for another. I wasn't even sure I wanted to go back, but something told me it was a good idea to keep my finger in both pies. Guillaume was no fool, and he was probably right when he said that whoever picked the wrong side was going to end up regretting it. Well, I'm no fool either. It's a tricky question, which horse to back in a two-horse race. I knew a gambler once, and he had the answer. Back them both at the best odds you can find. It's the way of the world and no one can change that. All I could change was the way I cut the pack. I needed to let Guillaume know where I was, and then they could sort it out between them. I'd go with the winner for the time being, or go on my own if I was lucky. The only question was how.

I looked in the mirror and decided that my new, boyish look quite suited me. Very gamine and Joan of Arc. It set off my cheekbones nicely. Well, if they wanted Saint Joan I would give her to them. I'd be the patriot girl whom every Englishman wants to tame. No need to build a fire, boys. I'm quite hot enough. I thought about using my charms to become Lovell's mistress but decided against it. No point in putting all my eggs in one basket, as his friend might be more inclined to give me what I wanted if he thought he was the object of my affections. I decided that the best way to play things was the hope of passion yet to come to both my gallant deliverers. Let them scramble for my credit. They did a lot of scrambling, those two, while the Québecois and the other one did the real work. They were constantly by my side, asking me how I was and whether I was recovered enough to travel. Lovell disappeared for a day, and I thought it was time to make my move with his friend. I moped, and politely refused wine.

'I say, Mademoiselle, are you upset?'

I sighed. 'I weep to leave my country, Monsieur, even if it is to go to a safe place until I can return. I weep to leave France. How would you feel if you had to flee England like a thief, perhaps never to see the blessed soil that bore you again? I have heard that when a gentleman of Venice was condemned to die, he would be taken for a last walk along a bridge that gave him a final glance across his city. They call it the Bridge of Sighs. Ah, how I long to take a final walk in Paris, to hear my native tongue spoken in the streets and to look back upon the life I have led and sigh at its passing. I know it cannot be. Your friend, the one in charge, he has told you that we must stay here until we leave for England and we must do as we are told.'

I looked up at him through my eyelashes and allowed my eyes to moisten in a most affecting way. He was not a subtle man. I could read the conflict in his face. He took on the appearance of a man with dysentery, unsure whether to subject himself to the uncertainties of a flight to the safety of home or resign himself to the immodesty of shitting in the street. I stifled a sob as he paced.

'Damn it all. I'd rather hang than leave England without drinking a schooner of ale or hearing the post-horn on Blackheath of a spring morning myself. I'll do it. Hugh is no man of stone. I'm sure he'd understand. Doesn't do to see a young lady in distress, after all. It's just not the act of a gentleman. Who is he to tell me that I should act dishonourably, anyway? Put your disguise on, Mademoiselle, and we'll take a stroll together.'

I changed into the ragged dress that one of my rescuers had

worn as part of his crone's disguise and wiped dirt on my face. I had not felt comfortable dressed as a boy. It was like going out unarmed. I knew that I had to let Guillaume know where we were rather than run away or be rescued while I took my promenade. The last thing I wanted was to be returned to my employers, as I had my doubts about Guillaume's reassurances that I would be allowed to go about my business once this affair was at an end. Ideally, my rescue would come too late and I would be spirited away to England with my credit as a faithful daughter of the Revolution well established. I could decide what to do for the best at my leisure. It was all working out rather well. I was just congratulating myself on my cleverness, when I realized that my would-be benefactor had met some resistance.

'I cannot let you leave, sir. Monsieur Lovell has left very clear orders.'

It was Bertrand. To tell the truth, if Hawkwood had been less of a fool he would have seen the sense in this. Luckily for me, he was not.

'You, Corporal, do not permit me to do anything. Know your place, Dubois. I would have thought that a quick glance outside would tell you all you need to know about what follows when the lower orders forget their station.'

'It is not I who gives the orders, Monsieur Perry, as well you know. You heard Monsieur Hugh's instructions.'

My escort flushed beetroot. I pretended not to understand English and busied myself with my shoes.

'My good friend Captain Lovell does not outrank me in His Majesty's service nor in society, however much he may think he does. I will do as I please and if you dare . . .' he spluttered over the words '. . . if you dare to stand in my way I'll see you kiss the gunner's daughter at Colchester Barracks Square before I break you to the ranks. So if you know what's good for you, Corporal Dubois, you'll show me the proper respect and prepare the horses at my order, sir. See to it.'

There is nothing more ridiculous than a man who stands on his dignity in the face of good advice. Luckily for me, there is nothing more servile than a devoted retainer. Foolishness and idiocy stared each other full in the face for a moment until centuries of 'do as you're told' prevailed and Corporal Bertrand Dubois remembered his place. As he dashed off to hitch up the cart he was enough of a Frenchman to curse under his breath. Sadly for him, he was too much of a soldier to prevent his hand stealing to his forehead in the ghost of a salute. I had witnessed a wise man take a bad order from a fool because the fool had breeding. Poor Bertrand. He paid a very heavy price for being so biddable.

Hawkwood and I rode the cart to the edge of the city. We hitched the horse to the rail outside a tavern and went inside. I bought us both wine and bread. After we had refreshed ourselves, I told him I needed to make my toilet and left him sitting at the driver's seat. I slipped into a courtyard in search of a latrine. There was a hue and cry in the street. An elderly man had been robbed of his purse. I had seen a group of those ragged children that seem to infest Paris flee through the gate into the courtyard I visited and thought that there was a good chance I could recruit one as a messenger. I found him hiding in the latrine. I opened the door and made as if I were going to scream. He cowered in the corner, staring up at me with infected eyes.

'You know I could have you on the cart to prison in a moment, don't you?'

His eyes fought against sores to widen to the size of eggs and he nodded.

'You are lucky today. Do you know who I am?'

He shook his head.

'I am Claudette Benoit. I am an agent of the Committee for General Security.' I paused to let that sink in. He looked on the verge of soiling himself, so I pressed on. No point in terrifying him so much he couldn't do as he was told. I smiled at him. 'Don't be afraid. There's more at stake here than one old man's savings. Do you know the police post by the Hôtel de Ville?'

He nodded his head epileptically. I pulled a scrap of paper from my clothing and scribbled a note. 'Take this to Commandant Bouchier. Tell him that you come from Claudette, and he will ensure that you are rewarded. It will be your safe conduct from this place. Now go.'

He sped off, mingling with the crowd and weaving his way towards the centre of town. I returned to the street and saw Hawkwood surrounded by guards. Shit. The man's French was so bad that he might as well have signed a confession as soon as he opened his mouth. I wandered up, trying to seem as if I was a curious bystander.

'Your name, Monsieur. I ask you for the last time.'

Hawkwood looked stricken, but seemed to be keeping his mouth shut. He had more brains than I had given him credit for. The situation could be saved. I put on my broadest Breton accent and panted as if I had been running.

'Gaston! What are you doing? Why are you detaining these men?' I stepped on to the cart and cuffed him round the head, then I turned to the guards. 'I am so sorry about my brother, Messieurs. He was born a half-wit. He is as deaf and as dumb as a statue in a churchyard. We have come to find my father. He enlisted in the guards. Our mother sent me to find him and sent my brother with me to look after my virtue on the road because these are dangerous times. She is not a woman who knows the world, as you can see. I spend more time looking after him than I do looking for my father. He gets very upset when people talk to him. He tries his best but he has no more sense than my father's sheepdog, bless him. He has a good heart though and wouldn't hurt a fly.'

I smiled prettily at them, giving them the benefit of my blue eyes and pulling my bodice tight against my chest. The guardsman smiled at me. They always do.

'What's your father's name, girl? We may know where you can find him.'

'Antoine Daube, Monsieur.'

'No, I have not heard of him. Look, girl, your father could be anywhere. At the front, even. Why don't you take your brother and go home? Find yourself a nice guardsman for a husband and raise strong children for the Mother Country.'

I smiled at him. 'Are you volunteering to make me a wife, Monsieur? I would be honoured to be a bride but I am a virtuous girl and could not kiss a man unless we were to be wed. I am no aristocrat, after all.' I winked at him, and his comrades roared with laughter.

'Take your cart and be off with you. If I were you I'd go back west. A girl like you won't stay virtuous for long in Paris.'

I jumped up beside Hawkwood and took the reins. It was all I could do to stop myself whipping the horse into a gallop. As we meandered out of the city, he whispered to me. 'I say, Mademoiselle, you're a cool one. You're quite the bravest girl I have ever met. You saved us both. It's really quite extraordinary. I have three sisters and none of them has half as much pluck as you, even though they are English. When we get back to England would you do me the honour of accompanying me to the theatre?'

You see? They're all the same under the skin. Rich or poor, gentleman or artisan, officer or soldier, even Englishman or Frenchman. There's nothing that the gentlemen can do that can surprise me because nothing they do is remotely surprising. I find it a comfort. I was young then, you see, and I thought that there was no game I couldn't win provided I kept my head.

There was a certain amount of unpleasantness when we returned from my final tour around the sights. Needless to say, Lovell was extremely displeased that we had gone out at all, and the fact that we had come within a paper's width of discovery did not improve his humour. He and Hawkwood conversed in a state of strangulated politeness, which I discovered meant that they were having the bitterest of arguments. I knew nothing of the ways of Englishmen at that time and found it all rather confusing.

'Perry, old chap. I really must protest. You know as well as I do that you shouldn't go wandering around Paris on your own. You put us all in danger, including the girl. It really won't do, don't you know. I did tell you that I required you to attend my return underground. Did you forget?'

'I really don't think you should talk to me like that in front of the servants, Hugh. It's most unseemly. There was no harm done to anyone. We have known each other since we were boys. Our long acquaintance should teach you that I can be relied upon not to put the cat among the pigeons.'

'Quite so. I recall our first meeting. You were fagging for my older brother and burned his toast. That was the first time I had to pull you out of a fire of your own making.'

'I did not make the fire, your precious brother did and was roasting me over it. You presume too much, old chap. If we were not such good friends I would be bound to ask you for satisfaction.'

'And if we were not such good friends I would accept. It is only because of my regard for your sisters that I do not, sir.'

'Your regard for my sisters does you credit. It was precisely because of my regard for our charge's tender sensibilities that I decided to exercise my initiative. You would have done the same. She's a cool hand, Hugh. She saved our bacon with the bloody guards, I can tell you. Jabbered at them until they went away. Told them I was her idiot brother.'

'Half correct at least. It does you no credit to plead Mademoiselle d'Auray's bravery as an excuse for your stupidity. None the less, we have her to thank that there seems to be no lasting damage. I'll thank you to keep to the rules in future. If you take us to the guillotine, we won't be able to help others like her, will we? There's more at stake than one girl's happiness, however beautiful she may be. You would do well to remember that.'

Lovell stalked off to one side of the cavern and sat on a chair, assiduously reading. Hawkwood stuttered, then thought better of his reply. He turned his back on his companion and stared at the wall. Meanwhile the two servants continued with the preparations for our departure. I lay on my chaise longue and sipped my wine. They argued like children, these Englishmen. It was almost a refreshing contrast to the idiotic Alain, who would have demanded to fight to the death. If it was to be my fate to spend time in England, they would need some study. I had relaxed and become lost in my thoughts when it happened.

I had never been involved in violence in a personal capacity. Oh, I'd seen it enough times. Alain's duel and public executions, mainly. I have always felt that I was observing it all from a distance and it didn't really concern me. It was easy to watch it unfurl and work out how it affected me, if at all. I'm not a coward – at least I don't think I can be, as I never panic or lose my temper even when times get extremely fraught. But I did not like being in harm's way and I resolved to avoid it whenever possible. The one thing I can say about this occasion is that it was all over very quickly. One minute the worthy Bertrand had refilled my glass, the next it was dark and bullets were flying around. The light was the first casualty, so when someone grabbed me by the hand I had no idea who was dragging me off and where I was about to end up. It was Lovell, of course. Men like him have an amazing capacity to fall into the midden and emerge with a bunch of lavender, as Mother used to say. About me, as a matter of fact. He pulled me out of the tunnels and bundled me on to a horse and we were away. Another house, false papers and a coach trip to Cherbourg followed.

We waited to see if anyone joined us, staying at the home of a family he described as trusted friends. I never met them. We skulked in an attic while they delivered food to the door. Lovell had become obsessed with security since Paris and the whole set-up made me think that Guillaume's exploits in this part of the world hadn't been as thorough as he had led me to believe. I kept my head down and waited for developments. I knew that the message had got through. The gunfight in the tunnel proved that. Whatever happened now, I was safe. The English thought I was the sort of brave aristo that would make a good mistress even if

I could never be introduced to Mother. Guillaume's lads thought I was their girl on the inside. Perfect. If there was to be a war to decide the fate of the world, I was going to win – and to Hell with the rest of them. Personally, I rather hoped that we would make it to England. Paris seemed like stepping backwards. I quite fancied pastures new. I hadn't given up on the prospect of the New World either. I had missed my money and I was looking forward to a reunion. You have to look after yourself when you live in interesting times.

No one turned up. Not Bertrand, whom I had thought of as being a bit of a survivor. Not the gamekeeper. Not Hawkwood, but that didn't surprise me at all. Even if he'd survived the fight he was the stuff of heroes. If ever there was a man to lead the last stand, it was he. The forces of revolutionary justice were also conspicuous by their absence, so it seemed that no one had been taken alive. It all began to get extremely boring, sitting in the attic and pretending to embroider a sampler. As you know, I get bored easily. I started to think about escaping myself, heading for Brittany and a ship to the Americas.

Lovell seemed to sense my dissatisfaction as he spent more time in the room and less on the arrangements for our departure. He told me about England at great length and assured me that he would present me in London society, where I would be well received on account of my beauty and bravery. I nodded, and pretended interest, but we both knew we were in limbo. Finally, I found myself on board a merchant ship flying the colours of the Batavian Republic. It was a poor thing that rolled most alarmingly. I was horribly seasick. Thank God my American trip seemed to have been postponed. I don't think my complexion could have survived the punishment. I kept noticing the small threads of broken veins appearing on my cheeks. I'm sure that this was caused by the strain of my vomiting. I was relieved that the voyage would only last a couple of days. I saw the famous white cliffs and felt as happy as any Englishwoman. A new life with the possibility of keeping my meals down lay ahead.

14

Perfidious in Albion

I DECIDED THAT I RATHER LIKED LONDON. I HAD INTENDED TO take the next ship to New Orleans, but I resolved to stay for a while. Quite apart from my unwillingness to endure another voyage, there was too much money to be made for me to pass up. Also, I was enjoying myself. It was an easy life and after my recent adventures I had realized that you can't put a price on peace and quiet. Not that it was all attentive Englishmen and walks in Hyde Park, you understand. There had been quite a lot of that, it's true, but if that were all London had to offer I would have been bored. As some roastbeef said, if you're tired of London, you're tired of life itself.

The first few weeks were rather dull. I spent a lot of time with Lovell. He was very subdued throughout. The deaths of his friends and servants at the hands of Guillaume and his men had been confirmed and he went into a bit of a decline. He was too much the reserved Englishman to do anything as honest as grieve for them, but his company took on a melancholic tone. There are only so many sighs and silent evenings that a girl can bear. We would go to the theatre, or riding, but the joy had gone out of the man. Wherever we went his gloom followed us like a reproachful servant.

I got bored with him eventually. It's a character failing of mine, I know. I am not suited to the life of a comforter. If that was what he wanted, he should have found himself a wife or a nurse – and me, well, I'm not exactly wife material.

It took me a few weeks further to recover my money from America. I had made the acquaintance of a banker who proved to be an invaluable help. He was very quick, as well, meaning that I had to endure the minimum of inconvenience to get what I wanted. I was reunited with my strongbox at the same time that I decided I had to branch out on my own. It was largely intact, as well, which was a pleasant surprise; I had had a vision of opening it to find it empty except for a few sous and a lot of dirty fingermarks on the lining. So there I was, a young girl possessed of a fortune and in need of a business in which to invest. I thought of buying land and going back to the family trade, but farming seemed hard work. Besides, I had travelled too far from Father's farm to have any desire to go back. I took rooms in the Haymarket and waited to see if I could find an opportunity.

London was a city at war, and where there is war there will always be men who want to fight. There was also a large population of Frenchmen, mainly the sort of arrogant idiots who spent their days despising the English while they waited to be returned to their former station by force of others' arms. I recognized quite a few of them from my days escorting Alain. They were not people I would have chosen to spend time with. Their principal attraction, their money, had usually been dissipated long before they ended up in London. I did reacquaint myself with one of Alain's friends, Raymond de Coutances, and it was through him that I discovered what had happened to my doctor, Simon.

Poor Simon. I expect that he was enchanted by the Revolution at first. All the liberty and fraternity stuff was exactly the sort of idiocy he would have found irresistible. He always did think of himself as an enlightened man, with his philosophy and his nature study. I knew that he had become Alain's father's personal physician. Apparently, he decided to stay at his master's side when even the biggest fool in the world could have seen that some ridiculous Breton jacquerie was doomed to failure. I had never thought of Simon as stupid, except in the usual way that men are. He was caught trying to escape from France with Alain's father, who was some kind of invalid. They were both disguised as old women, a pretence that I am surprised he didn't manage to carry off. They were put on a barge and towed into the Channel along with other enemies of the Revolution. The shore batteries sank the vessel, and that was the end of that. I have absolutely no idea why Simon decided to stay with a man who clearly slowed him down and was extremely easy to recognize, or why he decided to take part in some insane peasants' revolt in the first place. There was more to him than met the eye, obviously. He was a strange little man, and I must confess I nearly shed a tear when I heard about him. I received a number of offers of comfort, but I wasn't in the mood. I went back to my rooms and drank a glass of Muscatel in his memory. Simon Legris: I will even miss the irritation I used to feel every time he asked me to marry him. A little.

Well, shocking though the news was, life went on. I started to spend a bit of time with my fellow émigrés (as we were known), and I made the acquaintance of a lot of young women who had escaped with very little. I have never come across so many noble names attached to so many girls I once knew. Revolution seemed to have made elevation to the aristocracy ridiculously easy. Who would know this better than the Comtesse d'Auray, after all? I met an English sailor at around the same time. Captain Henry Clive of His Majesty's Royal Navy approached me in the street without the formality of an introduction. He demanded the right to escort me about the town, and insisted that I call him Harry. He was a lively man with a large circle of military friends, all of whom seemed equally obsessed with meeting my countrywomen. This set me thinking. I deduced that Harry and his friends did not have marriage in mind. It struck me that an establishment where English gentlemen could enjoy the tender passions of France would make me more money than if I decided to go into business forging coin. I didn't want to be a mere brothelkeeper. I was a countess, after all. Also, I had a shrewd idea that the English liked to have their romance dressed up as something their mothers would find more palatable.

I realized that if I were to set myself up in business I would require premises and so I went out on an excursion to view a house. I had become lost, fatigued and was not in the best of tempers when I decided to take refuge in a tavern in Covent Garden. It was a rough place, filled with whores, market men and the sort of respectable gentleman who had either strayed from his usual path to church or had come looking for company that would cost him only coin. I was taking coffee and dejectedly perusing the premises' details when I had the most extraordinary meeting. I could tell that I was being watched, but this is normal for me. I assumed that the man who kept stealing glances at me from an adjoining table was looking at something he couldn't afford and paid him no mind. He was a persistent fellow, who reminded me of a mouse, both in his features, which not even his mother in her most tender moments could have described as handsome, but also in the way that he approached me indirectly. He walked around the walls to my table as if he did not dare to cross the expanse of the floor. He sat next to me and introduced himself as a Mr Stuart Driscoll, a lawyer. I was at the point of telling him to go about his business when he said something that intrigued me.

'You are French, are you not? I'm sure a girl of your, ah, attributes will be looking for property.'

This was accompanied by a leer. I looked down at the engraving of the house on the table in front of me, and concluded that I was not dealing with an expert in seduction. I nodded almost imperceptibly, not wishing to encourage him but at the same time wanting to hear what he had to say.

'It so happens that I have become the executor of a remarkable estate. Have you heard of the late Doctor Graham?'

I had not.

'A great man, so some people say. Personally, I'm not so sure. He had some reputation as a scientist. His most renowned invention was a bed of singular electric properties.'

He had my attention. I resolved that if he attempted to cheat me I would have Harry thrash him through the streets, but I was beginning to see an opportunity.

'He ran an establishment in Pall Mall. A Temple of Fertility, he called it. It's all there, you know. The bed, the furnishings. Everything. An enterprising person could pick it up for a very reasonable consideration, if she had a good friend in the right place.'

He winked at me, moistening his lips. I took a deep breath.

Another idiot, another price. If I travelled to the ends of the earth I would find some man offering me a trip home in luxury and rubbing the sweat off his palms like a fly on a windowpane. I rose and offered him my arm.

'Monsieur Driscoll, I am the Comtesse d'Auray. I wish to instruct you as my lawyer in a property matter. I believe that lawyers should be most cordial with their clients, so call me Claudette, pray. Is there somewhere nearby where we may discuss business with more privacy? We could take a chair to inspect the premises of which you speak, perhaps?'

I knew that it was perfect as soon as I walked through the door. There were a number of statues of girls in various states of undress. All very Roman and tasteful, mark you, but exactly the sort of thing that would get the customers in the mood to open their purses. We climbed the stairs to the top of the house, me in the lead rolling my hips. I looked back over my shoulder and saw it was having the desired effect. He appeared to be in some kind of discomfort that necessitated the rearrangement of his britches. I'll be sure to get a good price, I thought. He directed me to the master bedroom. Then I saw it. If ever there was a centrepiece for an establishment like mine! It was an enormous bed. I walked around it, and noticed that the headboard was engraved: 'Be Fruitful, Multiply and Replenish the Earth.'

I smiled, thinking that it would be very fruitful indeed, multiplying my money and replenishing those parts of the earth that I occupied, when Driscoll started talking. 'It's all in perfect order, you know. We've kept it all maintained, as we thought that it would be worth far more as a piece that has its components.'

It must have been obvious to him that I had no idea what he was talking about, as he stripped off his frock coat and began to tinker with the bed. He pulled the remaining dustsheets away to demonstrate that it could be tilted to various angles. Impressive, I thought. He fiddled with some machinery at its head. Blue sparks climbed the chains to the canopy, arcing between them with great flashes of light. I stepped back.

He smiled at me. 'Oh, it's all perfectly safe. There's no danger of fire or injury. The good doctor thought that it magnetized the air and increased fertility. Who can say what the truth is?'

I felt the charged air lift the small hairs upon my forearms. It was a pleasant sensation. He carried on, 'Of course, when this place was the Temple of Health, the bedding was filled with aromatic herbs. It used to cost fifty pounds to spend the night here.'

He let his words hang. The unattractive leer had returned. Well, I thought, it must be mine. No question of it. I walked to the bed and sat, allowing my hem to ride up. It was time to begin negotiations. 'The price, Monsieur Driscoll?'

'For anyone else it would be prohibitive, but to you, Claudette, I could arrange for the transfer for as little as thirteen thousand guineas.'

I moistened my lips slowly, crossing my legs to reveal the border between my stocking and my thigh. I sighed and pulled my skirts down most modestly.

'I am afraid it is quite impossible, Stuart. Ten thousand guineas is all I can afford.' I paused to allow a look of disappointment to cross his face. 'In cash, at least. I am sure that a man of the law such as yourself could come up with some alternative consideration.'

I could hear his breath; fast and ragged like a swimmer. He sat beside me, and I leaned towards him, allowing my bodice to force my breasts upwards to show the rosy top of my areolas. I lowered my voice. 'You would earn my gratitude, Stuart. You would become a friend, and for a friend in my country, the door is always open.'

He seized me about the waist, pulling me towards him. Our lips met, stifling his excited squeal. As I lay back to allow his passage, I noticed a mirror suspended under the canopy. From one angle this allowed me to pass the time counting the spots on his behind. I noticed that my hair, which had grown quickly, looked most becoming when I spread it out across the pillow and contented myself with admiring my reflection while he finished.

It was not a pleasant experience. As I walked from the rooms with the deed of sale in my hand, I resolved it was to be my last. I have never been the sort of girl who would take on allcomers. For someone in my line of work, I was positively choosy. I have slept with men for three reasons: affection, advancement and money. I have tried to combine the three wherever possible. Sometimes it is not, and this was one such occasion. Driscoll had something I needed and I had something he wanted. I still had that something, but his attractiveness rested in my hand now and he'd get no second chance. From then on, I was to be a businesswoman. I would only get my dress creased if I wanted to.

We settled in rather well. It took no time at all to find my staff. Some of them were old friends of mine from my rue Cordeliers days, all kitted out with preposterous titles. Henriette, a blacksmith's daughter from the Gironde, had become Mademoiselle du Brabant, a duchess. Roxanne was the youngest daughter of the Comte de Provence. Illegitimate, naturally. I remember when she helped her mother sell flowers outside the Hôtel de Châtelet. A pretty girl even then, and one who was unlikely to spend her days as a florist. I supplemented my professionals with a smattering of genuine blue bloods. They seemed to take to the work. I suppose the real problem for them was not sleeping with different men every night. My establishment was very exclusive indeed, and I cultivated quality rather than quantity. Six months in London was a great leveller. English charity didn't extend to giving these people a pension, and you can't eat your aristocratic pedigree. Or wear it. In fact they all got on rather well, my girls. Sisters under the skin, you might say, and I was like an older sister to them all. After all, a girl needs experience to survive in this cruel, new world and that was a commodity I had to spare.

They got quite talkative, the gentlemen. Being military men, they talked about the army and the navy. What they were planning. Where they were going, you know the sort of thing. 'I'm afraid I can't see you next week, Nicole, my ship is to sail to Toulon.' They talked to me, the girls, and I stored these little nuggets. It became as much a part of the working day as the work itself. When the last client had gone back to barracks or to his wife, the girls and I sat around, drinking wine and discussing them. I'm sure they did the same with us. Captain Salter, with his potbelly and small manhood, spanked poor Henriette's backside quite raw. Liked to be tied up like an animal. He even asked her to piss on him, but had to wait for that pleasure as the dear girl had the wit to demand more money than he carried. Oh, and his regiment embarked for Flanders the next day.

It is always a shame to waste good money, and I could tell that the information that came to me from the girls was worth its weight in gold. I had Jean-Claude's private address and dropped him a line. Nothing I would worry about if it fell into the wrong hands. I thanked my father's old retainer for his service to my family, gave him my new address and told him that if he was ever in London he should look me up. The first thing the old villain did was send me a package of money as his 'investment' in my establishment. Outrageous! Still, you had to admire his instinct for survival. He was only doing exactly as I would. If he had to run, he'd made sure he had somewhere to go and something to live on. His next approach was a bit more cloak and dagger. I received a visit from a ballad-singer. I never understood what the English see in the lower classes caterwauling myself, but the clients loved it. 'Molly' became a bit of a fixture. She came in, sang about gin, faithless lovers and hanged thieves, then left with a little note sewn into her shawl. I kept my friends in Paris happy. As Guillaume said, you couldn't predict who was going to win the war and it was only good business sense to spread your investment. I was becoming quite the commercialist.

Things were going altogether rather well. Then Hubert Lovell resurfaced. I thought I'd seen the last of him. He wasn't even a customer. He called on me in what he described as an 'official capacity'. Very sinister. He was dressed in civilian clothes, so I assumed he wasn't checking the premises on behalf of the regimental surgeon. Not that it would have concerned me if he had been. I ran a clean house. He sat down next to me on the chaise longue in my private room and told me that I had attracted some attention from his superiors. 'Really?' I said. 'Well, I run a superior establishment.'

He put on the sort of serious expression that I always associate with men trying to save me from my immoral life. 'Claudette, you have no idea how it destroys me to see you reduced to this.' He cast a hand about him, over my gilded mirror and well-stocked wardrobe, which I felt gave his gesture less effect than he intended. 'When I saved you from the Temple Prison you were the most beautiful, brave girl I had ever seen. I even thought that I would make you my wife. You saved my life, and the lives of my men in France. Yet you have become a common whore.'

I drew myself to my full height and stared directly into his eyes. Saint Joan, again, you see. Always give the client what he likes. 'Hubert, I may be a whore but I am anything but common. I have done what I have to in order to survive and be beholden to none. You must remember what I have been through. I relied upon my family all my life. Now they are gone, along with the life I once had. You and your countrymen may defeat the Revolution. I hope that you do. I dream of the day that I can spit in the faces of the horrid little men who treated me so foully. But you can never put things back to the way they were. Too many people are dead for that. I can never go back. You ask why, and I'll tell you. I was raised to be a thing of beauty. I know nothing else and I will use all I have to make sure I never need to be rescued again.'

He looked crestfallen. I took his hand. There was a moment's silence in which I swear I could hear his heart racing. 'Claudette, I work for an organization called the Aliens Office. You will have heard of us.'

I was cold suddenly. Of course I had heard of the Aliens Office. All émigrés had. They were responsible for arresting spies. Surely he could suspect nothing. I clasped his hand and leaned towards him.

'My masters have become aware that your establishment is a conduit for classified information. You are suspected, as are your staff. I have seen the dossier, Claudette, and while I was shocked I am not so blinded by your beauty that I can ignore the evidence of my own eyes. I have come here with a proposition that you cannot afford to decline. You are to continue in your work, but report to me. I will provide you with information, which you will send to France using the methods that you have done to date.'

I nodded, and allowed a tear to form. It was caused by relief, but I counted upon Lovell to misinterpret me. He did not disappoint. His manner softened. His upper arm brushed my breast as he clasped my hand.

'I must know, Claudette. I trust myself a good judge of men. I did not imagine that you would be a traitor.'

I sighed, turning it into a sob that would have the stalls weeping. 'You cannot judge me, Hubert. You have no right. A man came to me here with news of my sister. I had presumed her dead, but it seems she lives. She is a prisoner and will go to the guillotine if I do not help them. My own dear sister – what choice did I have? You come to me like a man. You make your demands and will take what you want by force if I do not give it to you, my brave Englishman. You are not so different from those you fight. You both plunder that which is not given to you. No doubt you will say if I do not help I will hang. Good. I will help. You call me a whore. If I am a whore it is because men like you have offered me the choice of whore or corpse and, may my Father forgive me, I have not the strength to die.'

It was all very moving. Lovell tried to speak, but his throat caught. I kissed him on the lips and led him to my bed without a word. As I say, I was quite the commercialist in those days. I spread my investments wisely.

So that was my life in London. I would pass messages to Jean-Claude. Hubert wrote some of them, but not all. Had he had the wit to understand it, I would have explained to him that if he wanted to have the lies he sent believed, then they would have to be garnished with a liberal pinch of truth. I suspected he did not. I got money from the clients, from Paris and from Hubert.

It was a good life until I received a message from Jean-Claude that disturbed me. It came from Molly. I was instructed to meet Jacques on Millbank in three days' time. I was to promenade with Molly, who would sing. Jacques would follow us but we would not speak until we were alone. Guillaume was dead. Jacques was in some kind of trouble and must flee. I was to keep him out of mischief, apparently. The news did not shock me. Men like Guillaume are as likely to be executed as they are to be executioners. I supposed I could put the boy to work. I had been considering whether to employ an accompanist for Molly, and a hurdy-gurdy shouldn't be beyond his abilities. I was unsure about whether I would tell Hubert who he was. In the end I did not.

Few things make me afraid, but I do fear the weather in this city. It is not that I am unused to damp. What Breton could make that claim? It is just that when it is cold, and a fog rolls up from the river, I can feel it penetrate my clothing like a lecher's glare. It strips me naked, and who but a fool stands out in the fog with no clothes on? It's positively reckless. I pulled my shawl about me and pressed closer to the brazier. Molly stood in the firelight, a tin cup in her hand. There was a mixed crowd. Some sailors, probably from the ships tied at Millbank wharf, some gentlemen, undoubtedly officers by their uniforms, and a good smattering of the kind of ne'er-do-wells that congregate around a crowd after dark. I clutched my purse tightly. Molly sang.

> 'Tis said gin's a Mother's Ruin
> And I would a gin soak be
> For I'd rather raise a glass
> Than ever raise a family.
> Oh the parson he will tell you

That drinking is a sin
So the Devil take the parson
And pour me a glass of gin.

All very affecting if you like that sort of thing, I'm sure. The
crowd greeted it with approval. Coin chinked into Molly's cup.
She curtsied, thanked them for their kindness and we walked
away. I could see a small figure in our wake, but only out of the
corner of my eye.

Jacques adjusted to life *chez* Claudette without difficulty. He
became a bit of a favourite among the girls. I thought I would
have to be firm and introduce a policy of no fraternization, but
his interest in them seemed to be confined to conversation. I put
him to work about the place. He was most diligent, seemingly
as happy to change bedding as he was to serve drinks and eject
unruly customers. This last proved a surprising discovery. I was
on the verge of calling the two men I had stationed below stairs
to deal with the amorous and impecunious, when there he was.
Although he was only half the man's size and received a buffet
about the head that would have felled one of the statues, he
threw his opponent out into the street. 'Stronger than he looks,' I
remarked. I intended to placate Hubert with the story that Jacques
came from the same village as my family, but when he next called
he singularly failed to notice our new member of staff. He was in
high spirits and was very keen to discuss a business venture.

'Claudette, you will have heard of Admiral Nelson?' I had, of
course. 'Now this information is top secret. You must swear not
to tell a soul.' I swore.

'Admiral Nelson has been injured during the fighting in
Corsica. The poor man has lost an eye. Anyway, he has come

back to England to recuperate and to receive his latest orders. He is – how shall I put it? – an admirer of feminine beauty, and my masters are anxious that he should be entertained suitably, by way of recognition of his services to the Crown. We have in mind an entertainment upon a theme, possibly nautical or some such. You, Claudette, will provide this entertainment. You will be very well remunerated. It will be a party that people will talk about for months, although probably not with their wives.' He laughed. I joined in. They do hate to laugh alone.

'It will also be an opportunity for indiscretion of another sort. When the dust has settled, you will report to your friends in Paris that the fleet under Nelson's command is to sail for the West Indies. You will be personally responsible for the Admiral's pleasure to give this authenticity.'

I nodded. 'And the money?'

He laughed again. 'Claudette, when you reach the Pearly Gates Saint Peter will try to bed you and you will ask him for cash! Do not fear. We want this to look very good indeed. You have five hundred pounds to ensure that this will be a night to remember. Make sure that events are so memorable that no one will be able to recall their actions precisely, there's a good girl.'

It always irritates me when a client acts as if he knows me intimately. Naturally I suppressed this. Hubert would be as un-aware of my annoyance as he would be startled by my reason for it. Like all men, he assumed that he knew me because he had known me. The two are as far apart as, well, love and marriage. I smiled at his poor witticism, but it did set me thinking. I had to plan a party for the Admiral. A party with a theme. I considered the usual masked balls and Romans but discounted them. Oh no, I had been ordered to provide a notable entertainment. Hubert's harping on about my appearance in the afterlife gave me an altogether better idea. I was going to throw one Hell of a party.

It took a surprising amount of work to give a smart English townhouse a Hellish ambience, but by the eve of the Admiral's visit the former Temple of Health had been reconsecrated to a less benevolent deity. All my statues had been draped in crimson silk. The pictures were hung with black. Red cloth swathed the walls, stitched with silk thread to shimmer like the infernal flame. All the girls were in scarlet. Scarlet women, you see? The two exceptions were Molly, who wore the black of a damned soul and was to sing the Pater Noster backwards at midnight, and me. I wore white. My hair hung loosely over my shoulders. I had caused Jacques to build me a pair of wings from swan feathers, which I had strapped across my shoulders. He was clever with his hands in more than one way. I was a vision. An angel trapped in the Pit, calling out for a brave English sailor to rescue me. I lay on the Celestial Bed, watching the electricity spark and splutter above me and contemplated my reflection. I believed that if this Admiral had spent his last year in a Neapolitan whorehouse he would be no more able to resist me than if he had been at sea.

I had planned to compel Jacques to remain below stairs. Even if he remembered to shave, which was not guaranteed, his strange appearance and the curious hoots he emitted in unguarded moments could be distracting. I did not want the customers' attention on anything but the entertainment. This turned out to be unnecessary. As the final touch to my little vision of the infernal, I hired a troupe of malformed exhibits from a pleasure garden. I had them dressed as the Damned and positioned throughout the house with trays of glasses and other refreshments. They were a peculiar crew, limbless, twisted and altogether ferocious to look at, but extremely gentle and polite. I suppose they had a lot to overcome. I have always had a first impression to rely on, which has allowed me to get away with almost everything I have wanted. These poor creatures were unable to overcome that first flinch, however much they 'as you please'd' or 'yes madam'd'. Still, Jacques fitted among them like sand at the seashore. It was strange to see him as the least singular-looking in any gathering. I stationed him at the Master Bedroom door, champagne in a bucket of ice at his feet and two polished glasses on his tray.

I have only had the chance to see two nations at their pleasures, but I am sure that the way that people abandon themselves is as individual as a passport. Soirées in France were muted, intimate affairs with low lighting, muffled conversation and the subtle rustle of hands upon silk. The Englishman is a raucous, roaring creature. By the time Molly, who seemed to have mislaid her costume, stood to sing her Pater Noster, my cellars were sorely depleted. Groups of my girls and their naval escorts cavorted in various states of undress. Molly ended her performance to the sound of breaking glass. I chided myself mentally for failing to negotiate restitution. In fact, the only people who had kept their clothes on were the Admiral and I. I looked around my little Hell and smiled. If the real Devil chanced by, he would not have been disappointed. Hubert shouted my name. I approached his table and saw that Nicole had stationed herself beneath it and was providing him with a service that I would have described as an extra. I was struck by the self-possession of the British governmental official as we conversed. It is no wonder these people have an Empire.

'Claudette, the Admiral. Have you made his acquaintance?'

I had, but only briefly. I was sure that none of the girls would have risked taking my place.

'I go to find him, Hubert. I want to be the finale not the overture.'

The Admiral stood by a statue of an Amazon in the hallway. I took his arm. He was a man much smaller than his reputation. I am tall for a woman and he was of a height with me. His lips were fuller than I had expected. He looked soft, almost sensitive. I gazed into his face. Only his grey eye betrayed the truth of his pitiless renown. When he looked at me I saw his soul was as cold as a winter shore. The other eye was glass. It stared unblinkingly into its own distance but it had a more companionable gaze. Although I could see the desire behind his glance as he surveyed me (he was a man, after all), I felt a twinge of disquiet that I could not identify immediately. As he took me in with predatory nonchalance it came to me. He had a murderer's arrogance. I had met many killers, good men and bad ones. I had not the experience to recognize his type then. I doubt I could do so even now. Men like this are rare. Men like Admiral Nelson.

'You will be Mademoiselle Claudette, I suppose. Mr Lovell speaks very highly of you.'

I nodded, taking his arm. 'He is a dear friend.'

A moment of silence. The house was in uproar yet it was as if we stood behind glass.

'Who is she? The one you think about?'

He smiled. 'I will never underestimate the French again. If I had been as transparent to Admiral Villeneuve as I am to you I would be commanding a sunken fleet. Emma, her name is. She is of course married to another and hence beyond my reach. I was contemplating the irony of our surroundings. It was here that she met the man whom I intend to make a cuckold. No, not one of your redoubtable employees, Mademoiselle. She was a muse for the premises' last occupant, the celebrated Doctor Graham. There seems to be a history of the ladies of this house moving in the highest circles. She had become the wife of His Majesty's Ambassador to the kingdom of Naples by the time I was fortunate enough to make her acquaintance.'

I digested this. It was not going to be easy. Show a married man the way to your bedroom and all he will worry about is whether he can get away with it. Unconsummated love makes men loyal to an ideal of their beloved that can be hard to compete with. Still, I like a challenge and I have only met two men who turned down their chances.

'Tell me about her.' We were facing each other and I circled his waist with my arms. 'Is she as beautiful as me?'

I could feel his interest through his britches. Play your hand well, Claudette.

'She is different. You are as fair as morning. She is as dark as the lady in the Sonnets.'

I laughed. 'Then come with me. Make love with me. You will forget your love while you take your pleasure. I am no imitation of her, but myself. You will not be reminded of your loss as you look into my face. Perhaps you will learn something for her with me, even.'

I ground my hips against him as he decided. It was a tribute to my skill that he believed he had a decision to make. He pressed against me and croaked, 'Take me to your cloud, my angel. Show me your heaven.'

I kissed him on the lips. My tongue slipped into his mouth and I was surprised to taste gin. I took his hand to lead him to the stairs and he stumbled slightly. For the first time I realized he was very drunk. God knows, his voice had not betrayed him. I led him upstairs. If he was aware of the sounds of sex and the drunken singing that came from all around, he gave no sign. We passed Jacques at the door, and I relieved him of his champagne and glasses. We entered the celestial bedchamber. I closed the door behind me, but I did not lock it.

I had always been a lucky whore. I used to think that maybe the bad luck of my father murdering a tax collector that turned me into one was enough for this lifetime. The one thing about luck, though, is that it's like wine. Nice while it's still there but they both run out eventually. Mine ran out spectacularly that night. You hear so many stories about the nasty ones. Not just ones like Captain Salter – you know, the one that gave Henriette a raw arse – but the really nasty ones. There was a girl I knew in Paris. I can't even remember her name but I remember her scar. Right across the face it was, an ugly purple line that told more about men's natures than any amount of whores' gossip. He'd been up her with a knife as well. Put her out of business. It was only that all us girls used to pay her to act as a maid that kept her from the gutter. Lucky to be alive, so they say, which goes to show that luck means different things to different people. But I had always been Lucky Claudette. My pox was cured for free and the gentlemen only laid a loving hand on me. Until then.

The big myth is that you can tell. Believe me, you can't. I had no more idea what was going to happen than the girl with the scar. I thought that my Admiral was eating out of the palm of my hand. He started normally enough. A kiss, a 'Take off your skirts', a gasp as I took him in my mouth. He was ever so polite as well. 'Please would you mind going on all fours, Claudette?' Every inch a gentleman. I'd like to be able to say 'They all are,' and give everyone something to look out for. Nothing prepared me for it. One minute I was on my knees, groaning and even quite enjoying myself, then bang. A fist in the back of my head and I was spiralling downwards into the dark. I didn't know what hit me at first. If all he had wanted to do was beat me I'd probably have been out for the duration. But no, he had a way to get a girl's attention, this Admiral. It was so cold. I felt it inside me and it brought me back round in a second. It didn't feel like a cock. It was so hard and inflexible it took me a while to realize what it was. I felt the coldness seep out over my thighs and heard the bubbles effervesce on the sheets. It was the bottle. He had one hand around my throat and he was forcing the bottle inside me neck first. I screamed, or tried to. All that came out was an arid gurgle and he laughed, the bastard. I felt something split inside me and a rush of warmth mingled with the cold. I twisted my head and sank my teeth into his arm. He let go, and I screamed again. A real scream, lost among the sounds of the party below. He slapped me hard enough to rattle my teeth and began to choke me again. I could see his face, caught in a snarl, and heard his whisper, 'Fucking French whore. You don't like it like this, do you?' I thought about how sad it was that my best sheet should be ruined by the blood. I had always been so careful. How sad it was that I should have got through so much and that I would die like this. All I could see was his face, his smile and his cold, grey eye. His eye.

There was a sound like a melon being dropped on to flagstones and that awful eye rolled upwards. His grip slackened on my throat. He fell to one side and I saw Jacques. My saviour. He had a bloodstained bucket in one hand. My ugly, hairy, short saviour. I have never loved a man, except perhaps Father, and you know what a disappointment he turned out to be, but I gave my heart to Jacques in that instant. He was beside me, whispering urgently. 'Claudette, there is something I must do. It is an ugly thing and you must not see it. Turn your face away, I beg you. This English pig must lose his manhood now. It was the Boss's final order to me.'

He pulled out a knife. There was a tearing noise and he was at the window. 'We must go, Claudette.'

I went to him, each step an agony. I joined him at the window. He put his arm around me to support me and I kissed him. He stood upon the windowsill.

'You must hit me. I cannot leave with you. You must hit me and leave it to me to talk my way out of this.'

He turned. He could see that I was right. He raised the bucket and there was a burst of light.

When I came round the room was filled with Englishmen. There was no sign of the Admiral and no sign of Jacques. Hubert was at my side, and questioned me sharply. 'What happened?'

'Where is he – my hero? The Admiral?'

'Explain.'

'One of the deformed ones raped me. He dragged me into this room and did a terrible thing to me.'

His eyes slipped downwards. My thighs were covered in blood. The bottle lay at his feet. It was bloodstained almost to the base.

'And the Admiral?'

'He rescued me. There was a fight between them. I swooned. I must have struck my head.'

He patted my hand. As soon as I knew I had won, I leaned against him and I wept. It was absolutely the right thing to do, but my tears were real. I had not cried since I was a child, not even when they led Father away and my life changed. I cried for them all then: for Father, for Alain, for Guillaume and even for poor, silly Simon. I cried for me.

Part III

Warrens

15

The One-Guinea Brief

I LOATHE THIS JUDGE. HIS LOVE FOR HIMSELF HAS LOST passion's first blush and settled into a comfortable autumnal adoration that has transcended the mere physical. There are only two greater pieces of excrescence in the court. The first of these is my learned opponent. He's so well groomed he shines like a palamino. The very sight of him makes me shudder. The second, well, he's the client. A man so unutterably vile I have to grit my teeth and actively visualize the wine I intend to spend my fee upon before I can bring myself to shake him by the hand. I look at it all and it stares back at me like a reflection. Another Monday morning at the Assizes. Another trial. Here we all are and let's make the best of it.

I am defending a man called Sturrock who has stolen poultry. The case against him depends upon his equally unpleasant neighbour, a Mr Hunter. It is he who has just finished his evidence in chief. I rise, and fix him with my best baleful glare. I look angry, which I am. I am indifferent to Mr Hunter. It is probable that the world would be a better place if he did not inhabit it, but the full force of my displeasure comes from my hangover and the fact that I would dearly love to be almost anywhere in the world but here. I am a one-guinea brief, as the clients term it. One-day trials for a one-guinea fee. The great and the good in my profession command more than this, a lot more. They represent felons whose activities occupy months of the court's valuable time. They are paid not only the brief fee, but also a daily stipend throughout the case which is called a refresher. As my practice runs to cases that finish quicker than a bridegroom, I must seek my refreshment elsewhere. It was not always like this. Once I was in chambers in Lincoln's Inn and the world was at my feet. This doesn't make things any better, but the realization smoulders uncomfortably in my stomach as I start my cross-examination.

'Mr Hunter, you have told this court that you were able to recognize the twenty chickens that you saw in my client's yard as your own. Is that not correct?' A rumble of affirmation. Good to start the witness off with a nice easy one that gets him into the habit of agreeing with you. 'And you then called the constable? Could you tell the court how you described that which you claim to be your property to Constable . . .' I reach down and consult my papers, '. . . to Constable Blaydon?'

'I can't recall what I said, sir. I just showed him my chickens.'

'Exactly, you showed him chickens. Were you able to point to any feature of these chickens that marked them as your own?'

'I don't understand what you mean, sir.'

Got him! As soon as any witness tells you he can't understand the sort of simple question that could be used in an admissions examination at Bedlam, you can be sure that they know what you have in mind but have no answer for it.

'Well, Mr Hunter, it's a simple question but I will try and render it even more comprehensible for your benefit. If you were asked to describe my learned friend Mr Stork, he who prosecutes today, you might say he was a tall man, or that he has a moustache, for example. Can you tell the court what colour the chickens you directed Constable Blaydon's attention to were?'

'Brown.'

'They were brown, you say. What breed were they?'

'Bantams.'

'Would you agree that there are a great number of brown chickens?'

'They were my chickens. I should know my own livestock.'

'Indeed you should. I am not asking you about what you should know, but what you did know. Are not all bantams brown?'

'Yes.'

'Would it be fair to say that you pointed out these chickens because they were brown, a common colour for their species?'

He glared at me, and I smiled back at him. 'You choose not to answer? Perhaps you need me to put the question more simply again? Very well, did any of the chickens that you claim to be your property wear a moustache?'

'No.'

'Was any animal possessed of plumage of a colour other than brown?'

'No.'

'Did they cry out to you in recognition?'

'No.'

'I thought not. So you say that these birds are your property because they are brown and for that reason alone, then? A condition that they share with all their brothers and sisters.'

Silence. I look to the jury. One of them smiles at me and I know I have done enough.

'I have no further questions, Your Honour.'

The client is triumphantly acquitted, and after his release from custody hands me my fee with poor grace. I am enjoying a pipe on the court steps as I watch him meander across the square to a tavern. He is accompanied by his two vast, slatternly daughters. I notice his arm around each of them drapes over their shoulders and rests casually upon a breast. I muse that it would be a good thing if drink and the feeling of invincibility that seems to overcome the clients after an acquittal were to combine to produce a murderous rage. Either he should kill his offspring or they him. It would be a good thing for the world at large to be deprived of one or all of the Sturrock clan. Most importantly, it would be a good thing for me. A murder brief would have a refresher. I put this out of my mind. I am Robert Warrens of counsel. I am competent beyond my workload, and I make do. I get by. I subsist upon the chaff of criminality like some monstrous crab, combing the effluent for my sustenance. I am adapted to feed from the bottom and I make the best of it. As I walk back to my chambers every step feels as if I am walking to the gallows. The guinea weighs my pocket down and I fancy it marks me out as clearly as a leper's bell. Here walks Warrens, the one-guinea brief. It was not always like this.

I loathe this town. I have spent the last ten years here and I can feel its provincial ways settling around my shoulders like a shroud. It will be my coffin soon enough. It is always cold, and yet the natives act as if it is a land of eternal summer. I pull my coat about me defiantly, as I feel that as soon as I cease to fear the elements I will have become one of them. I do not wish this to happen, yet I have been here so long I have stopped dreaming of escape. I have no one to blame for my exile, not even myself. This makes things worse.

When I first arrived from London I raged against my situation and cast about me to find a culprit. This gave me a purpose that I lack now. In fact, a combination of circumstances brought me here. I came down from Oxford filled with education and ambition. My father was a financier, but I did not wish to follow his profession. I went to chambers in Lincoln's Inn where I briefly enjoyed the reputation of being a rising star. I kept apartments in Berkeley Square, and lived on my fees (which were increasing but not nearly sufficient to convey the impression that I was determined to make) and upon money I borrowed on the expectation of my inheritance. This allowed me to keep fashionable company and to secure the hand of Miss Madeline Knightly in engagement if not marriage. She was the daughter of Sir Steven Knightly KC, the head of my chambers. I had ambition then. Ambition and expectation. How those words ring to me now with the hollow booming of a lighthouse bell.

I have precious few expectations now, and little ambition beyond my next one-guinea brief and bottle of claret. I had precious few expectations then, had I but known the truth. My father specialized in high-risk investments. These brought him what seemed at the time to be unassailable wealth and privilege. His final venture was to invest everything in a trading company. Had this been successful, he planned to buy himself a peerage. Unfortunately, the laws that Mr Newton established governing the behaviour of falling apples also applied to stock, or at least to the stock upon which rested the hopes of ennoblement of the line of Warrens. The stock fell, and so did I. My father did not tarry to see the effects of his decisions. He drank a bottle of brandy and blew the back of his head all over a rather fine Chippendale chair with a pearl-handled pistol. The pistol, the chair and any other property of value were seized by bailiffs and sold to satisfy my father's debts. His wig was deemed too damaged by his passing to be worth their consideration.

Deprived of my expectations, I was unable to borrow and my creditors acquired a steely lack of forbearance that was quite unlike the avuncular tolerance to which I had become habituated. I found myself in lodgings at Newgate, incarcerated as a debtor. My older sister had married well. Her husband was a duke's son and she prevailed upon him to procure my release. When I returned to chambers I found the doors barred against me. Madeline would not receive me. I could find no other position at the London Bar. Wherever I went I could feel eyes upon me and hear the whispers of 'Warrens the bankrupt'. I fled and I found myself here. I bought myself a place in chambers with the £100 that my brother-in-law had given me on condition that I never return. Once I spat bile at the thought of his condescension and vowed to make him eat his words. Now, well, I make the best of it.

I run up the steps, hoping to convey that I walk from court through choice and not because I cannot afford to maintain a carriage. My young clerk, Spicknell, greets me with a smile that stops just short of a sneer. I pretend not to notice, and ask in false good cheer whether any brief has been sent for my consideration.

'Yes, sir.'

'And what has the client done this time?'

'Espionage.'

I manage to exert enough control to prevent myself asking

whether he has made a mistake and given me a brief that was intended for someone else. But only just. The room seems to lurch and I perceive its beauty for the first time. I see the contrast between the dun-coloured books and the whitewashed walls. I admire the elegance of motes of dust as they dance in a shaft of sunlight. I am reborn. This is no one-guinea brief. This is redemption wrapped in a pink ribbon. I become aware of my clerk addressing me.

'Are you all right, Mr Warrens?'

I shake my head as if I am clearing it, but in truth I have never seen the world with greater clarity. 'Yes, thank you, Spicknell. I am quite well. Have the papers taken to my room.'

'There's more, sir. There is a letter from Mr Justice Cooper that accompanied the brief.'

This does not bode well. I know this judge. His belief in the inadequacy of prosecutors leads him to intervene in proceedings with such savagery that I have often seen his name on the court list and decided that I would be better off packing up my wig and going home. Legend has it that he imprisoned a court usher for nine years by an accident that was predicated by his fondness for brandy during the luncheon adjournment. He would not accept his mistake, reasoning that he embodied the law and was incapable of error in this capacity. I grab this judicial missive from my clerk's outstretched hand and retreat into the relative security of my room. It is only after I have fortified myself with a glass of port and regained my composure that I break the seal.

My Dear Warrens,

I have heard of your stalwart and rigorous defence in the matter of Rex-v-Smithyman from my brother Judge

Summers. This, along with my own experience of the pleasure of having you appear before me on so many occasions in the past, made your name the first that came to my mind in connection with the delicate matter upon which I have sent you the brief under cover of this letter. I hope that you are in the best of health and that your busy practice allows you the leisure of accepting these instructions.

I pause. Cooper is not a judge who is known for his wit. Even those who still remember him at the Bar recall him being a bludgeon and not a rapier. Yet, 'your busy practice'? It has the flavour of a mockery so subtle that, were it not for the seal and the source, I might be led to question its authenticity.

As all Englishmen know, our precious liberty and traditions are assailed on all sides. The turmoil across the Channel has found admirers and would-be emulators here. I have heard the sedition of the corresponding societies has even infected the Jolly Tars of the Royal Navy. As this cancer grows within, it is exploited and nurtured by the King's enemies in Paris. The traitor plots our downfall, and is assisted in his perfidy by the spy. If men of good favour do not act expeditiously, then all we hold to be our birthright will be swept away to be replaced by anarchy, terror and a lack of proper respect for those whom God has smiled upon and, in his infinite wisdom, placed above the herd. For some such as I, the role in this conflict is clear. I am a judge and I will do my duty with a terrible wrath upon those of this ilk who have the misfortune to appear before me.

I cannot help but smile at this. 'Of this ilk'? And anyone else who has that misfortune regardless of ilk, no doubt.

Others' duty lies along less well-travelled pathways. Your duty as a defender of felons is to ensure that, regardless of the opprobrium that their crimes bring upon them in most people's eyes, your own natural revulsion and the strength of the evidence against them, the fair trial that is the fountainhead of English Justice is seen to take place. You play your part, Warrens, and the court is grateful for it.

The case of an enemy agent has been allocated to my court. I find that the man is without representation. His paymasters in Paris seem to have washed their hands of him. Well, as the Sadducees and Pharisees pass on the other pavement, it falls to the Samaritans of the English judiciary to ensure that this wretch receives the assistance that no doubt his savage and bestial contemporaries have denied to so many others. Let no man in Europe say that all are not equal before the majesty of the law. The brief contains the papers that are necessary for his defence. I would urge you to accept these instructions. I am concerned that there is no report of a confession and, turning to the depositions of the arresting constables, it seems that this man may be trying to lay down the foundations of some form of defence. No doubt he will draw upon the native dishonesty and subtlety of the races that favour the grape over the grain to escape his fate.

A fund has been established to remunerate those who ensure that our own system is not debased by the necessity of dealing with the enemies of all that we hold dear. You will find that the brief is marked at twenty guineas, with two guineas daily as a refresher. I hope that you will be able to accept the inadequacy of this remuneration. If you do not feel yourself able to overcome what could only be described as a comprehensible disgust for this client, do not hesitate to return these papers, safe in the knowledge that by doing so you do not invite our displeasure. I will bear no malice and will be merely disappointed that the brief must pass to a less worthy recipient.

The prisoner is incarcerated in the gaol at Hartlepool. If you are able to accept these instructions pray send word with your clerk and attend before me at the arraignment three days hence.

Yours sincerely

Cooper J

I am disconcerted. Everything about this letter rings false. It is clearly from Mr Justice Cooper, yet why is it addressed to me? What are the client's 'foundations of a defence'? I pick up the brief and study it, paying particular attention to the endorsement. There is no doubt about the fee, and in my circumstances I cannot afford to refuse. I am sure that the judge is aware of this, despite his protestations about my vaunted abilities and his hitherto undetectable regard for the role of the defence. I put my suspicions to one side and concentrate, as ever, upon the fee. Twenty guineas and two a day as a refresher. The letter seems to hint at more of the same to come as well. I will accept. I call Spicknell to my room and send him with my reply. He is instructed to procure me a carriage on his return. In the meantime I read the papers. These consist of the depositions of two parish constables sworn some three days ago. I have read many depositions. These are no exception to the rule that a constable's evidence will be consistent with that of his fellows. The two in my brief are identical to each inkblot.

This is the deposition of Charles Crooks, Sergeant of constabulary of the parish of Hartlepool, taken this day March the 19th 1795. I Charles Crooks do make oath and say as follows:

I was called to muster in the early hours of the 18th March. In truth I was not asleep as every man in the town was woken by the sound of the report. As I walked to the watchtower I could see fire on the horizon. I knew that a great ship was aflame and the explosion was the fire reaching her magazine.

I met my colleague, Constable Roger Bacon, and we agreed to make haste to the shore in order that we could commandeer all flotsam we could carry for the Crown. As we reached the shoreline I could see that every man in the parish shared our zeal and had assembled to do their patriotic duty. The wind blew great waves across the headland, and the spray and cold chilled all present to the marrow. Our patience and steadfastness were rewarded when I observed the wreckage being washed upon the beach. There was an unseemly stampede to the shore which Constable Bacon and myself were forced to contain using our cudgels. Fortunately, the militia cavalry arrived in strength at this point and together we were able to hold back the crowd and ensure that Crown property was not taken.

We noticed with sorrow that all the timbers washed ashore

were charred in a manner that suggested their exposure to a furious flame. This led us to believe that the treasury would be deprived of the revenue that would have been generated by the sale of the spirits and wine for which the wrecks of French shipping are justifiably famed.

I have to acknowledge the constable's professionalism. It's not merely a question of lying. Any fool can lie, and in my experience they frequently do. The beauty of this man's dishonesty is that he knows precisely the right lie to tell in the circumstances. I can almost hear the clink of glass from his greatcoat pocket as he raises his hand to take the oath. Had he not found his vocation he would have made an admirable client.

We resolved to marshal all the valuable items into a pile to facilitate their recovery. The assembled people became enraged at our appropriation of what they seemed to think was theirs to treat as their own. I became concerned for my colleague's safety as well as my own, and called the militia to form a firing line. I ordered the mob to disperse, but they declined to do so. We fired a volley of shots above their heads. One man hurled himself into the path of our bullets. He was clearly the worse for strong drink. He fell and the mob fled, voicing seditious chants.

There was a great deal of flotsam still washing up, making it impracticable to remove it all to safety. We stayed on the beach all night to prevent theft and damage to His Majesty's property. We divided ourselves into watches. I was woken as day was breaking and my attention was drawn to something swimming through the waves. It had the shape of a man but dived back into the deep repeatedly with supernatural strength and vigour. We hailed it, and when it did not respond, loosed a volley of shots. The creature became aware of our presence and ran from the sea towards the dunes. We followed.

The pursuit was a perilous one. The fugitive moved across the dunes with the speed of ten, leaping from peak to peak. Our horses could barely keep pace. We reached the outskirts of the town. As the eaves of the buildings closed upon us, our quarry gave a mighty leap. His hands fell upon the pole hung outside a barber's shop. As the sign bore his weight, it fell from the wall, depositing him waist deep in the cargo of a nightsoilman's wagon. He was incapacitated.

Unfortunately, our dedication to the task of apprehending the suspect left us both blind to the safety of others and, more importantly, ourselves. I attempted to rein in my horse. As soon as Bacon noticed the danger, he did the same. Our focus upon the chase had made us both oblivious to the proximity of a crowd of onlookers who had assembled around the figure held in the cart. We both ploughed into the press of bodies at speed. They threw themselves in front of the horses. Strong drink had made them unable to judge the angle of our approach. Minor incidents of trampling made our mounts slip. Constable Bacon and I were thrown clear, landing in the same wagon as the fugitive. After recovering our footing, we waded towards the suspect and made our arrest.

We observed the creature we had apprehended. My observation was that it was wearing the uniform of an officer in the enemy's navy. It was hirsute in the extreme. Its eyes were a liquid brown. Its brow was low and it displayed its teeth in defiance of the King's authority.

We pulled our captive from the filth. It smiled and performed a number of feats of acrobatics no mere man could equal. It begged for food. I observed it. Constable Bacon displayed his youth and credulity. He turned to me and enquired whether I shared his opinion that our prisoner was a monkey.

I was less sure. Although our prisoner was a short, hairy character my scrutiny revealed nothing that I could say precluded him from being French with any certainty. I compared him with the pamphlet that has been circulated showing the various aspects of the enemy. His resemblance to one of the more degraded visages it contained hardened my resolve. I caught his chin, pulled his face to mine and looked into his eyes. I thought I detected a glimpse of criminal cunning. Yet he continued to caper before the crowd, hanging by his feet from a tavern sign. His antics left me in some doubt. Not wishing to bring the name of the constabulary into ridicule by arresting a monkey, I decided to interrogate him.

I resolved to waste no time by taking him to the Bridewell. I was determined that my interrogation should follow the practice of the constabulary. I caused the prisoner to be bound hand and foot. He resisted with the strength of ten. Constable Bacon was thrown to the floor and bitten sorely upon the upper thigh before the prisoner was subdued with stout cudgel blows. I bound him with hemp twine. A brazier was dragged into the road. I pressed our captive into its side and demanded that he yield to the King's authority and reveal his identity. He screamed and chattered at a furious pace. Bacon and others in the crowd swore that he spoke in French and was hurling brickbats and defiances in the face of my questioning. The remainder of the mob retorted with cries that any but fools would know that the captive was a mere beast. The debate turned to dispute. Oaths and then blows were exchanged. The King's peace was in jeopardy. As I drew my pistol, the heat of the coals caused the twine binding the prisoner to part. He sprang past me with more than natural speed.

At this very moment the crowd parted. A carriage passed through the struggling mob. It paused as its rear wheel passed across a rioter's body. The prisoner saw his chance. He sprang on to the roof and felled the coachman with a single blow. As he made to seize the reins, a man emerged from within and pointed a brace of pistols full into the fugitive's face. He said something I could not overhear. As the latter turned to press his escape, the stranger struck him across the crown with his pistol butt. He fell, unconscious.

The stranger manacled the prisoner and handed the chain to me. He spoke:

'Take your prisoner to the Bridewell. Guard him with your life. He is a most cunning and dangerous enemy spy.'

The stranger was a tall man. He was well dressed and spoke with the authority that only good breeding brings. I asked who he was. He damned my eyes for my impudence.

'There is no time for this, Sergeant. If this captive escapes, you will hang in his place.'

I took the chain.

Bacon and I took our prisoner to the Bridewell. The

225

following morning we brought him before the Justices, where this deposition was taken.'

I feel dread seep into the pit of my stomach. It is so cold that port cannot warm it. Am I being asked to participate in some form of judicial sport, or is someone taking their sport at my expense? I check the seal again. It is undoubtedly genuine. I have passed the point at which I viewed myself as important enough to be the victim of conspiracy. Clearly, the judge feels that the client is trying to feign madness to escape the gallows. Well, if he is then good luck to him. If he does so well enough, then he may have a defence and I may be able to string the case out to a full trial at two guineas a day refresher. There's no such thing as a truthful client. They separate into those whose fictions can be made into plausible defences and the rest. I cannot believe that the idea that this man is not human can possibly be maintained and begin to drag my thoughts along the lines of pleading his lunacy, which will save him from a date with Jack Ketch but consign him to the Bedlam.

Spicknell interrupts my reverie. He has borrowed a coach and we must leave post-haste. As I descend the stair, I catch sight of the coachman. His face is buried in a pamphlet. I despise the press, and pamphleteers in particular. My youthful appearance in the *London Gazette* with its accompanying details of my bankruptcy still makes my face burn. This example has a picture of a brutish and simian Frenchman dragging a half-naked girl towards a guillotine on its cover, which seems somehow apposite. My clerk has decided to accompany me and for once I am glad of the company. Coach journeys bore me.

'Can you tell me what is in the papers, sir?'

I am surprised by the intensity of his curiosity. He has never shown the slightest inclination to question me about the nature of my cases before. But then, with reflection, I have not had a case that amounted to more than five minutes of dilatory conversation while he has been my clerk. I reprise the contents of the depositions for his benefit. He regards me with an expression that I struggle to place. I am forced to conclude he is being respectful.

'Sir.'

'Spicknell?'

'If the client's a monkey, how can he be a spy?'

'That would be so were our client to be a monkey. But that is a matter of evidence of which I remain to be satisfied. The criminal mind and its ingenuity never fails to amaze those who study it. What cunning and intelligence can be concealed behind the overhanging brow of the felon! Why, before you came to my service I had the misfortune to represent a man charged before the assize court with the theft of undergarments from a lady of good standing. The fellow professed lunacy. He repeatedly implored me to obtain face paints and hosiery for him to wear at his trial. A hulking, bearded man, he refused to answer to any name other than Mary. During our numerous conferences he spoke to me in a piping voice and smiled coquettishly at me from behind a fan made of pigeon feathers and string. He sought, you see, to avoid hanging for theft by this masquerade. Fortunately he did as he was advised and pleaded guilty. I was able to persuade them that the garments in question were beneath the capital threshold, so he was transported. When I last heard of him he was the foremost milliner in Botany Bay.'

'Will he hang, then, our client?'

'Without doubt.'

'Even if he is a monkey?'

'He's no more a monkey than I, Spicknell. If he is resolved upon this course, then we must attempt to persuade the court that he is a lunatic. If we are successful, the client will be confined in places that will make the gallows seem an appealing option.'

Our conversation flags as we draw into Hartlepool. I have always liked the smell of the sea. When I was a child my family would take a yearly holiday to our house in Broadstairs. The scent of tar and brine brings back memories of digging in the sand with my sister, when every morning held the promise of another day. I smile as I inhale, hoping that Spicknell will not pass any remark to spoil my mood. We pass through the market square and out towards the cliff top. I smell the gaol before I see it. It brings memories of Newgate, which I had hoped to bury, flooding to the forefront of my mind. The blend of urine, sweat and cabbage that is the aroma of incarceration fills my nostrils and I am unable to suppress a tremor.

The prison is not an imposing one, housing at most a hundred inmates. Its main gate is relatively modest in size, so I am able to raise a most satisfying booming as I rap upon it with my cane. A turnkey in a dirty coat answers. He has the air of a man for whom civility is an imposition.

'Yes?'

'My name is Warrens, Mr Robert Warrens of counsel. I am charged by the court to defend the Frenchman whom you have incarcerated here. I will see my client.'

The gaoler pauses. I can see the conflict between deference to my well-bred tones and the conceit of his own authority play across his face. Finally, he thrusts out a hand. 'Papers.'

I have none. I am not disposed to confess this and render the tedious discomfort of my coach journey redundant. I have a shrewd suspicion that the man is illiterate. I thrust my hand into my jacket and withdraw the order I had intended to hand to my wine merchant to celebrate my latest fee. He takes it, scrutinizing it with narrowed eyes. He returns it with a grunt that signifies his satisfaction.

'Who is the other gentleman?'

'Richard Spicknell. My clerk. He has come in the capacity of my scribe. Make haste now, my good man, I have little inclination to expend the day explaining my profession to you.'

The gaoler steps back, allowing the door to swing open, and we pass out of life and into a place of incarceration. The main building lours across a courtyard, its barred windows surveying those permitted the petty freedom of walking under the sky. I can feel a hundred resentful eyes as I start my promenade across the open space with Spicknell at my shoulder. I cannot help but square my shoulders and give my gait a military air to bear their weight. I have been here before, and set my feet upon the path to the low building to the side of the courtyard in which members of my profession are permitted to meet their clients. I have almost reached its door when I become aware of our escort's absence. I turn to see him standing at the gate regarding me with an insolent amusement. I shout to him to hurry. His smile causes a quickly suppressed impulse to strike him. He beckons and we return, all the while conscious that we have somehow been diminished before our silent audience.

'You are not permitted to see this prisoner in the usual place, sir. Governor's orders.'

'Where then? I take it that you do not have the temerity to refuse me an audience at all.'

'Follow me, sirs. I will take you to him.'

We start our journey anew and enter the main building. The stench is almost as overpowering as the memories it kindles. It takes all my reserves of control to enter the half-light. I remind myself that I am here as Warrens the advocate, a message that I repeat with each step. It soothes me like a rosary but cannot quite drown out the sounds of the gaol, which rise like a flood. Shouts, groans, fragments of conversation, snatches of song, stories of missed opportunities, poor choices, bad investments and betrayed loves lose themselves in each other and combine into a crescendo. It is the gaol's symphony, a song of innocent suffering and penance deserved. You can detect among its roar the cadences of hope unbidden, blackened and abandoned among the filthy rushes on the debtors' floor. It has its equivalent at every prison, and its sister at every madhouse. I have heard it at Newgate, where my own voice swelled the choir. I feel its rhythm as it shakes the bare flagstones beneath my feet with the slamming of heavy doors and the rattle of bars.

I become conscious of a halt in our progress. We stand before a thick door that is remarkable for the absence of a spy-hole. We have reached our destination. It is only when the door opens that I realize the indignity. I wheel upon our escort, and find that my anger has freed me from the mire. I can hear my voice, strong and harsh, and I am not afraid. I feel light, brittle and hard. I am the Angel of Justice and they will fear my wrath. I greet this emotion like a lost dog.

'This is the condemned cell, is it not?'

The gaoler realizes that he can rely upon the ambience of incarceration to deaden the blow no longer. His insolence deflates like a bladder at a privy.

'It's the Governor's express order, sir. I have no choice. Your client is a very dangerous man, sir. He is housed here to prevent escape.'

He cringes and I notice that I have raised my hand to him. Fury is my regeneration. I lower my hand to my side and my voice to sibilance. 'My client has yet to face a court. He has yet to be arraigned and you, you dare to house him in the condemned cell? Do not dare to protest to me that you follow your orders, sir. I am all too aware that the likes of you have no conscience to betray. I will see my client, then I will have an audience with your master. He will regret his decision to oust the presumption that a man is innocent until found guilty by jury. Do you understand me?'

The gaoler nods furiously.

'Unfasten the cell door and leave me. I will see your master at my leisure and not his.'

We are in. The room is vaulted. The only light comes from a grille far above us. A watery shaft descends to pick out a crude table and two chairs. The client is at his repose. I can make out his form on a pile of rushes in the far corner. The scorch marks of his interrogation are visible upon his uniform greatcoat. I feel an unwelcome surge of empathy. 'There but for the grace of God ...' I suppress my humanity and become a lawyer. The client shows no sign of being aware of our presence. I strain my eyes against the gloom. His breathing is not consistent with sleep. Very well, then. I have encountered difficult clients before. I station Spicknell at the door, sit at the table and open the brief. I spread the papers before me, picking up a document. I scrutinize it.

'Pray take a seat opposite me, sir. I am Warrens, your counsel. We have much work to do if I am to save you from the gibbet. I need your instructions to prepare your case for your arraignment.'

There is no response. I continue my perusal in a manner that I hope conveys my cynical indifference to his play-acting. I have just re-read the constable's deposition when Spicknell breaks the silence.

'Take a look at this, sir.'

'I have no intention of looking at the client until he conducts himself in a civilized manner.'

'But Mr Warrens . . .'

I steal a glance from under my wig. The client has taken his place opposite me. His manner is somewhat unconventional. He stands upon the seat with his arms hanging loosely by his sides. I am forced to concede that his appearance is somewhat simian. This troubles me slightly. I recall the judge's letter. I am determined not to be fooled.

'Good. I have roused you. Perhaps you could use the furniture in the way it was intended and we can make some progress?'

A low hooting follows. I return to the papers.

Spicknell coughs. 'You should look up, sir.'

'Spicknell, I have no intention of watching this pantomime. If I want to see a man pretend to be a monkey I will attend a carnival. As soon as the client has the courtesy to desist his idiocy and introduce himself like a civilized man, then he will have my undivided attention. Until then, I will occupy my time as profitably as circumstances permit.'

I return to the papers. I read the letter again and take comfort in its certainty.

'Sir. Mr Warrens.'

'Spicknell, I hesitate to be brusque but find myself in a place where your constant interruptions place me contiguous to impatience. Will you be silent? I am trying to work.'

There is a crack in the boy's voice. 'Look out, sir.'

I raise my head at the warning in time to receive what my senses confirm is a handful of faeces full in the face. It penetrates my eyes, mouth and nose. I am blinded by disgust.

'He's filling his hand again, sir.'

The client's whoops and shrieks ring in my ears as I rise. I stumble towards the door, Spicknell's guiding hand upon my sleeve. I turn in the aperture. My final view of the client is of him catching his excreta in one hand while investigating the contents of his chest hair with the other. He bares his teeth and I slam the door in my wake. I hear the soft impact of his missile against it as I stumble towards the corridor, desperately wiping my eyes. My vision clears sufficiently for me to discern a portly man with shiny buttons on his coat as we surface into the harsh daylight of the courtyard, blinking like foetuses. He seems to be waiting for us.

'Who the Hell is that?'

'It's the Governor, sir.'

'What the Hell does he want?'

'You asked to see him, sir.'

'For Christ's sake, Spicknell, get rid of him. I can't speak to anyone now. I'm covered in shit.'

I sweep past him and into the comforting confinement of our carriage. I am oblivious to the early part of our journey, which I spend cleaning my wig.

'Turns out he is a monkey after all, sir.'

There is nothing more irritating than accuracy in a subordinate.

'I know that, Spicknell. You may even say it was written all over my face earlier. It's certainly ruined my best kerchief.'

233

'So what are you going to do?'

'I shall defend this client to the best of my ability. You may not be familiar with this, Spicknell, but monkeys don't attract liability under the criminal law.'

'I did hear it mentioned, sir.'

16

Arraignment and Incarceration

I HAVE RESOLVED TO ARRIVE EARLY AT COURT, ALTHOUGH MY case will not be heard until the afternoon. This is somewhat of a departure, as I am notoriously tardy in my affairs. I have taken this decision to symbolize my renaissance, but as I walk to the court I feel my determination crumble like an overripe cheese. There is no building more likely to engender melancholy than this. The rational man within me, such as emerges when I sit before my fire, port in hand and *The Wealth of Nations* before me, ascribes the moisture that appears upon its walls during cold weather to the fact that it was constructed upon land reclaimed from a salt marsh. It is hard to remain rational here. I regard the rivulets coursing down the plaster in the robing room and fancy them to be the tears of those who have come here searching for justice and found only the law. If these walls could talk, their histories would have few happy endings.

I pull on my gown and descend. The hall outside the courtroom is filled with those awaiting Mr Justice Cooper's favour. There are my fellows, filled with self-regard and swapping anecdotes that seek only to illuminate their own eloquence. There are my opponents, quiet in the confidence that they will be deciding the fate of lesser men in an atmosphere that will not require such niceties as evidence. Finally, there are those who are excluded from the companionability of profession. The witnesses show me straws in their boots and promise me testimony that can only assist my cause for a modest consideration. I recognize most of them, which indicates that their stock has fallen. The rest, the associates of those who wait in the wings of justice behind barred doors, huddle together under a fug of tobacco smoke and the sweated fumes of past indulgence. I cannot bring myself to converse. I intend to secrete myself in court. I shall rehearse my submissions for the afternoon's hearing in this relative tranquillity.

The door opens and the clerk calls the list. I take my place in the queue to book in. The judge's clerk is a man with a hollow, desiccated face. His sallow skin is a delta of broken capillaries that speaks most eloquently of his fondness for drink. As I wind my way towards him, I am assailed by the stench of curdled milk that hangs about him like a cloak. My distaste rises behind my tonsils and I swallow as he bares lichen teeth at me in what I can only assume he believes to be a welcoming smile.

'Mr Warrens. What a delight it is to see you here so early.'

I grunt. This merits no response.

'Who prosecutes me today?'

'Why Mr Fawsley, sir. We do not expect him until the afternoon.'

The news does not please me at all. I know the man by

reputation. Needless to say, prosecutors of his illustrious pedigree are rarely found at the one-guinea trials that were my meat and drink until three days ago. The highest of high Tories, he sits in the Lower House as Member for the constituency of Cromer East, a borough so utterly rotten that it has been under the waters of the North Sea since Cromwell's Bare Bones Parliament. He rides to hounds, shoots most things that show the poor judgement to fly or run before the line of his fire, votes with the government whip and opposes the emancipation of Romanists and the abolition of slavery with the same relentless brutality with which he is reputed to demolish witnesses. Always for the Crown, loyal and savage as a guard dog, he is a thoroughgoing creature of the state. Still, I have found that the desire to avoid humiliation strikes those at the summit more sharply than the rest of us. I am convinced that no one would wish to destroy such a carefully cultivated reputation by entering the annals of history as the man who took a monkey to trial for espionage. I settle into my chair and lose myself in my thoughts as the business of the court commences around me.

A sharp rap upon the door causes the assembled multitude to clamber to their feet with varying degrees of respect and deference. Mr Justice Cooper enters the court, rubbing his hands with the air of a man about to embark upon an arduous yet pleasant physical task. He is a small man, who holds himself so erect he seems to be leaning backwards. He takes his seat and beams around him amiably.

'Good morning. Who is the first case?'

'Arthur Pring, My Lord. Mr Dickson defends.'

'And the charge?'

'Theft, My Lord. Of lead from the roof of a manufactory.'

The judge's mouth contracts to a sphincter of disapproval. He glares across the court to the dock, his bonhomie a distant memory. I raise my eyes from my papers and look at Dickson. I have never been able to decide whether I find Dickson objectionable because he is a sycophant or because this trait seems to have brought him success far greater than my own. I flatter myself by assuming it is the former. He excretes his exaggerated respect for the court from every pore.

'My Lord, if I may indicate that this will be a plea of guilty and ask for the matter to be put.'

The judge smiles with the anticipation of a man waiting for his hors d'oeuvres. The charge is put and the luckless Pring enters his plea. Cooper turns to Dickson.

'Now, Mr Dickson, what have you to say in mitigation?'

'Simply this, My Lord. You will have regard to my client's antecedents and will be aware that he is a twenty-seven-year-old man of hitherto good character. His offence is one that comes not from a background of criminality but as a response to recent destitution. He is a skilled man, a handloom weaver. He has recently found his trade in less demand as a result of the very manufactory that was the victim of his depredations. His spouse has passed away, leaving him solely responsible for their eleven children. He took the lead from the roof with a view to reselling it and providing his offspring with sustenance. You may feel, My Lord, that his unwillingness to burden the Parish with his responsibilities stands to his credit. It is a limited credit, I confess. He has nothing other than his family and his plea to fall back upon. I would ask that this court show him the mercy and compassion for which it is widely famed. You could deprive him of his life, or his liberty. I ask you to consider doing the latter. I implore you to keep his period of incarceration to a minimum. Allow him to reflect upon his actions, to suffer his incarceration and to return to his family a chastened man.'

I can barely stop myself laughing out loud. I cannot believe that he is appealing to, what did he call it, Cooper's 'mercy and compassion'. He might as well call upon his sense of fairness. The worst of it is that there is nothing that he could have said that would have altered the outcome by one iota. This realization casts me back into the gloom and I reflect bitterly upon the pointlessness of my profession. Meanwhile, the judge is conducting an onanistic version of the Socratic dialogue. It is an unedifying spectacle that is clearly contrived to show the world the agony that performing a vital public duty brings to a man of such obvious sensitivity. His eyes are shut and he rocks backwards and forwards, speaking in a stage whisper. I cannot help but listen, although it makes me want to vomit.

'I'd like to believe him, but look. His face is familiar. Even if he hasn't been before me in the past, the fact that I almost recognize him suggests that he comes from the criminal classes. Yet all those children. Left without a mother and now, to be deprived of a father. It makes me want to weep, but what can I do? I must be firm. I must be strong.'

He opens his eyes and I notice that the dreamlike indulgence that consumed his countenance has vanished. His eyes are red and as unsympathetic as virtue.

'Stand up, Pring. I am told about your reduced circumstances and your children. I am urged to take this into account and show you mercy. I am only too aware that your story is not an original one. There are all too many persons whom one sees about the town in similar straits. They seem in good health but have no work. If I were to accept the argument that hunger is an excuse for theft, or even mitigated the consequences of dishonesty, then I would open the floodgates to the idea that private property should not be protected against the poor. We can all turn our faces to France and see where that road will bring us. Indeed, there are numerous paupers who do not appear before the courts, even though their circumstances do not differ from yours. It is not your poverty that makes you a thief, but your dishonesty. This deserves punishment. If I were to allow you your freedom I would be sending out a message that it is permissible to steal from manufactories. This, in turn, would lead to an increase in prices as the manufacturers pass on their loss to their customers. That would create more paupers and, if your logic is followed, more thieves. It would also make victims of the honest investors who would see scant return for their risk. No, my duty is clear. I will temper my judgement with mercy and allow you your life. Twelve years. Take him down.'

There is something comforting about predictability, even if it simply confirms that that which you regarded as distasteful remains every bit as bad as you expected. I return to my papers and erect a barrier between my labours and the business of the court. I cannot entirely exclude the judge's voice, which booms malevolently in the background.

'Nine years.'

'Death by hanging.'

'Twenty years.'

'Transportation.'

'Take him down.'

'Take him down.'

'Take him down.'

I look up as a sharp injunction from the clerk calls us all to our feet to mark the judge's departure. I take in the scene and notice to my distaste that the learned Mr Justice Cooper shines pinkly through his perspiration. He leaves replete with satisfaction at his work. I cannot remain in court. The unfortunate necessity of spending my last fee on hiring the carriage means that I cannot afford refreshment. I will go to the Bar mess and seek out Fawsley. I am hopeful that I can negotiate the speedy demise of this case without the need to trouble the judge for a decision. If I am fortunate, he may even buy me luncheon.

The Bar mess is predictably empty. Cooper has executed, incarcerated and transported his way through the best part of the daily list in a morning. My learned friends have all fled back to their chambers to lick their wounds and rewrite the day's events in a more palatable style. There is a fire in the grate at the end of the long room, and I can see smoke rising above the parapet of a large winged chair stationed in front of it. My forensic skill leads me to the conclusion that its occupant must be none other than my opponent. I approach, stamping slightly to herald my arrival. I have no desire to take a man with Fawsley's reputation by surprise.

There is no response, and I find myself loitering behind the chair not really knowing what to do next. I cough, more to hide my embarrassment than to attract his attention. This prompts a reply. 'Put the port down on the table and get out of my light, there's a good fellow.' I can feel my face burning. My lips pull themselves around my teeth like a drawstring. I have been mistaken for a servant.

'I am not your servant, my good fellow. I am your opponent. I had hoped that we might occupy a few moments discussing our respective positions before the case is heard. I see, sir, that your luncheon seemingly takes precedence over your duty.'

I am about to turn on my heel when Fawsley deigns to speak to me. Faced with an honour like this, what can I do but remain?

'Ah, Williams.'

'It's Warrens, actually.'

'Warrens, then. What do you want to discuss? I have read the papers and it's a straightforward matter. Your client has no safe conduct, no passport and no parole. He sought to evade capture. He has no business here and is clearly, if not French himself, then in the pay of the enemy. In short, he is a spy. If you have come to try to arrange a basis of plea that puts his conduct in a more favourable light, then I'll do you the courtesy of listening to what you have to say before I reject it. There will be no horse-trading. The Crown has all the evidence needed to send your client to the gallows.'

I cannot repress a smile. 'That would be so were you to be in the happy position of having a defendant whose characteristics render him subject to prosecution.'

'You're not seriously suggesting that your client is a lunatic, are you?'

'Not a lunatic. No. Certainly not. It's far worse than that. My client – if that term doesn't confer more dignity upon him than he deserves – my client is not human.'

'Well, I can't argue with your beliefs, Warrens. In fact I share them. The bloody French have never struck me as being from the same stock as us, although I have met some of them who could pass for human in poor light. Can't say that sort of thing in court, though, can we?'

'I mean it, Fawsley. I tell you that the client is neither French nor a spy. In fact, were you to need to find a metier for him, his character suits him more to working with the operator of a barrel organ than espionage. He's a monkey, Fawsley, and as we both know, the escapades of monkeys have no place in the courts.'

Fawsley seems to be having difficulty maintaining his composure. He turns from me for a moment before fixing me with a smile that has all the warmth of the sun glinting off the faceplate of a coffin.

'I recall something to that effect in the papers, yes. I am surprised that a member of the Bar has fallen into the same pit that trapped two constables of the parish of Hartlepool. I had expected that the walls of ignorance that confined them would be relatively simple for a man of even limited education to climb. Clearly I was mistaken. Now, Warrens, I would advise you to listen very closely. My advice usually costs in excess of five guineas but I will cater to you *pro bono publico*, as they say. Your client is no more a monkey than you are. If you want to trespass upon this judge's notoriously short supply of good nature, then that is a matter for you. Your no doubt extraordinary eloquence is woefully insufficient to persuade me to join you in the Bedlam.'

'Yes, yes. That's exactly what I thought when I read the depositions. Come, Fawsley, all I ask of you is that you accompany me to the cells beneath the court and regard him through the spy-hole.'

Fawsley yawns with a theatrical flourish. 'Warrens, that is where you and I differ in our role. I represent the Crown. My client is found in gentlemen's clubs, at the Court of St James and in other agreeable places. You represent the defence. Your clients are found in the cells. If I were to start going into dreadful places and peering through spy-holes, then you would have to start appearing in all sorts of congenial settings to which you are obviously quite unsuited. It would make us both unhappy and benefit neither of us. Furthermore, even if I were to make an exception and look through your spy-hole it would do exactly as its name suggests. It would show me a spy, one I fully intend to prosecute and hang. Good day to you.'

I clutch my dignity to my breast and it flutters like a bird, febrile and arrhythmic. I cannot trust myself to respond without precipitating a duel from which I know I am unlikely to emerge alive. I can feel the pulse hammering at my temple and my eyelid vibrates with tension. I hate this man more than I can possibly express. I will make him eat his words. I want this more than anything. My brother-in-law, the judge, everyone who has ever shown me less consideration than I deserve, I would forgive them all for the chance to deluge micturition upon the Right Honourable Sir Marmaduke Fawsley, KC, MP. I had hoped to carve this case and claim my fee without the necessity of presenting it before the court. I offered him the chance to avoid seeming ridiculous. He rejected it. I hope to see him squirm and regret the day he threw my approach back in my face. I will be a man of stone.

I spend the rest of the adjournment smoking my pipe and trying to forget that I am famished. I pull my gown around me and lope, vulpine, into court, reeking of tobacco and resentment. I cannot bear even to look at my opponent, so I busy myself with my lectern, which is a venerable contraption that requires some technique to erect. I have organized my papers when the clanking and slamming at the back of the court announces the client's production from the cells. I turn and see him in the dock. I am relieved to see he cuts every bit as pitiful and non-human a figure as he did during our conference. I must confess that Fawsley's certainty has the effect of making me doubt my own senses. I realize that I am retreating into the very deference that Fawsley and his kind rely upon, and I am filled with a self-loathing that is only barely outstripped by the antipathy I feel for my opponent. I console myself with the thought that I will bathe when I return to my lodgings. I will bathe, enjoy a glass of wine and wash away the day's humiliations. But first I will win my case.

There are no other cases to occupy the court this afternoon so it is in with the judge and on with the show.

'Has your client had the courtesy to provide the court with a name?'

'I regret not, My Lord. However—' I am cut short.

'I will refer to him as "Pierre", then.'

'If that pleases you, My Lord, then I am sure that my client's capabilities do not extend to objecting.'

'Very good, Mr Warrens. Can your client be arraigned?'

'No, My Lord.'

Every pretence of good humour drains from the room. Cooper peers at me, his eyes narrowed. 'And why not, pray?'

I take a deep breath and remind myself that there is little that the judge can do to me. After all, I am in the hitherto unheard-of situation of being here at his invitation.

'It is a matter of jurisdiction, My Lord. One that I would submit is most appropriately resolved by way of preliminary issue.'

The judge regards me as if I have suggested that we resolve matters by competitively ravishing his daughter. I swallow, realizing that I have gone beyond the point at which the option of discretion is available. I have no choice but to press on.

245

'My Lord, I would invite your attention to my client.' I turn and gesture towards the dock. The client seems oblivious to events and has busied himself with his toilet. I cannot help but admire his flexibility, and I am relieved to note a reassuring lack of humanity in his exploits.

'Regard his hirsute nature, his overhanging forehead and the proportions of his limbs and body. I submit, My Lord, that you can use your experience of life and conclude that the unfortunate creature that stands before you is precisely that: a creature. A beast. An animal. A being more suited to appearing at the circus than in this court. To hold otherwise would be to reduce this court to the status of circus and hold it to ridicule. I invite you to dismiss the charge of espionage and discharge this monkey. I cannot call him the defendant as to do so conveys upon him a dignity that his species simply does not merit.'

I remain standing. I have made my submission and I await any questions from the bench. The judge's silence is somewhat disturbing. I notice he appears to be reading. I cling to the hope that he is researching some point of law that is at least vaguely favourable to my cause. He leans back, raising to his face what I had hoped was at least a book on a subject of marginal relevance to the case and I notice with a shiver of revulsion that it is a pamphlet. I recognize the picture on its cover. It is the simian Frenchman in the cap that had so diverted the coachman prior to my trip to the gaol. The bloody judge has been reading a pamphlet throughout my submission. I warn myself that calm must be maintained. I am stern, but no more so than I feel to be necessary in the circumstances.

'If I can assist you further, My Lord?'

Cooper yawns. 'I do not believe you can, Mr Warrens. What say you, Mr Fawsley?'

'The Crown say that we agree with the defence to this extent alone. If my learned friend's client is a monkey, then the Crown accepts that the court has no jurisdiction to try him. That remains a question that is to be decided. The venue for that decision is the trial and the tribunal given the power to make it is the jury. My learned friend advances a defence to you and asks you effectively to withdraw the prosecution case before the jury have had the chance to decide upon it. I submit that is wrong. The status of the defendant is a matter of evidence. No evidence has been called. The Crown's case remains he is a man and a spy. It is for a jury to decide the truth.'

Cooper beams at my opponent with such tenderness I feel like a voyeur. This does not bode well. 'Quite so, Mr Fawsley. A matter of evidence then, Mr Warrens?'

I am struggling. I can hear a hissing and popping in the background that sounds like spit on a griddle. It is rising in pitch and I experience some detached amazement that no one else has remarked upon it. I press on.

'With respect, My Lord, my learned friend seeks to misdirect you if his case is that you require evidence to decide a matter that is as self-evident as whether night follows day. You can take judicial note of the self-evident. I am not required to advance evidence to prove that rain makes a man wet or that the land stops at the shoreline. These are facts that are so obvious that to require strict proof brings the law into disrepute. I invite you to do no more than look at my client and take judicial note. That is all.'

'Very well, Mr Warrens. I am against you. I find that the

question of whether your client is a monkey is a matter for a jury. I have regard to this publication.'

The judge waves his pamphlet in the air, his finger indicating the lithograph of the simian Frenchman. The whining in my ears turns to a howl. I cannot hear a word this judge is saying. There appears to be some sort of disturbance in the court as I can vaguely discern shouts. I am both appalled and delighted to find that someone is expressing thoughts about this judge that I wholeheartedly share. Clearly I have at least one of the observers on my side. The man must have nerves of steel. He has just called Mr Justice Cooper a buffoon, an ignoramus and a catamite. I resolve that I will embrace him if he survives the day. My supporter accuses the judge of drowning justice in a bucket of piss. He is obviously nearby, but I cannot quite catch sight of him. I turn to thank him when I feel a hand upon my arm, which I shake off in irritation. My assailant is persistent and I find myself undergoing the indignity of a brawl, which, predictably, I lose. It is only after I am restrained that the fury that had occupied my form slips away as quietly as a defaulting tenant. I am appalled to find myself being held by a dock officer. The judge is addressing me. I am alone.

'Mr Warrens. As such a partisan of your client's cause you will no doubt enjoy the opportunity of sharing his lodgings. I am most displeased by your performance today. It is unworthy of a member of the Bar. Nay, it disgraces an Englishman. I hold you in contempt. You may appear before me at my pleasure tomorrow to purge yourself or serve a term in prison in default. Take him down.'

My inability to comprehend my situation spares me the full horror of being chained and placed in the cart. I am aware of jeering, and find myself seated with the client. As the wheels rumble across the cobbles I discern a hitherto invisible spark of humanity in the client's eyes. He leans towards me. He places a hand upon my arm and tells me to be strong. I am certain that this is a hallucination. I must keep this to myself, although at present madness seems a tranquil refuge. I swoon.

17

The Expert Witness

THE JOURNEY FROM COURT PASSES IN A BLUR. IT GIVES the impression of speed, although I am sure it takes over two hours. I am ruined, that seems certain. I have been imprisoned after swearing at a judge. My practice, such as it was, will surely suffer from this if I ever find myself in the happy position of emerging blinking into the light and have a practice at all. None the less, I know I will emerge alive. This is not my first experience of ruin, and while I cannot claim to have conquered adversity in the past, I seem to have discovered a capacity to acclimatize myself to the consequences of humiliation and failure that speaks of a robustness of mind. All is not yet lost. I will have to appear before Cooper tomorrow to purge my contempt. This will involve making the sort of cringing apology that will send my sphincter into spasm. I will eat my humble pie and make do with what crumbs remain in the aftermath.

Cooper will decide my fate. I doubt he will transport me, particularly if I purge myself with the sort of abject defeat that

I strongly suspect he will find irresistibly appealing. I anticipate incarceration. The question is how long I will be detained. The options span immediate release to indefinite detention. I search my mind for precedent, but find none. It all returns to the judge's mood. I resign myself to spending a few years in gaol and console myself with the thought that I could sell my house and use the proceeds to insulate myself from the typhoid and violence that make an already painful experience unbearable for the incarcerated poor. I am Robert Warrens, and if there is one thing I can do it is get by. Send me a bad situation and I will make do to the best of my considerable and as yet untapped abilities.

I learned to ride a horse when I was a small boy. It was the sort of accomplishment that the son of a wealthy man required. My circumstances have not permitted me the luxury of owning one for many years, but I am certain that I would be able to take to the saddle today. Another skill that never leaves is the ability to manage imprisonment with the minimum of inconvenience and discomfort. There is little to choose between Newgate and my current durance vile. I slip into the manner of the prisoner with the distasteful ease of a man putting on soiled clothing. I am presented to the same ill-natured gaoler who escorted me to my first meeting with the client. I establish myself as a gentleman convict by giving him two shillings. This secures private accommodation, a meal and the sort of wine that, were my situation better, would cause me to take a whip to my wine merchant.

Night crystallizes imprisonment. As I wait in the limbo between sleep and wakefulness my mind is stripped of its armour. All the conceits of being able to survive, all the rationalizations about having no great distance to fall are gone. I am imprisoned.

I cannot act upon an impulse to promenade at midnight. I am reliant upon the venality of those with power over me for the scantest kindness. The noises of the prison swell around me and I clamp my eyes shut to block them out. A treacherous tear forces its way through the bars of my lashes, making the very escape that I am denied. I will not weep. I repeat this phrase like a rosary. I will not weep. Finally, sleep catches me and bundles me away like a footpad.

I have not been able to stomach enough of the gaoler's wine to prevent me dreaming. I have never enjoyed happy dreams. I have vivid recollections of my drenched bedding being changed by a tutting nurse as I shivered tearfully and begged that my father be kept in ignorance of this latest transgression. As soon as I was able to take to drink, I did so with alacrity. It not only purged my dreams. Perversely, given its reputation, it allowed me to look back on nighttime incontinence as no more than a distasteful memory. Tonight, with the walls pressing in and the incoherent screams of one of my fellow prisoners lulling my senses, my drowned night terrors return with a vengeance.

My former fiancée, Madeline, had a particularly villainous small dog, which filled the part of her soul that yearned for children. She indulged it with a nauseating sentimentality that acted as positive evidence of the wisdom of the practice of separating well-bred offspring from their parents and consigning them to the care of servants while they are young enough to avoid the horrors of a surfeit of maternal affection. It was a terrier – a breed that I have always been led to believe is famed for its tenacity and good humour. Naturally, she loved it. In her eyes it could do no wrong. Her love took the form of sweetmeats, choice cuts of beef and veal, and a ruthless bullying of any servant who dared to protest at the task of cleaning its excrement or removing its fangs from his person. By the time she and I became affianced, it had grown enormously fat. Indigestion and indulgence had produced an irascibility of character that made it quite unsuitable as a pet, but would have been an admirable quality in a despot. The creature sensed that I was a rival for its mistress's affections. It did not view me as a serious contender but, in the manner of all despots, it knew that I had to be dealt with violently and quickly in order that my fate could serve as an example to others contemplating challenging its supremacy. No matter how well disposed I pretended to be, it would pass up no chance to attack me. For my part, defence was as impossible as surrender. If I ignored the brute it would savage me. If I retaliated even to the limited extent of shaking its jaws from my buttocks, Madeline would accuse me of inquisitorial savagery. I took to avoiding it and vowed that it would be the first casualty of our union.

Now, oppressed by walls I cannot scale, I dream of the dog. I am in the withdrawing room, apparelled in the kind of finery I could afford when I had expectations. My britches are complemented by a pair of silk stockings that cost enough to have unsettled me even in times when I thought that money was not an obstacle to creating an impression. I am to accompany Madeline to the theatre. A volcanic rumbling from the armchair alerts me to the dog's presence. It lumbers from its roost and crosses the floor towards me. I retreat to what I hope is the safety of the bay window. It continues its advance, snarling and revealing yellowing fangs. I limit its advance to a small channel between a revolving bookcase and the wall. It springs, fastening its teeth to my calf and destroying my beautiful stocking. I kick it smartly on the snout and it lets forth a satisfying yelp. As I do so, my fiancée sweeps into the room.

She surveys the scene like an examining magistrate. 'You kicked him, Robert!'

'Madeline, I . . .'

'You did, I saw you. How dare you kick my dog, Robert!'

'Madeline, the beast attacked me. Look at my leg.'

'You must have provoked him, Robert. My father always says you have a talent for provocation. You must apologize to him forthwith.'

'I will do no such thing.'

'Oh, but you will, Mr Robert Warrens. If you don't I will make my displeasure quite plain to my father.'

I curse, prudently confining my expressions of rage to the internal. 'Sorry.'

'No, Robert, I want you to make a proper apology. You must go down on one knee.'

I do not hesitate. I know where the power lies and how foolish it would be to upset her, at least until she is my wife and my father has elevated us to the peerage. I feel the prickle of carpet against my calves and wince as fibres attach themselves to the bite wound. I swallow to banish even the slightest taste of sarcasm.

'I'm really terribly sorry. I don't know what came over me. It's quite outside my character.'

The dog looms over me. Dear God, it's the size of a bloody carthorse. An icy wind billows the withdrawing room curtains and causes the judge's wig that the creature sports to fly out like wings. I scream, wake and realize that my night terrors have brought their moist accompanist. I reach for the foul wine and sleep again.

A pallid dawn is heralded by an icy blast through the bars that stirs me from my bed. A sea mist has enveloped the prison, placing the limited views of the outside world beyond my reach. The gaoler enters and presents me with a bowl of tepid water and a blunt razor, the better to make myself presentable for my judicial assignation. I permit myself to be shackled and led to a cart. As it leaves the gatehouse and starts towards the court I turn, and see the prison disappear into the mist. The cries of its inmates fade into the distance like those of gulls.

I await Mr Justice Cooper's pleasure in the cells. Needless to say, I am left until the conclusion of the court's business. A fine repast of sentencing ably finished off by the port and cigar that is Warrens. I have sufficient time to build myself into a froth about the injustice of my situation – a state that is considerably increased by the entrepreneurial spirit that has possessed my gaolers. My outburst has given me some notoriety, and this has led to a trade in glimpses of the famous assaulter of judicial gravitas. My wicket and spy-hole are in near constant use. I am sure that I recognize the eyes of some of my fellows. It is not without its consolations, as my keepers feel maintaining my goodwill to be part of their duties. My physical comforts are catered for and I have tobacco and wine. I eat two hearty repasts. I am even offered the services of a whore, which I decline as I have seen the drabs favoured by the condemned in these places and have no inclination to make use of them. I suspect that these kindnesses are motivated by the desire to see me do more than sit and stare at the wall. No doubt if I took the proffered whore, the spectacle would command a premium price. Light is fading at the cell window before my door is opened and a determinedly cheerful gaoler informs me that my carriage is ready.

The public gallery is empty but the well of the court is filled with my fellow men of the law. I survey them but ignore any greetings.

I hope my disposition in the cells left them disappointed. I fold my hands in my lap and drop my eyes, taking in every detail of the wear and sheen of my shackles. I recognize the stance as soon as I adopt it: the prisoner in the dock. I allow myself a moment of detached amusement at how speedily I have contracted to fit my environment before the familiar rap on the door announces the start of my ordeal. Cooper bounds in. I do not raise my head. He is unusually cheerful. I wonder briefly whether this means he has decided to include me in his general expression of goodwill or if the punishment he has in mind for me has acted as a tonic. His clerk sits and declaims: 'The case of Robert Warrens, My Lord.'

I risk a glance round the court. They are all here. Dickson, Fawsley, the whole of the north-east's legal establishment has gathered to watch me. I had no idea I was so well known. They all wear expressions that I am sure they have adopted in the fond conceit that they signify both stern condemnation of the transgression and pity for the wretch whose downfall will be revealed before them. They are mistaken in this. Dickson in particular looks constipated. The idiot even holds his hand at waist height as if it is resting on the pommel of a sword. The impression he hopes to convey is that of Roman senator. He looks like an invalid who has just discovered that his walking stick has been stolen.

I am asked to rise and identify myself. I await the charge and find myself stunned to hear Fawsley interrupt the proceedings.

'My Lord, unusual as it is for counsel not involved in the case to address the court, my conscience obliges me to speak. I was present in court when the matter arose and I ask the court's indulgence to allow me to put forward a plea on the prisoner's behalf.'

Cooper looks at Fawsley with an expression that suggests he has received a proposal rather than presided over a breach of etiquette.

'That rather depends, Mr Fawsley.'

He turns to me. 'Do you instruct Mr Fawsley, Warrens?'

I am too nonplussed to do anything other than nod.

'Very well, proceed Mr Fawsley.'

'I'm obliged, My Lord. I would submit that the arena of the criminal court is a harsh mirror before which all the frailties of a man's character are mercilessly exposed. Such is the nature of the adversarial system, and rightly so. It is only through this harshness that the precious kernel of truth may be revealed. We are all engaged in a brutal search for this scarce commodity. However, the unforgiving nature of our workplace can prove too much for those who are exposed to it. The fire that we deploy to scourge away lies can also burn those against whom its fury is not directed. Take alongside this the fact that we, as advocates, are asked to stand in our clients' shoes, and I would submit you have an explanation for my client's outburst. He is a man who has appeared before you on many occasions, no doubt, but none as redolent of dishonesty as that which gave rise to his outburst. You, My Lord, and I to a lesser extent, are accustomed to the very depth of human wickedness. We participate in serious trials, and as an advocate I walk the tightrope where the truth and my instructions converge. We have become like the ice bear. We have grown a pelt thick enough to protect us from the vicissitudes of our surroundings. My client was put in a position in which his duty forced him fearlessly to advance an argument that was without merit. He identified with his client – a quality that you may recall in your own time at the Bar. He is a man who is prone to the sin of anger, and this flaw was exhibited and magnified by the arena before which it emerged. No man, be he treasury counsel, judge, soldier or ploughman, is without fault. I ask that you discharge my client upon his apology, freely given in open court. He will not repeat his error. Perhaps, My Lord, you could be persuaded to regard his outburst as part of the process of his growing his pelt. I plead his inexperience and request your forbearance.'

I am both furious and absurdly grateful. I resent any reference to my inexperience, even though it has more than a grain of truth in it. I have to acknowledge that it was a fine piece of work. He knows how to play this judge. I could be facing a relatively short sentence indeed.

The judge addresses me. 'You have heard Counsel, Warrens. What have you to say?'

I stand. The view of the court from the dock is unfamiliar. It takes my breath and sends my mind into a vortex. I had hoped to match Fawsley's eloquence but all the phrases I long for hang just beyond my reach. I cough and stammer an apology. Cooper settles himself and gives judgement. I can scarcely believe my ears. I am to be released.

As I stagger from the cells and begin the walk back to my lodgings, I am assailed by the judge's clerk who thrusts a letter into my hand. I break the seal and read it as I walk. Its contents are so unexpected that I am forced to re-read them. Not only am I released unexpectedly, but also it appears that I am to suffer no professional difficulty. The letter sets out the date of the trial and bids my client and me attend to witness the jury being sworn. It is signed by the judge's clerk. I have received numerous similar missives in other cases. Its very routine nature is curiously comforting. Far away, across the market square and through the church towers and dwelling houses, I can hear the contents of my cellar calling to me. I hasten to my rendezvous.

It appears that I will be dining with my clerk. My housekeeper has transmitted this unlikely state of affairs to me. I have repaired to my bedroom, ostensibly to change for dinner but in reality to make some sense of the day's events by drinking a bottle of claret. I can find no explanation for it that does not involve either my acting under some kind of hallucination on the one hand or everyone else involved doing so on the other. Neither hypothesis is comforting. Neither is plausible. I have been rescued from a trap of my own making by the most disagreeable man in England – a man who not a day before had both mistaken me for a servant and been disappointed when he realized his error. I have been released by a judge who would never pass a sentence of ten years' imprisonment if the prisoner could be condemned to hang. A judge, mark you, who views transportation as an act of mercy. I have not even lost the brief he sent me. I stop to sniff my coat. The smell of the prison is unmistakable. It was neither a hallucination nor a dream. If I were a religious man, I would take comfort in the idea of the Lord working in mysterious ways. I believe, but question the desire the Creator may have to interfere in the minutiae of human affairs. I drain my glass and fall upon its successor. Perhaps the sense is that there is none. It has happened. It has stopped and I must move to the next hurdle, which appears to be dinner with my clerk. I rise and make my way to the kitchen.

My housekeeper is busying herself by emptying the numerous mousetraps that litter her domain. I greet her, and she informs me that we will be dining on roast chicken. I notice she has not executed the mice and has put them into a sack. This intrigues me. I enquire and receive the reply, 'I'm surprised that a London man such as yourself doesn't know this, sir. I send them to my sister. You know, the one who's in service to a medical man in Greenwich.'

I am unable to think of an apposite response, such is my consternation. I am reduced to question without comment. 'What on earth does she do with them? I have been here for a long time but I cannot believe that it has become fashionable to eat mice in London.'

'Not eat them, sir. Apparently our Constance skins them and sells the fur to ladies' maids who make false eyebrows for their mistresses from it. Eh, but it's a funny thing to do, wearing mouse fur on your forehead when the Good Lord gave you eyebrows for the purpose. There's no sense in trying to understand London ways now, is there, sir?'

'Are there no mice in London?'

'Our mice have denser fur, sir, so I'm told. Better for the ladies. Longer lasting. She gets a good price for them, does Constance.'

I shake my head. Seemingly the world has gone mad. I am released from custody to continue my defence of a monkey to find my housekeeper is farming mice. It is too much for me to bear. A rap at the door signifies Spicknell's arrival. I flee the kitchen in search of even the approximation of sanity promised by his company.

Spicknell has ensconced himself in the parlour and is monopolizing the fire when I arrive. My housekeeper provides us both with brandy, leaving the decanter as she goes about her business. Spicknell looks at me expectantly. But I am damned if I will satisfy his curiosity without a request.

'Will you be coming into chambers, sir?'

'I expect so, Spicknell. What is the talk of my exploits?'

'Well, sir, it is said that you damned the judge's eyes when he refused to believe that your Frenchman was a monkey and he sent you to spend the night in the gaol. You went back before him and Fawsley pulled your fat from the fire.'

I smile. One can always rely upon an over-mighty servant to puncture any attempt at conceit.

'That is all true, and all the more remarkable for it. Is there any rumour as to what prompted the judge to discover the quality of mercy so late in his career?'

'One or two, sir. I favour the one that has the judge at death's door and discovering virtues to keep him out of the Devil's clutches.'

'It would take more than one incident of mercy to keep Cooper out of the fire. If this is the case then I expect to see him in the town at weekends handing out alms and dandling orphans on his knee. He has allowed me to retain the brief, you know?'

This last piece of information surprises even that fount of sangfroid, my clerk. 'Really?'

'No, Spicknell, as the world has clearly gone mad, I cannot say that, simply because I have experienced it and I have a letter from Cooper's clerk notifying me of the trial date, then this is reality. It may just be the strand that the winds of lunacy have blown past me. None the less, what I have told you is true.'

I show him the letter. He makes a show of examining it before handing it back to me with a whistle. 'So it is true.'

'So what is true, Spicknell?'

'An acquaintance of mine told me that this brief was being hawked around chambers like a sprig of lucky heather on race day. No one will touch it. It's called a . . .' he gropes blindly for a half-remembered phrase '. . . a poison hospice.'

'Chalice, Spicknell. A poisoned chalice. Why is that, then?'

'Partly because of what happened to you, sir, and partly because the combination of Fawsley and Cooper is a prospect that
most advocates would travel to the ends of the earth to avoid.
Those that need the money are too scared and those that are so
well known that they're not scared don't need the money enough.
And that's quite apart from representing a client who throws
handfuls of his own shit at you.'

I cannot but acknowledge the truth in this. It occurs to me that
I should return the brief, but only for a moment. As my clerk
points out, I need the money. There is a certain cachet in being
the one who does something that everyone else is too frightened
to attempt. God knows it has never applied to me before. I
have always been happy to be the child who watches the daring
ones fling themselves from the highest branches, happy in the
knowledge that while I attract no glances of admiration, I am still
possessed of a complete set of working limbs. Now, through the
simple device of looking at the fee before the contents of the brief,
I find myself as Warrens the Brave. A novelty indeed. I would
become a winning and fearless advocate if I were to be victorious.
I cling to this image before discounting it as too fanciful. There is
little for me to fear that has not happened already. I have wiped
the client's excrement from my wig. I have been imprisoned. I
return to the comfort of knowing that it is hard to injure oneself
falling into a pit if one is already at the bottom.

We drink more brandy in silence.

'So what are you going to do, sir?'

'I am not sure. The last hearing left me in a quandary. Quite
apart from everything else, the damned judge won't accept the
evidence of his own eyes. You saw the client?'

'Yes.'

'Tell me that he is, in fact, a monkey. I believe him to be so but I crave reassurance that this is not another facet of the madness that has overtaken everything in the past few days.'

'Oh, he's a monkey and no mistake. You only have to see him.'

'Thank you, Spicknell. You only have to see him. Exactly. The bloody judge has seen him, though, and contrary to the reaction of every other person including you, he does not accept this seemingly obvious fact. This creates a problem. How on earth does one gather evidence to prove the bloody obvious?'

'I don't understand, sir.'

'You don't, Spicknell? Well, let me attend to your education. There are some things that are so obviously true that the law, when it is functioning as it has done until three days ago, does not require evidence to prove. That is a fortunate thing because the sort of fact of which I speak is extremely hard to prove. For example, if I were to say to you that I needed you to prove that the sun rose in the morning, how would you go about it?'

Spicknell purses his lips. I can see he suspects a trap.

'Well, you would only have to get up and see the sunrise to prove that, sir, surely?'

'So far as that day is concerned, yes. But think, Spicknell: you are being asked to establish that the day will always commence with the sunrise. How do you do it? The answer is that of course you cannot. The law graciously allows us to make the assumption that it will remain so, because it has been so since the creation. Therein lies the problem. I have the task of proving that the client is a monkey to a court that seemingly requires more proof than the simple admonition of 'Just take a bloody look at it!' Where the Hell do I find the evidence?'

A bell rings. Spicknell and I make our way to the dining room. My housekeeper brings in the chicken. We eat in silence, contemplating our dilemma.

'We need a witness, sir.'

'Brilliant, Spicknell. Why didn't I think of that? Do you suppose we could find a witness to the client's conception? Maybe there's someone we could call to testify that he was born to a mother and father monkey. I'll send you to find him presently. I am not sure that even the boldest "professional" would testify to that before Cooper, but I wish you every success in your quest. Look for a man with a straw in his boot and an expression of suicidal melancholy.'

'No, sir, I mean a witness who can identify things because he knows about them. Like the vetinarian you called to prove that the allegedly stolen purse was a bull's scrotum.'

This is like a slap of cold water across my sleeping face. An expert witness. Of course. It is breathtakingly simple.

'We couldn't call the same gentleman. He was a specialist in livestock. The client hardly falls within his expertise. What I need is a man who can speak about the nature and habits of jungle animals. A man with credentials so illustrious as to make them unassailable even by the most vicious prosecutor or by Mr Justice Cooper of Bedlam himself.'

It is a solution that brings a number of unanswerable questions in its wake. I rack my brains. Whom could we call? Who could put themselves forward plausibly as an expert in jungle animals? I know no one who has travelled further than Europe. A recess in my memory whispers about a dinner party held by my father when he was at the height of his wealth. There was a man there who had travelled to the Cape and who had kept the company entertained by his tales of lions and natives. He was a member of the Royal Society. I search for a name and find none. Damn. My thoughts are disturbed by the infernal clattering of my housekeeper as she clears the crockery. I decide to share my progress with my clerk, more in the hope that articulating my dilemma might signpost its solution than in the expectation of any assistance.

'As I see it, Spicknell, we need a man who is learned in what is known in fashionable circles as natural science. I doubt any are to be found in this region. There must be few men indeed who possess both the learning and the practical experience for our purposes. I recall that one of my father's friends was a member of the Royal Society . . .'

There is a crash from the sideboard. I notice with more than a little annoyance that my housekeeper has dropped a rather fine Staffordshire gravy boat. Although I affect a lofty disdain for the material which I feel befits my aspiration to asceticism, I am secretly rather fond of those few small things that I have managed to retain from my old life. This dinner service, for example. It lay buried in my father's garden along with some choice silver plate and a purse of coins. Retrieving it was a nightmare of lantern-lit terror that retains the capacity to make my throat constrict. The memory distracts me, allowing Spicknell to seize the initiative with irritating smugness.

'Pamphlets, sir.'

I do not care to be reminded of the trigger of my recent downfall. I am on the cusp of a highly satisfying admonition when he continues, 'And journals. The Royal Society must have them. Everyone does, these days. I was reading about the London Monster in one only recently. You have to put a notice in a journal that is read by the sort of gentleman who knows a monkey when he sees one.'

Silence settles over the room like a blanket of dust. Now is the time of Warrens. A church bell tolls in the night. It sounds like the herald of my resurrection. I assume the sort of artfully nonchalant expression that befits a man about to claim another's good idea as his own. When I address my clerk I detect a treacherous high note of excitement in my voice which I struggle with but cannot quite master.

'I cannot go to London myself, of course.'

Absolutely true. I could not bear the humiliation of returning to the scenes of my former near-glory in the guise of a provincial visitor. The sort of riff-raff I used to chide from my path with my cane would probably attempt to sell me keepsakes of my visit to the capital.

'You'll have to go yourself, Spicknell. Take the mail coach. You can lodge with my housekeeper's sister. She has a parcel to receive that has already been paid for so there's no need even for the price of your passage.'

He opens his mouth to protest but I silence him with a nonchalant wave. 'No time to waste, Spicknell. I shall compose the notice forthwith.'

I have written many letters asking for assistance throughout my career. Help is a commodity that many have to squander. Experience has taught me that few are prepared to part with their assistance freely. I need bait to lure my witness to me. Money is no object. Provided I make no specific promise I can offer the stars. I am unlikely to need this man's particular skills again, so I can cope with what will undoubtedly be an outraged withdrawal of good favour after the case is won. He may go to law to recover the debt, certainly. I know my knowledge of the law can trap his attempts at recovery in a mire of writ and counterwrit. No, if I have the measure of such a man, and from my memory of my father's acquaintance I believe I have, it would take more than money. I have a vision of solidity, full cheeked and fetlocked, dressed expensively but in a somewhat anachronistic style that spoke of a studied ignorance of the ephemeralities of fashion. Men such as these do not want money, although they are unlikely to reject its promise. Their lives are a constant quest for renown. If fame is the spur then I know how to apply it. I dip my quill and commence, Spicknell reading over my shoulder.

To whom it may concern,

A Commission and Stipend for the Practice of the Natural Sciences

I commence with my heartfelt apology for my presumption in addressing any among you in this precipitous manner. My name is Robert Warrens. I am a lawyer currently in chambers in the city of Durham. The reputation of the Royal Society as a crucible of men of science has penetrated even this most far-flung corner of our island. It is this renown that has caused me to take the unprecedented step of communicating with its members by way of this notice in order to enlist assistance.

It is my duty to defend a creature that has been arraigned before the court on a charge of espionage. It is a delicate and unusual case. The Crown allege that my client is a Frenchman who has entered this country without passport or parole in order to perform some unspecified and nefarious duty for his masters in Paris. I have had the opportunity of meeting this client in conference and I am of the opinion that the prisoner is no more than a harmless creature, a monkey or ape, which has chanced upon the shore following a shipwreck or some such mishap. Indeed, my experience of this client is that he neither conducts himself with humanity nor displays a capacity for human speech.

As I write, my mind reprises a most unwelcome scene of a prison cart, jeering faces, a small, hairy hand upon my arm and a whispered invocation of courage. I shake my head imperceptibly and put this aside.

The question of whether the client is a monkey or a Frenchman is at the very heart of the Crown and defence case. If he is in truth a creature, then the laws of man do not apply to him. The court has no jurisdiction to try him and he will be released, probably into the custody of any person willing to accommodate him. Needless to say, the Crown does not accept that he is anything other than an agent of the Revolution. The court requires that the client's genus is established by way of evidence. As a mere barrister, my opinion does not enjoy that status. Only a man well versed in scientific theory, whose own researches have taken him beyond the threshold of knowledge at which most men wait, can assist the court and save this poor animal from the execution that will follow any conviction. Only a member of that most illustrious Royal Society would have the skill and knowledge to assist. This is why I take the liberty of this declamatory communication. Your renown, your scholarship and your research have made you happy Fellows and Members the only men in England who can save this innocent life.

I feel that it is my obligation to inform you that should any among you feel able to accept this commission, his name is almost certain to reach national prominence. Indeed, the name of the man who gave evidence on matters scientific is likely to join that of Newton himself in the pantheon of those men whose fame shines beyond the immediate circle of those who seek knowledge in creation itself. I can only cling to the hope that the remuneration that I am able to offer, which could be considered to be substantial, will act as some compensation for the unwelcome glare of popular celebration that its acceptance will convey.

The remit of these instructions is simply to establish the client's origins and to report in detail the factors that have led to your conclusion. The client is incarcerated in Hartlepool. I am aware that the journey from London is lengthy and arduous and would be pleased to offer my humble hospitality should any among you accepting my commission have no other accommodation in the locality that would be more fitting for a man of scholarship and nobility.

I remain in your debt.

Your servant . . .

I dash off a letter to the editor of the journal and seal the notice and a promissory note within with a flourish. I hand it to Spicknell. He is to take the first coach south and is not to return without at least one learned doctor in his wake, or his position will be in the greatest jeopardy. As he takes his leave, my house-keeper hands him a suspicious sack that writhes as if it contains a snake. He takes this burden with a considerable lack of good cheer. I notice that his face is contorted with the effort of holding it at arm's length. I stand at my door and finish my pipe, musing on the day's events. So, my case is a poisoned chalice and I am known as the man who took communion from it? I will pay them all out. The poison will change into the sweet draught of victory in my mouth. Science will bring about transubstantiation.

18

A Report and a Rendezvous

THESE LAST TWO DAYS HAVE BEEN SINGULAR IN THEIR disruption of my household. I did not imagine that anyone who was able to call themselves a member of the Royal Society would take up my offer of accommodation. Had I envisaged that this was even a remote possibility, I would never have included it in my notice. It was just a matter of politeness, an expression of good manners and breeding, but it has cost me a great deal. Doctor McCreadie (for so he is called) descended upon me, complete with his housekeeper. Had I a suspicious mind I would surmise that her presence signified that their relationship went beyond propriety. Having met the great man, I am reassured that his person and character are so vile that he would find it impossible to form a liaison even with a servant. They arrived on the London coach, announced by Spicknell in the kind of tones that one would expect from a barker at a travelling fair. I greeted the doctor at the door and caused the guest chamber to be made ready. This was not an easy matter, as I have become such a stranger to hospitality that the room itself lacked even the bed upon which it could justify its name. My housekeeper fulfilled my command through the device of removing my possessions from my bedroom. I have spent two nights searching for sleep on a dusty floor – an experience that has made me look back upon my incarceration with not a little nostalgia. It was a privation I could have borne with cheerful fortitude had my guest not proved himself to be the most disagreeable of companions.

We dined upon roast pork. This precipitated a discourse on all things porcine, and in particular their feeding habits, which was given with such a relish that I found myself to be robbed of any hunger. I am now possessed of such knowledge of the construction of latrines in the Indies and their role as a porcine dining hall that I cannot foresee any circumstances in which I will ever eat pig again. I noted that Doctor McCreadie did not share my sensitivity. Not only did he manage to clear his plate with ravenous alacrity, but he found space in his ample stomach for the remainder of my repast as well. This was all washed down with four bottles of my finest claret. This too failed to measure up to his expectations. He found himself able to overcome his natural courtliness to explain his criticisms of my cellar to me at some length. I am afraid that I will be unable to share his advice with my wine merchant. Sadly, the thunderous grinding of my teeth and the clank and swill of my inferior wine disappearing down his throat drowned the hindquarters of his dissertation. I was happy to retire, and joyous to discover the arrangements that left me without a bed.

I rose early to discover that he had already departed for

the prison. The flood of relief to find myself reprieved of his company over breakfast was so palpable it equipped me to deal with the day's remaining vicissitudes. He returned late and took his dinner in my room. This was accompanied by yet more of my unsatisfactory wine and a quantity of my no doubt disappointing brandy. Only my pleasure at escaping his company that evening permitted me to bear the expense of his pillage of my beverages with something approaching equanimity.

Now he has gone, taking his housekeeper with him. I am informed that five of my silver spoons have taken their leave also. I am sure that they have been offered a better position or were simply pulled in by McCreadie's wake. He has left me two things: a letter and a note of his fee. I file this last in my writing desk as I remind myself that I will deduct the expense of his lodgings, the price of my spoons and a small consideration for my inconvenience, should I feel disposed to pay at all. He has asked for twenty guineas. I promised a reward that 'could be seen as substantial' and that is what he will receive. I remain confident that I did not pledge a reward that could ransom the entire Royal Family, the Archbishop of Canterbury and the Master of the Beaufort Hunt. I will dash off a missive assuring him of 'prompt and generous' payment at the conclusion of the case. That will get him to attend the trial. After that, who knows? If I were Doctor McCreadie I would not plan my next expedition to an uncharted shore on the back of any promissory note in the name of Warrens. I sit, pour myself what seems to be the final remnant of my brandy, break the seal and read.

To – Mr Robert Warrens, Counsel for the Defence
And To – The Presiding Judge

Report in the Matter of the Crown-v-an unnamed
Frenchman.

I, Doctor Charles McCreadie, make oath and say:
I am a fellow of the Royal College of Physicians and a
member of the Royal Society of Natural Sciences. I have
published a number of papers on matters relating to the
categorization, appearance, habits and habitat of species
domestic and exotic. These include 'A Discourse on the
Generative Habits of the Northern Grampus' and 'The Great
Apes of the Slave Coast – Their Society and Constitution'. I
have been the expedition naturalist upon three voyages of
which two successfully reached their destinations. I have
made a particular study of the fauna of the South and West
of Africa in my capacity of Ship's Surgeon and Natural
Scientist to the Dahomey expedition. I confirm that all
contained within this report is true or to the best of my
knowledge and belief correct.

I have been requested by Mr Robert Warrens, learned
counsel for the Defence in this matter, to comment upon
the creature or person whom he represents and to give an
opinion upon its genus and subspecies. To phrase this in the
manner in which I was addressed: 'Is the client a monkey
and, if so, what sort of monkey is he?' To this end I have read
the depositions of the Crown's witnesses and attended upon
the Defendant (the subject) himself in his place of incarceration at Hartlepool for five hours. The results of my enquiries
are as follows.

I took a moment to observe the subject before introducing myself to him in order to gain a first impression of his characteristics. I saw him to be of short stature, just under five feet in height. His features were essentially Negroid, with a flat nose, prominent lips and brow. He had the general appearance of that creature which is known as *Panus Sylvanus*, a tribal ape that is numerous in the western part of the African continent. I was able to rely upon my experience of this creature to detect several anomalous traits that cast doubt upon this classification. Firstly, the subject is considerably taller than an ape, an impression that is intensified by his posture. Where an ordinary ape stoops at the waist and proceeds upon his hind legs with the occasional assistance of its fore limbs for balance, the subject stands perfectly erect. His legs are not overly bowed and, while short in proportion to his torso, remain within the range found within the human species. Similarly his arms are not so disproportionate as to make his classification as either ape or human a mere matter of formality. He is covered in coarse black hair, as would be expected in the case of the animal he so closely resembles. Clothing largely concealed this pelt, but that which was discernible seemed to me to be uncharacteristically sparse around the upper face and cheeks, although it was extremely prominent along the jaw line, around the mouth and on the neck, forming a pattern similar to that of the human beard. I would give the opinion that a visual assessment is insufficient to reach any meaningful conclusion.

On interview I found the subject to be compliant if subdued. His initial reticence was overcome when he and I realized that we were already acquainted. I first came across this individual before the outbreak of hostilities when I was the guest of the celebrated scientific patron, the late Duc de Ladurie de Bretagne. At that stage he was employed as manservant to the Duke's personal physician. It was explained to me that the subject had been captured during an expedition to the Slave Coast of which the Duke's man was the sole survivor. I was informed that he had been living as part of a tribe of apes before they cast him out and he was rescued by his then master. The creature was the centre of much heated debate. It is capable of human speech, and able to display emotion, albeit of a mawkish kind such as weeping over the corpses of small birds killed during a hunt. The focus of dispute was not the creature's species, as the French took the rather superficial view that it could be classified as an ape without further enquiry. The issue that engaged the various persons present, which included a number of well-born individuals and members of philosophical societies, was whether the ability to reason and express some empathy indicated humanity. This was discussed interminably, with the French living up to their reputation as circumlocutors incapable of decisive action. I was permitted to participate in these enquiries and to conduct a full physical examination. I found those factors which point towards non-human origin to be superficial in nature, although I was prevented from reaching a firm conclusion by the sentimentality of the Duke's physician who expressly forbade my proposed dissection. The creature was judged human and given the name Jacques LeSinge.

My interview at the prison confirmed my initial findings.

The subject informed me that he had been expelled from the Duke's household after he had behaved with undue informality towards the Duchess, an incident of which I was aware. He described his journey through France and eventual arrival in the capital, Paris. He went on to recount his recruitment to the Revolutionary Navy and took a great deal of pride in informing me that he was commissioned at the rank of lieutenant. He recounted the events of the shipwreck (an incident for which he must bear a degree of culpability, as he confessed to starting the fire that was to be the vessel's undoing after falling asleep in his hammock while smoking a pipe) and was able to set out the events of his capture and prosecution with clarity. Of course I have no means of verifying this information save for that contained within the prosecution papers, but it would be entirely in keeping with my eventual conclusion.

I was asked to give an opinion whether the subject was a monkey. I can unhesitatingly conclude that he is not. Although there are obvious similarities that would bring him within this classification, my view is that he is a member of the human species. These particularities of appearance, hirsuteness and facial features, for example, are explicable by a theory that would, in turn, shed some light upon the reasons for his discovery. It has been long acknowledged that the events that befall a mother during her confinement are writ large upon the person of her offspring. For example, I have personally encountered cases in which a child has been born with additional limbs where enquiry has revealed that the mother was startled by a spider during the late stages of gestation. I believe that the subject's mother received a shock at the hands of an ape in her last trimester, causing this unfortunate effect upon her offspring's physiognomy. This child was cast out by the mother's people, and was adopted by the apes it so resembled. It remained among them until its differences began to manifest themselves at adolescence, whereupon it was cast out for a second time. Tales of children reared by animals appear in the mythology of all nations. The court will be aware of the well-known tale of the founders of Rome. The subject is a human child, deformed by adversity and raised to adolescence by apes, but blessed with resource and intelligence that have permitted him to adapt to his new surroundings.

I blink twice, but I am unable to dispel incandescent particles that drift across my retina like stars. I become conscious of these, and they divert me as I struggle to take in the consequences of what I have just read. I read it again. There are no hallucinations. It appears that the client is not a monkey after all, and despite all appearances to the contrary. Not only is he a man, he is a commissioned officer in the French navy. My thoughts return to the cart and I recall his hand upon my arm. I look into his eyes again and see that the complete lack of fear I find is not a result of incomprehension. Even sheep would become distressed if they were surrounded by a baying mob. I have seen courage, and dismissed it as a phantasm. A courageous officer of the enemy's navy . . . this thought sends my mind racing to the deposition.

I struggle with the papers on my desk until I locate it. Yes. 'It was wearing the uniform of an officer in the enemy's navy.' Exactly as I thought. I skim the deposition and reassure myself that I had not imagined the frequent references to a shipwreck. I have found my point. The client has been arrested after a shipwreck. He wears the uniform of a naval officer. There is no reference to any activity that could be described as espionage. There is no evidence of anything other than the client's being a prisoner of war. That is my point. Its discovery may have been serendipitous. It may not be the one upon which I have expended considerable time or upon which I allowed myself to be provoked to the point of incarceration, but it is as sharp as a bayonet. I can feel it as I weigh it up. It is lethal. I imagine the pleasure of sliding it under the ribs of Fawsley's prosecution and permit myself a murderer's smile.

The rules of court dictate that I must serve the report immediately. Sadly, I am permitted no ambush, although confronting Fawsley with this evidence and no time to react to it provides me with a pleasurable daydream that I graciously allow to divert me. No. I must abide by convention, as the consequences to me would be considerable were I to depart from it. I am to whip the prospect of passing a sentence of death from beneath the judge's nose. It would not do to offer myself up as consolation by a breach of etiquette that would place me in contempt again. This would smack of recklessness. I restrain myself from serving it in person only by reference to the certainty that its recipients would believe that I could not afford a clerk were I to act as my own delivery boy. I am not given to exertion, but I run through the streets to my chambers, repressing a battle cry through the force of will alone. My heart hammers at my ribs. This time it does not feel like a bell ringing out my doom. I will be victorious. The poisoned chalice has been filled with the most exquisite wine.

There is nothing like an unexpected knock on the door to turn one's thoughts to the subject of bailiffs. Although different night terrors may fill others' minds, it is creditors that hound me to wakefulness as the sound of knuckles upon oak fills my parlour. I have fallen asleep in my chair. As I adjust my wig, I review my debts to reassure myself that this caller is at my door by mistake. I reflect that I am as conditioned to start at an official knock as a hound is to the hunter's horn. I hold the certainty of my advancement close as a comforter as I compose myself. I can hear my housekeeper in the hallway. She is a quarrelsome woman, and I do not greatly rate the chances of any bailiff besting her. I listen to the discussion. The tones of the person she is shrieking at seem well modulated. So not the bailiffs. Who, then? It has been three days since I dispatched Spicknell with the letter. Three days in which I have resigned myself to there being no acknowledgement. Surely the judge cannot be in the habit of acknowledging his correspondence late at night? The prospect of mollifying Mr Justice Cooper after he has been kept waiting by my housekeeper spurs on my makeshift toilet. I am just smoothing my eyebrows with a moistened finger when the door bursts open. A tall man with a black moustache strides in, trailing my housekeeper in his wake. I am clear on only one thing. I have never seen him before.

'I tried to stop him, Mr Warrens, but . . .'

I hold up a magisterial hand. The interloper halts before me. I do not rise. I incline my head in a muted greeting.

'Good evening to you, sir. Your clothing would seem to mark you as a gentleman. Your storming of my front door suggests a footpad. I sincerely hope that my first impression is the correct one and I look forward to you presenting both yourself and your explanation.'

Some of my fellow advocates refer to spontaneous eloquence as a stream. It is not a simile that I favour, as if it were true then my own poor rivulet winds its way through an arid and hostile land. A deluge can cause it to flood to a torrent. When it does I can pluck remarks like this last from the ether with the ease of a swallow catching flies. It is too unpredictable to rely upon, but quite extraordinarily satisfying. This man possesses the adamantine poise of the true patrician, but I have shaken him. He coughs.

'I regret the manner of my calling upon you, Mr Warrens. May I introduce myself? My name is Hubert Lovell. I am an undersecretary in the Aliens Office. You may have heard of us? No? Well, we are a branch of government established to monitor and disrupt the activities of foreigners generally and the enemy's spies in particular. I do not invade your home in this capacity, however, but as the dutiful nephew of my esteemed father's brother-in-law, Mr Justice Cooper. I bring you an invitation. You are to attend at the judge's lodgings forthwith.'

I have to clasp my pipe stem to prevent my hand trembling. 'Mr Lovell, it may have escaped your attention but it is one o'clock in the morning. No doubt your calling keeps you constantly awake in pursuit of the King's enemies. Mine does not. I have much to achieve today.'

He turns to my window, opening the glass and one of the shutters. He is a tall man, but I can see the street past his shoulder. It is filled with militiamen. I decide to salvage what measure of free will I can.

'Ah, I see. Well then, unorthodox though it may be, it would be unmannerly to refuse an invitation from a member of the judiciary. Pray tell, will I need to dress for dinner?'

My host's messenger boy does not dignify this with a response. I put on my topcoat, thrust some papers under my arm and go out into the night. My companion takes me by the arm and escorts me to a rather handsome coach and four. The journey to the judge's lodgings is a short one. Despite his precipitous entry to my home, Lovell is a taciturn travelling companion. I assay light conversation, hoping to draw the purpose of my summons from him. He responds in monosyllables. My attendance has never been commanded in this way before. My imagination, always prone to morbidity, begins to run riot. Has Cooper reconsidered his uncharacteristic clemency? Am I to be flung back into the very cell from which I so recently and inexplicably escaped? An unspecified feeling of dread seeps into my stomach and is absorbed with the slow inevitability of ink on a brocade cushion. The coach rolls to a halt with a crunch of deep, well-raked gravel that announces our arrival at the threshold of power and influence. I am forced to expend the final reserves of my self-control to prevent my hand from trembling upon the handle as I descend.

Lovell exchanges a word with the footman and gestures curtly with his head towards the open door. I fill my lungs and precede him past Doric columns into the hallway.

I have never been inside the judge's lodgings before, and I am filled with curiosity despite my trepidation. I expected a monastic air, whitewashed walls and a medieval absence of adornment. Instead I am faced with wood panelling, plaster cornices and portraiture that could have graced the chambers of the club to which my father took me. Judges, rendered even more dark and forbidding by oil and wood smoke, glare at me as I pass. I cannot meet their eyes and am struck by the millennia of incarceration and forests of gibbets that stand as their monuments. This is a house at which mercy calls rarely, and enters only below stairs when she has the courage. In duet, we climb a staircase that rises from the centre of the entry hall. Lovell leads me along another gauntlet of deceased judicial faces, before halting at a door. He knocks, and the unmistakable tones of Mr Justice Cooper bid us enter.

I do not know what to expect, save that I anticipate the worst. My gaze ranges the room, searching fearfully for the escort that would accompany me to the gaol, but there is none. Mr Justice Cooper sits at a writing desk. Papers are fanned out before him with the studied negligence of a winning hand at whist. He is not alone. Fawsley, my nemesis and saviour, warms the seat of his britches at the fire, glass in hand. Lovell takes up a station in a winged armchair beside him. The judge is dressed like a country squire. His boots are splashed with mud. He smiles welcomingly, reinforcing the image of a man who has recently returned from an arduous but pleasurable ride. He is in his shirtsleeves, a state of undress he shares with Fawsley.

'Come in and sit down, Warrens. How civil of you to respond to my invitation. I take it you have met my nephew? Good. Fawsley you know already, of course. We were discussing cosmetics, of all things, before your arrival. I was explaining to Fawsley that I cannot see the attraction of this damned face paint the ladies are using at present. Most un-English. An English girl is characterized by her good health and pleasant disposition. Painting herself white with lead gives her a sepulchral appearance more suited to the French, don't you think?'

I have steeled myself for the worst. I could have borne incarceration with the fortitude of a Protestant martyr facing the Inquisition. I could have faced the sternest of injunctions with a resigned dignity. The invitation to join in with a discussion about fashionable ephemera comes as such a shock that I am moved to the verge of tears. I am quite unable to respond. Fortunately, Fawsley seems to hold strong views upon this subject.

'You are quite wrong, my dear Judge, quite wrong. You have spent too long on circuit and the exposure to the uncultured masses seems to have coarsened your taste. You are not describing English virtues, but the brutish physical attractions of women from the lower orders. We all know that for most young men of quality the first experience of the act of love comes with someone quite unsuitable for marriage – a servant girl perhaps.'

He looks around for approval. I look at the floor, not wishing to share the fact that my only excursions into the world of affairs of the heart have been of a soullessly commercial nature. Lovell takes up the baton. 'And you, my dear Fawsley, have given more evidence against yourself by that remark than you have shed light upon a question that deserves more consideration.'

The judge and Fawsley laugh, and I feel obliged to participate in this activity.

'What we are discussing is what makes an Englishman or woman, and what makes them three times the equal of any Frenchman, Prussian, Spaniard, Indian or Hottentot,' Lovell continues. 'We English prize health as a virtue, but that is not what makes us unique. I doubt even the French really enjoy sickness, although their hypochondria may suggest otherwise. Uncle, you are describing health. But health can be found among women of all orders, including those who may hide it behind paint. Ladies do not work in the fields, and do not acquire the rosiness to which you refer. A lady of good standing spends as little time outside as possible, save, perhaps, for a promenade in the park or riding to hounds. Her skin may redden when it is exposed to the elements. It is as well she disguises this with paint. It shows her to be a woman of quality. Prevents a mistake of identification.'

The judge interjects. 'That's exactly my point. When I was a boy one could tell a lady's family by her complexion. Hiding them behind this white mask means it is quite impossible to tell whether the damsel you are conversing with is a courtesan or a duchess. It's the most monstrous charter for the advancement of parvenus' daughters. I am sure it looks quite becoming. I feel there is need for some legislation restricting its use to mistresses so we all know where we stand. Can you raise this in the House, Fawsley? Talking as we were of manners, I find I have quite forgotten my own. Would you care for brandy, Warrens?'

'No thank you, My Lord. It is either too early or too late.'

'There's no need to be so formal. We are not in court now. You may call me "Cooper". We are all among friends, are we not? Perhaps coffee?'

The prospect of relaxing with this judge disturbs me. Passing time in pleasantries with the man who had all too recently condemned me to prison, a King's Counsel and a representative from an organization called the Aliens Office is unlikely enough a prospect to lend the proceedings a dreamlike air. We sit in a semicircle with the fire at its centre, the four of us. Cooper to my right, Fawsley to my left and Lovell beyond him. It is a semicircle that would have been rendered incomplete by my absence. All three look at me in a most unfamiliar manner, which I am only able to identify as affection after I have run through the entire catalogue of negativity. Cooper rings for a servant and turns to me.

'Well, Warrens, you are too astute to think that I have caused you to be brought here simply to have you participate in a discussion about face paint. I would stress that you are all here voluntarily. You can leave at any time. The only pressure I will apply to you this morning is that which it took to prise you from your lair. Government has three limbs: the legislature so ably represented by Fawsley, the executive of which my nephew is a fine example and the judiciary, myself. Usually their three limbs pull in different directions, and through this pressure a balance is achieved that allows the state to function but prevents tyranny being visited upon the nation. But think, Warrens – we are in a time of national emergency. There is no place for the niceties of government when we are at war. After all, if the arms of the state are to burst fighting each other to preserve liberty, then no guard is raised against the enemy without and no watch is kept upon the enemy within. It falls upon the three of us, and those we represent, to cooperate. There is no point in pulling against each other to keep Englishmen free, if by doing so we hand the country to a bloodthirsty mob who will take our freedoms and burn them in the marketplace.'

I try to look as if this makes sense to me, as if I can see why this discourse on the nature of wartime government is relevant to my being rousted from my bed in the early hours. Although I form my features into what I fondly hope is an expression of polite interest, I must be less of an actor than I had considered myself. Cooper coughs and continues in the manner of a man who has carefully constructed an argument only to find that his audience is unable to comprehend its subtleties.

'The criminal trial is, in a way, a microcosm of the nation itself. All three branches of the government play their part. A felon is prosecuted by the legislature. The servants of the executive investigate his crimes. Finally, he is told his fate by a judge. There is one additional element: the defence. You, Warrens. You test the evidence and the law. You represent the felon, but your true role is as the representative of freedom itself. The force you exert upon proceedings secures the liberty of the subject. This goes far beyond the personal freedom of some ne'er-do-well in the dock. It is a system that has served us well. Ordinarily I would not consider even a temporary departure from it. The Crown proposes, you oppose and that is the way it must be. But war is upon us. Our allies' defeat at Valmy makes real the prospect of invasion. Just as the branches of government must react to the times we find ourselves in, so must we.'

I make as if to interject. The judge bestows such a basilisk look upon me that I subside into my chair.

'Doctor McCreadie's report has presented me with a problem. I will be candid with you. You were selected for this case because I anticipated that your client would present himself to you in the manner he has. You would present your case accordingly and he would be convicted. Your client would hang and a terrible crime against the person of one of our most valued sailors would remain unexposed. I had anticipated that you would lack the resources to take the issue further than the evidence of your own eyes. I underestimated you.'

It is too much. I cannot remain silent. What on earth is he talking about? 'A crime against one of our most valued sailors?'

'I am at a loss, Judge.' I cannot bring myself to call him Cooper. 'I do not understand what you ask of me.'

The judge sighs, and is for a moment an elderly man. 'I cannot bring myself to repeat it. Nephew, it must fall to you to tell him. First, Warrens, you must swear that what you are about to hear will not pass beyond these walls. You must not disclose it. Not to your client, your clerk, your mistress or your mother. Do you understand?'

He produces a Bible from the writing desk and presents it to me. I place my hand upon it and mechanically repeat the oath. I am so overcome with curiosity that I can only nod like a halfwit. Lovell opens his mouth but is interrupted by the arrival of coffee. This is poured with what I consider to be an excess of ceremony. Lovell takes a deep draught as the footman closes the door behind him soundlessly. I wait. Lovell speaks:

'I do not propose to involve myself in the debate about whether your client is a man or a monkey, Warrens. There is no doubt that he is exactly what the Crown say – a cunning and dangerous spy. I am attached to a branch of government that is charged with the duty of frustrating the enemy. I have been to France frequently, both in this capacity and in order to conduct certain private business that enjoys official blessing if not sanction. I am the man the French call "The Pimpernel".'

He pauses, expecting a reaction that I am not equipped to provide. The what? What is a bloody pimpernel? Some kind of bell? The answer eludes me. Have I spent so long in this miserable place that my horizons have so narrowed that I am unaware of anything that is not of direct local interest? Clearly, as all present seem to think that it requires no further explanation. It seems that my ignorance is plain, as Lovell elaborates with an exasperation that suggests he is trying to teach a particularly stupid child its letters.

'"The Pimpernel" is the name given to an anonymous private citizen who has rescued a number of aristocrats condemned to death on the guillotine and spirited them away to the safety of England. I was aware of a faction within the Department of Public Security known as the "Bouchier Party" through my work in government service, of course. Their leader, Commandant Guillaume Bouchier, was responsible for the demise of a number of our people in Cherbourg. He was a Jacobin fanatic. A man possessed by the desire to end the rule of those empowered by God to do His bidding. A ruthless, cruel, pitiless servant of tyrants. I came across him and his men in the course of my own exploits and damn near lost my head for my pains. The man who nearly put a bullet through the Scarlet Pimpernel is your client, Warrens. I had rescued the Comtesse d'Auray from her dungeon. My men and I were hiding in mine workings, awaiting our chance to flee, when they came at us. God knows how they knew. I believe that the man who calls himself Jacques LeSinge used his abilities as a tracker to find us. It was pitch black, as black as the soul of the Devil you represent. We circled in the dark. I heard breathing and fired. There were two reports. I believed myself to be dead for a second, and then I heard his cry. I was unscathed. I thought my assailant dying and took the Countess to safety. I lost three men. Three good men, who had served my family well, abandoned to unmarked graves without even a Christian burial. I wish to God I had put another ball in him to make certain. I did not and I must live with the knowledge that my negligence set him free to perform an act of such atrocity . . .'

Lovell sniffs, and wipes his face upon his kerchief. I am unsure whether this is an affectation. A display of a conspicuously noble and wounded soul usually seeks an affirming 'there was nothing you could have done' or 'you must not blame yourself'. I am passing certain that any comment that detracts from his performance will stop it in its tracks, so I assume an expression that I hope conveys my deepest sympathy and regret. I will him to continue.

'I only became aware of his presence in London after the deed had been done. I even doubted the evidence that the Countess was able to give me after she had recovered from the ordeal to which he had subjected her, as I had assumed he would have met his fate at the hands of the Revolution at the same time as his odious master. It was only when I saw him down a pistol sight that I was sure. By that time, of course, he was already in the custody of the militia, so I was forced to exercise all my control to avoid finishing matters there and then. The law would have to take its course. There were too many witnesses to his capture who had already identified him as a spy for the bullet in the skull I favoured. You ask me what your client has done? I will tell you. He has ravaged the person of the Comtesse d'Auray, a woman of noble birth and great pulchritude. Not content with subjecting her to the sin of sodomy, he used the opportunity of his infiltration of her chambers to come upon Admiral Nelson like a footpad. I can scarcely bring myself to tell the full extent of his crime. Suffice to say that the commander of our navy, our bravest and most capable sailor, this English Paladin, will never enter the marital chamber at arms again.'

There is silence. I reprise the last statement. Surely he could not mean . . . ? A glance around my companions convinces me there is no misunderstanding. Bloody Hell! If there was ever a case that was sure to be discussed for decades! Cooper seems privy to my thoughts. He surveys me appraisingly.

'Warrens, you will of course remember your oath. I regret my choice of counsel for the defence. You have displayed a resource-fulness that I had not anticipated. I will not underestimate you again, or try to circumvent your reservations by subtle rhetoric. I need you to lose this trial. Your King needs you to lose this trial. England needs you to lose this trial. If you assist your Sovereign, you will find that he can be a most generous paymaster. Oh, I am not speaking of the few guineas you received as a brief fee.'

He raises his glass to the lamp, surveying its contents with feigned concentration. I am silent. What can I say?

'You have proved most tenacious in your pursuit of the truth, Warrens. I have always regarded this as a very laudable characteristic. Even,' he pauses, 'even a judicial one. Tell me, Fawsley, when does the Lord Chancellor invite soundings for appointments?'

'He takes them even now, Cooper.'

I am not an emotional man. I do not look on anger as an emotion as much as an entirely justified reaction to my circumstances. I have certainly never been at all prone to displays of public grief, yet I almost weep aloud at the preposterousness of it all. I, Warrens, a judge? His Honour Judge Warrens? Mr Justice Warrens? It has never been an ambition of mine, but then again it has never been a possibility. I have had no ambitions to fly, either. Now I have it in my grasp. His Honour Judge Warrens. Almost in my grasp, I should say, as the obstacle standing in my way is the complete impossibility of the request that is its precursor. I smile at the capriciousness of it all. I am a starving man with my face pressed against the pie-shop window. 'Would you like a pie? All you have to do is walk through the glass without breaking it.' My smile is misinterpreted.

'What do you find so amusing, Warrens?' The judge's voice is like a scourge. I am forced to express my thoughts.

'Well, Judge, I am surprised that you and Fawsley have not

seen the flaw in your plan. As I understand it the situation is as follows. You cannot reveal the true nature of the client's espionage in England without making the Admiral's fate public knowledge?'

A murmur of assent.

'Then the case cannot be lost. Consider this: if the client is a monkey and is found to be such then he is not guilty of espionage. Yet if the client is a man then he was arrested in uniform following a shipwreck. He is a prisoner of war and he is not guilty of espionage. I am flattered to be considered tenacious and judicial. I would assist, but I cannot. No one can.'

There is silence. They exchange smiles. Finally it is Fawsley who speaks. 'How do you intend to present the case, Warrens?'

'I will call Doctor McCreadie, tender him to your cross-examination and point out the complete lack of evidence of espionage.'

'What if you were to reprise your argument at the arraignment?'

I pause. 'I'd have to be some kind of fool, wouldn't I? I have a piece of evidence that destroys your case. Why would I fail to make use of it?'

'And your client. He has instructed you that he is a lieutenant in the French navy? Has he?'

'Well no, but . . .'

'As I recall, your instructions are as you kindly relayed to me when we met in the Bar mess. Your client capered, filled his hand with his own filth and pelted you. In short, you are instructed that you are defending a monkey. Your professional duty is to present those instructions. You are not obliged to suggest more plausible defences to the client. Good God, man, if you were to do this you would be breaking every rule of conduct ever written. You would be disbarred.'

This is true. It is a rule that if observed would mean a practice consisting of guilty pleas, but a rule none the less. His argument has but one flaw.

'My professional obligations require me to disclose the report to the client, do they not?'

It falls to the judge to be Mephistopheles.

'My dear Warrens, you cannot expect advancement without making sacrifices. You must not present this defence. Doctor McCreadie's report must never see the light of day. I would not ask any member of the Bar to betray his calling were it not for the calumny of this defendant and the real threat we are under. Are you blind to the discontent, the loss of deference? I see it every day. It is like a hydra. Every head I remove is replaced by two. Revolution will be upon us if we do not act to prevent it. I would happily hang every man, woman and child in England to stave off the sort of tyranny we see in France. You will be rewarded. You are not asked to betray your conscience entirely. You are asked to forbear from providing a criminal with material from which he could manufacture a dishonest defence. That is all. If you cannot find it in your heart to serve your country, then at least serve yourself. I cannot believe that the prospect of defending Mr Sturrock and his chickens again is so appealing.'

He is right, of course. What have I to lose? I'll tell you exactly. I have poor lodgings, cheap wine, appalling food and my fame as a one-guinea brief. Not much to weigh in any scale, yet they hang about me like leg-irons, pulling me down to what has become so much my level that I cease even to see it as humiliation. Against this all I have to set is my conscience, which, being intangible, is weightless. It is the only salvage from my downfall and seems a petty conceit in the face of my advancement. I feel the wind pluck at my clothing as I survey the riches of the earth from this high place. A gnawing practicality distracts me.

'But what of Doctor McCreadie? Even if I were to agree, surely he would bring the matter to public attention? I got the impression he intended to make a learned paper of the case.'

'You need not concern yourself with the good doctor, Warrens. His sins have found him out, poor chap. He liked the good things of life whether he could afford them or not. His debts were held by a number of institutions sympathetic to the national interest. A simple matter to have them called in simultaneously. He was only in Newgate for a couple of days before he expired. I understand he had no confidants, so the contents of his report are published exclusively in this room. I feel almost privileged in my gnosis, don't you, Uncle?'

Lovell's laugh is as cruel as a paper cut. Fawsley and the judge join in chorus. For a moment I look behind the polish and see a shadow of what I could become. I join their laughter, feeling that dissent could consign me to the same fate. I know that incarceration is hazardous. Gaol fever, assault, all loomed in from the dark. If a man had no money or no family, death could be a swift coincidence. Yet I am sure it was no happenstance that has reunited McCreadie with his maker. I realize that I hang above an abyss. Great leviathans lurch and wheel beneath me, offering me protection if I will be their slave. I make a choice, telling myself all along I can resile from it when I am beyond their clutches, that I am not committing myself. I am sure I do not doubt it.

'So what do you want me to do?' An enquiry, no more.

'We expect you to present your case. You will continue to assert that your client is a monkey. You will do so throughout the trial, no matter what may transpire. All we are asking is for you to go to court and present your client's instructions to the best of your ability. What could possibly be the harm in that?'

He is right. What possible harm can come from my doing that which I have done almost every day of my professional life? I grasp for another practicality, anything to allow me time to weigh up what I have heard.

'It has occurred to you that it is entirely possible that this defence may succeed? After all, the client displays almost exclusively simian features. Were it not for Doctor McCreadie I would not myself have recognized the subtleties that distinguish him from a true ape. I am not unconvincing as an advocate. I could procure acquittal without McCreadie. While you may have ruled that you cannot rely on the evidence of your eyes, Judge, you cannot exclude the jury from doing precisely that.'

The creatures of the state exchange smiles. They do not exclude me from their secrets, and I feel an unfamiliar gratitude. They appear happy to have a chance to explain an adroitness that would otherwise have gone unrecognized. It seems that the joyous task of explaining matters to me will fall to Cooper.

'Have you seen the pamphlet? I'm sure you have. I read it in court just before you had your outburst. It seemed to enrage you in the way I calculated it would. This has been circulating in the locality since we became aware of the capture. Every person who could conceivably serve on the jury has read it. Our friends have done their work well. Anyone seeing your client cannot help but be reminded of it, and its helpful illustrations.'

I recall the simian Frenchman, a hairy face glowering under a cap of liberty.

'We have a great deal of influence, Warrens. Do not underestimate us. We are professional men who detest the mere prospect
of leaving anything to chance. We are aware of the problem. The
pamphlet can only take matters so far. Fortunately there are only
a very limited number of persons whose property qualifies them
to sit on a jury. Of these, like all groups, there are those of wit
and intellect who would regard this pamphlet as a crude piece
of demagoguery fit only for fools and there are, well, those upon
whom the subtleties of this no doubt great piece of literature are,
frankly, wasted. They have just enough faculties to register that
this is what a Frenchman looks like. We will ensure that the jury
is composed of these. God knows, if everything has its use, as the
philosophers would have us believe, then we are probably offering
these individuals a reason for their existence. No, I feel sure that
there is no prospect of your client being found to be a monkey.'

I cannot prevaricate. I have to agree to betray the client or
. . . well, I have no way of finding out the consequences of my
demurring. It has been said that every man's life reaches a
crossroads at which he has to choose between that which is right
and that which is right for him. Dilettantes will tell you that the
choice a man makes will determine whether he is moral or venal,
Brutus, the noblest Roman of them all, or Iago the jealous. I
know this to be false. A man's life will present him with occasions
that require him to assent or dissent. That much is true. These
occasions have as little true choice as the decision to take a breath.
I would hold nothing dearer than the possibility of choosing to do
right. The ethics of my profession demand that I reject the judge's
proposal. They also demand that I decline to act for a client who
has told me he is guilty, of course, so I don't imagine that this
broken fence should detain me for too long. Betrayal does not

seem the right thing, yet I am filled with the vision of Sturrock on the day he paid my last fee. I can see his lascivious hand upon his daughter's breast with the clarity of a detail in a fresco. Am I really doing right by condemning myself to be his faithful advocate? Is there no course that is both right and right for me?

I sigh, realizing that there is no choice, and hence there is no rectitude. I have my back to a rock. It will not yield. Before me stands the foe. I cannot overcome his ferrous might. I am but flesh. I protect my client. My client the murderer and spy. My client who has made a fool of me and caused my incarceration (even if this was indirectly). My client who has pelted me with his shit. I am but flesh. I feel pain. I feel cold. I feel the prison gates behind me like a blow between my shoulder blades. I taste indifferent wine and poor food. I see Sturrock at the head of a legion I have represented and will represent again if I refuse, assuming I can refuse. I hold my choice and it is as insubstantial as a conscience. I accept. It does not have the flavour of choice. It tastes of destiny.

19

Trial

I T STARTS TOMORROW. IT IS PAST MIDNIGHT AND I AM SEATED
at my desk. There is brandy in the decanter. My papers are
spread before me. A candle provides the only light. I am the
very picture of the conscientious advocate. Yet that is all I am, a
picture. I am a representation of that which I once was. An actor.
I read the papers but know that no matter what they may relate
to me I will be saying the same thing to the court. I have a part
to play. I have my script. I take a pull at my brandy and feel the
warmth concentrate in my chest and migrate to my extremities.
It is some comfort. It flows into the vacancy that I feel and for a
moment I am delighted. Then my melancholy returns. It settles
about me like a damp coat. I push the papers to one side.

I have started a journey that I cannot stop. I am not even sure
that I want to. After all, its destination will see me ensconced
upon the bench. I have always supposed that I had no ambition
for judicial office. I thought myself immune to those feelings of
envy that I knew filled some of my fellows as soon as the judge

swept into court. The alacrity with which I lunged at this offer surprises even me. Clearly, the rhetoric of egalitarian humility in which I had clothed my rejection was exaggerated to say the least. I held myself out as not wanting to sit in judgement, knowing, as I thought, that others had already judged me unsuitable. If I am to look at this dispassionately it could be said to prove the easy disguises the mind puts on to make discovering one's mediocrity bearable. It transpires that my shortcomings were not as overwhelming as I have recently supposed. My mind wanders to other ambitions that I have never dared to voice. Perhaps they, too, could be within my reach. I hold this thought. It combines with the brandy and I am at peace for a moment.

I reach for the decanter and realize that I am excruciatingly tired. Dear God, I can barely lift it to my glass. I have not been sleeping well since my . . . since my what? How would one describe it? I have mulled this over at length and find I prefer the word 'arrangement'. There are less pleasant descriptions. Unless I remain vigilant the word 'betrayal' slinks into my thoughts like an assassin. I cannot allow it. I cannot permit myself to think that I have lost something irretrievable, even for a moment. I am not afraid to sleep. Sleep is fine. I never remember my dreams, if I dream at all. It is those moments between sleep and wakefulness that I fear. It comes upon me then, and I cannot but wake myself to resist it. It starts with a sideways pull to the pit of my stomach. A lurch, followed by an icy deluge. Then a fall. Not a plummet, but a graceful descent, sideslipping through my resistance to settle in a cold place. It is how I imagine a shipwreck once the fury of the waves has done its will and all is lost.

I am not religious. Oh, I believe in God. Everyone except heathens and revolutionaries does. I even go to church occasionally. I was baptized, or so I believe, and, if questioned, would describe myself as a Christian. I have never been given to the morbidity of excessive religious thought, which I have always regarded as being the exclusive domain of lunatics and hypocrites. My mother had a sampler, which I am sure she cultivated as a means of irritating my father. I cannot recall the precise phrase it bore, but it was something to the effect that it profits a man little if he gains all the riches in the world and loses his soul in the process. I used to find this ironic, given my father's fate. If he had sold his soul, then he had overestimated its value considerably. I find it intrudes upon me now, my mother's sampler. It irritates and goads me as only the most absolute and simplistic morality can. It names me damned. Even at my most optimistic, when the sun is high and I have a good quart of wine in my belly, I can see its relevance. It damns me. I had a duty and I betrayed it. I am condemned by a dead woman's needlepoint. When I am in my depths I can see it stitched upon me like stigmata.

I can dispel it, of course. I rise and confront it with the fury of a man correctly accused of cheating at cards. It is the simplification that offends me most. A man is damned when he chooses to sin. If I have sinned, and I do not necessarily accept this, then I have done so without the luxury of free choice. I have often wondered what would have happened if I had refused. I am sure that I know the answer. If I am in danger of forgetting it I need only remember the words 'Newgate', 'McCreadie' and 'the debtor's press'. I had no choice. It is as complex and as simple as that. I know this. My whole rational being knows this, yet once again I am awake at my desk in the early hours. I assume it is like a wound. It will itch and prick at me until time heals it. Eventually I will not feel it at all.

The dark seems thicker at this time in the morning. I go to the window and look out. It is palpable, settling at the edge of the circle of light before the window like snow. I drink more brandy and the fire returns. It is darkest before dawn, they say. In a few hours it will be a new day. I will rest my head among the papers a while. It will be time to rise and go to court soon enough. I will dream of England and tell myself that I have done my duty.

I find myself at the court with little memory of getting there. I have not seen the client in my capacity as his advocate since our first encounter at the prison and I do not visit him in the cell this morning. Convention has it that an advocate should take his last conference with his client at this stage, but I will not face him. It would not tally with the defence I am to advance. I used to enjoy the theatre when I lived in London. I was practically a regular at Covent Garden, so I can appreciate the importance of narrative consistency. I take my seat on the advocate's bench. Fawsley is already in court. He does not acknowledge me and I make no overture. It would be comforting to have my membership of whatever club it is that I have joined confirmed, but I can see that he, too, is playing his part. He is to be the stern champion of the state. I am to be the upstart defender of the indefensible. He will despise me and I him. I look round the court. The public gallery is empty. Our audience has yet to arrive but we players must remain in role. I open the brief and pretend to engross myself in the case. I cannot prevent myself from allowing an ironic smile to pass my lips. I look up, and catch Fawsley in the act of avoiding my eyes. He seems completely at ease, a man whose early mornings are spent in his bed, and who does not need brandy or philosophy to lull him to sleep. I find this curiously reassuring, as if I have seen another patient in a sanatorium who has been cured of an ailment identical to my own. I drop my eyes and return to my pretence.

This is no remand court. There is no other business but our trial, so I am spared the tedious banter and carping of men of the law. A distant clock chimes the hour and there is a susurration behind me as the public galley begins to fill. This ebbs and flows until there is a tumult of disjointed conversation and noise as chairs are moved across an unpolished floor and people discuss the coming entertainment. I do not turn to acknowledge them. I am above that. I sit and regard my props as I go over my lines. A rap upon the door silences the crowd. Mr Justice Cooper makes his entrance. Moments later the client is led from the cells to the dock in chains. I can feel the public intake of breath. There is an unreality about it all that seems obvious only to me. The judge greets us and inclines his head to Fawsley who rises. I half expect applause, and I am left with a vague sense of disappointment when the public gallery remains silent. My opponent confirms that there are no matters of law to occupy the court. We proceed to empanel the jury.

I have conducted many trials. Selecting twelve good men to judge the client has previously been a ritual that I have enjoyed. I assess, appraise and judge each one, finding them sympathetic, winnable or lost as they take their oath. It is an inexact process, but it brings me happiness when I am right and outright joy when I am able to win round the intractables. I can barely raise my eyes from the desk to watch them file in today. I know what I am to expect, and I am sure that I will not be disappointed. A jury of fools. Twelve men who are happy to believe that the truth does not lie in their own experience but in a pamphlet that confirms their worst fears. The first takes the oath. He is a small man whose wig fails to conceal his bald pate. He has a weathered face and discoloured teeth. There is something deeply objectionable about him, and I challenge. I do not have to show cause. I am permitted to discard without voicing my reasons, which in this case are purely to deprive a distasteful nonentity of his day in what approximates to the limelight. Depriving Mr Malcolm Butcher, a farmer, of his tavern tale gives me a rush of pure pleasure. I am shot a warning look from the bench but I continue. I am sure that Mr Justice Cooper is as aware of the conventions of our little drama as I am. I am Warrens. I object. I defend. It is what I do and the assembled public wants to see the show. If I acquiesced it would be as much a wasted day for them as watching dogs worrying a dead bear. I challenge two more, one because he reminds me of a wine merchant to whom I owe money and the other because, well, I have always found an excess of nasal hair abhorrent. My tactics can only delay. The jury box fills with the inevitability of an hourglass. Each juror seems more deficient an example of humanity than the last. They shuffle into public office with the lowing placidity of the ring parade at an agricultural show. It is done. The jury of fools has been appointed, the players are at their stations and the bench bids us proceed with a smile as thin as workhouse gruel. On with the show.

My learned opponent opens his case. I am not sure whether I care for Fawsley even now. There is a whiff of sanctimony about him. I can almost blind myself to it, reasoning that a man in my position lacks the leisure to choose his own acquaintances, but not quite. I do admire his skill. He opens the case with such brevity and economy that by the time he calls his first witness I am convinced of the client's guilt. Lacking diversion,

I occupy myself by speculating as to the cause of his cavernous open pores. I can count twelve on the left side of his nose alone. I begin an exhaustive examination of my quill as Sergeant Crooks takes the oath, concluding only after he has finished his evidence. Predictably, his testimony reprises his deposition with a preternatural accuracy that I consider in the light of my gnosis. Can it be that trials are always stage-managed and I have been the only participant unaware of this? I am so caught up in my reverie that I come within inches of failing to notice that I must rise to cross-examine. Have a care, Warrens! Only a poor player misses his cue. I haul myself to my feet, affecting an air of utter boredom.

'A few questions, Sergeant.'

He regards me with suspicion. I am struck by his extra-ordinary ugliness. The page does not do him justice. He resembles the product of a union between a pig and a baboon. If I had not been party to the bargain, I would have found the judge's refusal to accept the client was a monkey instantly more comprehensible.

'You say that when you and your, ah, colleagues, had my client at bay you heard him speak French, do you not?'

He grunts his assent.

'Would you describe your discourse in that tongue as fluent?'

A cruel trick and one that I would regret were this individual not lying so transparently. It brings the inevitable response.

'I don't understand your question, sir.'

'I do apologize, Sergeant. Have I outstripped you already?'

The judge's already high colour has taken on a pleasing terra-cotta hue. 'Mr Warrens!'

'My Lord?' I am the model of mild bewilderment. The result

may be predestined, the itinerary may be tightly scheduled, but there is nothing in the script that dictates that the Crown's witnesses must travel to their destination in comfort.

'Pray do not berate the witness and confine yourself to proper questioning, sir.'

'My profoundest apologies, My Lord. I had no intention of making an improper suggestion to this stalwart of the constabulary.'

Mr Justice Cooper considers the prospect of confronting me and decides that the potential humiliation of debating the licentious and non-licentious meanings of the word 'improper' is unlikely to enhance the awe in which the court is held.

'Proceed.'

'I am grateful, My Lord.' I turn to the witness. 'Very well, Sergeant, I will try to put my question in the most basic terms I can imagine.' I smile at him and address him as if I am presenting a child with a particularly desirable Christmas present. 'Do you speak French, Sergeant?'

A pause. He has regressed. He can see the lion and is deciding whether to flee or fight. His jaw clenches. Good. I like a fight.

'Not well, sir, but I believe I can recognize it when others speak it.'

I smile lazily. I am a shark. '*Also gut, mien gut man. Was ist eure name?*'

Silence.

'Your French not up to a response, Sergeant?'

'I have already told you that I don't speak it, sir. I knew that you were speaking it, though.'

I roll on to my back and coast through the water towards his dangling legs. 'Are you sure?'

'Most certainly, sir.'

'Very good, Sergeant. I will inform you that it was not French. Have you any response?'

'Are you sure, sir?'

'Perfectly. Would it surprise you to learn that I was not speaking French?'

He does not reply. He directs an imploring look towards the bench – the sort of glance I imagine he directed at his mother. Mr Justice Cooper rises to his defence like a lioness.

'Mr Warrens, this is a court. It is not a schoolroom. If you wish to teach the witness Dutch, then I suggest that you and he enter a private arrangement.'

I ponder this interjection with insolent leisure. I am not surprised that Fawsley greets it with an un-gentlemanly amusement that his fabled reserve seems unable to suppress. I shrug my resignation as a wave of laughter from the public gallery breaks over my back. I wait for it to subside before replying.

'My Lord, it is the sergeant's evidence that he understood my client to have addressed him in French. This, in turn, makes up the very foundation of the Crown's case that my client is a spy. Unless you are able to direct me otherwise, I cling to my belief that the purpose of a trial is to contest the evidence and allow the jury to reach a conclusion upon that which they have heard. This has included an opportunity for the defence to put their case to the witnesses in every trial I have conducted. Of course, if your Lordship is directing me that I may not, then I will abide by your ruling, but it would be such an unusual departure from precedent that I would feel the need for some form of instruction as to how it has come about and why.'

I allow my voice to trail off. Mr Justice Cooper shuffles the papers on his lectern. His reply is lacking in the grace that his office might suggest is within his capabilities. 'Proceed, Mr Warrens. But confine yourself to questioning the witness. You will have your opportunity to make a speech. The experience to which you refer will doubtless confirm that it would depart from precedent to allow you to take it halfway through the prosecution case.'

I return to the witness. 'Would you say that you have a good memory, Sergeant?'

'I would, sir.'

'Good. You are doubtless blessed by this.' The judge's glare thunders across my bows with the subtlety of a broadside. 'Are you able to assist the court by sharing your recollection of the nature of the seditious chants you attribute to portions of the population of Hartlepool?'

'Yes sir, I am. They were shouting . . .' He pauses. I nod to him to continue. He assumes the coarse dialect of the locality to lend his reply an authenticity. 'A constable is always able. To steal the bread from a poor man's table. By the squire is where he'll stand. To rob us of our common land.'

'Is that exactly what was chanted?'

'Yes sir.'

'And you refer to my client hanging from a tavern sign, do you not?'

'I do, sir.'

'And can you recall the name of the tavern?'

'Indeed, sir. It was the Rose and Crown.'

'And when you looked into his face and saw what you describe as criminal cunning, are you able to tell the court of the lighting conditions?'

'Torchlight.'

'Torchlight, you say. Not, perhaps, the most clear light, wouldn't you agree?'

He smiles. He thinks he has seen my point and will move to counter it. 'If you mean that the light was too poor for me to see what I saw, you are wrong sir. There were many torches.'

'How many?'

'Twelve. I had one. Bacon carried one, and members of the militia nine. There was one in a bracket outside the tavern as well.'

'An admirable recollection. You refer to your colleague Constable Bacon's expressing some doubt about my client's humanity. What words did he use?'

The constable blushes.

'Pray do not be embarrassed. Use the precise words.'

'He said, "Fucking hell, it's a bloody monkey," sir.'

I smile. The trap is almost sprung.

'You refer to my client as hurling what you term as "brickbats and defiances" at you and your colleagues. I hope that I have accurately noted your evidence. Am I correct in my recollection?'

'You are, sir. I have held the office of constable for nigh twenty years and never have I heard such fury.'

'So it remained in your mind, then?'

'Oh yes, sir. I am unlikely to forget it.'

'Etched upon your memory, then?'

'Sir.'

I bend and make a play of consulting my notes. The court is silent as it waits for the next question. I glance up and notice the witness has the constipated look of a man resisting the urge to smile in deference to the majesty of the occasion. I lower my voice to a near whisper to ensure the jury hangs on my every word.

'What did he say?'

He has the wit to realize his predicament. The smugness drains from his face. He is forced back to a perennial response.

'I don't understand the question, sir.'

There is a snort of derision from the public gallery. It is solitary, but I can feel the season change. It is the cuckoo that announces the coming of the spring of Warrens. I look at the jury directly, smile and shrug. I am rewarded by three childlike grins. I conclude that it would be premature to interpret it as sympathy. It may be merely wind.

'It's a very simple question. I am sure you will understand if you muster your powers of reason as I ask it again.'

There is an eruption from the bench. I ignore it.

'What did he say? What words did he use to express his "brickbats and defiances"?'

Silence. The Sergeant looks between Fawsley and the judge in desperation. I plough on before they can ride to his rescue.

'You have astounded us all with your prodigious memory today, Sergeant. You have told this jury that the curses my client pronounced are etched upon your memory. I am asking you to show us your etchings.'

There is a positive gale of laughter. I notice with satisfaction that five jurors have joined the merriment. I allow it to subside before pressing on. I can feel a tingle in my fingertips. It is so unfamiliar that it takes me a moment to place it. I am enjoying myself.

'Well? Does your memory fail you?'

Mr Justice Cooper yawns. He removes a fob watch from his robe and consults it with exaggerated concentration. 'Gentlemen, it is one o'clock. We shall leave matters there until after luncheon.'

I am outraged. I rise to protest to see that I am about to address my objections to his retreating back and resume my seat with poor grace. I muster my papers then stalk out of court in an exaggerated display of anger. I repair to the Bar mess but find that I have no hunger. My digestion is an intricate knot, and I can stomach no more than a half decanter of Burgundy. I am sipping my wine and reviewing the depositions when I am interrupted by a quite unmannerly kick to the sole of my shoe. It is my opponent. I cannot resist the impulse to order him to bring me my pipe. He flushes, and it dawns on me that he has no recollection of the incident in which our roles were reversed.

'A word, Warrens.' He gestures to the door. I follow him without urgency, pausing on the threshold to light my pipe. Fawsley seems to be in a state of agitation.

'What the hell do you think you are playing at?'

He is a pre-emptor, a trait that could easily be elevated to a flaw in his character. My reply is a mirror of the witness.

'I don't understand, Fawsley. What do you mean, "What am I playing at"? I am fulfilling my part of the bargain. I am defending my client in a show of sound and fury that will doubtless signify nothing in the face of the preparations that you and your colleagues have made.'

We stand at the corner of the street. The day is overcast, but as we speak the sun breaks through to shine upon us. The open pores upon Fawsley's cheeks strike me inconsequentially. He maintains his smile. I had thought it bereft of warmth when I first encountered him. It is as bleak as tundra now. He addresses me through clenched teeth.

'You are in danger of winning this trial, you fool. Rein yourself in, or you will ruin everything.'

I open my mouth to respond, but he cuts me off. 'Do not underestimate us, Warrens. You are here to give us a good show. That is all. You will be rewarded if you do as you are told. I do not recall an acquittal entering into our contract. If you put yourself in breach by your antics you will find that your previous experience of debt collection is a mere nursery game. I am sure you would benefit by reflecting upon Doctor McCreadie. Making yourself surplus to requirements would be very rash indeed, wouldn't you say? I am sure your physician would not recommend it.'

The sun hides again and a blast of wind fresh from the North Sea slices through my clothing. I shiver. Fawsley smiles again, making me long for the clemency of the elements.

'Good. I can see we all know where we stand. Look at the judge if you need any more aides-memoires. I am sure you will find the robes most becoming. If not – well, defending chicken thieves may come to represent your finest hour.'

He spins on his heel and marches away, his black robes flying about him. I watch his progress as I collect myself. My breath is shallow and fast. I know that I have no choice. I can see the signposts on the road that point me towards where my own self-interest lies. Yet I can still see my mother's sampler in my mind's eye. 'It little profits a man.' A treacherous voice tells me that I could win, and win a trial I know is rigged to boot. What triumph that would be. I would win back my soul. I would be a free man, beholden to no one and triumphant. I would be at a pinnacle. The shipwreck asserts itself. A free man? Ridiculous! The only freedom that would bring me is the choice of whether to stand passively awaiting my doom or assay some pitiful flight. Freedom indeed. My soul would not buy me a solitary glass of bad wine in Newgate, assuming I was fortunate enough to have the chance to drink one. I sigh, light my pipe again and hunch my way back to court. I will make do. An unbidden spark reminds me of the savage joy of victory but I snuff it out. I will get by. It is what I do.

The public gallery hums like a hive. I take my place and see that Sergeant Crooks has returned to the witness box. The rules of court prohibit him from discussing his evidence during the adjournment, but rules are not made to restrain those paid to enforce them. He has a confidence about him that suggests that he has been well prepared. We all await the judge. Our cues have been taken and I am struck with the irony that both of us have benefited from a voice from the prompt box. I sip my water and avoid my opponent's eye. Enter the judge stage left and I rise to play my part, encumbered by the chains of my obligation.

'Sergeant Crooks, I last asked you what words you heard my client utter. Do you recall that?'

'I do, sir.'

'And you have no difficulties in understanding the question?'

'No.'

'So what is your answer?'

'I do not recall the precise words, sir. I can only say that I was disturbed by their ferocity.'

I cannot resist this. I consider leaving the point and realize that it would be more damaging were I to do so. I shiver like a greyhound. I am trained to the hare and cannot help myself but run when the chase is on, though my heart may burst with the exertion.

'You cannot even paraphrase them? Despite your prodigious memory?'

More laughter. I have found that nothing whets the appetites of the public gallery better than a constable in distress.

'No, sir.' He recalls the luncheon's coaching and interjects his best and most damaging point. 'After all, sir, your client spoke in French.'

'Ah yes, Constable. He spoke in a language that you do not understand, have never heard spoken and yet you possess an ability to recognize. So how do you know he was berating you rather than, say, asking you for a glass of wine?'

He has the exaggerated conceit of the petty tyrant. I can see that his role as the comic relief has not pleased him. There is a telltale pulse at his temple that suggests an ill-considered outburst is to follow.

'It's Sergeant, sir. Besides, it was how he said it not what he said. He bared his teeth and screamed at us. I have never seen the like before or since. He was like a wild animal at bay.'

He snaps his teeth to try to bite it back. Too late. I can see Fawsley out of the corner of my eye, but I am far beyond his remonstration. I feel curiously distant, as if I am in the audience and not on the stage. I am willing my character to pursue the point and, being in every respect as convincing as Hamlet, I am pleased to note that he does.

'A wild animal at bay, you say. He was at bay, was he not?'

Silence. The answer is as obvious as a blemish. I do not wait for it to be vocalized but press on, hurtling towards a conclusion with a recklessness I had forgotten I ever possessed. The blood sings in my veins like a chorus, encouraging new feats of rhetoric. I am saved. I will win. I am filled with the knowledge that I can do nothing else. I have been tempted but I have not fallen. It little profits a man. My Golgotha may await me but now, in this instant, I am no one-guinea brief. I know that Fawsley is wrong. Whatever may befall me I will still have this moment.

'What made you discount your colleague's opinion that my client was a monkey?'

'The gentleman said he was a spy, sir. He ordered us to arrest him.'

'Is this gentleman in court today?'

He looks around. 'No, sir.'

'Have you seen him before?'

'No.'

'Or since?'

'No.'

'Yet you take his word over your colleague's? Over the evidence of your own eyes?'

'He was a gentleman, sir.'

I pause momentarily to digest this. I have travelled too far along the road to redemption to stop.

'I suggest to you that he was dressed as a gentleman, is that not the case?'

'Yes, sir.'

'And spoke like a gentleman, I'm sure. Now tell me, Constable, what did my client look like?'

The response was automatic. No comment of mine could have been more eloquent than the laughter it precipitated.

'It's Sergeant, sir. I don't understand the question, sir.'

'I will endeavour to simplify it for you. Would it be fair to say that my client stands no taller than a child of eleven?'

A grunt of assent.

'That he is covered in dense hair? That he is able to caper, shriek and hang by his legs from a tavern sign? That he behaved when trapped, in your words "like a wild animal at bay"?'

Another barely audible grunt.

314

'And yet you deny that he is a monkey on the basis of the word of someone whom you have not seen before and who has not come to court to justify his conclusion before this jury? That is your evidence, is it not?'

Reluctant agreement.

'Could you discount the suggestion that this individual was not an escaped lunatic? A figment of your imagination?'

He cannot. He has lost his assurance and hangs in the dock like a scarecrow, a dejected collection of straw in uniform. I put him out of his misery.

'No further questions, My Lord.'

I resume my seat to a smattering of applause that is quelled by a bloodthirsty glare from the bench. It has been some time since this judge has transported the entire public gallery, but the legend lives on. I bask in my satisfaction until I am distracted by a tug at my sleeve. It is a turnkey.

'What do you want?'

The man stammers, 'Your client, sir. He wants to speak to you.'

I do not turn to see what is going on, although I am becoming aware of an altercation in the dock. I hiss from the corner of my mouth, 'My client is a monkey. I am not in the habit of discussing matters with animals, be they wild or domesticated. He's probably hungry. Give him an apple or something.'

There is an ominous hubbub behind me, punctuated by the clank of fetters. It is too indistinct for me to discern what exactly is being said or by whom, so I ignore it. The evidence has concluded, and it is time for closing speeches. I have no witnesses to call and I am not permitted to call my client even if I were minded to do so. Fawsley rises, bows to the judge and turns to the jury. It is a pregnant moment, which he exploits to the full. Silence falls behind me as even the client awaits the case for the prosecution.

'Gentlemen of the jury, it is your task to judge the facts in this case. It is hard for the Crown to convince you, and rightly so. We bring this case and must prove it beyond reasonable doubt. We must produce evidence that makes you sure that the defendant is what and whom we say he is. This defendant is charged with espionage. The evidence must make you sure firstly that he has committed or intends to commit acts against the security of the nation and secondly that he has done so on behalf of a foreign power. We must also prove that this took place at a time at which our country was at war, a fact that I am sure you will not find it hard to accept. We say that this defendant is a Frenchman, we are at war with France and that the absence of any explanation from the defence as to his presence allows you to infer an intention to commit acts against the national security.

'Consider this. The defence make the following admissions. Firstly, that the French vessel *Thermidore* exploded and foundered on the night that the defendant was apprehended by the constabulary and militia. Secondly, that the defendant has no parole or passport that would permit his presence in the country at time of war. Thirdly, that he did not seek official protection when he had the chance so to do. This last is significant. Many Frenchmen now reside in England. Their presence among us cannot be described as welcome, but they are not spies. They are unfortunates seeking refuge from the vile revolutionary regime that has settled upon their unhappy country like a succubus. All of them have this in common – that when they arrived upon our shores they sought out the authorities and asked for sanctuary.

Yet this man fled the constables and had to be captured by force of arms. The Crown do not say that all Frenchmen in England are spies, but ask you to conclude from how this individual has conducted himself that the only reason for his presence is that he intends to cause us harm.

'And how did he conduct himself? Well, you have heard the evidence of Sergeant Crooks. When he was challenged he fled. You may ask yourself whether a shipwrecked sailor would have run rather than surrender, if shipwrecked sailor was all he was. When cornered, he fought. You may ask yourselves if an enemy soldier in uniform would have carried on against such overwhelming odds. After all, in either case he is no Englishman. When compelled to give account of himself, he adopted a scandalous pretence. It is to that pretence I will turn now.

'Members of the jury, you have a difficult task. Do not allow your arduous responsibilities to be made more difficult by distractions. You have heard the evidence of a sergeant of the Hartlepool Parish Constabulary, a man of good character. He has told you that this defendant, this man, spoke French in his presence and hearing. That is the fact. My learned friend Mr Warrens showed us all he was an educated man. He showed us all that if one is minded to misuse one's education, it is a simple matter to tie up an honest man in the silken twine of dishonest words. Do not allow yourself to be distracted by discussions about the words 'animal at bay' and their meaning. Do not allow yourself to be misled by these tricks, for tricks are what they remain. You will be asked to examine the defendant and conclude he is a monkey. Examine him. Take note of his features and compare them with your knowledge of the enemy. He is short, but are there not those among us who are short? He is hairy, but are not the French renowned as a hirsute race? Ask yourself why a man in his position would advance such a defence and conclude, as we invite you, that the only reason for such a desperate stratagem is the desperation of a man lying to save his neck. After all, we are Englishmen. Had he claimed to be a prisoner of war then his plea would have been accepted and he would have been treated with the courtesy that we bestow even upon our enemies. He did not. Ask yourself why he did not. The only answer to this question is the one we invite you to find. He did not claim to be a prisoner of war, because he is a spy.

'Gentlemen of the jury, in due course you will be invited to retire to deliberate upon your verdict. I ask you to do nothing more than your patriotic duty. Return the only verdict that the evidence will support. It is one of guilty.'

It is a fine piece of work. Once again I am forced to acknowledge Fawsley's skill. Now it is my turn. I moisten my throat and begin.

'Gentlemen of the jury, this has been a fortunate day for you. I understand that we would usually be charged a penny to see the monkey, yet here we all are. The monkey sits behind me. We may look at him for free. Some of us are actually being paid for our trip to the menagerie.'

The shouts of laughter are stamped flat by cries of 'Silence in court.'

'Make no mistake. He is a monkey. His pelt, his features and his carriage all point to this. You have been asked to have regard to the evidence of Sergeant Crooks. Allow me to repeat this exhortation. Have regard to his memory. It was so reliable that he could remember everything save for those details that may prove inconvenient to the Crown's case, and ask yourself if you could regard this as coincidence. You may be blessed with charitable indulgence. You may be saying to yourselves that it could be a coincidence. Well then, consider his assertion that he recognized that my client was speaking French, a language he could not speak but yet possessed a preternatural ability to identify even when it was not actually spoken. You may feel that this was another coincidence. We seem to be collecting them. You may even feel that the sergeant is cursed with a common character flaw – that of being unable to admit that he is wrong. His colleague thought that my client was a monkey. He based this upon the evidence of his own eyes. He saw my client hang from a tavern sign by his feet. Now, members of the jury, I have no doubt that the French are a dexterous race. We have all heard of their ingenuity in the construction of buildings. They have even taken to the skies suspended beneath vast bags of hot air. I have yet to hear it is common among them to hang by the feet. I do not recall this being said of Joan of Arc. I have read Shakespeare's plays, as we all have. Do the French hang by their heels before Agincourt in *Henry the Fifth*? They do not. I would invite you to conclude that the sergeant's evidence is a bag of hot air. Do not allow yourself to be suspended beneath it like the ingenious French.

'Yet this evidence is crucial to the Crown. It is the only evidence that my client can speak at all, let alone discourse in the language of the enemy. You have heard the assertion that he would have been treated with courtesy had he claimed to be a prisoner of war. Discount that out of hand. My client is a monkey. Expecting him to claim to be prisoner of war is a fantasy. You may as well expect a lost dog to ask for directions. The very facts to which my learned friend refers point towards the truth.'

There have been mutterings behind me throughout my speech. I have ignored them. After all, it would be inconsistent with my case for me to turn and take the client's instructions. As I touch upon the issue of the client as prisoner of war, they rise to a crescendo that cannot be eclipsed by my own efforts. I turn and see that he seems to be engaged in some form of combat with the turnkeys. He throws one off his back and shouts across the court. I am unable to pass this off as anything other than speech, and to make matters worse, it is in perfect French.

'*Menteur. Traître. Il est où, Docteur McCreadie? Vous savez qui je suis. Je suis Lieutenant Jacques LeSinge de la Marine Revolutionaire. Vous m'avez trahi. Vous êtes fini.*'

It is no less damaging to my case for being true. 'Liar. Traitor. I am Lieutenant Jacques LeSinge of the Revolutionary Navy.' All true and within my knowledge. 'You have betrayed me.' Correct in every respect. His only error is his last remark. 'You are finished.' Well, partially untrue. One of us is certainly finished. Fortunately the client has ensured that it would not be me. Every eye in the court is on him. Every ear strains to hear what he has to say. Like all good advocates he has an innate knowledge of when he has made his point. He sits.

The judge's summing up refers to the client's outburst with indecent relish. It is only the prospect of free victuals that keeps the jury out for a day. As they troop in, each avoiding my eye, I know. I notice that the judge shares my prescience. He dons his black cap before the jury confirm that they have managed to elect a foreman, let alone deliver a verdict. 'Guilty' comes the response, and death by hanging is its refrain. I do not turn to face the client. We part as we met, with a ball of his faeces hurled at my head. Fortunately, my inattention spares me the indignity of wiping it from my eyes.

Epilogue

20

Warrens

IHAVE NEVER ENJOYED A HANGING. I HAVE ATTENDED A FEW and although the festivity and drama of the occasion can be pleasurable, I have enough of the aesthete in me to find that very pleasure distasteful. It has always been so. When I was a student I would gather with my fellows to enjoy the spectacle, but I always contrived to be virtually insensible with drink by the time the preliminaries had been completed. This gave me a quite uncalled-for reputation as a sot, but better a sot than a milksop. Squeamishness is an unbecoming characteristic in a young man, and I thought it prudent that it be disguised. I attended his hanging, of course. I felt it was my duty.

The mayor and burgesses of Hartlepool had decided to make an occasion of it. Scorned by the residents of Durham and Newcastle as unsophisticated, the opportunity to celebrate nascent municipal pride that the execution of such a notorious felon provided could not be allowed to pass. Engineers and shipwrights were commandeered to construct a gallows of lavish proportions. Their hammering and sawing kept the populace from their slumbers, but all agreed that the commanding view this edifice provided was worth the privations visited upon them by its construction. The usual delays and formalities were dispensed with by order of the Learned Mr Justice Cooper. The client was to be taken to a place of execution with almost as great a dispatch as he was taken to whence he came once sentence was pronounced. I have no doubt that those who stage-managed the trial wished to avoid the possibility of the client's notoriety attracting the sort of tender sympathy that could lead to petitions for mercy or parades of young women in white bearing offers of matrimony at the foot of the gallows. Sympathy is a hardy plant and, being the first shoots of martyrdom, it was to be given no chance to germinate.

It is a long way from the prison to the gallows. The route was lined with the ranks of the curious, and took in several taverns. The sound of his progress approached like a flood tide, and as it neared me I was filled with an impulse to meet him at one of these, to buy him a last drink to show him that I was a civilized man and not the coward and traitor he undoubtedly thought me to be. It was a pleasing fancy, but I suppressed it out of hand. We had made our choices, such as they were. He would abide by his and I by mine.

He died well. His courage impressed the crowd, and I count myself among them in this if nothing else. He scorned the benefit of clergy with a curt inclination of his head as if such superstitions did not merit more of a response. He was not silent, though. He took full advantage of tradition and made a speech. It was in his native tongue, and this is what I heard. I hope that my poor skills as a linguist can do it justice.

'Citizens. Every man's life is a journey. I have travelled far and I do not fear my end or count any step as wasted. Like all men, I do not know how, where or why I started life. I, at least, have the privilege to know where and why I meet my end. Death stands at my shoulder now. I can look him in the face and say I have never lied. I have never perpetrated an injustice upon another, nor suffered injustice without resistance. If I have stolen, I have taken only from those who have stolen from others weaker and poorer than themselves. If I have caused harm, I have done so in rightful vengeance upon those who cause harm to us all. For are we not all brothers, we wretched of the earth, and are the treasures of the world not our common treasury? I am a man. I will die a man. Will you live as beasts? To arms, citizens.'

It was all lost upon the intended recipients, of course, but moving none the less. I fingered my letter from the Lord Chancellor in my pocket as the noose was placed around his neck. It was a comfort to me. As he twitched upon the rope's end, I was filled with a morbid fear that I would pull my hand away to find it stained with blood. As the small body hung motionless I extracted my hand to find that it was only ink. There was a disturbance and as the militia moved in to restore order, I caught sight of Lovell in the crowd. He was standing next to a blonde woman of an extraordinary serene beauty. I wondered whether my new status as His Honour Judge Warrens brought such things within my reach. I will find out, no doubt. 'It little profits a man', as my mother's sampler said. I expected to feel somehow reduced, but I do not. A man may save his soul to little profit. I am leaving this godforsaken outpost and if my conscience is heavy, it is considerably lighter than my purse.

21

Claudette

I WAS SCARCELY WELL ENOUGH TO TRAVEL WHEN THEY CAME for me. I had spent weeks on my sickbed. Hubert paid for the best physicians. Unnecessary, of course. I could have afforded them myself easily, but it does not do to refuse the charity of powerful men. They pronounced me cured. I do not think the Admiral has caused me the sort of injuries that would prevent me from working like the poor girl with the scar I mentioned, but I feel something is broken inside me and I have no stomach for it. I had always imagined that I would have at least one child. I even fantasized about a husband in my weaker moments. It seems that now my dreams can never come true, so I have put them behind me. I am sure I will have my moments in the future. None of them will ever be weak.

They came in the evening. I was taking a glass of wine at the bay window that overlooked the garden. The sun had just fallen behind the houses and I was alone in the twilight. My maid admitted them. Two men in identical dark brown coats. They could have had Aliens Office written upon their hats. My first thought was that my time had come. I had had a lot of time to brood about my miraculous escape from the gallows. I have always been quick, and I knew I had put up a good show at the time, but as the weeks wound on without any sign of Hubert I began to worry that he was less convinced than his solicitous payment of my medical bills may have suggested. It was an uncomfortable time for me, made worse by being confined to the house and unable to flee England as my every instinct told me I must. I was almost relieved that it was at an end. But no. These were not the execution party. They were just my new protector's errand boys. I was handed a letter and advised that a carriage awaited me. I had no time to read it. I only recovered from my confusion enough to break the seal when we had already left London. Slow, I know, but you must remember I was unwell. It takes a lot to recover from a shock like that.

There was more to come. I who had always been the one who controlled things now found myself a prisoner of events. The letter was from Hubert, of course. I cannot recall his precise words. I have the letter somewhere even now, but its eloquence does not support the effort of seeking it out. It was very to the point. The outrage that had been perpetrated upon me was not to go unpunished. The assassin and ravager had been captured and I was to witness the final act of his vengeance in person. Then we were to be wed. Simple as that. I would have laughed, only it still hurt me. I suppose I should have been flattered. He was no Cyrano de Bergerac, but presenting his exploits as an attempt to win my heart and protect my honour was rather sweet when you think about it. It was food for thought on what transpired to be a very long and very uncomfortable journey.

I have no idea where our destination was. If you pointed me to a map of England I would be quite unable to pick it out. I am told it is called Hartlepool and is in the north. It was bitterly cold and I have no desire to visit it again. Hubert met me from my coach and escorted me to the shore, where we were to witness the hanging. He seemed almost childlike in his desire to see me happy and prattled on about his own cleverness and the machinations he had arranged to bring Jacques to the gallows. I did not reply. I think Hubert took my silence for the horror of seeing my attacker again, as he took my arm with some force. I have noticed that Englishmen often mistake physical effort for passion. It can be quite charming, but I wasn't in the mood. I assume I'll marry him. It doesn't sound like I have much choice. Better a ring on my finger than a rope round my neck and both are within his power. I suppose I should be grateful, but it's not in my nature. The real question is whether I'll stay or not. Marrying Hubert sounds uncomfortably like betting everything on one horse and I haven't forgotten Guillaume's advice. I haven't given up on the New World either.

Poor Jacques. If there were any justice in the world he would sail away unscathed and the Admiral would hang. But there isn't. He was a real man to the last. He gave a speech encouraging the roastbeef to rise up in brotherhood, would you believe. Very brave and moving it was. I think that I must have been one of the six people present who understood a word of it. There was a bit of a riot, but Hubert explained that it wasn't a revolution. The taverns had run out of gin. Still, I hope that he saw it before they took him and it gave him some comfort. If you can't have hope, comfort is the best you can wish for. It's my new philosophy. And I do wish Jacques the best you can hope for, a poor thing though that may be.

I could almost feel the rough texture of the hemp against my skin as they put the noose around his neck. My hand flew to my throat and I started to weep. Hubert hurried me away. He was sure I was upset by seeing the monster again and I didn't disabuse him. I never lose my temper and I rarely cry. Who did I cry for? I have asked myself the same question and I can find no answer.

22

Simon Legris

I SHOULD NOT BE ALIVE. I REMEMBER THE BARGE EVERY TIME I close my eyes. I cannot help it. I had to support my Master to the dock. The soldiers who captured us took his chair. When I remonstrated with them that he should have this dignity in the face of death they struck me with their rifle butts and knocked me unconscious. Perversely, it was this that saved me. I could not stand with the others so they laid me upon the bow. The shot struck the boat in the middle, blowing it apart. The blast flung me into the sea. The cold water revived me and I was able to grab hold of some wreckage. I floated for days in the mist before I found myself washed up.

I had influenza. I was delirious but, as ever, I had survived unscathed when those more deserving of life had perished. I had stayed with my Master to the last. I should feel that my obligations were discharged by this, but I do not. If I had not made him a cripple then who knows? Maybe he would not have been captured. Trying to flee with a man in a chair was rather arduous. As I reflect, it seems as doomed to failure as everything else I have ever attempted. If I had not prevailed upon him to send the Young Master to Africa with me, perhaps he would not have remarried. It was his family that made him decide that he would stay and fight. A man without the hope of a future would have fled in time. I have been the cause of so much and yet I live on like some damned soul in a Greek play, forced to witness the consequences of my acts for eternity and have no power to alter them. I cannot even have the comfort of madness. The ancients say that those whom the gods seek to destroy they first make mad. I remain sane. If the gods exist they seem to intend to use me as an agent of destruction not destroy me. I am convinced they do not exist. It is this conviction that comforts me, although I have found myself ruminating on the question of whether, if God does exist, atheism is a form of madness itself. I could continue for ever, but I know that I must not. I have other things to do, even now.

I recovered with almost indecent ease. I could not stay in the west. I had thought of it as my home, but there is nothing for me there but memories of people who have been caught up in my wake. So I came back here. To Paris. To my practice and to the company of whores. My consulting rooms are less grand. I have one specimen, a small owl in a glass case. I keep him in memory of my Master as I have lost all desire to travel and I have no faith in my abilities as a scientist. They called themselves *chouannes*, my Master's men. The little owls of Brittany. Little owls who fought a hopeless fight and waited for help from England that never came. I suppose it could be dangerous, keeping him. Symbols have a terrible power in these troubled times. Yet I cannot bring myself to throw him away. Animals have always destroyed those around me, so maybe he will keep me safe. Look at Reynard.

I heard a distressing story the other day. There are so many newspapers spreading scandal about the English these days that I pay them no mind usually. This one caught my eye. It told of the stupidity of the English who had captured the mascot of one of our ships and hanged it as a spy. The article referred to a monkey. Tears sprang to my eyes as I read. One cannot rely upon a journalist to distinguish between a monkey and an ape and I knew it was Jacques. I was transported to the green gloom of the forest although I stood on the Place de la Révolution. He always wanted to return before I made him a man. Now he never will. Poor Jacques. Another name to add to the list of my glorious dead. I am not certain I was right to save his life. If I had not raised my musket all those years ago he would have died in the forest and become part of the soil. He would not have been able to save me. I cannot help but think that my continued survival has not been to mankind's unqualified benefit.

I recall a picture I saw once in a book. I believe it must have been back among the brothers when I was still a child, as I cannot imagine that I have owned a book of such overtly religious images. It was called the Wheel of Fortune. As it revolved it elevated some and crushed others. I have been elevated once and I have developed a taste for luxury while I was at its apex. I have sunk, yet I have not been crushed. It can be comforting to believe that I will rise again and enjoy luxury as an old man. My clientele are unlikely to permit much of it, but there is always hope. Somewhere there is a golden patient waiting the arrival of his or her dedicated and solicitous physician. When I am not crushed with melancholy I allow myself to wish. I find that as the horrors of the barge recede, my humours reach some semblance of an equilibrium. I can permit myself such thoughts from time to time.

Acknowledgements

With thanks to Doctors Dominic Anderson (medicine) and David Longley (philosophy) without whose help it would all have been impossible. To Martin from IT Rescue in Catford, who did exactly as the name suggests and saved me from my own stupidity. To Sandra Watson, who knew how to fix the computer and didn't mind being asked. To Louis and Kiera, who have had too many holidays by the pool disrupted in the name of research. To Miles Dell for the photograph. To my wife, Michaela, for whom long-suffering would be an inadequate description and whose encouragement and support gave me the time and courage to write this book. Finally, to Simon Schama, Professor Doyle, Georges Rudé, Franz Fannon, Elizabeth Sparrow, Jean de Brunhoff and all the other great minds whose work I have shamelessly pillaged and parodied.

Also, thanks to Maggie, Jamie and Nicky at Crawford Pearlstein and Jane Lawson and Marianne Velmans at Doubleday in the hope that their faith and hard work was not misplaced.